For Vlada and Kitty.

BASED ON A TRUE STORY OF LOVE,
LOSS, HOPE AND SURVIVAL

The Missing STAR

A NOVEL

JULIE CANEPA

FIRST U.S. Edition

Cover design by Augusto Silva
Typesetting by Ronald Cruz
Photos courtesy of Vladimir Munk
United States Holocaust Memorial Museum. "Partition of Czechoslovakia."
Holocaust Encyclopedia.
https://encyclopedia.ushmm.org/content/en/article/czechoslovakia.
Accessed on June 5, 2023. Copyright of United States Holocaust
Memorial Museum.

Library of Congress Cataloging-in-Publication Data has been applied for.

ISBN 979-8-9868387-3-1

Printed in the United States of America.

Contents

CHAPTER ONE

What are little boys made of?
What are little boys made of?
  Snips and snails
  And puppy-dogs' tails
That's what little boys are made of.

  ROBERT SOUTHEY

VLADA 1929 - 1933
PARDUBICE, CZECHOSLOVAKIA

Vlada Munk and his father, Karel, stood, unmoving, as the large, wooden gate that separated the distillery compound from the outside world slid slowly to the side. Vlada inhaled deeply in anticipation of what was beyond the gate, tightening the grip of his tiny hand around his father's. Time stood still for a moment, and then two enormous russet-colored beasts stepped majestically into the factory yard, bound together by a wooden yoke.

They stomped and snorted, their breath visible in the cold morning air, and their colossal bodies swaying from side to side. Vlada stepped back, his eyes wide with fear, and he looked up at the mammoth creatures passing within inches of him. Karel pointed to the rear of the beasts, where their cargo was revealed: they pulled a train car carrying chemicals, its wheels following the railway track that led from the train depot nearby and into the compound.

The factory yard at the distillery was a living, breathing organism, a hub of activity and industry. The enterprise never ceased to amaze four-year-old Vlada each time he stepped outside the family's ground floor flat and into the yard. Each morning before work, Karel took Vlada by the hand and they made their morning rounds, stopping first at the main gate, where the guard on duty allowed Vlada to play with his ring of keys. Then they walked along the iron fence bordering Palackého Street in front. The tour was never complete without a stop at the stable that butted up against the high, brick wall in the back of the yard, where the mighty pair of oxen chewed great mouthfuls of straw, their large tongues protruding. Vlada's earliest childhood memory preceded the visits to the oxen, a memory of his family's move from the tiny first-floor flat on the distillery grounds to the second floor upstairs.

Since their marriage in 1923, Karel and his wife, Hermina, lived comfortably in the tiny flat. The family's home was in a two-story, square gray stone affair, that faced an expanse of the factory yard, and it was there on a brisk winter day that Karel walked purposefully toward the house. His left hand pressed his hat tightly against his bald head, his right hand gripping the collar of his wool overcoat up against the wind. Karel opened the door into the kitchen of the first-floor apartment, allowing a rush of cold air in.

Hermina looked up from the kitchen table, her dark hair tucked behind her ears. She stopped chopping vegetables and wiped her hands on a towel. "Darling, you're home early," she said, standing up, helping Karel with his coat. Vlada padded out of the bedroom rubbing his eyes, his brown hair tousled from a late afternoon nap, pulling a large stuffed bear on wheels behind him.

"Tati!" He ran to his father and hugged him around the legs. Karel picked up Vlada and lifted him into the air. "I have an announcement," he said, and settled Vlada on his hip, puffing his chest out ceremoniously. "Starting next month, I will be responsible for the day-to-day technical operations of the distillery."

"Darling! What wonderful news. We must celebrate!" Hermina kissed her husband's cheek.

"We have been offered the second-floor apartment." Karel watched Hermina's face light up. They were both aware that the flat on the second floor was twice the size of their current space.

"I can't believe it, Karel." She threw her arms around her husband's neck, encircling Vlada as well. Vlada giggled.

Hermina began to sniffle and turned away. Vlada saw his mother's cheeks were wet with tears. "Why are you crying, Mami?" Karel and Hermina looked at each other and began to laugh.

"These are happy tears, my sweet boy," she explained. She tickled him and he laughed, pushing his mother's hands away.

When moving day arrived, Vlada refused to budge. He lay in his tiny wooden bed clutching his favorite wool blanket, arms crossed over his chest, his chin set in protest. He watched as his parents and the moving men carried lamps, chairs, pillows, and stacks of Karel's books up the stairs to their new home. At the end of the day, Vlada sat on his bed in the fading light, befuddled by the empty rooms around him.

"It's time," Karel announced sternly. The movers each grabbed an end of the child's bed and lifted Vlada, his small hands tightly gripping the sides and carried him up the stairs. The men took the steep stairs one at a time, the only sound their grunting and heavy footfalls, ascending the flight with their precocious cargo. Hermina peered nervously over her husband's shoulder, holding her breath.

Resembling an Egyptian king on a litter, holding a wooden toy across his chest like a scepter, Vlada was greeted at the top of the stairs by his father. "Welcome, Pharoah." They all burst into laughter — Karel, Hermina, the movers. "Welcome to your new home." Vlada looked around at the adults warily and then joined in their laughter.

The second-floor flat was laid out in a square, echoing the building's exterior. It was punctuated down the middle by a corridor. On one side was a dining room, Karel and Hermina's bedroom, a living room that doubled as Vlada's bedroom, and a pánsky room for entertaining. On the other side was a large kitchen, a maid's room, and a bathroom with a sink and bathtub. A balcony off the kitchen overlooked the factory yard.

"Come, Vlada," Hermina coaxed her son from one room to the next. He walked on tiptoe, peeking his head around each corner, regarding each new room with suspicion. At the end of the tour, Hermina stood in front of the polished double doors that led to the pánsky room. "This room is for grown-ups, not little boys," his mother cautioned. She grasped both doorknobs and threw open the French doors with a flourish, and stepped, breathless, into the center of the room. She sat in the only upholstered chair, spread her skirt out around her and motioned for Vlada to join her. Vlada scrambled over and climbed up.

Hermina hugged Vlada to her and spoke barely above a whisper, her breath tickling his ear. "When I was a girl we lived above the family store — my parents, my five sisters and my two brothers. This apartment is much larger, and it is just for the three of us." Her voice trailed off. Vlada tried to wiggle away. "My mother, your Babicka Emilie, will be impressed with our new home, maybe even a bit envious." Her voice lost its dreamlike quality. "Now let's wash your hands. It's time for dinner."

Hermina set the table for the family's first meal in their new home with the finest tablecloth she could find. Candles flickered on the table, casting the new surroundings, cold and unfamiliar just a few hours earlier, in a warm and welcoming glow. She carried a large porcelain tureen from the kitchen, a wedding gift from her parents, and placed it in the center of the table. And finally, ceremoniously, she lifted the lid, fragrant steam escaping that filled the room with the scent of savory spices and roasted meat.

"*Svíčková na smetaně!* My favorite, Mami!" Vlada grinned and grabbed his fork. His mother ladled stew meat and root vegetables into a bowl and placed it in front of him, her eyes shining in the candlelight. Karel reached for his wife's hand.

"I like it here," announced Vlada, slurping his stew, his objections to the move entirely forgotten. Vlada spotted a photo taken when he was an infant hanging on the wall, prompting him to engage his parents in a favorite family game. "Tell me again about the day I was born, Tati," teased Vlada. The scene played out in a familiar way. Karel would tell his version of Vlada's birth first, after which Vlada would ask his mother the same question.

"Well, Vlada," Karel spoke in an officious tone, "the regional weather station was in Pardubice that year. It is on record that the 27th of February 1925 was cloudy and overcast during the day. No precipitation, no snow cover. The air temperature ranged between -0.6 °C and a high of 6 °C. A light north wind was blowing. The mild temperature may have caused buds to sprout prematurely on the bushes in the factory yard."

"Karel," Hermina scolded her husband. She took Vlada's small hand in hers and their eyes locked in a way that had become their habit. "Inside the downstairs flat that day there was only sunshine, Vlada, my sweet." Hermina breathed in and sighed contentedly. "I remember pushing you in the pram, a gift from Babicka Emilie, on a cold day in March to the photographer. You were so alert. You never let me out of your sight!"

"And I never cried, right, Mami?" Vlada said proudly. He looked to his mother to validate his words.

"You never forget a thing, do you?" Hermina told Vlada that Pirka, the photographer, kept his studio very cold. Even when she undressed Vlada and laid him, alone and naked, on a large scrap of fur, he remained stoic. She smiled at him, gently shaking her head. "No, you never cried." She pushed his bangs away from his forehead. "You were my brave little man."

One warm afternoon during their first summer in the new flat, the air was dry and static. Dark clouds rumbled overhead. It was Sunday and the distillery was closed, and Karel allowed Vlada to accompany him to the laboratory. "I want to show you something, Vlada." Karel directed his son's attention to a glass and wood contraption that hung from the wall.

"This is a barometer, Vlada. It measures air pressure. Do you feel the change in the air?" Vlada nodded. "That means a storm is coming. It is coming soon, and it is going to be a big one." Vlada's eyes widened. "Don't worry," said Karel. "Nothing bad will happen."

Vlada woke that night to the eerie sound of trees bending and cracking under the strong wind that howled and drove the rain sideways. Karel, Hermina, and Vlada stood in the kitchen in their pajamas and watched the storm play out, bright white streaks of lightning brightening the pitch-black sky, immediately followed by thunder that rattled the windows. Vlada clung to his mother's side as the flashes of lightning and booming thunder inched closer together.

Without warning, the rain stopped. An eerie quiet descended over the property. "I think it's over," said Karel. He opened the French doors leading to the balcony and immediately the quiet was shattered by a thunderous crack. An explosion followed that rocked the factory compound, shaking the house to its foundation. "Stay back," cautioned Karel. "I have to go down and look around."

"Tati!" Vlada cried. "Don't leave!"

"It's okay, Vlada," said Karel. "Stay inside," Karel warned Hermina. He disappeared quickly down the stairs, Vlada jumping as the door slammed shut behind him.

Hermina sat at the kitchen table, holding Vlada on her lap, and together they watched the flames licking up from the mangled shell of the building that had once been his father's laboratory. Black smoke billowed skyward, shrouding the night in a thick, choking fog. Vlada heard sirens in the distance and jumped from his mother's lap to peer out the balcony doors. He watched as the machinist who lived below them ran to the wooden gate, sliding it open to allow the fire trucks to enter.

"Look, Mami," Vlada pointed to the firemen. The men jumped from the sideboards of the truck and removed a long wooden ladder from its side. Vlada watched the men intently, but soon he returned to his mother's lap, his eyes growing heavy. Hermina felt Vlada's tiny body soften into hers. She slipped her arm under his legs and carried him to his bed in the living room.

Hours after the last embers had been extinguished, Karel and Mr. Prochazka, the distillery director, stood in the factory yard inspecting the damage. Hermina heard Karel's footfalls on the stairs and opened the door of the flat to find her husband covered in soot. She went to the kitchen and came back with a wet cloth. Karel sat down at the kitchen table, exhausted. "Lightning struck a vat of alcohol in the distillery, causing it to catch fire," Karel explained. He took the cloth and began wiping the ash from his face. "We will have to leave the grounds until the necessary repairs are made. We can stay at the Bergmans."

The next day, Karel gathered Vlada's things for the family's temporary change of residence. "I like Pepik Bergman, Tati," Vlada said. Pepik and Vlada were the same age. The boys had met and played together on a few occasions. Their parents both attended the synagogue, Pepik's more often than Vlada's.

"Will you have to go to the synagogue, Tati?" Vlada asked.

Karel laughed. "No, Vlada. That is where we differ from the Bergmans. The Bergmans are Zionists," explained Karel. Vlada looked at his father, tilting his head. "Zionists are Jews who believe Israel is their homeland and one day they hope to move there."

"And leave Czechoslovakia?" Vlada's small face took on a quizzical look. Vlada could not imagine any circumstances under which he would ever leave the distillery, or Pardubice, let alone Czechoslovakia. This was his home. He was going to have a talk with Pepik about this.

The minute they returned to the flat after the shock of the fire and the family's brief stay with the Bergmans, Hermina felt her shoulders relax. Vlada had the same sentiment. He bounded up the stairs in front of her, and skipped happily from one room to the other. He stopped at the living room window that faced onto the street below. "Mami, look! She's back!" From his vantage point, Vlada could see the organ grinder, in her threadbare sweater and head scarf, struggling to pull her cart across the street.

"Please, Mami, please." Vlada pleaded with Hermina to let him cross the road and give the old woman a coin in exchange for a song. He could not resist the organ grinder's siren call.

Hermina smiled to see her son in such good spirits after the fire. "You were well behaved at the Bergman's. And it is time you learned to properly cross the street." She took a thick gold coin from her change purse and dropped it into the palm of his small hand.

"Do exactly as we talked about, okay, Vlada?" Vlada nodded and ran down the stairs ahead of her. When they came to the street corner, Vlada did as his mother instructed, looking first to the right, then to the left for cars or a horse-drawn carriage, of which there were fewer and fewer. When he determined that the coast was clear, he looked to his mother for approval.

"Now, Mami?"

"Yes! Now, Vlada! Run!" Vlada's feet left the curb, and he ran at top speed across the street, arriving breathless on the other side.

"Hello?" he said to the organ grinder. The face that looked back at him was wizened and gray, its only color coming from rouged cheeks. The old woman held her hand out and waited for Vlada to deposit the coin. Vlada dropped the coin in her dry, lined palm. With a magician's sleight of hand, she palmed the coin, slipping it into the pocket of her baggy skirt, and began to turn the hand crank that operated the bellows inside.

The organ began wheezing out a tinny polka and Vlada clapped his hands together with delight. A huge smile spread across his face. The organ grinder sped up and then slowed down, turning the crank in an exaggerated fashion for the benefit of her young audience. Vlada laughed and clapped his hands, waving to Hermina, who watched the sweet scene from across the street. When the song was done, Vlada's shoulders fell in disappointment. One coin for a pleasure that had gone by all too quickly. He carefully looked both ways again and ran back to the spot where his mother was waiting for him.

In between deep breaths he told his mother about the encounter. "She looks like Babicka Emilie, Mami." He turned and raised his hand to wave to the organ grinder, but she was already pushing her cart up the street, her back to him, in search of another, more lucrative corner.

Years later, under Nazi occupation, traffic would change direction according to German road regulations, forcing Vlada to reverse the first right, then left habit taught to him that day by his mother, a habit that kept him safe for most of his young life. The change in traffic patterns, and portending of future events, would lead to many fatalities.

One morning at breakfast Karel made an announcement. "There will be a delivery here later today, darling," Karel said, a sly smile spreading across his face.

"And what form will this delivery take?" Hermina looked at her husband, and then at her son, who was covering his mouth with his hand. She peeled Vlada's hand from his face. Underneath, he was grinning. Karel shot Vlada a warning look, putting his finger to his lips. Vlada nodded seriously.

"Oh! You two are in cahoots. Off with you, then!" Hermina worked in the kitchen all morning, roughly chopping potatoes and root vegetables. She set the vegetables in a deep pot filled with water and placed it on the stove. She was interrupted by a muffled knock at the door. Two men stood on the landing awaiting entry, having slowly labored up the stairs under the weight of a large cabinet.

Hermina's eyes grew wide at the sight of them, her eyebrows raised in genuine surprise. She inhaled deeply, then led the men through the flat to the pánsky room, instructing them to set the cabinet down. They obliged her with a resounding thud. Hermina stood back, taking in the burnished walnut cabinet, its fancy, curved legs, and curved glass on three sides.

Hermina greeted her husband at the top of the stairs that evening, kissing his cheek. "It's perfect, Karel," she said. After dinner, they retired to the pánsky room. Karel and Vlada watched as Hermina arranged her small but precious collection of hand-cut Czech crystal on the shelves of the cabinet. Next came the Meissen figurines. She gingerly placed the "Apple Seller," a lovely porcelain maid whose apron was full of fruit, next to the "Dancing Couple" and the tiny, corseted "Opera Singer." Hermina stood back and admired the results.

"Now come, Vlada. It's our turn," Karel motioned for Vlada to come closer. "Close your eyes."

"Tati," Vlada giggled. He was giddy with excitement at the treasure that awaited.

"Okay. Now open them," Vlada looked down at the small box in his father's hand. He pushed open the lid, revealing three medals sitting on royal blue velvet. Vlada lifted the first medal out of the box; it had a red and white ribbon and four concentric circles.

"That is the Czech War Cross, given to those who served with distinction," Karel said, giving Hermina a wry smile. They both watched Vlada place the medal carefully on a shelf in the cabinet. Vlada reached for the second medal, holding it up, and examining it closely.

"Ah. That is the Victory Medal," Karel ran his fingers over the words encircling the lion in relief on the medal. "*Světová Válka Za Civilizaci* (The World War for Civilization)." Karel was quiet for a moment. "Very optimistic don't you think, darling?" Hermina's eyes met his. It seemed presumptuous to think they had forever conquered evil at the end of the Great War. Vlada placed the medal on the shelf, lion side up. "I like it," said Vlada.

Vlada removed the last medal from the box, its red ribbon faded to the color of rust over the 10 years since it had been conferred. A thin blue and white stripe ran through it, and a winged horseman sat in the center of the cross.

"That," his father said proudly, "is the Medal of the Revolution." Karel took it from Vlada's small hand. "This was awarded for service toward the independence of Czechoslovakia. As a member of the Czech Legion, it would seem I played a role in that," Karel said, his voice tight. "When you are older, I will tell you about my train ride across Siberia." Karel set the last medal down on the shelf and Hermina closed the cabinet door with a click. Karel filled two glasses with brandy and handed one to Hermina. She held the slender glass in her hand, poised just inches apart from her husband's.

"*Na zdraví!*" they said in unison. The glasses made a gentle clinking sound.

A few weeks passed and one afternoon Karel came up the stairs to the flat with two large rectangular packages wrapped in brown paper, one under each arm. Hermina was in the kitchen making lentils and fried eggs.

"What is it, Tati? What is it?" Vlada followed his father into the dining room. Karel motioned to Hermina to join them. They gathered around the table waiting for Karel to reveal the package's mysterious contents.

Vlada's face was level with the table as his father cut away the paper from the first package. Inside was an oil painting of a natural landscape in a frame, with an envelope bearing Karel's name on it taped to the back. Karel opened the second bundle, a painting of Prague, with Prague Castle rising in the left-hand corner. Vlada lowered his head, his disappointment evident; there was nothing here of interest to little boys.

"It's from Jaroslav Grus, darling." Karel held the painting up for her to see. Vlada heard his mother breathe in sharply. "He was a Legionnaire like me, Vlada. We became quite good friends on that train ride I told you about. Now, let's find a good place to hang these, shall we?"

Hermina proudly regarded the beautiful paintings and the new china cabinet. Those items and her hand-woven rugs lent a warmth to the flat that filled her with contentment. It seemed complete. So her shock was visible when, upon answering the door one afternoon, she was greeted by three stout delivery men. Vlada heard his mother exclaim and followed her downstairs to see what was happening. An upright piano sat on a truck behind them.

"You must have the wrong house," Hermina told them. "You might try the Fehlig's? Or the Cernys?" As she spoke, Karel strode across the factory yard toward the men.

"Hello, gentlemen. You are in the right place," he said. "One floor up, please." The men released a string of curses as they struggled with the piano up the stairs, and their coarseness made Hermina blush. Upon reaching the second floor, the men rolled the piano the rest of the way to the pánsky room.

"Karel! This is too much!" Hermina protested. He pulled out the bench and motioned for her to sit. She removed her apron and took her place at the piano. She flexed her fingers, allowing them to hover over the keys and then plunged them down, launching into a bright and playful tune.

"That, Vlada, is Mozart," his father explained. *Eine Kleine Nacht Musik - A Little Night Music.*

Vlada had never seen his mother play the piano before. Her right hand moved busily, her left hand adding notes in just the right places as Vlada looked on. Vlada clapped his hands together with delight when she finished. She patted the bench next to her. Vlada sat down next to his mother, plinking the keys with both hands. His mother had made it look so easy.

Four years had passed since the explosion at the distillery and Vlada had begun to attend school. On weekdays he waited outside the gate of the distillery, climbing onto the back of the Bergmans' horse-drawn wagon where Pepik and Tomas were waiting. After the factory fire and the family's relocation to the Bergmans', Vlada had grown close to the brothers, Vlada generously informing Pepik that as far as little brothers went, Tomas was quite tolerable.

But today was Saturday and Vlada leaned on the railing of the balcony, looking out over the factory yard. The afternoon sun glinted off the distillery's roof, which had been replaced after the destruction of that fateful night. Vlada caught movement in the yard and quickly dashed into the kitchen.

"No breakfast today, Vlada?" Hermina stood at the sink, washing dishes, the slice of bread with butter she prepared for him sat on a plate, untouched.

"I must go now, Mami. The games are waiting!" Hermina stopped him as he ran past and held Vlada by the shoulders. Their eyes locked. "Slow down, Vlada." She pushed his tousled brown hair to the side, combing it with her fingers.

"Lada is waiting, Mami. Goodbye." Vlada ran down the stairs, scouring the factory yard for signs of life but all he saw were a few hens wandering the yard and pecking absently at the dirt. Vlada's face lit up when he spotted Lada making his way towards him.

"Lada!" Vlada waved his friend over. "I thought I saw you. How about a game of hide and seek?" Lada Jenik was a lanky boy, the son of the factory chauffeur. His family also made their home inside the distillery compound. He was one year older than Vlada.

"Sure, Vlada." Lada face broadened into a wide grin. "Who hides first?"

"You count first and I will hide – and remember what I told you!" The good thing about Lada was he rarely peeked during hide and seek, allowing Vlada to avoid discovery for long stretches at a time. Once Vlada got a cramp from crouching so long before Lada found him.

Vlada had shared his secrets on how to avoid discovery with his friend. He spoke in hushed tones, as if what said was a matter of national security. "There are only two things to remember, Lada," he whispered conspiratorially. "You must remain still, and you must remain silent."

Lada buried his head in his arm and counted out loud, leaning against the official counting spot, the large wooden door that led to the factory yard. "One, one thousand. Two, one thousand." Vlada made the first round an easy one. Lada found him within seconds. "You got me, Lada, fair and square." Vlada stood up, surrendering his hiding spot. The two boys noticed Milan Prochazka, the factory director's son, walking across the yard. Milan walked, head down, kicking stones in his path, and giving chase to a hen that got in his way. Milan was bored. This was good news for Vlada and Lada. Vlada picked up a stick and brandished it in Milan's direction. "*En garde!*" he shouted.

"Ah, so it is the Three Musketeers today," Milan scoffed. "I'll play, but only if I get to be D'Artagnan."

Vlada did not like Milan's plan. "I should be D'Artagnan," Vlada insisted. "I am the youngest." Vlada liked D'Artagnan for his bravery and intelligence but kept that to himself.

"Okay, then. Have fun," replied Milan said, turning to walk away.

Vlada stepped in front of Milan. "Wait. All right, then, I will be Athos."

"And I am Porthos," replied Lada, picking up a stick and brandishing it jauntily.

"We know," replied Milan and Vlada in unison. Lada always played Porthos because he thought he was the strongest and funniest of the musketeers. Milan chose a stick and scrambled up one of the piles of coal.

"Un pour tous, tous pour un!" Milan declared. They played for an hour. Lada and Vlada kept Milan engaged by allowing him the most heroic scenarios. But they soon exceeded the limits of Milan's attention span, and he wandered off to other pursuits.

The loss of Milan warranted a change of scenario. "Watch out for the Reds!" directed Vlada. The dormant train cars in the factory yard were now occupied by Czech Legionnaires, like Vlada's father, crossing the whole of Russia on the Trans-Siberian Railway. The boys hung off the sides of the car as it crossed the imaginary frozen tundra of Siberia.

"I can see Vladivostok, Lada," Vlada shouted, holding his hand to his forehead. Vladivostok was the Legionnaires last stop in Russia when the fighting ended. After a long journey, the boys disembarked the train in their home country, hands clasped over their heads in victory, to a hero's welcome. They had ended the war and liberated Czechoslovakia.

One day after school, Vlada returned home to find his mother standing in the kitchen of the flat, holding a leash. On the other end was a long-haired mutt with silver fur and dark eyes. "Vlada, meet Čigy," said Hermina. "Čigy, Vlada." Vlada looked from the dog to Hermina, his eyes gleaming, a grin spreading across his face. He clapped his hands together and called the dog to him. Čigy walked to Vlada, sniffed, then turned and ran back to Hermina, curling up and settling in at her feet like they were old friends.

"Čigy is going to love you, Vlada." But his mother was wrong. The fox terrier did fall in love, but not with Vlada. Čigy reserved his affections for Karel and Hermina. He was rewarded for his slobbery displays of unconditional love with a training regimen that was decidedly lax.

One evening, Karel and Hermina set out for the Veselka Coffee House to meet with friends. The disobedient pup ran alongside them, keeping pace inside the iron fence that ran the length of the distillery. The dog found the few bars in the fence that were wide enough to slip through and happily joined his owners in the street. "No, Čigy! Go home!" Čigy ignored Karel's commands and was forcibly hauled home by his leash. Their happiness at returning the dog home successfully was short-lived. Čigy had escaped again and was snatched by the town dog catcher.

Vlada accompanied his father to the kennel, where his father paid Čigy's "bail." The outlaw was released, unrepentant, into the custody of his loving family. A few days later the predictable cycle of capture and release played itself out all over again. His parents feigned exasperation at the dog's antics.

It was St. Nicholas Day, the start of the Christmas season, the day when the trio of St. Nicholas, the Angel, and the Devil went from house to house and judged whether children had been good or bad. Bad children were given coal, or worse yet, hauled away in the large bag carried by the Devil. Vlada thought he had been very good but there might have been a few incidents he hoped could be overlooked. He had set his shoes out on the landing, filled with hay from the oxen in the factory yard, in the hopes that it would be exchanged for candy.

Vlada was nervous about his prospects and the sharp knock at the door of the flat made him jump. He held his breath, convinced his transgressions had been discovered and it was the Devil who had come to remove him from his parents. He trembled as Hermina opened the door. To Vlada's delight, the Bergman's maid, Adelka, stood on the landing. His smile faded when he saw Adelka's usually cheerful face contorted in pain.

Hermina ushered the young girl inside, her shawl covered with melting snow, and gave her a seat at the kitchen table. "What is it, dear? Please come in out of the cold."

"The Bergmans sent me to tell you the news. Tomas has died of pneumonia." Adelka began to cry, her shoulders shaking. Hermina put her arm around the girl and waited as she regained her composure. "I must be going," Adelka said, pulling the damp shawl around her shoulders. "I have more stops to make."

"What happened to Tomas, Mami?" asked Vlada. "He hasn't ridden the cart to school in a long time. Pepik told me that his brother was having trouble breathing."

"He was a very sick boy, sweetheart." She went to Vlada and hugged him tightly. Vlada's eyes narrowed, and he pulled away from his mother, frowning and shaking his head. Vlada had escaped the Devil, but Tomas had been taken away from his family that day. As far as little brothers of friends went, Vlada had liked Tomas and he had told Pepik as much. And now Tomas was gone.

Vlada thought about the time he had jumped in the Vltava River to swim on a hot summer day. The current of the river was stronger than he expected, and he was pulled under the water almost immediately. He struggled to get back to the shore, splashing and searching for something to hold onto, desperately gasping for air. That is what it must have been like for Tomas. Vlada shuddered at the thought.

Vlada forgot about St. Nicholas. He went to bed and dreamed he was in the river again, battling the current. A hand reached down from the riverbank to pull him up to safety. It was Tomas.

CHAPTER ONE

What are little girls made of?
What are little girls made of?
Sugar and spice
And everything nice
That's what little girls are made of.

    ROBERT SOUTHEY

KITTY 1934
TEPLICE, CZECHOSLOVAKIA

The story always began the same way: "There we were in Venice in a gondola in November, gliding down the Grand Canal ...." Bettina Löwi described the waves of nausea that had swept over her, the vile morning sickness she had endured while pregnant with her daughter Kitty that had found her retching in spasms off the side of the narrow boat. The trip to Italy was ruined beyond repair. The implication was obvious to even the most casual listener: if Kitty had committed such grave offenses in utero, one could only imagine what else she was capable of at the age of seven.

"We had it on good authority the Venetians had concluded their summer holidays," Bettina prattled on in German. "No one told us the rest of Europe would be there, too." She balanced a delicate china teacup and saucer on her lap, daring it to spill onto the skirt of her plaid wool suit. She extended her pinky finger, lifted the cup to her lips, then set the cup back down in the saucer with a decisive clink.

Kitty sat frozen in a gold damask chair across from her mother in the parlor of the flat. She was a doll, like the ones that lined the high shelf in her bedroom, trotted out to impress visitors. Bettina had instructed Oila, her governess, to dress Kitty in one of her best dresses. Oila obliged. Kitty's long dark hair hung in shiny twin ringlets. Now Kitty was twice imprisoned; first by the rose-colored, ruffled dress usually reserved for formal photographs and second, by her forced presence in the parlor. Kitty sat, doomed to listen to Bettina recount the ruined holiday story to her latest victim, their new neighbor on Masaryk Street, Mrs. Müller.

Bettina dabbed at her mouth with a small square of starched ivory linen, the initials "BL" sewn into the fabric in a flowery script, the shade of her lipstick an exact match to her fingernail polish, the rim of her teacup bearing the same waxy imprint. Kitty turned her head and rolled her eyes.

Bettina had pinned her hair up into a tight bun, showing off her long neck which bore a gleaming strand of pearls. Kitty likened Bettina's hair to spun gold, like the straw spun by Rumpelstiltskin in the fairy tale, or the sugar the pastry chef wound around a croquembouche in the pastry shop window at Christmas.

"There, there," Mrs. Müller cooed in a sympathetic tone to her new acquaintance. "That must have been simply awful." Bettina was an oddity in the small town, her company sought after not because she was a fascinating conversationalist or a good listener, but for another reason: she had been born in America. Chicago. That made her exotic, a curiosity among the ethnic Germans who made up the bulk of the population of Teplice, a small spa town tucked in the northwest corner of Czechoslovakia near the German border. They knew nothing of what brought her there and rarely asked. Bettina told her story anyway.

"My parents were Czech," she explained. "They emigrated to America. Each time my mother had a child, her mother insisted the family return home so she could bestow her blessing. The Great War prevented my parents from making the return trip home to America. I met my husband Karel in the neighborhood where we lived in Prague when we were barely teenagers. Years later, when he proposed, he was working in Germany. I refused to move there, so here we are."

The "here" she referred to was the Sudetenland, a chunk of the Austro-Hungarian empire ceded, wrongly according to those of German descent, to Czechoslovakia after the Great War. She left out that she was Jewish.

Kitty shifted in her seat. "This is what grownups do for fun," she thought, planning her escape and glancing at the half open French doors that led to the foyer. The gilded clock on the mantle struck three. When she thought she could not bear it a moment longer, Karel Löwi, Kitty's father, appeared in the doorway. Kitty's face lit up.

"Good day, Frau Müller. And did she tell you the gondola story?" Karel laughed. Frau Müller nodded. "I remember it well. The canal was choppy from the sheer number of boats. We were bobbing up and down. Arturo, our gondolier, was masterful. He did a splendid job navigating our queasy passenger back to terra firma." Karel winked across the room at Kitty. In his brief but well-timed appearance, her father had sown doubt that Bettina may have confused being pregnant with being seasick. Kitty jumped from her chair, the crinoline beneath her dress scratching at her bare legs. She ran to her father, crashing into him, her arms encircling his legs.

"Kitty!" Bettina protested.

"May I steal my helper from you ladies?" Karel charmed the women with a smile. Kitty thought she saw Frau Müller blush.

"Of course, Karel," Bettina replied. Kitty had acted the part of the perfect child as instructed. It was a stellar performance. Bettina had no more use for her. With a wave of her hand, Bettina dismissed Kitty. "Send Hanuš in if you could," added Bettina. She was not as much asking as ordering. She turned back to her guest.

"Hanuš is my firstborn. He was due on Valentine's Day, 1925," Bettina said, launching into another of her often told tales. "The sky had been overcast for days. Suddenly it became clear and bright. The wind rattled a loose window in the bedroom and then there he was, on February the sixth, a week early, round, and warm and pink." At this point in the well-rehearsed story, her mother's tone changed, and she shrugged. "Kitty was born on June 15, 1928." She added, disinterested, "It rained, as I recall."

Kitty pitied Hanuš. "I have three people who love me whereas poor Hanuš has only one," reasoned Kitty. "Number One. I am daddy's little girl." Her father was the one person with whom Kitty knew she could get away with anything.

"Number Two. I have Otto." Otto Polesi was Kitty's cousin. He lived with the Löwis at their home in Teplice. Otto's parents operated under the firm belief that he would obtain a better education in Teplice than the small village where they resided. Otto and Hanuš were similar in age yet it was widely agreed that Otto was "the gentle one." In a household where her own brother was her nemesis, Otto was Kitty's stalwart companion. They made a childhood pact to marry each other one day should they each be lacking in acceptable suitors.

"Number Three. I have my Oila," Kitty reflected. Oila, one Maria Koppensteiner, was Kitty's governess and constant companion. Kitty had bestowed the nickname "Oila" on her governess at the age of two when she was unable to pronounce the word "fräulein." By some coincidence that same year Kitty began referring to her mother by her given name. But that is another story.

"Thank you for rescuing me," Kitty whispered to her father, her patent leather shoes clicking on the parquet floor, her father's hand warm and strong in hers as he led her out of the family's apartment and down the stairs to his office on the first floor. Karel Löwi received a generous salary from his position as director of the Brüder Willner Factory, a cardboard manufacturing company, and the owner provided Karel with the spacious, eight-room apartment commanding the second and third floors of the building. The Löwis made their home in the elegant three-story villa with gold brick accents and a blue slate roof; it was the only home Kitty had ever known. On a clear day, the long windows of the house filled each room with sunshine, the crystal chandelier in the center of the foyer splashing the walls with a thousand points of refracted light.

Karel opened the door to his office on the first floor, seating himself behind the massive walnut desk that took up half his office. He had a thick head of brown hair which he sometimes allowed to grow so long it curled around the tops of his ears. He was neatly dressed in a shirt and tie, and a vest that complemented his suit jacket. Kitty thought he was the most handsome of all the other fathers she knew. She told him so with regularity.

"How would you ever get along without me here to help you?" Kitty asked. She stood at one corner of the desk, stapling pieces of paper together with a rhythmic "thunk." She had appointed herself her father's official secretary. Her job was of such great importance that it required frequent visits to his office on the first floor — visits of which her mother profoundly disapproved.

"I don't know what I would do without you, Kitty." Her father spoke to her in German, the language of his youth. He watched as she dutifully pressed a rubber stamp onto an ink pad and then stamped the imprint onto an envelope. Karel shook his head and laughed.

Kitty's dark hair was wound in tight curls. Oila had been hard at work the night before in anticipation of the afternoon tea with Frau Müeller, separating thick strands of Kitty's wet hair and wrapping them in long strips of fabric. They had dried overnight, and the resulting ringlets were nothing short of magical. Everyone who saw her mentioned her resemblance to Shirley Temple, the American child actor. Karel had to laugh when he heard the comparisons. Shirley was precocious and sweet. His Kitty was downright mischievous. But Kitty and America's sweetheart did have one thing in common: they could act a part when needed.

"Back to work, then," Karel said. He turned his attention to a pile of invoices in a stack on his desk. Kitty knew that was her cue to leave. She skipped out of the office, her footsteps echoing outside the office, in search of further amusement and Otto.

Kitty found Otto kicking a ball in the high grass behind the villa. "I am the nurse, and you are the soldier," Kitty explained to her cousin. Otto had lived with the Löwis for a full school year. He was accustomed to the rules that governed playing make-believe with Kitty. Today they were playing war. It was one of Kitty's favorite games. Kitty was supervising the care of the wounded. Otto obliged.

"Sit down and let me have a look at you," she ordered the injured soldier. Otto sat on a stump in the yard behind the house, feigning injury. The yard was at once a stage and a setting that stirred Kitty's imagination. One day she and Otto were on safari, cutting a swath through the tall grasses toward the back of the property. Another day they were archaeologists uncovering the crumbling stone steps of some ancient ruin, the remains of an outbuilding that had seen better days.

Today, the sun was shining for their war games, warming the day; they had been playing for hours and Otto's brown hair was thick with sweat. Kitty inspected his make-believe battle wound. "Tsk, tsk. This is quite serious. I'm afraid I may need to operate."

"Noooo," Otto cried out in fake protest. Kitty threaded an imaginary needle and began to sew the wound closed, weaving it back and forth. She imitated the basic mending skills she had learned from Oila. For play-acting it was quite convincing; Otto thought he felt the pinch of the needle each time her fingers touched his skin.

"There, now," said the nurse. "Back to fight the enemy with you."

A while later, Kitty heard the lunch bell ring. "Hurry, Otto, or we will be late!" Kitty jumped up and ran from the backyard, and up the back stairs, Otto following close behind. They cut through the kitchen to the dismay of Cook, who was carrying a large tureen of soup through the French doors to the formal dining room. Kitty skidded to a stop, flopping herself down in her appointed seat at the long table.

If the Löwis were religious about anything, it was the noonday meal. The grandfather clock in the parlor struck noon, and Kitty found her father already seated at the head of the table. The meal was passed in the same manner each day: Karel inquired of his children and Otto about the status of their studies and afterward opened the discussion to include their leisure pursuits. It was always the same. When the meal concluded, her father took his leave from the family, retiring for a brief nap in his chair in the parlor, and at one o'clock sharp he headed back down to his office for the remainder of the day. There were no exceptions to this program.

Otto and Hanuš took their seats at the table. Bettina strolled in last. She sat across from her husband at the long dining table covered in a starched white lace tablecloth, exuding ennui.

"Well, children. Summer vacation begins today," Karel announced.

"No ballet! No piano!" Kitty said excitedly, leaping out of her chair. She ran to the head of the table and threw her arms around her father's neck. She blamed her mother for forcing her to take ballet lessons and gave her father credit for the respite from it. In a world where success was gauged by the color of your tutu, white being the best, green the worst, Kitty had thus far not been able to move past green. She now despised green.

Piano lessons were no better. No amount of sweat and practice held any hope of improving her skills. No matter how she begged, she could not convince Bettina to release her from a pursuit that brought her shame and embarrassment.

Bettina cast a disapproving glance at Kitty. Her father spoke. "Yes, Kitty. That is true. You know we must get the household ready for our departure to Jesenice."

Every summer at the end of the school year, the family, including Cook, a maid, and Oila packed up everything they needed to live for six weeks in the town where her father had lived as a boy. After his father's death, Karel had purchased a villa there, a sweet two-story terra cotta affair, in which his mother, Bettina's sister, Flora, and Flora's family resided. Kitty's best friend, Aja, and her family spent their weekends in Jesenice.

After lunch, Kitty walked through the kitchen and sat on the back steps, alone for a moment. She remembered a night at the end of last summer at the villa in Jesenice. The grownups were gathered at a long table in the backyard playing cards. Kitty was dozing in her room above, listening to the hum of their voices, their muted laughter drifting through the open bedroom window, the sound lulling her to sleep. A crack of thunder split the night. Someone cried out, Kitty was sure it was Bettina. Fat drops of rain began to fall slowly at first onto the dry yard, kicking up the dusty ground. A moment later the heavens opened, and Kitty could hear chairs being knocked over as everyone ran for cover into the house, the grownups' laughter following them inside. In town, the rain was inconvenient, especially if you forgot your umbrella. In Jesenice, it was enchanting.

Kitty had remained standing on her bed, looking out the window and watching the lightning as it flashed over the lake and the orchard in the distance. The rain smelled of dust. Jesenice was a magical place. She could not wait to start packing.

A group of children, brown from the summer sun and barefoot, milled about the courtyard in front of the villa in Jesenice. "Let's put on a show." Kitty announced. *Peter and the Wolf*, she added. Kitty was a ringleader, a showman, and, thanks to Oila, could not stand idleness in herself or others. If there was nothing to do, Kitty would make something from nothing. She understood that being in charge had its benefits: she could give herself all the plum leading roles. Kitty grabbed Aja's hand.

Hanuš groaned. Kitty's brother was a handsome boy with a thick shock of dark brown hair that obscured his dark eyes. He was the oldest boy among the cousins, except Frantisek, Otto's brother, and an unwilling participant in his sister's amusements. Today he wore *lederhosen* over a white V-neck undershirt, his summer uniform. His cousin, Otto, wore the same, which caused Hanuš no end of grief. In his mind, they were barely friends, let alone twins.

The other children knew the story of *Peter and the Wolf* quite well, having been forced to act it out on many occasions under Kitty's direction. Aunt Flora had collected all manner of clothing which she kept in the basement of the villa for just such occasions. Sometimes the children treated the grownups to a real show; other times the drama was improvised.

Kitty, Otto, and Aja went to the basement, foraging for the proper costumes. A few stragglers from the neighborhood, Liesl and Gertie, were added to the cast and Kitty assigned them minor roles. Hanuš was the Wolf, and Otto doubled as the kind Grandfather and the Bird. Aja always wanted to be the Cat, and the neighbor Gertie played the Duck, doubling as a Hunter with Liesl. Of course, Kitty was Peter. Otto's older brother Frantisek was nowhere to be found. Hanuš vowed that next summer he would assume the role of Frantisek, a disinterested teenager who kept his distance from the bothersome children.

Each member of the cast was expected to hum their characters' signature tune as they acted out their part in the play. It began with the Wolf attacking and feasting on the Duck, prompting Peter to capture the Wolf in a noose. Peter then tricked the Hunters into bringing the Wolf to the zoo and for that Peter was a hero, leading her fellow actors in a parade signaling the end of the play, the Wolf bringing up the rear. After the play was over, the actors disbursed. Gertie, Liesl and Aja went home. Otto, Hanuš, and Kitty wandered back to the villa in the waning dusk.

The following morning Kitty came down the stairs to the kitchen, greeted by the smell of onions and fresh thyme frying in goose fat. Aunt Flora was chopping onions for potato salad while Bettina, her hair covered in a babushka, her cheeks flushed, pounded pork for schnitzel.

"Mother, why are you cooking?" Kitty blurted out without thinking. "The only time you are in the kitchen is to get a glass of water or to talk to Cook." Flora burst into laughter.

"Kitty!" Bettina scolded her, feigning insult.

"You have to admit she's right, Bettina," Flora teased. Aunt Flora had a kind face, she was always smiling, her brown hair tucked up in a bun, her long neck lending her an air of casual elegance. Bettina and Aunt Flora had similar noses but that was where the resemblance ended. Bettina wore her hair down in Jesenice, she was taller than Flora and, in every photo taken of her that summer she could be found regarding the camera with suspicion.

"Uncle Erich is picking up Uncle Leo and Aunt Tessie in Prague. They will join us here for the day. Do you see Cook anywhere? She is on vacation. Now take this bowl and fill it with berries. We are making *bublanina* for dessert." Kitty's cheeks reddened. Of course, she knew Cook was not there. Kitty was not stupid, yet there were moments like these when she was made to feel that she was. She took the bowl and walked outside to the yard. The raspberry bushes behind the villa were thick with fruit. Oila had taught Kitty how to round the berries off the stem to keep them intact. In her anger, Kitty grabbed multiple stems at a time, crushing the berries, staining her hands ruby red. She stuffed a handful in her mouth, but their sweetness was no match for her resentment.

Uncle Erich, Karel's brother, pulled his car into the cul-de-sac in front of the villa. Kitty ran outside in time to see Uncle Leo, Karel's older brother, opening the car door for Aunt Tessie. Leo took Tessie's hand to help her out of the car.

Kitty had overheard her mother and her aunt talking about the couple before their arrival. "They are 'smitten' with each other," said Bettina. Kitty presumed that must mean they liked each other quite a lot. She looked up at Uncle Leo. It was whispered in the family that Kitty's father Karel had gotten the brains in the family while Leo had gotten the looks. Kitty did not understand the sentiment; surely her father was the most handsome man ever. However, when she saw Leo and Tessie together Kitty had to admit they did make a striking pair.

"Why, hello," Tessie leaned down to greet Kitty. Tessie wore a belted black dress with a cowl neck and a scalloped pattern that was edged in gold, elegant attire for the rural setting. "So good to see you again, Kitty."

"I'm Kitty Löwi and you are very pretty," Kitty said, lowering her eyes. "I like your dress." Tessie bent down to shake Kitty's hand.

"We've met before, darling, and I like your dress, too." Tessie smiled. Her lips were painted a deep red and her nails were polished. Tessie kissed Kitty on her forehead. Tessie laughed and took a handkerchief out of her purse to wipe the lipstick from Kitty's face. "There, that's better." It was decided. Tessie was officially Kitty's second favorite grown up. Second to Oila.

Oila led the children down the path from the villa to the water, a distraction so the adults could catch up and finish the lunch preparations. There was no breeze that afternoon. The lake was still. A dragonfly hovered above the water, darting high and low at a whim. Kitty had named the dragonfly Konstantin. She was sure that it was the same dragonfly she saw nearly every day, the same one that managed to evade Hanuš's butterfly net. A fish punctured the calm surface of the lake every so often to take a chance at Konstantin. Everyone called it "the lake" when it was in fact a pond fed by the Jesenický potok, a brook that wound its way through the town.

Frantisek had appeared out of nowhere, and he and Hanuš broke into a run. "Get me away from these babies," Hanuš said to Frantisek, scrambling to reach the clearing at the water's edge. All summer Hanuš had been vying for his older cousin's attention. The two boys ran off to a well-known fishing spot, leaving Otto behind with the girls.

Oila spread out a blanket on the shore. She tucked her dress underneath her legs and sat down, her feet stretched out in front of her, a camera on her lap. Oila's dark eyes crinkled in the corners, smiling as the girls took off their socks and shoes. Kitty and Aja had swimsuits on under their dresses, which they quickly shed, discarding them on the blanket.

The two girls ran to the water. A light breeze had picked up, blowing from the north, causing gentle ripples in the water. The sun shone on the surface, sparkling like diamonds. After a moment's hesitation, the girls plunged in, giggling, and splashing, scattering liquid jewels in every direction. They were good swimmers, paddling back and forth. "Ah!" Kitty squealed when a fish brushed past her leg.

"Otto!" Kitty waved to her cousin to join them in the water. He jumped up and ran in without stopping, flopping his whole body forward, splashing Kitty and Aja. They splashed and swam in the clear water of the stream for over an hour. It was unclear who had bored of fishing first, Hanuš or Frantisek. Hanuš rejoined the others just as they were exiting the water. When they had dried off a bit, they kicked a ball around the grassy clearing, pausing once to pose for a photo for Oila.

"What about Frantisek?" Hanuš looked around for his cousin so he might join them for the photo. Gone again. Kitty, Otto, and Aja lay on their stomachs, their heads propped up on their hands, legs kicked up behind them, Aja holding the ball in front of her, her dark bangs covering her forehead. Hanuš sat cross-legged next to them, barefoot. Oila laughed. "You look like a bunch of ragamuffins!" In the photo all the children are smiling from ear to ear, their faces brown, flushed with sun and heat.

Voices could be heard coming down the worn path. The voices grew louder until they eventually reached the clearing, revealing their owners. "It's the Germans," Hanuš said. He stood up, just in time to see a group of boys thrashing at the tall grass with long sticks. Two of the three boys, close in age to Hanuš, looked familiar.

Kitty frowned. "Oh, it's you," Kitty said to one of the boys. They stopped what they were doing. One of them laughed.

"Oh, so you are still here, eh?" The boy who spoke first was called Rolf. "Shall we pick up where we left off the other day?" Rolf had sandy blond hair that was long and swept to the side, sometimes falling over his piercing blue eyes. Kitty had a crush on him. She had learned the previous summer that ignoring him or being mean made him want to spend more time with her. Together with Aja and some of the other kids, they played "war" together. For reasons Kitty could not explain, the German kids always played the role of the bad guys. Kitty was Florence Nightingale.

"Sure, why not?" replied Hanuš. With that, the games began. The German boys used their sticks as guns, hiding and lying in wait in the tall grass on the edge of the clearing. Hanuš, Otto and Kitty ran to the pine trees, using clumps of dirt as grenades. Hanuš had a strong arm for throwing so he was elected to send out the grenades. The clumps of dirt landed close to the boys.

"Kaboom!" Otto made the sound effects of the grenade blowing up. Rolf stumbled out of the high grass, holding his head. Kitty ran to his aid.

"Where does it hurt?" she asked him. Florence Nightingale did not play favorites, she sought only to save lives. No matter what side they were on, Kitty nursed them back to health. Rolf pointed to his head, feigning injury. "Let me see what I have here." She looked in her imaginary nursing kit and pushed Rolf's hair away from his forehead, dabbing at it with an imaginary cloth. "I am going to have to bandage your head," she announced. She reached into the kit for bandages, which she proceeded to wrap around his head. "There. Now you mustn't move around. Sit here."

Another wounded soldier cried out. "Help!" This time it was Otto. He ran to Kitty, holding out his arm for her to inspect.

"What's the matter with you?" Kitty asked, her voice cool. It no longer seemed a coincidence that every time Rolf needed tending to, Otto needed care as well.

"I have been shot," Otto said. Kitty pulled his hand away from his arm.

"It's only a flesh wound," Kitty said. "Get back out there and fight!" The noises of battle carried on in the background, grenades landing and exploding while shots rang out from the make-believe firearms. Enthusiasm waned as midday approached and the weapons missed their intended targets.

"I'm hungry," Hanuš said, effectively declaring the games concluded. It was no secret that no matter how deadly the games came to pass, Hanuš came out unscathed. The ragtag crew dispersed leaving Hanuš, Otto, and Kitty to make their way back to the villa.

A huge table had been set outside on the stone terrace behind the villa. Lunches at Jesenice were late, languid, and long. The hum of the conversation, the clink of silverware, and laughter came easily among the family. Thin curtains fluttered in the window of the kitchen. Platters were emptied, bellies were filled, and the conversation grew sparse. The sun had lowered in the sky, leaving the backyard in the cool shadow of the villa.

Aunt Flora pushed her unfinished dessert away and stood up. "One last walk together!" she announced. A groan came from Uncle Leo and Kitty's father. "Come now. It's tradition," she added. The maid began clearing the plates from the table, leaving the adults no choice but to stand and join the others for the post-meal jaunt.

Kitty watched as the adults – Uncle Leo brandishing a cane, her father in suspenders, her mother in a button-down shirt, sleeves rolled up, Uncle Erich with his pants tucked into his socks, a light overcoat around his shoulders in case of a late summer chill – set off down the country road, kicking up dust, laughing and joking among themselves.

The summer was near spent; six weeks gone by in a flash. It had been consumed in the best possible way, days spent swimming, the adults hiking the long country roads surrounding the villa and lounging in the grass by the water's edge. On the last afternoon, the sun cast its late summer melancholy from an angle in the cloudless sky. It warmed the faces of the group that made their way back up the well-worn path from to the water in the direction of the villa. Kitty and Aja held hands, leading the way. They were followed by Oila, then Hanuš, brandishing his fishing pole like a weapon. Last was Otto.

They arrived at the terrace behind the house to find Frantisek eating alone at the long table.

"Lucky you, Frantisek," said Hanuš. "Summer is over, and we are stuck with your little brother for the school year, not you." The previous year Aunt Flora had expressed concern to Bettina that the local school left much to be desired. Bettina had offered to help. Otto had lived with them during the school year, attending the local school with Hanuš.

"First a little sister, now a boarder," Hanuš had grumbled to himself. Although the cousins were only months apart in age, they had until then only tolerated each other. On the first day of school the previous fall, dressed identically in the school's uniform, double-breasted jackets, collared shirts, and shorts, the two boys were mistaken for twins. Hanuš was beside himself. The memory of it angered him now, inciting him to do something rash.

Hanuš grabbed the wings of a butterfly that had alighted on a tall flower in the yard, pinching them together so it could not escape. It had pale brown wings with feathery edges and orange dots. He put it under a glass on the table, its wings beating against the tight space. Kitty reached for the glass to knock it over. Hanuš swatted her hand away. Within minutes the butterfly was dead.

Tears streamed down Kitty's face. "You are horrible! You killed it!" Oila had come out in the yard.

"Come with me, Kitty. It's time to wash up," Oila reached for Kitty's hand and led her, sobbing, back into the house. Oila sat Kitty down on the bed in the room she shared with her brother.

"Why, Oila? Why?" Kitty cried. "Why did he have to kill it?" Oila slowly washed Kitty's face and hands with a cool washcloth.

"There is no acceptable explanation for people's cruel actions, Kitty." Oila started to say more then stopped. Kitty turned to let Oila brush her hair, soothed by the rhythmic motion. When Kitty was calm, Oila covered her with a light sheet and kissed her on the forehead. "Good night, dear Kitty. Sweet dreams."

It was their last night in Jesenice, the last night of summer before heading back to Teplice. The light was changing in the tiny bedroom. The last remnants of sunlight danced on the wall through the branches of the tree outside the bedroom window. The shadows grew longer and filled the wall as the sun sank beneath the lake on the horizon. Kitty lay sprawled out in the bed, her cheeks flushed, a damp film of sweat on her forehead, her dark curls tumbling over the pillow. One suntanned arm hung off the edge of the bed. The rhythmic chirping of the crickets that hid in the tall reeds down on the water's edge lulled Kitty into a deep sleep.

Hanuš came in. He flopped down across the other bed, his long legs filling the length of it. He fell fast asleep face down, his dark hair stuck to his forehead. The bottoms of his bare feet were toughened from a summer spent running everywhere without shoes. Fireflies lit up the night, punctuating the darkness, flashing their secret Morse code. Summer in Jesenice was over. A new school year beckoned. It was time to go home.

Chapter Two

VLADA 1934
PARDUBICE, CZECHOSLOVAKIA

The sun, angled low in the sky, cast long shadows behind the trees in the factory yard. There was no talk of school yet, but Vlada felt its presence encroaching on the endless parade of warm days capped with clear skies and wispy clouds. The evenings seemed to go on forever; Vlada playing yet another game of hide and seek under the star-filled heavens with Lada, laughing and running joyfully, sweat drying on their brows in the evening's chill, the sound of crickets and his parents' voices drifting down from the balcony of the flat.

At night, he settled into bed and Hermina kissed him on the forehead. "I want to see my friends at school, Mami, but I don't want summer to end." Hermina brushed his bangs to one side of his forehead, looking at Vlada's face, tan from summer excursions to the mountains and castles nearby.

"And I don't want you to grow up, Vlada," Hermina said wistfully. "But I don't have a choice in the matter."

On a morning late in August, Vlada burst through the door of the flat, sweaty, and red-faced. Hermina sat at the kitchen table, peeling turnips. She dropped the turnips and stood up. Vlada stood in front of her panting, one hand behind his back. "What has happened, Vlada?" she asked nervously.

Slowly, he brought his hand out in front of him and presented her with a fistful of golden beets dangling from their greens. He pressed a finger to his lips, breaking out in a conspiratorial grin.

Hermina breathed out a sigh of relief. "Oh!" she replied, smiling. She took the contraband from Vlada's outstretched hand, pretending to sink under the weight of the bounty. "You are getting good at this!"

"You can thank Lada, Mami," said Vlada. It was the annual sugar beet harvest. Every day, carts from a nearby farm filled to overflowing with golden root vegetables passed within feet of the distillery walls on their way to the sugar refinery for processing. Lada had perfected the art of pilfering beets from the passing carts, and he shared his technique with Vlada, who proved to be a quick study.

"Watch this, Vlada," said Lada. In his hand he held a slender piece of wood with a nail embedded in the end. He lay in wait behind a wagon on the street and waited for a cart to pass by. At the last moment, Lada leaped up and began running, keeping pace behind the cart. He whipped the wood toward the pile of beets in the back of the wagon before it outpaced him, and Vlada heard a resounding "thwack." The nail had connected with its intended target.

It was Vlada's turn. "Run, Vlada, run," Lada encouraged his friend under his breath. Vlada got a late start and struggled to keep up with the cart. They both heard the "thwack" as the nail punctured the flesh of the beet. "Ha! Got one!" Vlada shouted enthusiastically. Lada put his finger to his lips. This was dangerous work. If the driver of the wagon caught them, they would both get a solid whipping.

The boys spent the rest of the morning taking turns running after the passing wagons. They met behind the coal truck in the factory yard and spread out the fruits of their labor in front of them, breathing heavily from their exertions. "Nice work, Vlada," said Lada, counting the number of beets in his friend's pile. "Seven! That's a record."

Vlada sat at the kitchen table while his mother prepared the beets. She scrubbed them in the sink and then she peeled and grated them. After that, she placed them in a pot of boiling water on the stove. Karel appeared just in time for lunch. "Beets, eh?" Karel said, shaking his head. He walked to the stove and watched as steam billowed up from the rapidly boiling liquid. "All right, Vlada. What is happening to the liquid in the beets? And why are droplets of liquid forming on the ceiling above the pot?"

Vlada walked to the stove and observed the boiling pot. "Evaporation and condensation, Tati," he beamed at his father.

"My future chemist," his father replied, patting Vlada on the back. "You have a future if you don't get arrested first!" Karel took a spoon and began to stir the beets in the pot.

"Away from the stove. Both of you," said Hermina, a playful grin on her face. "The experiment is over." Hermina poured the beets through a strainer, steam rising and dampening her cheeks. She discarded the beet solids and held up a jar filled with thick golden liquid for Vlada to see. "Our secret, Vlada," she said. "We are partners in crime."

The double doors to the pánsky room were kept closed when the room was not in use, sealing in the smell of the leather book bindings, dry parchment pages, and Karel's pipe tobacco. It was the last Sunday morning before his return to school, and Vlada entered the room, a book tucked under his arm, and inhaled deeply the room's familiar aroma. He lay down on the carpet on his stomach and began flipping the pages of the book. It was one in the *Skolak Kája Mařík* series by Czech author Felix Haj.

Vlada stopped to look at one of the book's illustrations. He thought he and the main character, Kaja, looked a lot alike, and he could easily picture himself having the same adventures. Kaja was a wild child who grew up in a hunting lodge and roamed the Czech forests and mountain ranges, thick with fir trees, chasing after geese and groundhogs. Best of all, Kaja attended school at his own discretion.

Vlada shared his father's love of books. Karel's book collection filled the pánsky room's built-in shelves to overflowing. "These are the great Russian novelists and playwrights, Vlada: Tolstoy, Dostoevsky, Chekov," his father had told him as he placed each book on the shelf a few months prior. "In a few years, you will be ready for Čapek." Čapek was a Czech novelist and screenwriter who had earned his reputation writing science fiction. But his series of interviews with Tomas Masaryk, the first president of Czechoslovakia, gripped his father's imagination. He held Čapek's book, *Talks with T. J. Masaryk,* reverently in his hand.

"I sent a copy to Čapek to sign." Vlada knew the story well but sat quietly as his father told it again. "He returned the book to me signed only with his initials. Inside was a two-page letter explaining why he thought Masaryk should be credited as the author."

One afternoon, Pan Zak, the distillery machinist, met Vlada in the factory yard and invited him to view his book collection. "I hear you are quite a reader, Vlada," Pan Zak said. The wiry bachelor was kind and soft-spoken and he rarely had visitors. "Books make the best companions, don't they?" Vlada stepped inside Pan Zak's flat on the first floor. It took a moment for Vlada's eyes to adjust to the dim light in the room, and then his eyes grew wide. Bookshelves lined the front room from the floor right up to the ceiling.

"Jules Verne!" Vlada exclaimed with delight, running his fingers across the titles on one shelf. He looked at Pan Zak for permission, and then reached for a copy of *Twenty Thousand Leagues Under the Seas: A World Tour Underwater.*

Vlada quickly returned it to the shelf and selected another volume. A satisfied smile spread over Pan Zak's face as Vlada perused *The D'Artagnan Romances* by Alexandre Dumas. "Books are of no use just sitting on a shelf, Vlada. They must be read to be enjoyed. If you promise to take care of the books while you read them, you may borrow freely."

Vlada could not believe his good fortune. He felt like an archaeologist discovering long-lost artifacts in a place that time had forgotten.

Pan Zak looked at the title of the next book Vlada selected from his extensive collection. It was bound in red leather and stamped in gold. "Ah. *The Archipelago on Fire,*" Pan Zak said, nodding his approval. He pressed the book into Vlada's hands. "Enjoy."

A year had passed since that first day in Pan Zak's library. Vlada had thought Pan Zak was sentimental when he spoke about books like they were people. "Each time I finish reading a book, I feel as if I am parting with a dear friend," Pan Zak had told him.

Now, each time Vlada turned the final page of a cherished book, he clutched it tightly to his chest, taking his time as he walked down the stairs before reluctantly surrendering it to its rightful owner. "Pan Zak was right," thought Vlada. "Books are like friends."

Vlada's reverie was interrupted when his father appeared in the doorway of the pánsky room. "Vlada, shall we go and see what Mr. Lochman has for us today?"

A trip to the bookstore in the center of town combined two of Vlada's favorite activities: spending time with his father and reading. He looked up from his book, grinning widely. "Really, Tati?"

A warm autumn breeze moved the clouds from east to west overhead as father and son left the distillery compound and walked east on Palackého třida, past the butcher shop and the horse racetrack. Vlada's cheeks reddened as they passed the track. He and Lada snuck into the racetrack grounds regularly that summer and hid in the tall grass to watch the horse races, never once paying the entrance fee. Vlada knew his father would not approve.

Karel was lost in his own thoughts about the racetrack. "There is a reason why they call it The Devil's Race, Vlada." Vlada heard his father's dramatic delivery, and he shivered in anticipation of the tale. "On their first lap over the dirt and grass track, the strongest horses fly like lightning. Up, then over the great hedge, clearing the ditch. Vlada's eyes were on his father, hanging on his every word. "On the second lap, a mighty horse and its rider crest the towering hedge. But the evil that is the Great Taxis Ditch will not be denied. Its watery depths have meant the end of many a fine horse. If the ditch is very angry, the rider may perish as well." His father winked at him, but Vlada remained horrified. He imagined the trench as an abyss, a gaping maw, like the dark sea monster in the Jules Verne novel, enveloping its prey with a horrible sucking sound.

Vlada knew what happened to the horses who succumbed to the ditch by virtue of a broken leg. They were euthanized on the spot. The proximity of the butcher shop to the racetrack was a convenient, if gory, circumstance. He felt a pang of guilt thinking that one of those strong, regal creatures might end up in his favorite dish, *Svíčková na smetaně*. His mother marinated the meat of the lean, young animal with vinegar, oil, and vegetables for several days in the basement where it was cool. When the meat was tender, she cooked it, and served it with cream gravy and dumplings. Vlada's stomach growled just thinking about it.

"Remember the time Mami went to the butcher to buy meat for Čigy?" Vlada grinned. Karel chuckled, launching into his best imitation of the indignant butcher. "How dare you come in here to buy meat for a dog? I sell only the best horse meat, for humans!" Karel shook his head, smiling fondly at his wife's efforts to spoil the dog. "Only the best for Čigy, right, Vlada?"

The two walked on, past the synagogue and the barracks of the Military Riding School. The school was home to cavalry officers and riding instructors. Its cache was heightened by the presence of a local hero. Captain Rudolf Poplar had represented the Republic in two Olympic games, competing in Paris in 1924, and Amsterdam in 1928, in the field of equestrian jumping. He was a source of pride for the townspeople of Pardubice.

When Vlada was seven, his father had taken him aside and delivered sad news. "I am sorry to tell you that Rudolf Poplar has suffered a grave injury, Vlada."

"What happened, Tati?" Vlada's eyes grew wide with concern.

"It seems that during a lap of the *Velká Pardubická*, Poplar's mare, Ella, missed the jump at the small rails. She landed on her rider with her full weight. Poor man. He died on the way to the hospital." Karel's face was solemn.

"Was Ella hurt?" Vlada held his breath waiting for the response.

"Ella is fine," his father assured him. Vlada breathed a sigh of relief. A few days later, Vlada stood next to his father as the tragic mare, Ella, and the entire riding school cavalry accompanied Poplar's casket as it was pulled through the streets of Pardubice. The officers wore full military dress – their signature crimson coats and camel-colored jodhpurs – and rode astride their powerful steeds, the animals' coats curried to a high shine.

Karel looked down at Vlada, who was smiling broadly as Ella trotted by. The mare's hooves clopped loudly over the cobblestones in front of them, her massive black head bobbing up and down. Vlada nodded back at her, overcome with delight that Ella had not ended up on the dinner table of some local family. Vlada secretly vowed he would never eat horse meat again.

The copper roof of the Green Gate rose ahead against a crisp, blue sky, the Renaissance clock tower soaring over the other buildings at one end of the Old Town Square. Vlada had climbed the stairs to the top of the tower many times, trying not to look down until he reached the top, where he marveled at how tiny the people appeared down below.

Today, Vlada broke into a run, skipping across the cobblestones of Pernstynkse Square. A flock of pigeons scurried ahead of him, refusing to become airborne unless offered no choice. The Ladislav Lochman bookstore was tucked away under the Green Gate. They entered the store and Karel went in search of Mr. Lochman to place an order for a book. Vlada walked slowly through the towering stacks, allowing himself to be swallowed up in the labyrinth of bookshelves. He made straight for the children's book section, where he began eagerly scouring the shelves.

"Aha!" Vlada slid a book off the shelf. It was a new addition to the *Skolak Kája Mařík* series. He sat down, opened the book, and began to read the first page. He was unable to concentrate, distracted by a clamor of raised voices, his father's among them. The discussion echoed through the bookstore, something about the president of Germany's successor and the new title he had chosen for himself: "Fuhrer." It was clear from the tone of the exchange that no one seemed in favor of the development.

A moment later, Vlada looked up to find his father standing in front of him. "Time to go, Vlada," said Karel, hurriedly. Vlada looked down at the book in his hands. He closed it reluctantly, preparing to return it to its place on the shelf in front of him. "What's that you have there?" Karel took the book from Vlada and flipped a few pages. His father exhaled deeply, his earlier agitation fading. "Shall we add this to your collection?" Karel asked, handing the book to him.

"Yes! Thank you, Tati." Vlada led the way to the cash register, the book tucked proudly under his arm.

At the front of the shop, Vlada proudly handed the book to Mr. Lochman, who lifted his glasses to his face, peering down at it. "Ah! You are a lucky boy," said Mr. Lochman, eyeing the title of the book, his eyes crinkling at the edges when he smiled. "This is the last copy." He was bald, like Vlada's father, and wore a vest with a pocket watch and chain. He wrapped the book in brown paper and handed it to Vlada. "That will keep it safe for your journey home."

A light rain had begun to fall, but the sky remained bright. Vlada held the book tightly against him. His father seemed to have forgotten his earlier irritation and paused for a moment in the shelter under the Green Gate. "Is it too rainy for a walk to the castle?" He teased, winking.

"Never, Tati! It's a perfect day!" Vlada bounded in the direction of Pardubice *Zámek*, the stark white Gothic castle on the banks of the Elbe and Chrudimka Rivers. The castle was protected by thick stone walls, great earthen ramparts, and corner turrets with holes for firing at intruders. Vlada loved to close his eyes and imagine the battles that must have raged outside the lofty castle walls right here, in his own backyard.

"Where shall we go first, Vlada?" Karel asked, already knowing the answer.

The castle was one of Vlada's favorite places and he knew the grounds by heart. He led the way up a wide stone staircase and stopped at the top in front of a heavy, wooden door, where he waited patiently for his father to join him. Karel lifted the latch. The door groaned and they entered a cavernous room. Vlada ran and stood in front of an intricately carved wooden chest. It was rumored to have contained the jewels of the Pernštejn dynasty and Vlada checked it every time on the outside chance the jewels had been returned.

They left the room and traveled across the castle courtyard to another set of stairs. The wind had picked up and it whistled down the stone staircase. Vlada bolted up the stairs, his footsteps echoing off the stone walls. "Hello! Hello!" called Vlada. "Hello! Hello!" His voice echoed back.

"We have time for one last stop, Vlada. Your mother will be waiting for us for lunch," said Karel, when they had reached the top.

A moment later, they stood in front of a decaying mural. Men dressed in black armor approached on horseback from the lower left corner, while spears seemed to grow out of the ground on the right. The mountains in the landscape were painted in shades of royal blue and aqua. In the center of the painting sat Delilah, her face obscured. Lest there be any doubt that it was her, in one hand she gripped a clump of Samson's hair and in the other, the dreaded scissors sat poised to cut.

"Tell the story, Tati!" Vlada looked pleadingly at his father.

"Delilah tricked Samson and earned his trust," recited Karel. "He confessed to her the source of his might: his hair. She betrayed him and cut off his hair, leaving him powerless. Or so she thought." Vlada stood very still, awaiting the denouement. "Samson harnessed every bit of his strength one last time and brought the pillars of the temple down upon the two of them, killing himself and all who had betrayed him."

The tour was complete. They began walking in the direction of the distillery. Vlada was eager to share with his mother the adventures of his day; the visit to Lochman's bookstore, the purchase of the new book, climbing the castle steps to see the secret oak chest, and the Samson and Delilah mural.

Karel grew quiet on the walk and the two fell in step next to each other, the sound of their footsteps the only sound on the quiet street. Vlada thought back to earlier that morning. His parents had been discussing the death of the president of Germany, von Hindenburg, and his mother's voice had been anxious, shrill.

Vlada shook his head. The sky was clearing, and he hugged his new book to his chest. It had been a perfect day, and nothing was going to spoil it.

The family's new maid, Klara, was a shy girl who was eager to please. It was laundry day, and her job was to keep watch over the huge pots of water that boiled on the stove in the kitchen of the flat. She lifted the bedsheets from a basket and into the hot water, poking them down and stirring the pot with a long wooden stick. If Vlada had not known better, Klara might have been making soup. Hermina worked beside Klara, her dark hair falling in her face. His mother paused for a moment to tuck her hair behind her ear before wringing out the excess water from the sheets left to cool in the kitchen sink.

Their first maid, Emilie, had fallen for a cavalry trainee. As Hermina had feared, Emilie quit and ran home to her parents, incapacitated by shame and a broken heart. "I hope this girl will not meet the same fate," thought Hermina, watching Klara as they struggled to carry a heavy basket of damp laundry out to the balcony to dry.

"Laundry day," grumbled Vlada under his breath. Even though it fell every six weeks or so, to Vlada it felt like a weekly occurrence. The two women would work all day and Hermina had created a quick dish over the years to ensure the family would not go hungry while they toiled: a corn meal mush slathered in blueberry jam that, in Vlada's not-so-humble opinion, was barely palatable. He went so far as to deem it unworthy of serving to the geese who lived in the factory yard.

"Čigy!" Vlada called the dog, removing his plate of corn meal from the table and walking downstairs. Čigy ran over and sniffed at the plate Vlada put in front of the dog, who greedily licked it clean. It seemed laundry day was only a problem for Vlada.

The following day, Karel took a poll. "Who wants to go for a bike ride?" He was aware of the hardships of laundry day, some real, some perceived. He hoped to follow it up with a pleasurable activity. Vlada's eyes lit up at his father's suggestion. He looked to Hermina for confirmation.

"Of course, Karel. Where shall we go? Vlada?" asked Hermina. For Vlada it was a difficult choice. The world surrounding Pardubice was a wonderland full of castles, mountains, and forests.

"I vote for Kunětická Hora," said Vlada excitedly. Kunětická Hora was a Gothic castle perched on a hill on the outskirts of Pardubice. It was surrounded by high, fortified stone walls that could be seen from the city's flat landscape below. The castle had survived many a siege upon its walls and was rumored to have been impervious to attack. It was destroyed by a tragic fire during the Thirty Years' War.

"Kunětická Hora it is." replied Karel. Hermina packed a picnic lunch. They mounted their bicycles and rode the eight kilometers to the bottom of Kunětice Mountain, which, at 82 meters above sea level, might have been better referred to as Kunetice Hill.

Vlada skidded his bike to a stop at the base of the hill, kicking up gravel. He dropped it on its side and began to hike up the overgrown path that led to the ruins at the top. Where epic battles awaited him. Karel and Hermina coasted to the base of the hill, setting their bikes down gently next to Vlada's. They carefully picked their way over the rocks and up the castle's worn stone steps, mindful of the cliff on one side that led to a sheer drop.

The view from the top was the perfect reward for the challenging climb. "Ahhhh," Hermina sighed, taking in the staggering view of the city and beyond. Down below their perch, on the ground, sheep grazed in the brush. Karel pointed to a deer nibbling on grass in the clearing. Karel and Hermina stood next to each other on the stone rampart, their eyes locked in a loving exchange, their arms entwined around each other's waist. They stood that way for a while, gazing off into the distance in comfortable silence.

Vlada shouted from his post on the grassy ramparts nearby. "No one shall pass!" He imagined himself in a hammered suit of armor, chainmail beneath it, a menacing helmet to protect his head, defending the castle against invaders. Vlada's shouts shook his parents from their reverie. The sun hung low in the sky and the air had begun to cool. Vlada's stomach began to grumble from hunger.

They descended the crumbling staircase, picking their way across the rocky path and down the hill until they were back where they had started. "It is a shame it has fallen into such sad shape," Hermina said, looking up at the crumbling ruins.

"I think it's perfect, Mami," said Vlada. They rode their bikes for a bit and then pushed them the last few blocks into the town at the base of the hill. They entered a small, family-owned restaurant that served Karel's favorite pork cutlets and potato pancakes. His parents drank beer and made a toast to the end of summer. Vlada's eyes were heavy from his dinner, but pedaling home in the cool early evening air on the country road reinvigorated him.

Vlada began to sing. "*Pes jitrinicku sezral, docela malickou.*" Karel joined in. "*Prisel tam na nej kuchar, prastil ho palickou.*" As they coasted down the hill in the direction of Pardubice, they sang merrily the folk song about the dog eating the sausage and getting caught by the cook. Hermina began to pick up speed on her bicycle. She held her legs out to the side of the pedals, laughing as she passed Vlada and Karel.

"Slow down, darling!" Karel shouted after her. She was ahead of them now. Vlada pulled his bike up alongside his father.

"Mami, wait for me!" His mother did not slow down, at one point becoming nothing but a speck in the distance.

The public elementary school in Pardubice was tucked away on Smilova Street, some distance from the distillery. Vlada traveled to school daily, along with his friend Pepik and Pepik's little brother, Tomas, in a horse-drawn cart belonging to the Bergman family.

With the school year came piano lessons every other Tuesday. Madame Ambrozova was Vlada's piano teacher. She was a kind, but very old woman with false teeth.

"I hate Tuesdays," said Vlada to Hermina. He watched the clock on the mantle in the pánsky room, willing it to stop ticking closer to the piano teacher's arrival at half past three.

"Vlada, your manners," Hermina scolded him, remembering her own mother's sacrifice, mending flour sacks for extra money, to save money for her daughter's piano lessons.

Madame Ambrozova arrived at the flat and made her way toward the piano, a powdery cloud of perfume trailing behind her. Vlada squirmed next to her on the bench, trying to make sense of the sheet music in front of him. He muddled his way through the scales then stopped.

"*Ještě jednou prosím*," Madame admonished Vlada, tapping her toe on the floor of the pánsky room to keep time. Vlada wanted to be outside in the factory yard with Lada, playing tag or kicking a ball around, or anywhere else for that matter. He positioned his fingers on the keys instead. He felt Madame's eyes on his hands, bidding him to run through the scales again. Suddenly, Madame uttered a strange, guttural sound. Vlada turned, startled, to see Madame Ambrozova fall off the piano bench where she had been seated next to him and onto the floor. She gritted her teeth and thrashed wildly, her arms and legs sweeping the floor.

"Mami, come quick!" shouted Vlada. The teacher continued to writhe on the floor. Her dentures popped out of her mouth, skittered across Hermina's handloomed rug, and clattered onto the wood floor. Vlada watched in horror as the woman's body went rigid, then limp, in a matter of seconds.

Hermina ran into the room. "Go tell your father to ring for the doctor," she instructed. Vlada stood up but did not move. He stared at the tableau in front of him: Madame Abromova on the floor, the dentures a few feet from her hand, and his mother kneeling next to her. "Vlada," his mother repeated gently. "Go get Tati." Vlada moved slowly, his limbs heavy. He sped up as he reached the door of the pánsky room and did not stop running until he reached his father's laboratory at the distillery.

Karel feared the worst when he saw his young son's face, red from his exertions and inhaling deep gulps of air. "Is it Mami, Vlada?" Karel's voice asked the question calmly, firmly gripping Vlada's shoulders.

"Not...Mami," Vlada stammered out the details of the catastrophe. Karel breathed a sigh of relief and picked up the phone, summoning the doctor. He put his arm around Vlada, who was still breathing heavily, and they walked together back to the flat. Vlada climbed the stairs behind his father and stayed in the kitchen. He could hear his parents' hushed voices but no sound that led him to believe Madame was alive.

The doctor arrived at the flat in no apparent hurry, to find that Madame had been revived. Her son, who had also been called, knelt beside his mother, offering her a sip of water from a cup. "My mother has epilepsy," the son explained. "This has not happened in a very long time." He lifted his mother up to a standing position. Vlada had gravitated to the doorway of the pánsky room and regarded the piano teacher suspiciously.

"I can assure you, it won't happen again," Madame Ambrozova whispered wanly, her comment directed at Vlada more than his parents. She looked him in the eye as her son led her out of the flat. Vlada backed away as she passed.

Hermina straightened the sheet music on the piano and pushed in the bench. Karel took her by the arm and spoke in a low voice. "Darling," he began. "There is nothing further to be gained from these lessons." Hermina bit her lip and nodded, disappointed her son's musical career would end on such a note, never to progress further than the "Chop Waltz."

Chapter Two

KITTY 1935
TEPLICE, CZECHOSLOVAKIA

Erich Löwi, Kitty's uncle, wound the forest-green Tatra 77 through the streets of Teplice, wincing every time he hit a bump in the road. "Sorry! So sorry," he apologized over his shoulder to the two passengers in the back seat, pushing his round eyeglasses up the bridge of his nose. Like Erich, Oila tensed as the car bumped along the cobblestone streets, but Kitty hardly noticed, instead staring out the window of the car, eyes wide, as they passed familiar landmarks –the pastry shop, the library, and the hotel - she had not laid eyes on in months.

It had rained earlier that morning but as the day warmed, mist rose off the street as puddles evaporated. Uncle Erich slowly brought the car up in front of the villa on Masaryk Street and came to a stop. Kitty was overjoyed at the sight of home and she squeezed Oila's hand so tightly that Oila cried out. Kitty pushed the scratchy gray wool blanket from her lap, her cheeks flushed from its unnecessary warmth. She had allowed Oila to cover her with it when the nurses transferred her from a wheelchair outside the hospital into the waiting car. For nearly six months, Kitty had been sequestered in a private room in the hospital recuperating from a ruptured appendix. She had no need for the blanket now. She was home.

Uncle Erich opened the car door and helped Kitty out. Oila got out and stood next to her.

"It seems like it was all a dream, Oila," Kitty said. She stared up at the villa, and a wistful smile crossed her face. "I almost forgot what home looked like." The last time Kitty had seen the house was from a stretcher.

It had been a Saturday night in late October. One of the last things she remembered was Bettina poking her head into her bedroom to say goodnight. Her mother had hovered in the doorway of the dimly lit room looking like a beautiful mirage, shimmering, elusive, and far away, her lipstick flawless, every golden hair on her head perfectly in place. She wore a plum-colored dress, cinched at the waist, and shiny pointed black heels on her feet.

Oila sat in a chair next to Kitty's bed, pressing a cool cloth to Kitty's feverish brow. She inhaled sharply when she saw Bettina, momentarily dazzled.

Bettina stepped across the threshold, pulling on her gloves. "Good night, darlings. Feel better Kitty." She approached the bed and stopped, her attention turning to Kitty's dresser. She walked to it and straightened a small porcelain figurine of a cherub, moving the trinket an inch to the left. Bettina looked at Kitty, and her eyes narrowed, momentary concern flashing over her face. Then she turned abruptly and walked back toward the door. She blew Kitty a kiss from her gloved hand and left, her perfume lingering in the air.

Oila's fists clenched. She shook her head, breaking the spell Bettina had cast over her. "How could something so beautiful be so thoughtless?" Oila wondered. She turned back to the bed where Kitty lay motionless and pale.

Hours passed. Kitty periodically cried out in pain. "Oila, help! It hurts!" Perspiration glistened on her forehead. Oila bit her lip and dipped the washcloth in the basin on the nightstand, dabbing at Kitty's brow in vain.

The front door opened in the downstairs foyer, and Oila heard the animated voices of Bettina and Karel. She left Kitty, descended the stairs, and strode across the foyer toward her employers. Karel stepped forward, his brow etched with worry. "What is it, Oila?" he asked.

Oila looked directly at Bettina. "You have to call the ambulance," said Oila. "Follow me." She led Kitty's parents up the stairs to Kitty's bedroom. Hanuš stood in the hallway in his pajamas rubbing his eyes. Bettina entered the bedroom first, then turned and stepped back out into the hallway, dabbing at her nose with her handkerchief. Oila pushed past her, a foul smell filling her nostrils. Kitty let out a faint groan, her dark hair pasted to her pale skin.

"What's wrong with her?" Hanuš asked, standing behind his mother and peering into the room. Otto had awakened, and Uncle Erich, too, and now the whole family stood in the hallway outside Kitty's bedroom.

Karel rushed into Kitty's room, placing the back of his hand on Kitty's forehead. "She's burning up!" he cried. He turned to Bettina, who stood in the doorway. "My God, woman. What are you waiting for? Call for the ambulance!"

Bettina bristled at her husband's tone. "Of course, Karel," she replied. She turned and slowly walked down the stairs. Oila loudly exhaled in relief and slumped into the chair beside the bed.

When the ambulance arrived, two orderlies in starched white uniforms lifted Kitty and transferred her to a stretcher. Kitty's moans continued unabated as they carried her down the stairs and wheeled her out the front door. Hanuš and Otto stood in the foyer. Otto stood motionless, his brow furrowed with worry, and watched the ambulance, siren blaring and lights flashing, speed away with his dear Kitty inside.

Oila hurried down the stairs holding a bag of Kitty's things. She noticed Otto's distress, and quickly put the bag down and stood in front of him, speaking in a calm tone. "She is going to be all right, Otto," whispered Oila. Hanuš looked away. The ambulance had gone, and there was nothing left to see.

Uncle Erich had dressed quickly, his car idling in front of the villa to take Oila and Karel to the hospital. Oila settled in the back seat of the car and Karel jumped in front next to his brother, slamming the door. Oila looked up at the house as Erich sped off in time to see the silhouette of Bettina standing in the doorway with the two boys, Otto and Hanuš, one on either side of her.

The hospital corridors were silent and smelled of disinfectant. Oila stood up when the doctor approached the door of Kitty's hospital room. He was graying at the temples and wore thin wire frame glasses that sat at the end of his nose, giving him an air of authority. "Your daughter has suffered a burst appendix. The offending organ has been removed," he said drily. The door to the room was open. Kitty lay on the metal hospital bed, covered with a white sheet, not moving, her cheeks flushed. "We cleaned the abdominal cavity as best we could. From the bacteria present, the rupture must have happened days ago. We will watch for sepsis now."

Karel's jaw tightened. "Thank you, Doctor." He and Bettina often joked about the way they played favorites with their children. Karel would never have let Hanuš suffer like Kitty on his watch. He walked to the bed and kissed Kitty gently on the forehead. He looked at his watch and then at Oila.

Oila spoke first. "I'll stay, Karel," she said quietly, taking Kitty's limp hand in hers. "For as long as I have to."

"Thank you," Karel replied, shaking his head. He gave Kitty one last look and left the room.

A week prior to Kitty's symptoms and increased abdominal pain, Bettina had suggested Oila try some home remedies. "Have you given her vinegar and honey? That always worked for me," she said to Oila. "What about a hot compress? Cook can fill the water bottle for you."

"I have tried both of those. We also tried peppermint tea," Oila replied. "Nothing seems to be helping."

Bettina shook her head, her lips pursed. "Well, then. If we absolutely must," Bettina sighed deeply, and walked out of the room to phone the family physician.

Dr. Bauer, an ancient man with thick jowls and silvery eyebrows, poked and prodded Kitty on his exam table until a sheen of sweat covered her face. "It's a simple stomachache," the doctor stated matter-of-factly. He removed his stethoscope and placed it on the table, signaling the end of the appointment.

Oila anxiously greeted Kitty and Bettina at the door when they returned home. "Nothing serious," Bettina smiled haughtily, removing her gloves. "The doctor prescribed a daily dose of bismuth."

A few days later, Oila found Bettina in her bedroom, seated at her vanity, dabbing her face with powder from a small gold compact. "Kitty is not improving, Bettina," said Oila.

Bettina's hand stopped in mid-air; her body tensed. She closed the compact with a click, but remained seated, responding to Oila's reflection in the mirror. "Oila." Bettina's voice struck a formal tone. "You have been a part of this family for years," Bettina tucked a stray wisp of hair behind her ear and pinched her cheeks. "But I am Kitty's mother. I make the decisions about Kitty." Bettina paused. "And I say we give it until Monday." It was Friday night. Bettina turned back to her own reflection in the mirror and dabbed a handkerchief to her lips to blot her lipstick.

Oila looked at Kitty where she lay in the hospital bed, her arms tucked tightly beneath crisp, starched sheets, and listened to her measured breathing. "How did this happen?" Oila wondered. She was not referring to Kitty's illness; she was puzzling over the nature of her relationship with Bettina, a relationship so fraught with tension that each decision related to Kitty turned into a battle of epic proportions. It was a dangerous rivalry, one Oila had not chosen to engage in but from which she found it almost impossible to extract herself. This time it had gone too far, so far that it had endangered the life of her beloved charge.

It wasn't the first time. Oila thought back to the fateful day at Jesenice, the summer Kitty turned two. A light breeze had been blowing from the north that day, causing gentle ripples in the lake. It was one of those perfect June days, and the family had made the summer pilgrimage from the flat in Teplice.

Bettina and her sister, Flora, had prepared a celebration for Kitty's birthday. The courtyard in front of the house bustled with activity. Family members, friends and neighbors arrived in cars and on foot from the nearby town for the day's festivities. A huge pot of goulash simmered on the stove in the kitchen, and the smell of beef, paprika and onions filled the house. Children ran in and out of the house, where they were scolded and sent outside to play until the supper was ready.

Oila set a stack of china plates on the long table in the back yard. She wiped her brow with the back of her hand and then froze. "Has anyone seen Kitty?" she asked the question to no one in particular, her voice drowned out in the laughter from the adults and shrieks from the children as they chased after one another. Oila struggled to remember the last time she had seen Kitty. It had been in the front courtyard with the other children. That was over an hour ago.

Oila walked through the crowd of partygoers, asking, "Have you seen Kitty?" Her search brought her to the edge of the yard, and the trail that led to the lake's edge caught her eye. "Not the water," she thought. She ran the length of the trail to the clearing at the end and found Hanuš, Otto, and Frantisek, engaged in a competition to see who could skim stones the farthest across the calm water. "Hanuš? Frantisek?" Oila's voice was tight. "Have you seen Kitty?"

"She was right behind us a few minutes ago, Oila" Otto answered. He drew his arm back to throw another stone. The look on Oila's face caused him to drop the stone on the ground. "We'll help you look for her, Oila."

Oila had turned and was on her way back up the trail to the villa. She found Bettina talking with her sister and her mother. She touched Bettina's arm, pulling her aside. "Bettina, Kitty was walking on the trail from the villa to the pond with the other children. Now she is gone."

"My goodness, Oila. She can't have gone that far," Bettina said. Oila looked at her, eyes widening, her shoulders heaving as her breath came in deep gulps. "Oh, all right. Let's go find that mischievous child," Bettina said.

Oila shouted down the trail, her hands cupped around her mouth. "Kitty! Kitty!" She stood in one place on the trail and turned around and around, her eyes searching frantically for Kitty in the brush that rose around the trail. She knew what Kitty was wearing. She had sewn it herself - a pink cotton shift with white piping and a flowered pocket and collar. She could picture Kitty's dark tousled curls and pudgy, sun-kissed cheeks even though it was still early in the summer. "Kitty!" Her voice cracked and her eyes began to fill with tears. Oila had a grown son in Austria, and she felt the passion of a mother's love. She loved Kitty as if she were her own.

Oila and Bettina searched the tall grass near the pond. There was no sign of her. Oila began to backtrack, nervously stumbling. Halfway up the trail, she stopped. A thick pine forest bordered the edge of the property. "Let's split up," Oila said to Bettina. "You go to the left and I will go to the right."

Bettina was tiring of taking orders, but she did as Oila suggested. Oila walked toward the tall trees, holding her breath. A small, barely perceptible movement in the grass caught her eye. Kitty stepped into the center of a large clearing in front of the trees. She squinted her eyes in the bright sun. Tears streamed down her plump, flushed cheeks. Her feet were bare and scratched from walking on pine needles and rocks. Oila was ten feet away from Kitty. Bettina was an almost equal distance on the other side of her daughter. They both called out to her at the same moment.

"Kitty Löwi! Come here this instant," Bettina barked. Kitty stood still, crying, her tiny body heaving with each sob.

"Kitty, darling," Oila called out to her in a gentle tone. "My poor little dear. Come here." Kitty turned to the right. She saw Oila, kneeling, arms outstretched, tears of joy streaming down her cheeks. She ran into the arms of her governess. Oila fell backward hugging Kitty to her. Oila began to laugh, deep belly laughs of relief. Kitty looked confused. Then Kitty began to laugh, a sweet giggle that came out in ripples. Oila hugged her, rocking back and forth in the pine needles and rough grass.

Bettina stood alone on the edge of the field watching the scene between Oila and Kitty unfold, her cheeks reddening. Word had spread of the search for Kitty and guests and family members now lined the trail, hoping to aid in the search for the missing toddler. Aunt Flora ran to Kitty hoping to divert the crowd's attention. She dropped to her knees, hugging Kitty. "You mischievous girl! You gave us all a fright!" But Kitty's fealty to her governess, rather than to her mother, had become obvious to all. Bettina had been publicly humiliated. The damage had been done, and now there existed an invisible, immoveable wall between Bettina and Oila. It had been a faint but discernible one before that day. Now it was in bold relief.

Otto and Frantisek walked back up the trail with Hanuš bringing up the rear. Hanuš observed the happy reunion and kicked at the dirt. "Oh, you found her," he said, rolling his eyes. Everyone burst out laughing. Everyone except Bettina.

Oila stood and looked out the long windows of Kitty's hospital room. Sun streamed through from a high angle in the sky, casting shadows of the windowpanes across the floor. Oila recalled the first moment she had lain eyes on Kitty. She had arrived at the Löwi household for her interview for the position of governess on a similar sunny morning, years prior, just after breakfast had been served. Looking back, Oila could see that she and Bettina had been on a crash course with each other from the very beginning.

"Good morning, Mrs. Koppensteiner," said Bettina, looking Oila up and down and clicking her tongue. Bettina turned and led the way to the nursery without further conversation. Oila's eyes narrowed. She walked behind Bettina in silence, her shoes making scuffing sounds on the shiny parquet floor as she struggled to keep up with Bettina's quick pace. Formality was seen as frivolity, noted Oila. She could hear Kitty crying all the way from the entrance to the flat. Her cries grew louder as they approached the room.

Oila entered and peered down into the bassinet. Kitty lay on a starched sheet in the otherwise empty crib, tiny and distressed, her cheeks wet with tears. She had a head of dark hair and thick dark eyelashes. Oila waited for Bettina to pick up the crying child. A minute passed. Oila asked, motioning to the crib. "May I?"

"By all means," Bettina replied.

Oila took a soft blanket from the layette and swaddled Kitty in it. She picked her up and put her over her shoulder with experienced ease. She patted Kitty's back, cooing in a low tone. "There, there," she murmured. Kitty stopped crying. Oila held her out to look at her. "You are a sweet little beauty," she said. Kitty began gurgling and smiling. Before she could stop herself, Oila kissed Kitty on the forehead.

Bettina shifted from one high-heeled foot to the other. "Well, then. I see you have things under control. Lunch is served at noon in the dining room." Bettina was halfway out of the room as she uttered the last sentence.

As truth would have it, there was nowhere Oila would rather be than by Kitty's side. When Kitty's fever dreams finally subsided, they were replaced by something even more concerning. An infection had taken over. Kitty did not regain consciousness; instead, she lay motionless, her breathing barely perceptible. Karel pleaded with the doctor. "Surely there must be something you can do for her?" As if on cue, Kitty groaned from her bed.

"I can't make any promises, Mr. Löwi," said the doctor. "Her organs may be affected."

Oila thought she might break under the pressure of willing Kitty to open her eyes, each night faithfully sleeping upright in a chair next to Kitty's hospital bed. After weeks spent that way, Oila collapsed in the hospital corridor, weakened by exhaustion. The next day two orderlies wheeled a second hospital bed into Kitty's room, under orders from the doctor, who came to oversee the installation. "It won't do to have you injured when this young lady wakes up, Mrs. Koppensteiner," he said with a wink.

A few weeks later, Kitty's eyelids fluttered. "Oila?" Kitty called out into the room, her voice cracking. Oila jumped from the chair by the bed, dropping the book she was reading to the floor.

"I am here, Kitty," Oila replied. She reached for Kitty's outstretched hand, gripping it tightly. Kitty turned to look at Oila, lifting her head from its resting place on the pillow.

"Oh," Kitty cried out, her head falling back on to the pillow. Oila let go of Kitty's hand for a moment and grabbed another pillow from a nearby bed. She lifted Kitty's head gently and put the pillow behind it, propping her up.

"Don't try to do too much," said Oila. She retook her post in the chair by the bed and with her free hand, brushed a strand of hair from Kitty's forehead, her eyes brimming with tears.

Kitty held her hand up and gently touched Oila's cheek. "Can I go home now?" Oila laughed.

Christmas came and with it, a visit from Bettina. She walked into Kitty's hospital room dressed in a gray suit, high heels clicking against the spotless linoleum floor. She wore a felted hat with a fur pompom perched at a jaunty angle. In her hands she held a large rectangular box wrapped in gold foil and tied with a wide, red ribbon.

"Hello, darling," she said. She placed the gift on Kitty's lap with a flourish. Kitty struggled to pull herself up on the bed, wincing in pain. She was too weak to move the heavy box off her lap, much less open it. She turned to Oila for assistance. Bettina saw the look pass between them. "Well, Merry Christmas then." She turned and left before Kitty or Oila could reply.

Spring arrived and with it the color returned to Kitty's cheeks. Kitty walked slowly down the hallway of the ward, arm in arm with Oila.

"Kitty, I feel like I am watching you take your first steps," said Oila proudly. Kitty shuffled forward, smiling as she passed two nurses seated at a desk down the hallway from her room.

One of the nurses spoke. "Very nice, Kitty. This is the farthest you've walked so far."

Oila shook her head at the nurse and put the finger of her free hand to her lips. "Shhh, don't flatter her," said Oila.

"Oila, go home," Kitty urged her gently. "Look how well I am doing!" She did a little jig and then stumbled, losing her balance. Oila caught her arm. A pained look crossed her face.

"That was a close one, Kitty," chided Oila. "And don't be silly. You know I can't leave. What if you need a sip of water or an aspirin?" Oila covered Kitty's hand tightly with hers. "You are not getting rid of me yet."

After months in the hospital, Kitty stood in front of the villa with Oila beside her and breathed in traces of the dusty rain that had fallen earlier. The tightly closed lavender buds on the lilac tree were just beginning to crack open. Kitty's gaze fell upon Bettina's prized rose bushes, thick droplets of water weighing down the deep-green, waxy leaves. The colors of the garden, of everything, were more vibrant than in Kitty's fondest memory, and her senses were overloaded.

Kitty's eyes rested on a thick circle of white and fuchsia petals that circled the base of a large tree in front of the house. "Oh, Oila!" Kitty cried out. "I missed it! The magnolia." She looked at Oila for a response. For the first time, she saw the dark circles under Oila's eyes that had intensified over Kitty's hospital stay. Kitty's eyes welled up. She had never known that kind of devotion, certainly not from her mother.

Hanuš walked down the front steps to where Kitty was standing. "Well, look who showed up just in time for summer vacation," Hanuš said, a sullen look on his face. Kitty had missed almost the entire second class of school. Her teachers had stopped sending lessons home when it became clear she was too ill to keep up. Hanuš had still not decided whether to be jealous or angry.

Otto ran down the steps toward the car, nearly crashing into Kitty. "Kitty!" Otto cried out. "Can I see your scar?" They turned and walked together up the front steps and into the foyer of the flat. Kitty's father was waiting there, his face ashen from months of worry.

"Welcome home, Kitty." Karel knelt on one knee in the foyer as Kitty approached him. He enveloped her in his arms.

Bettina chose that moment for her entrance. "Hello, Kitty. Perfect timing. You are just in time for lunch." Bettina turned to lead the family to the dining room. "Cook has made your favorite: spaetzle."

After dinner, Oila ran the water for Kitty's bath in the claw foot tub in the upstairs bathroom. It had been their typical bedtime routine. Kitty undressed. Oila winced at the sight of the long scar from the appendectomy on Kitty's pale skin. No longer red and angry, it would serve as a lifelong reminder of Kitty's brush with death.

Kitty sunk her thin frame into the warm water, raised her knees and joined her arms around them, floating her hand over the surface of the water. "What do you think will be the first thing I do when we get to Jesenice, Oila?" asked Kitty with an impish grin.

"Well, now, let me see? Will you ...talk with your grandmother?"

Kitty laughed. "Noooo!"

"Will you ... make up the beds?"

Kitty laughed again. "Of course not! Guess again! This is your last chance!"

"Will you find Aja and jump in the pond?"

Kitty splashed her arms in the water in her excitement. "Yes!"

"Out with you now," said Oila. Kitty stepped out of the tub, allowing Oila to wrap her in a fluffy white towel. Oila had set out Kitty's favorite nightgown on the bed. They had made the nightgown together. Kitty recalled the trip to the textile shop in town to pick out the blue and white seersucker fabric; she had chosen the pattern. When they returned home Oila had pinned the pattern to the fabric. Fascinated, Kitty watched as Oila cut out the arms and the bodice and the front and back of the nightgown.

Oila allowed Kitty to push the fabric along on the sewing machine she kept in her room, joining the long seams on the sides, removing the pins that held the fabric together before they reached the needle. Kitty had learned to respect the needle, taking care to keep her fingers away from it as it bobbed up and down doing its work.

Kitty loved sewing. She loved threading the bobbin, she loved the sound of the machine, and most of all, she loved pushing the pedal with her knee to adjust the speed.

Kitty sat obediently on the edge of the wrought iron bed, her back to Oila. She closed her eyes as Oila brushed her hair, which was now halfway down her back after her hospital stay. Oila separated sections of her still-damp hair and wound each section around white strips of cotton. "There, now. All done," Oila announced.

"Read me a story. Please!" begged Kitty.

"Kitty, it's late and we have a busy day tomorrow," Oila wanted to be firm, but it was Kitty's first night back home.

"Please just one story. *Max and Moritz*." *Max and Moritz* was an illustrated book about two mischievous boys and their escapades. Kitty's father had given it to her. It was one of his favorites as a boy. "When I grow up, I am going to write stories about the adventures of two girls, me and Aja."

Kitty climbed beneath the covers. She loved it when the weather grew warmer, and the layers of winter blankets were replaced with embroidered eyelet sheets. She ran her hand over the velvety bumps of the chenille bedcover as she sat propped up, her thick dark plaits in contrast against the white goose down pillows. When Oila removed the strips of fabric from her hair in the morning, they would leave behind thick dark curls.

Oila shut off the light and left a lamp flickering on Kitty's bureau. The house had electric lights, but it was her fräulein's habit to light the lamp, and Kitty loved it. The lamp cast shadows into the dark corners of her room. Oila would use it to guide herself to her own room next door where she would read by the lamplight for hours after.

Kitty looked around her room. She loved the wallpaper, cream with tiny roses that climbed up trellises to the ceiling. She had never paid much attention to it until Oila pointed it out to her. The porcelain music box, a gift from her father, sat in silence on her bureau. When opened, a tiny ballerina sprang upright and spun in circles to the tinkling tune of *The Dance of the Sugar Plum Fairy*. The wooden rocking chair sat in the corner, its primary use for calming Kitty and Hanuš when they were babies.

"I am so glad we are going to Jesenice, Oila. Father needs a holiday. Grandmother will look out for him while we are there, won't she?" Kitty worried constantly that her father might have another heart attack, having suffered the first one while listening to the man they called the Führer on the radio.

"And what will become of Uncle Erich, Oila?" Uncle Erich lived with the Löwis. He was single and he worked as a traveling salesman. "I heard Bettina talking to Cook about him after lunch. Something about finding him a nice girl." Kitty's eyelids grew heavy as her voice drifted off.

"*Och!* Good night, my little gossip," said Oila. She kissed her charge on the forehead, but Kitty was already asleep.

CHAPTER THREE

VLADA FALL 1935 – FALL 1936
PARDUBICE, CZECHOSLOVAKIA

Vlada turned left at the corner of Smilova Street, slowing down as he approached the high, iron fence that surrounded the two-story elementary school and cobblestone courtyard looming up ahead. He thought back to how happy he had been to see his friend, Jirka Friedman, waiting for him out front on the first day of the new school year. Jirka's birthday was in January, a month before Vlada's, and Jirka liked to tease his friend that he was the "oldest."

"At least my mother doesn't cut off all my hair at the end of the summer like yours does," Vlada had teased back. It was true. Jirka's mother shaved his sandy blonde hair at the start of each school year. Jirka bucked tradition with the dress code as well, arriving at school in unofficial V-neck shirts, his haircut and clothing making him the target of ridicule while Vlada obediently followed the school dress code, sporting a white button down, short sleeve shirt, and long khaki shorts to school each day.

Vlada had missed his quirky friend. He had spent the summer hitting tennis balls at the tennis club in town with his mother, doggedly working to improve his game. Playing tennis and fishing at his father's rustic camp in Polabiny left Vlada little time to play with friends his own age.

One day, not long after school started, Jirka grabbed Vlada by the arm and pulled him aside in the corridor. They hid at the end of a long row of wooden student lockers. "What's going on?" Vlada spoke quietly, searching his friend's face for clues. Jirka looked around, waiting until the last student had left the otherwise empty hallway before speaking.

"It's us, Vlada," Jirka replied, keeping his voice low. "They are only acting differently towards us Jews."

Vlada's eyes narrowed. After a brief pause, he shook his head. "Nonsense, Jirka," Vlada realized he sounded unsure of himself. "If you are talking about Professor Jicha, he always treats us badly. This year is no different." The Latin teacher, a slightly pudgy man, had developed a vexing habit of sneering at the two boys, seemingly when they answered a question incorrectly.

"No, Vlada. Ask your parents. They will tell you I am right." Jirka walked away, shaking his head, leaving Vlada alone in the hallway, pondering the implications. Vlada did not want to confirm Jirka's suspicions, but he thought back to an incident that had been awkward at best. Vlada had walked up to a group of friends engaged in conversation in the courtyard. When he entered the group, the conversation came to an abrupt halt. Vlada had felt ill at ease, his face flushed as he stuttered in response. The circle of boys tightened, leaving Vlada outside the group, embarrassed and alone.

Jirka had noticed items missing from his locker. The incidents, taken separately, might just be coincidence. They vowed to investigate and report back to each other.

Vlada chewed on a slice of bread with butter the following morning at breakfast, absentmindedly scratching Čigy on the head underneath the kitchen table. He sipped his "coffee," roasted wheat mixed with milk and sugar, as his mind played back his conversation with Jirka. He fidgeted in his chair, shifting his weight from side to side. Vlada had always been able to talk to his parents about anything. Why did he feel so nervous bringing up what was happening at school? Just ask them, he told himself, annoyance rising inside of him. If the conversation went badly, Vlada would blame Jirka.

"Mami, Tati. Jirka Friedman thinks something strange is going on at school." Vlada blurted out the statement, immediately regretting having spoken. Karel looked up from the newspaper he was reading.

"Something strange? What do you mean, Vlada?" His father leaned in closer to the table, his voice was tight. His mother stood at the kitchen sink, the clatter of dishes suspended.

Why did I start this? thought Vlada. He vowed to make Jirka pay if this turned into a mess. Vlada inhaled. He would simply tell his parents what Jirka had said, and they would tell him that it was utter nonsense, and he would be done with it. "Jirka said he thinks it has something to do with us being Jewish." Without intending to, Vlada had raised his voice, startling his mother. Hermina dropped the glass she was washing. It clattered into the porcelain sink and shattered. Čigy jumped up from underneath the kitchen table and trotted to Hermina's side.

"I'm sorry, Mami." Vlada stood up from the table to help her pick up the shards of glass.

"It's all right, Vlada." His mother's voice sounded far away.

Karel folded the newspaper, pushed it to the center of the table, and sighed. "Sit down, Vlada. I am sorry that we have not discussed this with you." His father's speech was measured. "Laws were passed in Germany recently, laws that are very bad for the Jewish people."

Vlada sat up straight in his chair. Jirka had been right. "But we don't live in Germany, Tati," said Vlada. He looked down at the table, uncomfortable, then back up at his father. "And besides, we are Czech first, right?" Vlada could hear his voice come out in a high pitch.

Vlada struggled to remember the last time his parents had observed any of the Jewish holidays at the synagogue across from the military barracks. His thoughts traveled back to the day he had proudly placed his father's Legionnaire medals in the new china cabinet. His father was a military hero. He had played a prominent role in Czechoslovakia gaining its independence, sacrificing years of his life for its ethnic identity. Freed from Austro-Hungarian rule after the Great War, they were now Czech first. Being Jewish was their secondary identity.

Karel breathed in deeply. "Unfortunately, Vlada, there are people in Czechoslovakia who agree with those laws," said Karel.

Vlada sat frozen in his chair, eyes darting around the room, frowning.

"It's time you were on your way to school now," said Karel, standing up from the table, his usual genteel tone creeping back into his voice. "We can discuss this more in the evening."

Vlada stood up, his face hot. He grabbed his rucksack where it hung on its peg and left the flat without saying goodbye. Vlada's cheeks burned. His father had just lied to him for the first time.

Vlada tightened his grip on his rucksack as he walked to school; he walked distractedly, his mind struggling to make sense of his father's words. He stepped off the curb to cross the street and heard the shrill caution of a car horn. Vlada jumped back, the car coming within inches of him, his heart racing at the close call.

He was going to have to figure this out on his own.

Throughout the fall, Vlada, Jirka, and a few other Jewish boys felt the sting of sideways glances, their classmates making snide remarks in German under their breath. Vlada and Jirka met frequently, discussing the offenses, but they failed to understand how restrictions on German Jews were creating ripples all the way to their school in Pardubice. They decided the only option was to ignore their offenders. Vlada did not mention the strained environment at school to his parents again.

During the first day of winter vacation, Karel climbed the stairs to the flat, carrying a small evergreen tree by the trunk. He set the tree atop a table in the dining room.

"Oh, darling. It's perfect," Hermina clapped her hands together excitedly. They decorated the tree in the Czech tradition, Hermina taking each fragile blown glass ornament out of a cardboard box and handing them to Karel and Vlada to hang. Čigy curled up under the dining room table at Hermina's feet, sighing deeply, and the family's conversation turned to their annual ski vacation in the Krkonoše mountains.

Hermina tasked Vlada with packing his suitcase for the trip. She showed her affection for her son in small ways every day, but a nagging refrain had invaded her mind. "What if I am not always here to help him someday?" she worried. She created a plan: she would assign him small tasks which she was sure he would accomplish with ease, and they could both feel proud of his increasing autonomy.

Vlada approached the task with enthusiasm. He carefully placed the clothing he needed for the trip – warm socks, long johns, shirt – in a small suitcase his mother had given him. When he was finished packing, he closed the suitcase, the lock imparting a satisfying click.

"All done, Mami," Vlada told his mother. "Want to check it?" He watched for her reaction.

"I trust you, Vlada," his mother replied. Vlada did not know what to do with the packed suitcase. He set it awkwardly by the front door, puzzled at the change in their usual routine. He missed his mother doting on him.

On the eve of their departure, Karel bid the travelers goodbye; he promised to quickly complete his work projects and then join them on the mountain. Mother and son hurried to the bus station under gently falling snow, their suitcases bumping against their legs.

The bus traveled over flat roads for two hours and Vlada dozed, his head lolling on Hermina's shoulder. He awoke to the bus bumping its way down the last stretch of their journey. The snow-covered Krkonoše mountains of Northern Bohemia rose ahead in the distance, skimming the edge of the Polish-Czech border. A collective sigh rose from the travelers, everyone was transfixed by their majestic beauty.

An army of horse-drawn sleighs and their drivers were waiting at the bus depot. The horses snorted and stamped their hooves on the snow-covered ground. Vlada's eyes sparkled with excitement. They carried their bags over to one of the open carriages and a mustachioed driver loaded their bags onto the back of the sleigh. He offered his hand in a noble gesture to support their climb into it. Hermina brushed a light dusting of snow from the leather seat and covered their laps with a heavy, woolen blanket.

The driver snapped the reins and the sleigh lurched forward. It picked up speed, the wooden runners cutting swaths through the packed snow, the bells on the sleigh jingling sweetly, marking time with the rhythm of the horses' canter. The sleigh climbed higher and higher on their journey to the top of the mountain, and Vlada grinned, thoughts of school and any troubles a distant memory.

"Mami, I think this might be my favorite place in the world," he beamed, his cheeks flushed from the brisk pace of the carriage as they passed snow-covered trees, branches heavy under the weight of a fresh dusting that sparkled in the fading light. Mother and son sat close together, their breath coming out in great clouds each time they laughed or spoke.

They arrived at the small row of cabins scattered across the mountain, the horses snorting and tossing their manes as they drew to a halt. The driver held out his hand, and Hermina stepped down off the carriage and into the snow. The porch light shone from the front of the cabin and snow swirled lazily in front of it. The driver placed their bags in the snow. Hermina opened the door to the rented cabin and sighed deeply.

"Mine too, Vlada," Hermina said, sighing deeply. "Mine, too."

In the morning, the sun filtered in through a crack in the cabin's shutters. Hermina flung them open and was greeted with a crisp, cloudless blue sky and a fresh dusting of snow.

"Oh," she exhaled. A year had passed since they were last there, but the beauty of the place – fresh tracks in the newly fallen snow, the pristine whiteness covering every inch of the great mountain – always had the same effect on her. Her shoulders relaxed; the tension of recent worries replaced by a feeling of calm. She glanced around the cabin. It was simple yet sufficient, a single room with two wooden beds, a small kitchen area and a bathroom. The front door opened onto a wooden porch and a dazzling view of the mountains.

Vlada began to stir in his bed. The smell of freshly brewed coffee and toasted slices of *bábovka* his mother had brought from home lured him from the bed to a seat at the kitchen table.

"Good morning, sleepyhead," said Hermina, smiling. "Are you ready for a day on the mountain?" Vlada looked at his mother, already dressed in her ski pants, her dark hair held back by a wool headband that covered her ears.

"Yes, Mami," he replied. He could hear a different tone in his mother's voice. She was playful, relaxed. It seemed they both had left their troubled thoughts at the bottom of the mountain.

Hermina was a gifted athlete. She had taught her son her favorite sports – skiing, tennis, ice skating – and together they shared a love of recreation. Vlada recalled how in the summer they used their membership at the local tennis club often. Sometimes Hermina had allowed Vlada to bring Čigy to the club and a circle of younger children always formed around the dog, Vlada puffing out his chest with pride, feeling important and gripping Čigy's leash tightly. Hermina always bought Vlada ice-cold lemonade after they played a rousing game of tennis.

Vlada recalled the last time they had gone ice skating. Vlada had taken to it quickly, cutting across the ice of the outdoor skating rink in the center of town, his sharpened skates leaving arcs of white in his wake. Afterward, he and his mother had walked arm in arm from the rink, cheeks flushed from the cold, mittens crusty with ice. Their noses had followed the scent of roasting *kostany* and the chestnut vendor, a ruddy-faced man who always wore a fur lined vest, knew them by name.

"Vlada, Hermina. Fill it up?" the man always asked the same question. They had laughed as he filled a bag with the toasted treasures near to overflowing. Vlada always grabbed two chestnuts in each hand, stuffing them in the pockets of his trousers to warm his legs on the short walk home.

Hermina had taken a chestnut from the bag. She peeled the hard skin back where it had been scored and popped the mealy nut in her mouth. "These remind me of my days in Prague as a young girl, Vlada," she said, chewing, and tucking a few chestnuts in her pocket for Karel's arrival. "When I met your father and fell in love." She had winked at Vlada; he had blushed and turned away.

Now, Vlada ate his slice of *bábovka* in the kitchen of the mountain cabin, chewing quickly and alternately slurping his coffee. He watched his mother pull on her ski boots. He went to the bed where his suitcase sat open and began rifling through it. He searched the bag, emptying it of its contents. He sat down on the bed, shoulders slumped.

"What is it, Vlada?" asked Hermina, looking at the clothing he had strewn all over his bunk.

"I forgot my ski socks and my mittens. I guess I can't ski today," he said, his lower lip quivering.

"Well, lucky for you I have an extra pair of each." She pulled heavy socks and mittens from her suitcase and handed them to her son. "I saved you this time. Next time you might not be so lucky." She tousled his hair.

Hermina pulled a wool vest over her wool shirt and stood in the doorway of the cabin. Vlada pulled on his coat, wool cap, and mittens, and stood in the doorway next to her. She looked at her son, his eyes almost level with hers. "Vlada! You are almost as tall as me!" She stepped outside and scooped up a handful of snow, threatening to throw it at him.

They made their way to the ski lift that would take them to the top of Sněžka, the highest peak in the country. Their legs dangled off the seat as the lift took them ever higher up the mountain. At the top, they slid off the seat, and paused for a moment, taking in the view. Vlada imagined this was what it must look like on the surface of a planet in outer space. Everything was white, snow-covered, and the wind at the top blew the snow so smooth it sparkled like alabaster. The wooden lodge to one side of the mountain top was the only reminder of civilization. The lodge was round with jewel-like windows resembling a slide projector, where every click rewarded the viewer with a slightly different image. It was quiet at the top, so quiet. Only the bravest of souls skied from Sněžka.

They skied run after run, their skis cutting into the side of the mountain, crisscrossing from one side of the trail to the other, their shadows growing long and thin, like creatures from another planet. The sky changed over the course of the day, at times a layer of clouds ringing the summit. They only thought about stopping when a sliver in the sky became tinged with pink.

"There is no place like this on earth," his mother said, her eyes scanning the view of the mountains before turning to head back to the cabin for the night. They stamped their boots outside the cabin, and went inside, cheeks flushed, laughing.

Karel sat at the kitchen table reading the newspaper. "Tati! You are early!" Vlada ran to his father and hugged him. His father was stiff, his thoughts occupied with the newspaper headline declaring that enlistment in the Hitler Youth was now compulsory for all German boys. Karel's frustration increased weekly as the news worsened out of Germany. And his hero, President Masaryk, had resigned because of poor health and old age.

"Karel," Hermina reprimanded her husband. Karel looked up, suddenly aware of his surroundings. He hugged Vlada tightly to him.

"Looks like you had a good day on the mountain, you two," Karel said, forcing enthusiasm.

"Yes, Tati," Vlada grinned broadly. "And tomorrow is the start of the new year and you know what that means." Vlada's birthday was just two short months away. He would be eleven years old.

Vlada sat down at the kitchen table next to his father. Hermina placed a cup of hot tea in front of him and began describing their day in detail to Karel. Vlada blew on his tea and sipped it, comforted by the familiar background noise of his parents' conversation, and thought about what he wanted for his birthday.

On a fine spring day, Vlada ran all the way home from school, chest heaving, out of breath. He and his classmates had been anxiously waiting for the principal to reveal the destination for the field trip that marked the end of their last year of primary school.

"Mami, they have announced the end of fifth class field trip," Vlada blurted out as he entered the flat.

"Slow down, Vlada." Hermina poured her son a glass of water and watched as he gulped it down.

He wiped his mouth with the back of his hand. "Mami, would you please come on the trip as a chaperone?" Vlada pleaded, his eyes locking with his mother's.

"So serious, Vlada," Hermina teased. "Well, it depends on the destination." She paused for a moment. "Does it begin with an "R" by any chance?"

"Mami, how did you know? Don't tease. Will you? Will you? Please?" The news that the class was going to Ratibořice had been shared with the parents in advance. The class would tour the château and grounds that were the setting of Vlada's favorite book, *Babicka*.

"I would be honored, Vlada," she held her arms in front of her. He ran across the kitchen and threw his arms around his mother's waist. Hermina treasured the moment and then just as quickly, it ended. Vlada pulled away and began to talk nonstop. His mother sighed.

"Have you ever been there, Mami? I am so excited. What shall we bring for lunch? Do you think we will see any animals? I think we will see Viktor's canal and the old mill. The teacher said so, Mami." Hermina listened to Vlada chatter on and went back to stirring the *zelňačka*, her mother's recipe for sauerkraut soup, brimming with smoked sausage and potatoes. Vlada was still chattering when Karel walked up the stairs for dinner. "Tati, guess where we are going for the end of fifth class field trip?"

Vlada wanted to read *Babicka* again before the school trip. He spent warm spring afternoons reading and lying indoors on the carpet in the pánsky room.

"Go outside, Vlada! It's a beautiful day!" Hermina said, hoping to coax him to put down the book and go outdoors.

"Let me read to you, Mami." Hermina gave in and sat down in the comfortable chair that was her father's favorite when he came to visit. Vlada licked his finger, turned the page, and began to read.

The wagon stopped at the gate, and Wenzel helped a little old woman to alight. She was dressed in the garb of a peasant, having her head wrapped up in a large white kerchief. This was something the children had never seen before, and they stood still, their eyes fixed upon their grandmother.

Hermina had forgotten how beautiful Němcová's prose was. Listening to her enchanting vignettes, she understood how the book had earned its place in the annals of Czech literature. She closed her eyes and gave herself over to the story. With no further protest forthcoming, Vlada continued reading. When he got to the part where the children were in awe of Babicka's wrinkles and her four teeth, Vlada stopped.

"That makes me think of my Babicka, Mami!" Vlada was referring to his maternal grandmother, Emilie Gesmai.

When Hermina responded, her words were tinged with sarcasm. "Indeed, Vlada." Wrinkles and missing teeth were similarities between the two grandmothers, one real, one fictional, but that was where the comparison ended. Hermina's mother had lived a life of challenge and privation. She had suffered indignities at the hands of her own husband, Hermina's father Adolf. The many hardships she had endured colored her approach to life. They had made her hard, in sharp contrast to the soft edges of Němcová's saintly matron.

The night before the class trip to Ratibořice, Vlada flipped through the pictures in his volume of *Babicka*, skimming through the book one last time.

"I want to be prepared, Mami. I don't want to miss anything," said Vlada excitedly. "I wrote a list of all the landmarks. I hope we see every single one!"

After an hour's ride, the bus pulled into the parking lot of the castle grounds. The children let out a cheer. Their teacher, Pan Hlavaty, struggled to make himself heard above the din of the students. "Mind your manners and file off the bus quietly, please," he shouted. He organized the class into groups. Hermina and another mother were put in charge of four children, including Vlada. Vlada waved to Jirka, who was in another group, a pair of binoculars slung over his shoulder, and they all set out along the mossy banks of the Upa River, surrounded by a canopy of leafy oak and slender linden trees.

"It's just like she described it, isn't it, Mami?" asked Vlada, skipping ahead. Hermina walked slowly, entranced. It had been a long time since she had been in this part of the countryside. They continued up the hill that overlooked the verdant space that was *Babiččino údolí*, Grandmother's Valley, each step reminiscent of a scene described in charming detail in the book.

The earthy scent of the forest and the fresh air were a far cry from the smell of coal in the factory yard and the pungent smell of industrial alcohol that emanated from the distillery. Hermina breathed in deeply as she walked. She became aware of the faint sounds of nature around her: the wind whispering through the mighty oaks and the delicate linden trees, the gentle rippling of the brook to their right. She heard the rush of the waterfall up ahead growing louder with each step they took in its direction.

"How absolutely lovely," she mused. As her pace slowed, Vlada and another boy in their group ran ahead. Vlada stopped and turned around to confirm his mother was still on the trail. When she was within earshot, he shouted to her.

"Look, Mami!" Vlada ran to the long cement dam that spanned the river, Viktorka's weir as it was known in the book, and jumped onto it, the spray from the fast-moving waterfall splashing his cheeks. "It's so cold!" He shouted, wiping the water from his face. Hermina quickened her pace, frantically waving to Vlada to move away from the water's edge.

"Vlada!" Hermina shouted, but Vlada could not hear her above the roar of the waterfall. Suddenly, Vlada slipped on the wet pavement. Hermina jumped up on the embankment, grabbed his arm, and pulled him away from the edge to safety.

Vlada looked around, embarrassed. "I was fine, Mami," he said, looking down at the rushing water below. He stepped back away from the water's edge, his earlier bravado evaporating into the misty spray.

"I saved you, Vlada," said Hermina, holding him by the shoulders. "How many times does that make now? Do you think you are a cat with nine lives?" She hugged him tightly to her. He pulled away but stayed close to his mother for the rest of the outing. They walked with others in the group, passing the landmarks lovingly described in the book – the old mill, the Baroque castle, the Old Bleaching Ground, a timber frame cottage that was home to the miller. Hermina paused to look at the rustic old building; its shingle roof, and small second-story window brought back memories of the airless living quarters she had shared with her parents and seven siblings.

"This reminds me of the old family store and the house where I lived when I was a girl, Vlada." A bittersweet memory flashed in her mind of herself as a girl sweeping the floor in the shop, the dust flying up in the air and floating in the stream of sunlight that came through the ground floor window.

"See, Mami? Aren't you glad you came?" The path led them back full circle, to the landmark the children most wanted to see. Inside a small iron fence stood a sandstone statue, *The Grandmother and Her Children*, a monument commemorated to *Babicka* herself. Adorned with her signature kerchief, the stone replica depicted the kindly old woman, her grandchildren in an orderly column in front of her, and the family's two dogs.

Vlada's eyes fell upon the stone figures of the dogs "There they are, Mami! Sultan and Tyrol! Just like in the book." Vlada ran and stood in front of the dogs. Pan Havlaty assembled the group in front of the statue for a photograph, and Vlada was caught frowning for posterity.

It was a fairy tale setting come to life, a lovely natural setting that had thus far been allowed to maintain its childlike wonder and innocence, a place where the darkness of the outside world had not yet crept in. In later years, a dark cloud would descend over the property when the beautiful château, once home to secret negotiations against Napoleonic coalitions, would be occupied by German forces.

Hermina stood in the kitchen of the flat holding a letter from her mother in her hand. Vlada sat at the kitchen table doing homework. "Babicka Emilie would like to come for a visit, Vlada," she said. Her mother's solo visits since her parents had parted ways were rare, and elicited mixed emotions among the entire family. For Karel, his mother-in-law's presence was hard to ignore, resorting to covering his head with a newspaper while taking his nap after lunch during her stays.

"Babicka Emilie is so strict, Mami! She and Grandfather are so different," Vlada looked up from his studies, blurting out his response. Although simply put, Vlada's statement rang of truth. Hermina was painfully aware of the differences between her parents.

When Grandfather Adolf visited the family, he commandeered the upholstered chair in the pansky room. Vlada loved to stand next to him and watch him light his pipe; it was an elegant ritual Grandfather loved to perform for Vlada, his best audience. He began by breaking up the tobacco and rubbing it between his bony fingers. Then, he filled the bowl of the pipe with the tobacco, tamping it down just enough to draw air in after it was lit.

"The first light is the test, Vlada," said Grandfather, his hand circling the tobacco in the bowl with his engraved gold lighter, the threads of tobacco dancing as they caught fire and then sputtered out. The second pass was where the magic happened. "Now, you draw, but don't inhale," he explained, the sweet smell of the tobacco filling the room, his grandfather's jowls jiggling as he puffed steadily on the pipe. The heady smell was intoxicating to Vlada. As the smoke swirled above their heads, sunlight glinting off the chain of his pocket watch, Grandfather drank a glass of cold beer, and told Vlada stories his mother did not think a boy his age should hear.

"There was a beautiful woman in the town, Vlada," Adolf began, simultaneously winking at his grandson. Vlada had difficulty following the story. It involved the woman in question being given a considerable number of items from the family store at a "discounted" price. Babicka Emilie found out about the discount, and the woman, and put a stop to both.

"Adolf, he is just a boy," Karel observed, hoping his father-in-law might temper his speech in front of Vlada. "You're a bit of a bad influence." His father-in-law did not deny it.

It had been years since Babicka Emilie and Grandfather Adolf had been in the same place at the same time. Hermina remembered how her mother had struggled to keep the Adolf Gesmai store in Nové Mitrovice solvent as one after another of their children left the family nest. One afternoon, Hermina discovered and read her mother's diary, begun with so much promise on the day she married. She was shocked to read of her mother's despair over the failure of the family business, her husband's infidelities, and her profound isolation.

"For all my patience I got a poor reward," her mother had written. "He did all his wicked acts in front of my eyes. I didn't have a living soul to complain or confide to. No one cared about me."

No sooner had Hermina moved to Prague and married Karel in 1923, than her parents sold the store and moved in with their older daughter, Ida. Their tenure with Ida and her family lasted just over a year; it turned out Hermina was not the only sibling to read her mother's journal.

Emilie wrote: "Poor Ida, she was unhappy from the beginning – he was a selfish, lazy, despicable fellow. When drunk, he was a bad knave." In Emilie's opinion, her daughter Ida had married a man just like her father. Ida did not appreciate her mother's assessment of her husband and not long after, Emilie and Adolf were sent packing.

Emilie and Adolf's later married life became one in which they wandered, separately, from one of their offspring's houses to another, thrusting themselves on their children for as long as each one would have them. It only took a few more years before the unhappy pair parted ways, this time for good.

Hermina remembered feeling mildly insulted when, after the birth of Vlada, she read Emilie's journal entry about her new grandson.

"Hermina and Karel Munk, Pardubice: Vlada (1925)." Vlada was barely a footnote in his grandmother's journal.

Emilie arrived for a visit in the fall, just as Vlada was beginning his first year of gymnasium. The family's maid, Klara, was given leave so that Hermina's mother could co-opt the maid's room in her absence. Vlada observed that as he had grown older, his grandmother disciplined him less and seemed to like him more. Emilie thought Vlada a great student, marveling at his recitation of the entire poem *The Ballad of Charles IV* by the Czech writer Jan Neruda. She laughed out loud when Vlada acted the part of the king spitting out the bitter wine. Even Hermina was shocked to see her mother enjoying the moment so. To the whole family's surprise, it was turning into a pleasant visit.

Karel arrived home during Emilie's visit carrying another painting by his Legionnaire compatriot, Jiroslav Grus. He unwrapped it, revealing a modernist interpretation of a bouquet of tulips in a gilded frame. He hung the colorful painting on one of the walls of the pánsky room.

"I love this one, Karel," said Hermina. She stood back and admired it. "His style is changing."

Babicka Emilie was impressed. "Hold on to that one, Karel," she said, genuinely appreciative of the work. "It could be worth something someday."

It was no secret amongst Hermina and her siblings that their brother, Karel Gesmai, was their mother's most favored child. Hermina held no animosity toward him for it. He had made their mother proud, graduating from Charles University in Prague as a physician in 1924. Now Doctor Karel Gesmai, the golden boy, was getting married in Prague, and Emilie refused to attend.

The morning of Karel's wedding, Babicka Emilie sat at the kitchen table in her bedclothes. "I don't like her," Vlada overheard his grandmother say to his mother.

Emilie had approved of Karel's previous girlfriend. The young woman's parents owned a fancy, white tablecloth restaurant in the city. Coming as she did from humble beginnings, Emilie was easily impressed by the girl. She had high hopes that the relationship would end in marriage. When she was told they had broken it off, she moaned over her son's poor judgment.

"How could this happen? She was lovely, just lovely," Emilie's voice trailed off, lamenting the broken courtship.

A few months later, Karel Gesmai proposed to Marta Benešová, a young woman of negligible pedigree. Emilie was fit to be tied. She refused to speak of the girl, let alone attend the wedding. Hermina was puzzled by her mother's attitude toward her future daughter-in-law. She wondered if the pages of her mother's diary might provide a clue and guiltily poked around in her mother's room until she located it. She scanned the pages quickly and found an entry about Marta.

"She is cheeky and unfeeling," her mother had written. Hermina could not have disagreed more. She and Marta had formed a bond of friendship almost immediately upon meeting. They shared recipes and had a similar fashion sense, walking for hours arm in arm as they window shopped past the clothing boutiques in Prague. Marta was smart and funny, and Hermina thought her a perfect match for her more serious-minded brother. She looked forward to embracing her as a sister.

Vlada liked his Uncle Karel. Vlada and his mother often took the train from Pardubice to Prague to visit him. He always had the latest model car, and Vlada experienced a thrill each time Karel pulled up to whisk them around the city.

On the morning of Karel and Marta's wedding, Hermina pleaded with her mother one last time. "Please won't you stop this and come along, Mama," Hermina implored Emilie.

"Hmmph," Emilie uttered impatiently, turning, and walking out of the kitchen. Hermina blew a kiss to Vlada and turned and left the flat with Karel for the wedding in Prague, leaving Vlada at home with Emilie. Vlada found his grandmother slouched in the same upholstered chair his grandfather loved in the pánsky room, looking at him like a forlorn child. Čigy had curled up under the chair by her feet, and she scratched the dog's head absently.

"Read to me, Vlada," Emilie insisted.

"What on earth would she like?" Vlada wondered. He was currently enamored of Josef Kopta, but he doubted his grandmother would enjoy the *Third Company* books about the author's years in the Czech Legion. He scanned the books on the library shelves and pulled down *Guard No 47*. It was the story of a guard who becomes temporarily deaf. His hearing returns, but he continues to act as if it has not so that he can hear what people are saying about him. Vlada sat down on the rug cross-legged, feeling satisfied with his book choice.

Vlada read to Emilie enthusiastically, but she sat still in the chair, her hands clasped tightly in her lap. He read on, expecting her to shower him with compliments as she had when he recited *The Ballad of Charles IV* for her by heart a few days earlier, but she only gazed out the pánsky room window, nodding every so often to indicate she was still listening. At one point he stopped reading to see if she would notice.

"Go on, Vlada. Keep reading," she said, her voice distant. Immaterial to the text, she began to weep quietly, sinking deeper into the chair, pulling at her handkerchief, and fraying the edge.

"Hermina, my Hermina," Emilie cried out. Vlada looked helplessly around the room. He closed the book, and they sat in silence. Vlada sat glued to his seat, afraid to leave his grandmother alone in the room. He sat with her until the room was engulfed in darkness. When his parents returned home, Vlada did not mention the incident to his mother, but examined her closely for a reason behind his grandmother's episode. He found none and breathed an inward sigh of relief.

Later, during his grandmother's last visit to Pardubice, the family walked together through the busy streets of the town on a blustery day. Babicka Emilie clung to Hermina that day, barely letting go of her arm during the entire outing.

Karel had brought along his camera and suggested they record the day for posterity with a photograph. "Stand just there," he instructed. He posed his subjects, Hermina, Emilie and Vlada, in front of the statue of the Czech aviator, Jan Kaspar. Emilie refused to smile, her face set in a grim line. At the bus depot, as Emilie prepared to board, Vlada was close enough to hear his grandmother's parting words to her youngest daughter as they embraced. Hermina pulled away from her mother abruptly and looked at her in disbelief.

"Stay away from Marta, dear. No good can come of it."

CHAPTER THREE

KITTY 1936
TEPLICE, CZECHOSLOVAKIA

Bettina stood up from her chair in the parlor of the flat on Masaryk Street and brushed her hands over her taupe silk skirt, smoothing the wrinkles that had appeared. She tossed the fashion magazine she'd been reading onto the chair and looked at her reflection in the large, gilded mirror above the mantle, tucking a wisp of golden hair back into her chignon. A pleased but slightly haughty smile spread across her face before she walked purposefully into the foyer, unruffled by the cacophony of sounds and activity that greeted her there. She had instructed the staff to prepare the house for the family's absence over the next few months. It was the beginning of summer vacation. Jesenice beckoned.

Oila stood in the formal living room with the housemaid, Lina. They took turns taking crisp white sheets from a stack on the settee. They unfurled a sheet, allowing it to billow down loosely onto each piece of furniture, tucking the sheet in and around the bottom of the chair or table after it settled. The other housemaid, Liesl, rolled up the tapestry rug from the floor, dragged it through the kitchen, out the door and into the backyard. With some difficulty, she threw it over the clothesline and began to beat it with a braided switch until her cheeks were red and shone with sweat from her efforts. Kitty followed Liesl out into the yard, hoping to give the rug a few good whacks.

Cook stood in front of the long kitchen table and scowled at the maid passing through her sovereign territory. Plump and pleasant, Cook was rarely seen without her white, bibbed apron, the sleeves of her shirt rolled up in readiness for the next task. She had worked for the Löwis under Bettina's authority since Hanuš was born. Cook was normally quite good-natured, an invaluable character trait while in the employ of Bettina. Today she was fit to be tied.

Oila entered the kitchen in search of a glass of water, and wiped her brow. Cook shook her head, hoping to catch the eye of her compatriot. "I don't know why today of all days she chose to have company." Cook exhaled the words in a stream of exasperation. The kitchen was filled with the aroma of sugar and butter. Cook lifted a still-warm pan from the table with both hands, turned it upside down, and gave it a sharp rap on the counter, emphasizing her displeasure. The cavities of the pan released a dozen sweet, golden madeleines onto the workspace. Kitty licked her lips at the sight of the yellow cakes, joining everyone in the kitchen after her job "supervising" the beating of the rugs.

"Those are not for you, my dear," Cook winked at Kitty. "I will see you later." Kitty smiled fondly at Cook, acknowledging her remark. She waited, the counter at eye level, as Cook scooped a cup of powdered sugar from a canister and poured it into a sieve set over a bowl. Cook grasped the sieve by its handle and tapped it gently, a fine sugary dust falling over the tiny shell-shaped cakes.

"It's snowing!" exclaimed Kitty. Cook picked up each dusted shell and placed it carefully on a floral china plate.

Cook looked down at Kitty's flushed cheeks, her dark hair gathered in long ponytails, and exhaled deeply. Her love for Kitty was second only to Oila's. Kitty had undergone an awkward plump phase after the Christmas holidays, having indulged in too much stollen and *strudel* and Cook's specialty, Austrian cookies. Cook felt a kinship with Kitty at the time, both indulging in sweets to lessen the effects of family and household tensions, Kitty with her mother and Cook with her son, who was disrespectful and cold after the death of his father. Cook's waistline disappeared then, and she doubted it would ever make a reappearance, whereas Kitty had returned to her normal weight with the arrival of spring, spending all her time playing outside, away from the daily upset.

The loss of baby fat, as Oila called it, did not prevent Bettina from reminding Kitty of those few months when she struggled to button the dresses Oila had lovingly made for her. One Sunday in the spring, Bettina and Karel had entertained guests for afternoon tea. When the visit concluded, the housemaid brought a tray of leftover spiced cookies back to the kitchen and set them on the counter in the empty kitchen.

Kitty and Otto came through the kitchen door from the backyard where they had been playing tag, laughing excitedly. Their eyes fell immediately upon the plate of cookies. They glanced around the empty kitchen; Kitty looked at Otto with wide eyes, questioning their good fortune. Just then, Cook appeared, and seconds later, Bettina. A strange tension filled the room. Cook walked with her ambling gait toward the plate, but Bettina got there first. She picked up the plate and heaved the cookies into the kitchen garbage pail.

"Kitty does not need those. They will go straight to her waist, and we don't want that," said Bettina sharply. She turned on her heel and left the kitchen. The corners of Kitty's mouth fell into a sorrowful pout and tears welled up in her eyes, clinging to her lashes before spilling over and down her round cheeks.

"It's okay, Kitty," said Otto quietly. "Let's go back outside." He took his cousin by the hand and led her out the door and into the sunshine.

Cook followed the children outside a few minutes later and found Kitty in the tall grass behind the house, pulling up weeds and sniffling under the shade of a tree. Otto had disappeared into the house. Cook knelt next to Kitty. "Whenever sweets make their way back into my kitchen, I promise to save some for you," she vowed to Kitty that afternoon.

Cook began cleaning the kitchen now, preparing it for the family's departure for Jesenice, clanging the pots and pans together without a thought for the noise, her anger reignited by the memory of Kitty's heartbreak over Bettina's heartless actions that day. As if on cue, Bettina came into the kitchen.

"Frau Müeller will be here any minute," said Bettina expectantly, clapping her hands together. "I'll take these, Cook," Bettina added, picking up the plate of madeleines. "Have Liesl bring the tea into the dining room."

Frau Müeller had visited the Löwis' home for tea a few months earlier. They were newcomers to Teplice and the family had moved into a nicely appointed villa next door. It was smaller than the Löwi's residence, a fact Bettina mentioned with some frequency. Like most other residents of Teplice, they were Sudeten German, ethnic Germans living in Bohemian Czech lands.

"I would bet the Müellers are Roman Catholic," Bettina heard a woman in her bridge club imply. Bettina cared little about what religion they practiced, but she did care about social status, and it was rumored that Frau Müeller's husband was rapidly ascending the ladder in the local government. Bettina aspired to have friends in high places.

The doorbell rang. Everyone in the household was occupied with efforts for the family's departure, leaving Oila to open the front door. Frau Müeller stood on the landing, dressed in an ivory tweed suit, her purse clasped tightly in front of her. She looked Oila up and down. "Aren't you the governess?" she asked. Her eyebrows knitted together, questioning the staff hierarchy before even setting foot in the house.

Oila smiled broadly. "Yes, Frau Müeller," Oila replied. Her mouth was tight, but the corners turned up into what passed as a smile. She turned and led the guest to the dining room, where the table had been set with a linen tablecloth, delicate china plates, and silverware. Bettina came in from the kitchen carrying the cakes and set them on the table. She kissed Frau Müeller on both cheeks. "Oh, how lovely to see you. Do sit, please."

Oila and Lina continued covering the furniture with bedsheets in the adjoining room, within earshot of Bettina and her guest. Oila listened to Bettina's lilting voice, plying her guest for information. "How are you finding the villa? The neighborhood? Have you met the Altmanns on the other side of you? How is your husband enjoying his new position?"

Frau Müeller cast her gaze around the room as the two women conversed, commenting on the home's lovely appointments. "That china cabinet is absolutely lovely, Bettina," Oila heard Frau Müeller comment. There was a pause and then Frau Müeller's voice tightened. "Is that a menorah?" Oila stopped what she was doing, straining to listen to the conversation between her employer and the guest.

"Why, y-yes." Bettina stuttered out a stilted reply, her back stiffening defensively. "Isn't it lovely? It has been in the family for years." The menorah sat on a shelf in the middle of the china cabinet. It was a Löwi family heirloom, the silhouettes of two brass lions holding up each side of the base that held the nine candles.

The conversation in the dining room, only moments earlier light and gay, was exchanged for an uncomfortable silence. Oila heard a muffled exchange and then a chair scraped abruptly across the hardwood floor of the dining room.

"I really must be going," Oila heard Frau Müeller say. "If you'll excuse me, Bettina." Oila heard Bettina launch into a gentle protest, but her guest had quickly gathered her purse and was making her way to the foyer, Bettina hustling along behind her.

"Do come again?" A flush spread across Bettina's cheeks, and her voice lost its usual certainty. Bettina cleared her throat but did not speak again as she stood awkwardly in her own foyer, watching Frau Müeller walk quickly onto the landing and down the steps. Bettina bit her lip and looked around the foyer helplessly. Her eyes darted back and forth, searching for an explanation for her guest's hasty departure. Suddenly Bettina's eyes narrowed, her fists clenched, and a look of recognition crossed over her face like a shadow. Her eyes flashed in anger. Oila stepped back behind the French doors and out of sight. She had seen that look on Bettina's face before. A storm was coming.

"I think this was the best summer at Jesenice ever for two reasons." Kitty prattled on in the back of Uncle Erich's car to whoever might listen. Hanuš and Otto dozed in the back seat next to her. Karel and Bettina occupied the leather upholstered front seat next to Uncle Erich. It was a warm day, a fitting end to another summer filled with golden, unhurried days, spent in a place far removed from the concerns of the outside world.

"Any guesses what they are?" Kitty continued, undaunted by the lack of response. Uncle Erich drove in silence toward the villa on Masaryk Street.

During Kitty's months in hospital, she had grown stronger every day, after her illness broke. The same could not be said for the world outside her hospital room. A sickness began to spread from Germany over the border into Czechoslovakia. The disease exhibited its symptoms in two ways. Like a rash that when scratched, spread, flags began to appear around the villages of the Sudeten region, including Teplice, flags placed proudly outside the doorways of the homes of their German-speaking neighbors.

Kitty had seen the flag before, two black horizontal stripes with a large, blood red swath sandwiched in between. After her discharge from the hospital, the flags cast a pall over the neighborhoods when Kitty and Otto walked to the park in the center of town. Kitty felt a forbidding sense of unease at the sight of them, the hair on her arms standing up when she passed by the houses bearing them. "I feel it too, Kitty," Otto told her, before the family departed for Jesenice.

The sickness also revealed itself through interactions with people they thought they knew. Kitty and Otto bought candied orange slices from a friendly German shop owner in town who knew both children by name. One day, they stepped inside the dim interior of the sweet shop and stepped up to the counter. Mr. Hoffman, the owner, stood behind the counter wearing his signature striped apron. He had his back to them as they entered.

"Good day, Mr. Hoffman," said Otto, cheerfully. "One bag of candied orange slices, please."

Mr. Hoffman did not turn around but continued to dust a shelf of cans and dry goods in front of him. "We are sold out," Mr. Hoffman replied in a gruff voice. Otto was confused. He looked in the case in front of him and saw rows of the sweet slices next to marzipan fruit and chocolate candies.

"Very funny, Mr. Hoffman," replied Otto. "I see them right here in the case."

"Yes. There they are," added Kitty. Kitty's mouth watered at the sight of the other candies. Mr. Hoffman remained silent. Kitty looked around the store. She and Otto were the only customers. She took a step back from the counter, her eyes narrowing, and she tugged pleadingly at Otto's shirt.

Mr. Hoffman turned around slowly, brandishing the feather duster in his hand like a stick. His face was red and splotchy. "I told you we are sold out." His voice was low and threatening.

Otto's eyes fell upon something behind the counter. He looked up at Mr. Hoffman and froze for a moment, then he reached for Kitty's hand and pulled her after him and out the front door of the store. "What is it?" asked Kitty. Otto did not answer but continued to pull Kitty further down the street away from the storefront. They turned at the next corner and Otto stopped, breathing heavily, and looked at Kitty.

"Why are you being mean? Kitty asked, rubbing her wrist where Otto had gripped her.

"Didn't you see the newspaper on the counter?" Otto asked. "He likes...." Otto looked up and down the street to see if anyone was within earshot. He whispered the next word. "Hitler." Kitty's mouth formed into an "o" of recognition. Her lip began to quiver. Otto had just said the name of the bad man that had caused her father to have his first heart attack.

"We are never going back there again," Kitty said firmly. That was two months ago.

Now Uncle Erich maneuvered the green Tatra slowly through the bustling center of town. They passed the sweet shop, and Kitty saw the ominous red and black flag above the doorway, whipping in the warm breeze. Mr. Hoffman must have hung it up during the summer while they were away. Kitty elbowed Otto, accidentally stepping on Pavla, where the dog lay sleeping on the floor of the car. Pavla yelped. Otto looked up just in time to see the additional proof of Mr. Hoffman's vile sentiments.

The car bumped along the cobblestones. Bettina put her hand on her husband's knee in the front seat and gripped it tightly. "Karel," Bettina said quietly, looking out the car window. The car had rolled to a stop outside the villa on Masaryk Street.

Fluttering from a pillar on the Müeller's front porch, flapping enthusiastically in the late summer wind, was the Sudeten flag. Karel reached toward Bettina, squeezing her hand. Kitty saw a look pass between her parents. She recognized it. It was the look that meant "We will talk about this later."

The house staff were waiting expectantly at the bottom of the stairs. "Welcome home," said the housemaids in unison. Everyone exchanged greetings, and Karel and Uncle Erich emptied the car of the family's suitcases. "Och," said Oila, grabbing her own suitcase and looking up at the house. "It's good to be home." Bettina cast one last glance in the direction of the Müeller's house and began to ascend the stairs.

Kitty and Otto bantered back and forth as they walked up the stairs to the villa. "Can you guess now, Otto?" she asked him. "Why was this the best summer yet?"

Otto gave an exasperated sigh. One of the hardships of being close to Kitty was you had to play on her terms. "Okay. The first one is easy: Pavla," Otto replied. The dog had accompanied the family to the villa for the summer. Karel had made a gift of Pavla to Kitty after her lengthy hospital stay. She was a handsome boxer with golden fur and dark brown eyes, and the mutt instantly became a source of tension between Kitty's parents. Bettina thought the dog an unnecessary reward for her daughter's year of lost education.

Kitty fell in love with Pavla the minute she laid eyes on her. She squealed watching Pavla paddle along in the lake at Jesenice. She and Aja stood near her as the dog furiously shook the water from her fur, laughing at the spray that flew everywhere and tickling the dog's belly afterwards. Kitty, Aja, and Pavla, or 'the three girls,' as everyone grew to call them, were inseparable the entire summer.

"Correct," Kitty replied. "What was the second reason, Otto?

Karel's boss at the factory loved Kitty almost as if she were his own. Kitty's frequent visits to her father's office to act as secretary were always followed by a visit to "Uncle" Josef's office, where he greeted her visits with a welcoming smile. Uncle Josef's children were grown, and he missed the carefree days of their childhood. Kitty sat in a chair in his office and recounted her latest adventures with Otto, and in return, Uncle Josef, hand to his lips, offered Kitty a peppermint candy from a drawer of his desk. When she was stricken with appendicitis, he was beside himself, inquiring daily about her condition.

When Kitty returned home from the hospital, Uncle Josef was there to greet her. He reached down to hug Kitty, and then stepped back, revealing a fire engine red scooter with black rubber grips on the handlebars and white tires. The busy streets of Teplice were no place for the scooter, but Karel had agreed to bring it to Jesenice. Kitty and Aja rode the scooter every day, Pavla running behind it, nipping at their heels. Hanuš and Frantisek made unreliable companions for Otto. On the days when they ignored him and set off into the woods, Kitty shared the scooter with Otto.

"Otto." Kitty prodded her cousin for a response.

"You never give up. Do you, Kitty?" Otto exhaled, delivering an exasperated reply. "The scooter, of course."

One by one, the family members shuffled into the dining room of the flat the morning after their return from Jesenice. Oila looked at the children and shook her head fondly. Hanuš, Otto and Kitty were suntanned and lackadaisical. The summer had been particularly carefree and boundless with the presence of the dog and a steady stream of visitors. Now there were precious few days to spare before the new school year required a morning routine and the discipline that came with it.

Bettina took a sip of water from a crystal glass on the table, and then tapped it with a spoon to get the children's attention. The loud clinking served its purpose. All heads turned toward Bettina. "Kitty. You, Hanuš and Otto will be attending the Czech school this year," Bettina announced, her tone both opening and closing the topic for conversation. Kitty inhaled sharply.

"What? The Czech school?" she asked, incredulous at the news. "Their lessons are given in Czech. How will Oila help me with my studies? She does not speak Czech." Kitty looked from Oila to her mother, willing someone to explain this turn of events. "What is wrong with the Jewish school?"

"School is school," Hanuš piped in. He bit into a slice of toast, ripping a piece off with his teeth. Otto was silent. He moved the eggs on his plate from one side to the other with his fork. His mother had given him strict instructions to observe all the rules of the Löwi household.

"Bett..," Kitty began. Oila glared at Kitty, who corrected herself. "Mother. I missed the entire second class. Frau Becker was kind enough to advance me to the third class without testing me." Kitty pleaded, trying to catch Oila's eye for some show of support.

Karel entered the dining room. "It has been decided, Kitty," he said in German. Kitty gritted her teeth and let slip a sigh of frustration. She loved her father, but this was simply too much. Even he did not speak

Czech well. He could barely roll his "r's" properly. She sat at the table, biting her tongue. She hated grownups. All except Oila.

On the first day of school, Oila fastened the back of Kitty's favorite polka dot dress and stood back to look at her. "You are growing like a weed." Kitty stood in front of the full-length mirror. The hem of the dress was above her knees where last year it had been at least an inch below.

Kitty's dark hair was parted on the side and separated into two pigtails. Each pigtail was wound into a long, shiny curl. Kitty's eyes were downcast, her face pensive. Pavla padded into the room, her nails clicking on the hardwood floor. Kitty took the dog's face in her hands. She would never say so, but she thought the dog looked a lot like Oila.

"Be a good girl, Pavla," she said. Her voice was distant, distracted, as she kneeled to rub the dog's velvety ears. "I will be back before you know it." Kitty sighed deeply, a frown falling over her face.

When Kitty failed to respond to Oila's comments, Oila waved a hand in front of Kitty's face. "Penny for your thoughts, Kitty," she said.

"I think I am growing up, Oila," replied Kitty. There was a melancholy tone in Kitty's response. "I don't think I like it."

Oila took Kitty by the hand and sat her down on the edge of her bed. "As long as I am here, you don't have to grow up," Oila told her. She smiled, but Kitty did not smile in return. Oila had witnessed Kitty to be an intuitive child; she sensed and felt things on a level that was beyond her years. While she loved Kitty dearly, today Oila approached her childish distraction with a sense of foreboding. She issued a silent prayer. "Please, God. Keep Kitty safe."

The three children gathered in the foyer to begin the trek to the new school. It was within walking distance, and Hanuš led the way. Otto walked behind him, and Kitty brought up the rear. The air was sultry, a hint of summer lingering in the air, and the sun adjusted its angle in the sky making it clear it was not yet ready to give over to fall. By the time the trio had arrived within a block of the new school, a delicate sweat graced their foreheads.

A group of boys about Hanuš's age were gathered in a circle up ahead, looking intently at something on the ground. The Czech school did not require uniforms, but the three boys were dressed alike: khaki shirts with dark knotted neckerchiefs, dark shorts, and wide black belts. Otto and Kitty began to walk faster and were soon by Hanuš's side. The group of boys stepped away as the trio approached, revealing the object of interest. The rotting carcass of a small rabbit, a swarm of flies buzzing around it, lay on the ground.

"Don't look, Kitty," Hanuš told her, walking sideways to block his sister's view of the animal. Kitty obeyed and looked in the other direction.

The boys imitated Hanuš in sing-song voices. "Oh, don't look Kitty-cat, you might be next," the tallest of the boys said in a threatening tone. Kitty broke out in a run, Otto trailing behind her, and they ran the rest of the way to school.

The first day at the Czech school was a blur for Kitty. She liked her teacher, who complimented Kitty on being a "quick study." Kitty thought it meant she was picking up Czech fast, and she stood a little taller after the teacher's comment. Kitty had missed a year of school and could do maths better than most of the other girls, a fact that did not sit well with her new classmates. She heard one of them refer to her as a "smartypants." Most of them appeared haughty and clannish, and Kitty did not care for them. By the end of the day, the feeling seemed mutual. She walked home with Otto, kicking stones ahead of them.

"The other girls at school are babies," Kitty told Otto. They approached the dead rabbit. This time, Kitty stopped to inspect the animal's condition. "I wonder if those boys killed it." Otto was the first to turn away, and they walked the rest of the way home in silence.

The children walked to school on the second day and found the boys in the uniforms had been joined by three more. They stood, obstructing the sidewalk, a block away from the school.

"Well, what have we here?" The boy who spoke puffed out his chest. It was the same boy who had teased Hanuš the day before. Kitty swallowed hard. He was not handsome, and she would like to have told him so. He wore a woolen cap over his dirty blond hair and his face seemed permanently set in a sneer.

"Leave us alone," said Hanuš. He kept walking past the group, his head held high. The gauntlet parted in the middle and allowed Hanuš to pass. Kitty and Otto followed Hanuš. Confidently, they walked past the imposing group and saw the lead troublemaker's mouth fall open in surprise. He stomped his foot and pushed another boy to punish him for letting them pass. A satisfied smile crossed Kitty's face, and she ran to catch up to Hanuš. The feeling stayed with her throughout the day, and she made quick work of her multiplication tables.

Kitty, Hanuš, and Otto walked the same route to school the rest of the week with no sign of the uniformed offenders. Kitty skipped all the way home at the end of the first week. She was learning Czech fast. Her teacher said she was "a natural." Hanuš's friends at the new school nicknamed him "Honza," and he seemed quite pleased with himself. Hanuš returned to his insufferable self, and Otto held the middle ground. Things were returning to normal.

The next Monday they woke to drizzling rain. Everyone at the breakfast table was quiet. Rain coursed down the windows in rivulets. "The sky is crying," Kitty said sleepily, yawning. Hanuš donned a rain slicker in the foyer, and Kitty and Otto shared an umbrella, splashing in the puddles on the sidewalk. Hanuš walked behind them, head down to escape the rain. They did not notice the gang until it was too late. Up ahead, half a dozen boys blocked the sidewalk, wearing identical rain ponchos and woolen berets.

Kitty and Otto stopped, forcing Hanuš to look up. Hanuš walked past and drew closer to the boys. Suddenly, Hanuš darted to the side and the boy on the end stuck his leg out to trip him. Hanuš was too quick for him and succeeded in getting to the other side of the line unscathed. Kitty bit her lip, gripping the umbrella with one hand while rain dripped off it in a steady stream. They copied Hanuš and ran to the right side, but the boy on the end was expecting them now. He stuck his leg out, and Otto went stumbling forward onto the wet ground, dropping his lunchbox in the process. Kitty stopped, still holding the umbrella, alone and surrounded, her breathing quick and choppy.

"Czech, mate," said a boy in the middle in German. "Get it?" He laughed and a few of the other boys laughed along. Two boys on the left turned and started to walk away. "Forget the girl, Ulrich," one of them said over his shoulder.

Kitty squeezed the umbrella tightly, looking for an opening. A moment later, she saw Hanuš's face push through the middle of the four remaining boys. One of the boys fell forward, his hands skimming the ground. Otto came around from the left and two boys Kitty had never seen before circled in from the right. Otto, Hanuš, and his new friends ran to Kitty and surrounded her, all of them drenched from the rain.

"Let's go," she heard Hanuš say to the rag tag group assembled to protect her. They began to move forward, with Kitty safely in the center. The pack of uniformed youth scattered as the circle of boys plowed forward. It was going to be a long year.

CHAPTER FOUR

VLADA 1936
PARDUBICE, CZECHOSLOVAKIA

Ivan and Milan stood in front of the Grand Cinema movie theater in the center of town, waving their arms at Vlada, beckoning him to walk faster.

"Hurry up, Vlada," Ivan scolded his friend. "The movie is going to start any minute now." The sun was blinding, and a thin film of sweat shone on Vlada's forehead from his walk across town. The three friends had met nearly every Saturday afternoon that summer at the theater, buying their tickets at the box office for the matinee and settling into front-row seats, letting the cool darkness envelop them. For two hours, Vlada's love of books was temporarily displaced by the on-screen adventures of American film actor Tom Mix.

The boys watched the screen intently, never taking their eyes off the hero as he galloped across rolling plains littered with boulders on his trusty steed, Tony the Wonder Horse. Along the way, Tom encountered gangs of villains and saved farms from the evil tax collector. When the film's final credits finished scrolling, the boys exited the theater, hotly debating which of Tom's narrow escapes from death-defying situations were worthiest of merit.

"Did you see the way he swam up to the ceiling as the cellar was filling up with water? He must have held his breath for two whole minutes!" Ivan puffed his cheeks out imitating his hero.

"What about the clever way he escaped from that pack of wolves?" added Milan, shaking his head reverently.

It was no secret among his friends that Vlada's favorite Tom Mix film was *The Miracle Rider*. It was the stuff heroes were made for: a greedy oil baron threatens the livelihood of an entire Indian reservation, and the oil baron gets his comeuppance when Tom devises a scheme to run him off the tribal land. Vlada eagerly anticipated the moment Chief Black Wing came on screen, and made Tom Mix an honorary chief of the tribe. Chief Black Wing wore a royal headdress made of leather and hundreds of feathers, and his long dark braids hung down over a beaded tunic. Vlada had seen the film twice and was awestruck by the chief each time.

"What I wouldn't give to see an Indian in real life," Vlada added wistfully. The other boys nodded in agreement.

"Are you sure you wouldn't rather see Shirley Temple?" Ivan teased, pushing Vlada off the sidewalk. Vlada shot Ivan a cautionary look, indicating that the topic was off-limits for further conversation.

Vlada had complained when his mother made him accompany her to the Grand Cinema to watch Shirley Temple in her film *The Littlest Rebel*. "What if my friends see me, Mami? That movie is for girls," Vlada protested. Later, he admitted to his mother that it was a pretty good movie. It was a musical drama set during the United States' Civil War. Vlada had never seen a black person in real life, and observing the interaction between Shirley Temple's character Vergie and the actor who portrayed the slave fascinated Vlada. When his friends found out he had gone to one of the child actress's films, their teasing had been relentless.

When not in the company of his friends, Vlada spent hazy summer afternoons at his father's rustic cabin at Polobiny on the marshy outskirts of Pardubice. The radio broadcasts and newspaper headlines told of the endless anti-Semitic decrees in Germany, and Karel experienced each shocking account as if he were a boxer absorbing physical blows to the body. He sought comfort in the simple pleasures at the cabin, fishing for carp off the end of a long wooden skiff and playing fetch with Čigy on the banks nearby. The area near the cabin was prone to flooding in the spring, the water rising to the meadow and sometimes the field beyond, but Karel preferred the silence of the cabin at its muddiest to dry ground and bad news.

Vlada coasted on his bicycle down the gentle, sloping hill to where the cabin stood, skidding to a stop. He waved to his father who stood on the shore of the stream, casting his fishing line high over his head and into the water, a rum-soaked ball of bread on the hook as bait.

"How is the fishing today, Tati?" Vlada shouted, cupping his hands to his mouth.

"Get your pole, Vlada! They are really biting today." A smile spread over Karel's face at the sight of his son. "Čigy is not here to bark at the geese and ruin the silence."

Vlada ran to the side of the cabin where, propped against a wall, was a wooden fishing rod. He walked to the edge of the stream where his father stood, took a ball of bread from a tin, pushed the hook through it and cast it out over the water. Father and son shared the lazy summer afternoon side by side in comfortable silence, casting and reeling in, the troubles of the outside world lost in the muffled sounds of life in the marsh. Vlada listened to the chirping of the crickets, and breathed in the marsh's mossy redolence, not sure if he wanted summer vacation to come to an end.

The school courtyard was empty when Vlada arrived for the first day of middle school. He stood at the bottom of the steps leading up to the school's entrance. "The first bell must have rung already," thought Vlada. His summer musings had made him late for school. He was a student in good standing, and generally well-liked by his professors. He looked forward to seeing Jirka and his other friends. He took the cement steps two at a time and pulled the heavy door open.

But his good mood evaporated the moment he entered. Pan Jicha, the Latin teacher, stood with his arms crossed in front of him, huddled in conversation with an older teacher. Vlada had to walk by them to get to his class, and although they spoke in hushed tones, he was certain he heard the word "Jew."

A chill washed over Vlada. He recalled his conversation with Jirka at the end of the previous school year. "You watch, Vlada," Jirka had warned him. "If things continue like they are in Germany, we will be feeling it here before you know it." Vlada knew his father feared that as well. It was the reason Karel could not sleep at night.

The anti-Semitic sentiments emanating from Germany had crept across the border under cover of night like the villainous horse thieves in a Tom Mix movie, covertly scaling the Ore Mountains, slipping into the shallows of the Bílina River, and arriving in Pardubice. Last year's distant and nebulous warning now had been fed on vile propaganda perpetuated during the summer months. The prejudice had become bolder, more public and threatening. Vlada imagined the poisonous rhetoric had a physical form, like the cephalopod from *Twenty Thousand Leagues Under the Sea*. It was strong now, strong enough to reach its deadly tentacles across the Czech border and strangle any Jews in its path.

Jicha's eyes followed Vlada with a menacing stare as he walked to his homeroom. Outside of school, this pudgy, balding man might seem perfectly harmless, but inside the walls of the school, he wielded an arrogant power over those he was meant to guide and educate. Vlada broke out in a cold sweat, suddenly chilled despite the warmth of the day. He needed to find a friendly face. Ivan and Milan were not Jewish so they would not be much help. He had to find Jirka. Vlada's cheeks burned with humiliation, but he felt his shame quickly turn to anger as he walked down the hallway in search of his friend.

"What have I to be ashamed of? I am Czech first," thought Vlada. "I have just as much right to be here as any of the other students." Middle school had held such promise, it came with seniority over the elementary students and increased freedom at school and at home. Now, Vlada felt small and inadequate. He saw his ability to harness that small bit of power slipping through his fingers because something else, something corrupt and deceitful, was going to ruin it.

Jirka set his books down on the desk next to Vlada's, and studied his friend's demeanor, a look of recognition spreading across his face.

"Oh. So, the fog is lifting now, eh, Vlada?" Jirka half-teased. He stopped his ribbing when Vlada forced a weak smile.

He was jealous of Jirka. Jirka was on the offensive. He had come prepared for the monster while Vlada had arrived unarmed.

Jirka scribbled something on a small scrap of paper and slipped it into Vlada's hand. Vlada took the note and went to his desk. He sat and looked around. When he was certain that he was clear of anyone's line of sight, he opened the crumpled note beneath his desk. The short sentence gave Vlada chills, but he knew Jirka was right.

"We need a plan of attack."

With a flourish, Pan Jicha finished scribbling on the chalkboard. "And what does Mr. Munk have to say this morning? Please translate, Mr. Munk. *Festina Lente.* That means 'Make haste slowly' in case you were wondering. Chop, chop. We don't have all day." Pan Jicha's verbal assault on Vlada continued unabated. "'*Aquila non capit muscas.*' Hello? You will never be able to read Cicero at this rate, young man."

Vlada sat frozen in his seat, a look of shock on his face. He had barely taken out his pencil when the Latin teacher had set upon him. What little knowledge of Latin Vlada possessed became an inaccessible jumble in his brain as he struggled to respond to the teacher's unwarranted taunts. Flustered and stammering, Vlada threw out his best guess. "Music soothes the savage breast?" Vlada's shoulders slumped, immediately sensing that his answer was incorrect.

Pan Jicha let out an exasperated sigh. He turned and focused his attention on Jirka, continuing his attack. "Mr. Friedman," he sniffed with displeasure as he said Jirka's family name. "Can you be of any assistance to your poor friend here? No? I thought not."

Finally the school day ended and Vlada ran all the way home. Both his parents sat waiting for him at the kitchen table of the flat, eager to hear about his first day in middle school.

"How does it feel to be back, Vlada?" His father smiled. It was not clear by his smile whether he was expecting a good report or just hoping for one.

"What is your favorite class this year, Vlada?" his mother asked excitedly. Vlada struggled to keep his shoulders from falling. He wanted to tell them just how bad the day had been. He wanted a hug from his mother, and he wanted his father to stand up for him against Pan Jicha, even if it meant speaking with the principal. Vlada wondered how he could tell his parents what had happened at school, how he had felt humiliated and worthless. "I am almost twelve years old. I must handle this on my own."

So he lied. "It was wonderful, Mami. Everyone was so happy to see each other. We had great fun during recess and the teachers were all in good spirits." Vlada spoke rapidly, the lies tumbling out one after another. They sat at the table and Hermina set down bowls of Vlada's favorite sauerkraut soup with crusty bread while his parents peppered Vlada with more questions about his day. When the interrogation was over, Vlada exhaled a sigh of relief.

"Tati, do you think it would be possible to get a tutor for Latin?" Vlada casually asked. He let his question hang in the air, hoping it would not prompt his father to ask more questions. "I think it is going to be a bit challenging this year."

"Oh, that Pan Jicha," his father clicked his tongue. "He is a strange bird, isn't he, Vlada? If you think it would help, then of course we will do it. I think I know just the fellow."

Vlada smiled weakly. He went to bed that night and had nightmares of Latin class.

Within a week, Pan Jicha had moved Vlada and Jirka's desks to the back of the classroom. The intentional exile of the boys provided them with the unexpected benefit of being able to pass notes indiscriminately out of Jicha's line of sight. Jirka handed Vlada a note which read *Sic gorgiamus allos subjectatos nunc*. He had written the translation on the back. "We gladly feast on those who would subdue us." Vlada could not have agreed more. "We just need to know who our friends are, and who is a foe," Jirka added.

Vlada had always liked the chemistry teacher Pan Vana. He respected the small man in the crumpled suits who shared a love of the same scientific area of study as his father. Pan Vana was fair in his grading and good at explaining complex concepts like kinetics. Every time Vlada got on his bicycle he heard Pan Vana's voice explaining that the coefficient of energy was zero while standing still, knowing that the minute he started peddling, the energy increased.

"Vlada," Pan Vana said in an imperious tone that contradicted his disheveled appearance. "Could you please explain to the class the difference between hydrolyzation and oxidation?"

Vlada stood up from the desk, mouth agape, his eyes searching anywhere in the room for help.

"Isn't your father a chemist, Vlada? You should know this," Pan Vana continued haughtily. Vlada stiffened, then collapsed back into his seat without answering.

That evening at supper, Vlada tested his father for his reaction. "I think Pan Vana is jealous of you, Tati," Vlada told his father.

"We were in school together, Vlada," Karel replied. "I think he saw himself in a larger role, running a lab and doing research. I can only think he is unhappy as a teacher." Vlada cared little about Pan Vana's job satisfaction. If the man meant to grill Vlada daily on chemistry facts, Vlada would be forced to add one hour of memorization in his chemistry book every night to avoid further humiliation.

Pani Babikova had garnet hair and a bold manner of dress that teetered on the edge of what the school elders deemed acceptable. She insisted the students call the classroom she presided over for art class the art *studio*. An avid devotee of the Impressionists, she let it be known that in her estimation Monet, Cassatt, Degas, and Renoir were the best artists that had ever lived.

"What about Jiroslav Grus?" Vlada asked the art teacher one day, wondering what she thought of the Czech artist who happened to be his father's good friend. Pani Babikova refused to answer, branding Vlada impudent from that moment forward.

"For our first project this year I would like to ask that you bring fruit from home to assemble into a still life," Pani Babikova announced one morning to the class.

Vlada informed Hermina of the art teacher's request that day after returning home from school. His mother was a gifted artist, and her talent took many forms: drawing, music, rug making. Also, his father was a fine artist in his own right, prompting Vlada to ponder his lack of artistic talent given both his parents' relative skill in those areas.

The following morning, Vlada watched his mother pack two large red apples in his rucksack. When Vlada was just a few blocks away from school, he remembered the fruit. He reached into the bag and took out one of the apples, biting into it, the satisfying crunch filling his mouth with a combination of tartness and sweet juices. He continued walking at a leisurely pace, apple in hand, distractedly taking occasional bites from it until he spotted the school down the block. He looked down to find there was nothing left of the first apple but the core. He quickly stuffed the evidence in his bag and went inside.

Vlada walked into the studio to find the class buzzing with excitement, each student proudly setting up their still life models on the pedestals the art teacher had provided. Vlada walked to his pedestal and reached into his rucksack for the other apple. When no one was looking, he took a few small bites out of it. Ivan caught Vlada in the act and shot him a warning glance from across the room, shaking his head at his friend, eyes rolling, questioning Vlada's judgment. Vlada shrugged, but stopped eating the apple, placing it on his pedestal instead, and turning it so that its half-eaten side faced the wall.

Pani Bobikova entered the room. She placed a record on the record player, lifted the needle, and waltzed around the room to the tinkling sounds of Chopin, friend to the Impressionists, his *Nocturne in E flat major* filling the corners of the studio. She called the class to attention and then began wandering from one student to the next, stopping to take in each student's first rendition of their subject matter on their canvas, offering suggestions and expertise. "The shadow is a little too dark there, Marek…Very good perspective, Ivan…Lovely, Pavel. Just lovely."

Suddenly, she shrieked as she caught sight of the half-eaten apple. She approached Vlada's pedestal and circled around it to get a better view. "Barbarian!" She pinched the edge of Vlada's ear, dragging him past Ivan's painting – which, Vlada thought, lacked perspective – and out of the classroom to the principal's office where the teacher hoped appropriate discipline would be exacted.

Jirka tried to console Vlada's bruised ego when they later met up in the boys' lavatory. "She is a temperamental artist, Vlada," said Jirka. "Don't take it too hard."

"Easy for you to say," Vlada replied. "She didn't almost tear your ear off." Vlada rubbed his reddened ear, and the boys laughed uneasily.

Vlada began the walk home from school nursing the indignity of his abrupt exit from the art studio earlier that day. His ear was still red where Pani Bobikova had pinched it. He had walked a few blocks when he noticed Vladimir Jedlicka, a Czech youth in the same class as Vlada, walking parallel to him on the other side of the street. Vlada lifted his hand to wave at his classmate, but the boy's sneering countenance made him think better of it. Vlada awkwardly lowered his hand to his side. Vladimir was definitely a foe.

Strains of an unfamiliar rhyme reached his ears, and Vlada slowed his pace. *"Zide žide cerf pro tebe přijd,"* Vladimir sang in a low sing-song voice barely audible to anyone but Vlada. Vlada had heard the curse before but had never been on the receiving end. He looked across the street at his classmate in disbelief; they sat at the same bench in school together, their parents knew each other, they had been casual friends. Vladimir continued the taunt. *Jew, Jew, the Devil will come for you.*

Vlada looked up and down the empty street. There were no other witnesses, but he knew a threat when he heard one. Vlada's lip curled in disgust, he became alert and poised, his anger rising, his muscles flexing. He had been driven to anger before. Pan Jicha made his blood boil almost daily. But Vlada contained his anger at school. He knew he could not afford the luxury of addressing his aggressors in the confines of the building.

On the street there were no witnesses, and no repercussions to endure from teachers or administrators. Vlada's whole body was charged with a frenzied energy demanding that he engage in some critical and necessary action. This was a new and exhilarating sensation. Vlada realized he wanted revenge, revenge for being belittled, insulted, and threatened. He tried it on, this new feeling, turned it around, examined it. He had never been in a physical fight before and found himself wondering what his clenched fist would feel like on Vladimir's flabby cheek. He guessed the touch of his knuckles hitting the soft flesh of Vladimir's face would feel quite good. He had seen other boys at school scuffle, slap and throw punches, seen the fake fights in the Tom Mix movies. He would do nothing now, here, alone, but he would talk to Jirka about getting the boy alone somewhere sometime soon.

Jirka and Vlada met in the park after school the next day to discuss the current state of affairs: the slurs, the derision, and the other small but frequent indignities they and a few other Jewish students were now subjected to daily.

"We need to follow a few simple rules, Jirka," Vlada told his friend. He drew a book out of his rucksack. He showed Jirka the title – *The Good Soldier Svejk* – but there was no spark of recognition. Jirka shook his head. Vlada was surprised his friend was not familiar with Jaroslav Hasek's satirical story about a simple, good-natured soldier who feigns enthusiasm for war and prevails over his misguided and idiotic military leaders. Vlada shared with Jirka the simple soldier's unwritten rules for survival and success under the most challenging situations.

"Never be late. Never be the first or the last. Never volunteer. Never make them notice you." Vlad periodically glanced up to make sure Jirka was paying attention.

Jirka nodded in agreement, committed to following the rules. "What shall we do about Vladimir?"

"We will deal with him," Vlada said, his eyes narrowing as he pictured what his next interaction with Vladimir might look like. He felt like the balance of power was shifting and he liked the idea of reclaiming his honor. At least now they had a plan. He hoped it worked.

CHAPTER FOUR

Kitty spun in circles, her mittened hands out at her sides while snow fell gently over the Neuer Markt square in Vienna. "Look at me, Oila!" Kitty squealed with glee. It was early Sunday morning, and the square, lined with elegant cream-colored stone buildings with wrought iron balconies and ornate molding, was empty. Oila and Kitty were on their way to Catholic Mass.

"I think everything in Vienna is prettier than it is in Teplice, Oila. In fact, I am sure of it," Kitty said. Oila looked around at the light dusting of snow. It sparkled off every surface, like a million tiny diamonds.

"Silly girl," Oila replied. "I think you may be right."

Kitty stopped spinning and looked at Oila. "Thank you for bringing me here, Oila," Kitty said. Her small face was serious, her cheeks pink from the cold.

Oila brushed the snow from Kitty's coat and took her mittened hands in hers. "You know I have always talked of bringing you here. Now here we are." Oila's voice was hoarse when she spoke. She turned away, leading Kitty over to the center of the square.

"Kitty Löwi, I give you ... *Donnerbrunnen!*" Oila held out her hands to indicate an aqua bronze and granite fountain. For years, Oila had told Kitty about the famous fountain, describing it in detail. The seated figure of Providentia, the Roman personification of foresight, rose from the center, one side of her billowy tunic lowered, leaving her breast exposed. Surrounding her were four naked cherubs, each holding a fish twice their size, allegories for the Danube. "In the summertime, the fish spout streams of water that fall back into the pool," Oila recalled, her voice echoing a dreamlike quality.

Kitty gazed up at the figure of the woman. "Oh, Oila. She's beautiful!" Kitty exclaimed. "I wish I could throw a coin in the fountain and know my future." The statue cast her unseeing gaze off to the right. "What do you think she's looking at, Oila?" Kitty eyes followed the statue's line of sight, and finding nothing of interest in that direction, she turned and looked in the other direction, her eyes landing on a building at the other end of the square.

"She's looking in the wrong direction," Kitty said. She pointed to a building that was seven stories high, a Viennese confection, every window framed with intricate white molding in the Baroque style. A lone round window occupied the top floor. Kitty pointed to the window. "That is where I am going to live when I grow up. I will look out the window onto the square, and every time Bettina comes to visit, she will have to pass by the naked angels in the fountain," Kitty said, giggling at her own joke.

Oila choked back a laugh. "If we were in Teplice, I would have no choice but to reprimand you for your cheekiness," said Oila with mock seriousness.

Kitty understood Oila's lack of reprimand as a signal that she could continue. "You know, Oila," Kitty said, a mischievous look on her face, "I don't think Mother has seen me naked since the day I was born."

"Kitty Löwi." Oila looked at Kitty, shaking her head. Church bells began to peal in the distance. Oila shook her head, listening for the number of bells to mark the time. "Hurry. We are going to be late for Mass." Oila took Kitty by the hand and began to briskly walk in the direction of the church.

Kitty looked around as she walked. People had begun to mill about the square. The sun had risen just over the tops of the buildings, casting everything under its warm glow and melting the sparkling snow, but not dispelling the magic. Kitty's first morning in Vienna was off to a wonderful start.

The day before Christmas, Oila tiptoed into Kitty's bedroom in the early morning hours while the rest of the household, save for Cook, was still asleep. Oila set an oil lamp on Kitty's nightstand "Kitty. Wake up."

Kitty rubbed her eyes, adjusting them to the light. "I was dreaming that Pavla wanted to play with some other dogs and Bettina wouldn't let her." Her voice was childlike and thick with sleep.

Oila sat on the edge of the bed. "Here is Pavla now, Kitty. None the worse for wear." The golden boxer was Kitty's devoted companion. Pavla was tiny for her breed, and Kitty had named her to reflect her petite stature. The dog snored contentedly on the floor near Kitty's bed until she heard her name a second time. She rose and stretched, sniffing the air, which confirmed her decision to go downstairs to see what Cook might have dropped for her this morning.

"I have a surprise for you, but you must keep it secret until breakfast," said Oila.

"Am I still dreaming, Oila?" Kitty asked, groggily. "I know how to keep a secret. Why, just the other day Otto and I...." Her voice trailed off and her head fell gently back onto her pillow.

"A simple yes or no will do, *mein kleine*," insisted Oila.

Kitty nodded her head. "Yes, Oila." Kitty sat up now, listening, propped up against the bed pillows.

"My precious, determined girl," Oila said, her eyes shiny with tears. She cleared her throat, wiping her eyes with the back of her hand. "Kitty, remember I have spoken to you about my son. His father was killed in the great war when Franz was just a boy. Perhaps because of that he joined the army."

Kitty nodded, yawning, losing interest. "Yes, Oila."

"He is grown up now and you are all that I have. I want you to come on winter holiday with me. It may be the last time..." Oila's voice trailed off.

"A trip to Vienna?" Kitty was fully awake now, excitement in her voice. "Can Pavla come?"

"Dogs are not permitted on this trip," Oila explained. "Would you like to take one of your dolls?"

Kitty looked up at the shelves above her bureau. The two long shelves were lined with porcelain dolls with long, shiny tresses, some blond, some brunette. They wore extravagant dresses of velvet and lace and held fans and fancy parasols. One day Otto had scared her into thinking the dolls were watching her every movement with their fixed, glass eyes. Kitty had not been able to look at the dolls the same since.

"Their faces are cold and set, and their crinolines are scratchy," Kitty replied. "Let them stay where they are, Oila. They are no match for my sweet Pavla. I will miss her terribly. Do you think she will be all right without me? What about Father? Do you think it is safe to leave him? With his condition?"

In the fall, Karel had surprised the household with an extravagant purchase. Two delivery men arrived at the house with a large box. The men made their way to the parlor, bumping into the door, and then disappeared into the room for at least thirty minutes. When they departed, Karel called the family into the parlor and showed them his new toy: a top-of-the-line Blaupunkt radio. Karel explained the features of the newly purchased item like a showman extolling the abilities of the world's strongest man. "We are the first family to own one, the salesman tells me," Karel bragged. "He said it has an 'enchanting, rich sound,' and that by just a turn of the knobs, we can bring the world into our home."

"You sound like the advertisement, Karel," Bettina joked but smiled to herself, pleased to know she had something the Müellers did not.

The receiver, encased in a dark wood veneer, was given a place of honor on a table next to Karel's favorite leather wing-back chair; the two pieces complimented each other nicely. Karel began to listen to the radio nightly and Kitty joined him. She sat directly in front of the radio, watching the tiny blinking light behind the speaker as voices in English, French, and German relayed the news of the week. The news about events in Nazi Germany under the Führer, Adolf Hitler, was bleak. Kitty caught phrases like "more anti-Jewish legislation out of Nazi Germany and Aryanization of Jewish property" until Bettina came in the room. "Shut that off, Karel," Bettina demanded, nodding her head in Kitty's direction.

Early one evening not long after supper Lina, the housemaid, found Karel lying prostrate on the floor of the parlor, the radio blaring a hair-raising speech in German. "Help! Help! Frau Löwi," Lina shouted. Bettina rushed in, a genuine look of concern on her face, and ordered the maid to call for an ambulance. Oila and Kitty were sewing in a room upstairs, unaware of the drama unfolding in the parlor until Kitty ran down the stairs and saw her father being lifted onto a hospital stretcher, just like the one Kitty had lain on a few years earlier.

Kitty was inconsolable during her father's hospital stay. "Is Father going to die?" Kitty asked Oila numerous times a day. "I should have been in there with him."

"No, Kitty. He is not going to die," Oila answered patiently. Kitty would not be convinced. She sat on the floor of the parlor, Pavla curled up beside her, staring at the radio, a look of distress on her face. Kitty refused to sit at the dinner table, keeping instead to her vigil in the parlor, willing her father's safe return.

"You must get some sleep, Kitty," Oila pleaded. "You are getting dark circles under your eyes. Your father would not want to see you like this."

On the second evening of Karel's hospitalization, Bettina strode into the parlor. "Kitty, enough," she declared. Oila lifted Kitty from her post on the floor and led her to the dining room for dinner.

Three days later Karel returned home, pale, and weak. He stood in the doorway of the flat catching his breath after the exertion of walking up the front stairs. Kitty ran at full speed toward him, hugging him and almost knocking him down. "Ah, careful, Kitty," said Karel, in a weak voice. "At least someone is happy to see me."

They walked arm in arm together into the flat. "I can't bear to think of you lying on the floor of the parlor for even a minute. I will never leave you alone in there again," Kitty said, sniffling. From that moment forward, she barely let her father out of her sight.

Hanuš watched his father quietly from across the table at dinner that evening. "How did it feel to be the man of the house for a few days, eh, Hanuš?" his father asked. Hanuš did not reply but went back to studying his soup. When everyone had finished eating, Karel stood up. "Well, care to join me in the parlor, Kitty?" Kitty saw the flash of jealousy in Hanuš's eyes.

"Race you to the chair, slowpoke," Hanuš teased. He ran ahead to the parlor, beating Kitty to the damask chair that served as home base in hide-and-seek.

"That wasn't fair, Hanuš. You had a head start. Move over." Kitty had learned not to accuse her brother of cheating outright. She squeezed herself into the chair next to him, making them both uncomfortable. Karel tuned the radio while Kitty looked on, fascinated, the broadcast switching from music to the news from England to a German language program, all within the span of a minute.

Hanuš looked from his father to Kitty, sneering. "This is it? This is what you do in here every night?" Hanuš stood up and walked out of the room.

"Aah," Kitty said, stretching out comfortably on the chair, crossing her legs until they were touching the woven cane sides.

Bettina appeared in the doorway of the parlor in a silver brocade dress and a cloud of Guerlain's Vol de Nuit. "Aren't you coming, Karel?" she asked, eyebrows raised in a question. A strand of pearls hung from her neck and her pale shoulders were covered in a fur stole. It was her parents' habit to go out after dinner and meet friends at a local club. Karel often played cards with the other men, not always with the best results.

"I think I might stay in and catch up on my rest, dear." Karel replied. His voice was kind, ignoring his wife's lack of sensitivity to his recent ordeal. "I've only just come home from hospital. You go ahead."

"Very well," said Bettina. Kitty watched as her mother applied her lipstick one last time in the parlor mirror. After her departure, Kitty made a face. Karel gave her his best stern look, then he settled into his chair and let out a sigh. Kitty watched him closely while he lit his pipe. A haze of smoke drifted lazily upwards as he puffed, the sweet smell of tobacco drifting into every corner of the room. Pavla padded in and curled up at the foot of Kitty's chair. Oila came in and stood in the doorway, shaking her head at the trio. "Three peas in a pod," she said, a contented smile crossing her face.

"I am not a pea, Oila," Kitty protested. "I am a caterpillar, and this is my cocoon," Kitty gestured at the chair surrounding her. "And one day I am going to turn into a beautiful butterfly."

"No doubt, Kitty. No doubt," Karel added.

Kitty took one of her mother's fashion magazines from the rack next to her chair. She studied the image on the cover, a sketch of two gloved models in chic belted suits walking arm in arm. Inside the magazine were tissue paper patterns that were used to sew outfits just like the ones on the cover. Kitty rolled her eyes. "I am wearing Chanel," Kitty mocked, the back of her hand to her forehead in dramatic fashion. "Don't you know, it's all the rage in America?" She added, "Too bad Bettina can't sew a stitch to save her life."

"Kitty," Oila scolded, out of habit more than resolve.

Karel chimed in. "Kitty, what did I say about calling your mother by her first name?"

"Yes, Father," Kitty replied. It was a hard habit for Kitty to break, especially because she had no desire to do so.

Oila brought Kitty back from her reverie, and her concerns over her father's health. Three months had passed since Karel's heart attack without further incident.

"The doctor said your father is doing very well now, Kitty," Oila continued. "Now listen carefully. I am going to ask your parents at breakfast this morning if you can accompany me on holiday to Vienna. Please be on your best behavior."

How could she tell her precious charge the truth? That what they had together, already threatened on her daily trips to school by ugliness and hate, might soon be under even greater attack? That this trip might be the last one they would ever take together?

Breakfast began on an uneasy note. "Nazis. Despicable," Karel slammed the newspaper down on the table. His face was red and splotchy, the veins in his forehead bulging.

Kitty began to whimper. Her thick dark eyelashes held back a rising tide of tears. Her toast with butter and jam sat untouched on the china plate in front of her. "*Mach Vas, Mater*. Do something." Kitty pleaded with her mother to calm her father.

"Karel, you are scaring the children," Bettina spoke without looking up, continuing to tap at the hardboiled egg perched in a gold-rimmed egg cup. "Please try to calm yourself. We don't want a repeat of what happened a few months ago."

Karel smoothed his tie, breathed in deeply, and composed himself. "I am sorry, Kitty," he said, acknowledging her distress. "I am fine. It's okay." Kitty sniffled and took a bite of her toast.

Oila cleared her throat. "Bitte, Herr Löwi. Frau Löwi." Oila had been in the Löwis' employ since Kitty was born. She was considered a member of the family, and as such, she addressed her employers by their first names, so the use of their surnames immediately brought all conversation at the breakfast table to a halt. Hanuš stopped eating. He did not want to miss a thing.

"Please, proceed, Oila," said Karel.

"I wondered if it might be possible to have Kitty accompany me on my winter holiday this year." Oila barely finished speaking before a jumble of voices joined in all at once interrupting her, one overlapping the other.

Bettina looked at Oila and then her husband. "Oila, this is a lovely offer. I just wonder if we shouldn't be concerned about the timing. What do you think, Karel? Given the latest developments?" Everyone around the table was quiet. Hanuš sniggered, gleefully assuming Oila's request was about to be denied by his mother. Kitty held her breath, crossing her fingers underneath the table and waiting for her father to answer.

"Oila, this is most generous of you. What do your parents say about the situation in Austria? Do they think it is safe for now?" asked Karel.

Oila adopted a conciliatory tone. "I would never put Kitty in harm's way. I do think the opportunity for a trip like this may not arise again, Karel. At least not for quite some time." Karel and Oila exchanged a knowing look.

"I believe that is an accurate assessment, Oila." Karel cast his wife a sideways glance and continued. "We have no doubt that Kitty would be in the best care with you. Let us know what we can do to help with the arrangements."

Kitty leaped out of her seat. She ran to Oila and threw her arms around her neck. "Oh, Oila," Kitty cried. "An adventure."

When breakfast was finished, Oila motioned for Kitty to join her in the parlor. Kitty sat in the damask chair and looked down at her feet. "Oila," Kitty exclaimed. "I can touch the floor." Just a few short months before Kitty's feet had barely brushed the carpet as she sat in the chair.

Oila clapped her hands together. "You are becoming a young woman, Kitty. That is why you must come with me," explained Oila. "And you know I can't trust anyone here to take care of you while I am gone."

Kitty laughed. "Father is working again; Otto is at home in Jesenice. Hanuš is useless. And Mother wouldn't notice if I were missing for days. I must go with you," said Kitty.

Oila smiled and then her tone turned serious. "I need you to remember one thing on our trip, Kitty," Oila said. She paused. "If anyone asks you what your religion is you must tell them that you are Catholic." Oila exhaled. She waited for Kitty to show that she understood the import of Oila's request.

"Oila, you know I am hardly Jewish. I am Czech," Kitty said matter of factly. When Oila did not respond, Kitty looked at her, her eyes narrowing. "Why can't I just say I am Czech?"

"If only it were that simple, meine kleine," Oila said, looking down at her hands, avoiding Kitty's gaze. When she looked up, Kitty was staring at her intently. "We are just going to have to keep it a secret, Kitty."

"Oh, I am good at keeping secrets," Kitty replied, relaxing a bit.

"Are you now?" They both laughed.

A week earlier, Kitty could not have imagined the grandeur of the towering and gilded ceilings in a Viennese church. Now she found herself in front of a gently curved boat the color of straw that was being tossed wildly on a wave of sea and clouds. A figure with a snow-white beard leaned back in the boat, one leg dangling precipitously off the edge, one hand raised to the sky. The man gestured wildly at the robed man on the shore. Kitty craned her neck to take in the painting two stories above her, tilting her head to one side, then the other, eyebrows raised, her mouth unknowingly curved into an "o." She jumped, momentarily disoriented, as the pipes of the church organ sprang to life.

"This way," Oila said, in a voice barely above a whisper. Kitty looked up at her governess, who motioned for Kitty to enter a pew nearby. They were in St. Peter's Church in Vienna, and it was the most beautiful building Kitty had ever seen.

"The Mass is in Latin," Oila had explained. "Just watch what I do, and you will be fine. When I sit, sit. When I kneel, kneel. I know it will be difficult but try not to speak during the Mass. When it is time for Communion, remain kneeling in the pew until I return." Oila had struggled with that part. It was rare for a child Kitty's age not to partake of the Body of Christ. She would rather lie and say that Kitty had not recently confessed her sins than have her receive Communion and commit sacrilege.

Wherever Kitty turned her gaze, she saw glittering gold. Every molding and cornice, every railing and font, appeared to have been dipped in a lustrous color. "I've never been inside the Teplice Synagogue, but I am sure Father and Bettina would have told me if it looked anything like this. It's so beautiful, Oila," Kitty said in her best whisper, holding onto the cuff of Oila's coat sleeve. Kitty pinched herself and tried to remember if there was a time she had felt happier than she did at that moment. The only thing that came to mind was swimming in Jesenice with Aya on a summer day.

Kitty and Oila took their seats at the same moment the organist, perched several stories high in the gilded loft, launched triumphantly into another hymn. Male voices joined in a chorus from one of the second-floor balconies, creating a harmony that echoed upward toward the vaulted ceiling. "This must be what it is like to be in heaven," Kitty whispered.

People filed into the church, settling in the pews, opening the kneelers and dropping them with a thud, and rustling the pages of the missalettes. Oila bowed in the direction of the altar before entering the pew. She pulled the padded kneeler down. "Kneel with me, Kitty." Oila made an exaggerated sign of the cross for Kitty to follow and then clasped her hands together, bowing her head in silent prayer.

Kitty likened the Mass to a ballet. Everyone knew their part. They danced in toward the altar for their solo: the priest, the lectors, the altar servers. They seemed to plié into position, arms outstretched in an intricate, white-robed dance. When it was time for communion, Oila played her role, one in a humble procession of many that led to the priest. A white wafer was transferred from a golden chalice to Oila's lips. Moments later Oila rejoined her in the pew. "What does it taste like?" Kitty asked, intrigued. Oila let the wafer dissolve in her mouth in silence.

The city of Teplice had a few large buildings to its name. The synagogue took up nearly a whole city block. Vienna was different. Kitty mistook churches and government buildings for palaces and the scale of the city defied her imagination. It took Uncle Erich ten minutes by car to get from one side of her hometown to the other. Lost in the sea of stories-high, ornate buildings of Vienna, Kitty thought she might never see the edges of the brilliant city. "You could fit one hundred Teplices inside Vienna," thought Kitty. And there were so many people everywhere. Kitty had never seen so many people – walking, eating, riding the tram, in the church.

When the Mass was over, Kitty and Oila walked to the tram. They held hands as the Vienna Tram 71 glided along, past the five gothic spires of City Hall at the Rauthausplatz. The gray stone building, long gothic arched doorways mirrored by windows above, seemed to go on forever. "It looks like a palace!" Kitty pressed her face against the window and looked out at the bustling streets of the city. Pedestrians, cars, and motorbikes sped in all directions under overcast skies. "There is nothing like Vienna on a sunny day, Kitty. I wish we had better weather," said Oila.

"I love Vienna under any skies, Oila," Kitty replied, her eyes wide, cheeks softly flushed.

The tram wound its way around the city, passing block after block of grand buildings with wrought iron balconies and pillared verandas. Kitty looked on in wonder. "Let's get out here," said Oila. She pulled the overhead wire that ran the length of the tram, signaling the conductor that they wanted to get off. "This is *Stephansplatz*. In a few more months there will be a market here with umbrellas and all kinds of trinkets to buy," explained Oila.

Kitty pointed to one end of the square where a gray stone church with a colorful mosaic roof and gothic spire towered over them. "Ahh, yes. That is St. Stephen's Cathedral, Kitty. Another one of my favorites," Oila said wistfully. She looked at Kitty, who continued to crane her neck to look up at the tops of all the buildings around them. "Your head is going to get stuck that way if you are not careful," warned Oila.

Oila navigated the streets of the city with ease. "I have a special lunch planned for us. This way, Kitty. Just a few more blocks," Oila instructed.

Kitty followed a few steps behind Oila, slowing down and staring in wonder at the sights of the magical city. "The women are so beautiful and well-dressed, Oila. And all the men are fat," observed Kitty.

"Kitty," Oila scolded Kitty, but what she said was the truth. "You are honest to a fault. I can only hope it does not get you into real trouble one day." Viennese men were portly, Oila acknowledged. They were a pleasant lot, grown comfortable in a certain lifestyle for which they were totally unapologetic.

Oila ducked in the doorway of a restaurant, parting the long black velvet curtains that kept out the cold. She pulled the curtain aside for Kitty to enter and watched for her reaction. Kitty's eyes shone. Chandeliers with tiny red lamp shades over each light hung from the ceiling of Café Diglas. Coffee cups dangled whimsically in between the crystals of the chandeliers. Stools lined a long, dark wooden bar that had been buffed until it shone. Red leather chairs surrounded square tables with crisp, white tablecloths.

"Oh, Oila," Kitty squealed with delight. They took off their coats, Kitty handing hers reluctantly to the woman at the coat check. "Will I get my coat back, Oila? Bettina will be so angry if I don't." Oila patted Kitty's back reassuringly.

A man at a wooden stand in the front of the restaurant spoke to Oila. "Would you and your daughter like a banquette?" Kitty drew in a breath and looked up at Oila, covering her mouth with her hand, and holding back a laugh.

"Yes, please," Oila responded, without correcting him.

"Right this way." A waiter had appeared, holding two long menus in his arm, directing them to follow. He wore a black vest over a starched white shirt and a long white apron.

"He looks like he is wearing a dress," Kitty whispered, following behind.

The waiter seated Kitty at a tufted red velvet banquette. He pulled out a chair for Oila across the small table from Kitty. They sat across from each other giggling at the waiter's mistaking them for mother and daughter. Kitty had to speak loudly to make herself heard among the din of conversation and clinking of silverware and china. The waiter arrived with a gold rimmed snifter of brown liquid and placed it in front of Oila. She lifted the glass to her lips and took a sip. From that moment forward, Kitty thought Oila's voice was more gay than usual.

They placed their orders, and Kitty alternated between bouncing on the seat of the banquette and looking up at the chandeliers. The waiter placed two plates in front of them, and Kitty's eyes grew wide. She looked from one plate to the other, shaking her head and licking her lips. "Even the food in Vienna is beautiful, Oila," said Kitty, her fork hovering over her dish, hesitant to spoil the chef's splendid composition.

"Eat, *mein kleine*," Oila gently replied. Oila took a forkful of cod fillet and put it in her mouth, chewing slowly and savoring it. "I have missed the cooking of my country, Kitty," said Oila. "I am so glad you are here to share it with me."

Kitty spoke between spoonfuls. "Do you think Cook can make beef goulash with sausages when we get back home, Oila?" Kitty said, raising another spoonful to her lips. "This is the most delicious thing I have ever eaten."

Oila whispered something to the waiter when he returned to the table to pick up their empty plates. He smiled and nodded and quickly returned with a beautifully arranged plate of apricot and plum dumplings. Kitty rolled her eyes each time she took a bite out of one, leaving Oila in stitches. "You are quite an actor, my dear. Now, I hope you have saved a bit of room. I must insist that you try the sachertorte. You cannot leave without tasting it. It is Vienna in a dessert," Oila said proudly. Kitty groaned. Her stomach felt like it might burst. Oila flagged the waiter down. "One slice of sachertorte, bitte. And a double serving of schlagsahne."

The waiter returned and placed the slice of cake with a double helping of whipped cream on the table in front of them. "You first, Kitty," offered Oila.

"It's too pretty to eat," said Kitty. Shook her head, her eyes sparkling. The cake was encased in a smooth chocolate ganache. The signature "S" for Sacher was piped in chocolate and apricot filling peeked out from the layers of chocolate cake. Oila went first, slicing her fork through the velvety icing, dipping the cake back onto the plate, her fork coming up with a generous dollop of whipped cream. She took a bite and closed her eyes. When she opened them, Kitty was following suit. Kitty closed her eyes, imitating Oila. When she opened them, she announced, "Delicious." They laughed and continued to take alternating forkfuls of cake.

"There is one more place I would like to take you, Kitty," Oila paused to allow the suspense to build. "My milliner. I want him to make a hat for you. I have told him and his wife all about you." They stood up from the table, gathered their coats on and walked out onto the street. As they strolled, the bells in the north Roman tower of St. Stephan's cathedral began to toll. They put Kitty in a serious mood.

"Oila?" Kitty asked quietly.

"Yes, my dear?" asked Oila.

"Why did you never marry again? You are so kind and so beautiful," Kitty said. Oila laughed. She stopped in the middle of the sidewalk, taking Kitty's hands in hers, her dark eyes meeting Kitty's gaze.

"Because I have you, *mein kleine*," Oila replied.

They walked a few city blocks, the streets and sidewalks littered with a flurry of handbills. Kitty began to skip, kicking the pieces of paper in front of her feet like fallen leaves on an autumn day. "I have never seen so much paper in the street before," said Kitty. Oila picked up one of the flyers from the ground and looked at it. She quickly crumpled the paper and threw it back on the ground where she had found it.

"What was it, Oila? What did it say?" Kitty asked. Oila did not reply but put her arm around Kitty's shoulders and walked her quickly past a fence where more of the same flyers appeared. Kitty caught a glimpse of one of the handbills, picturing a caricature of a man with an oversized nose. "*Der Stuermer*? What does that mean, Oila?"

Kitty stopped Oila's forward motion and stood in front of the fence, inspecting the image on the handbill. It was the front page of an anti-Jewish newspaper. Kitty had just enough time to read the paper's headline before Oila gently pushed her away. Kitty repeated the sentence aloud as she walked, searching for its meaning. "*Die Juden sind unser Unglück!* The Jews are bad luck? Why are Jews bad luck, Oila?" Kitty asked.

Oila continued to herd Kitty down the street. She walked faster looking for the sign for the milliner's shop, trying to sort her thoughts. On the way, they passed one empty shop after another. "I don't understand," said Oila, shaking her head. "This is one of the city's busiest streets and all these shops have closed."

"Wait a moment, Kitty," said Oila. She put her hand above her brow and peered into the window of one of the closed storefronts. The sign outside read "Lichtenstein Juwelier." "I know this jeweler. I had my watch repaired here last summer. There's nothing inside. Not one thing. It's like it never existed," said Oila. There was a tension in her voice that had not been there minutes earlier. Dusk was fast approaching. On the next block the fading light revealed more abandoned shops, a shuttered pharmacy, and an empty café. Each window of the café bore a crudely painted Star of David.

"Why would someone paint a Star of David on the windows of this cafe, Oila? Someone is going to be in trouble, aren't they?" Kitty assumed the perpetrators would be discovered and punished for their crimes. They passed the neighborhood synagogue next and found it abandoned.

Oila grew anxious, biting her lip, her eyes darting. She pulled Kitty forward down the darkening street. She scoured the storefronts, looking for something, anything familiar. "The milliner is just around the corner here," Oila's voice sounded flustered. "I wrote to the owners, Mr., and Mrs. Redelsheimer. I told them I was bringing you here for a new hat because you love mine so much. It was to be a surprise," Oila said, dragging Kitty by the hand, forcing her to keep up. Her pace quickened, her voice agitated.

"Oila, wait. You're hurting me. Please slow down," Kitty begged of her. Kitty twisted her hand to free it from Oila's, rubbing it with her other hand. Kitty was growing tired, and Oila was acting oddly. "Why are you walking so fast?" asked Kitty.

The street was deserted now, save for a few men who lingered in the doorways of the abandoned shops. "Who are those men, Oila?" Kitty asked, feeling their eyes on her as they passed.

The sun dipped down behind the buildings, plunging the street into darkness. Oila pressed forward, then turned around and led Kitty back down the same way they had come. "Are we lost? Oh, Oila," Kitty cried. She clutched Oila's arm as tightly as she could. "I'm frightened, Oila!"

Oila had been down this street more times than she could remember. She looked to the left and then to the right. "I am right here, Kitty. Just a minute. Now I'm all turned around. Let me get my bearings." Kitty heard a tightness in her governess's voice. At the precise moment

Oila stopped walking, the electric streetlights flickered to life. Light flooded over her like a spotlight on an actor on a stage. She stepped off the sidewalk and into the cobblestone street. She stood back, her shadow falling across the windows of the shop in front of her. Her face fell. There, painted in each large display window, illuminated by the streetlight was the word "*Jude.*"

Kitty breathed a sigh of relief, and walked toward Oila to get a look at the shop. "Is this it, Oila! Are we here? Kitty asked. "It looks closed. Where have they gone? Am I not to get a hat?"

Oila did not answer. "What is it, Oila? What's the matter?" Kitty followed Oila out into the street. She looked up at the sign above the windows and sounded it out. "*Red-el-sheim-er – Redelsheimer!*" She lowered her gaze, and read the words painted on the storefront windows. "Why would someone do such a thing?" Kitty asked Oila.

"Kitty, you know how there are Germans in Teplice that are unkind to Jews?" asked Oila, her face lined with sadness.

"You mean like the boys who throw stones at us on the way to school?" Kitty asked.

"Yes, Kitty. Like them," said Oila. Her voice had lost its spirit. "There are some people like that in Vienna."

"Why is Oila telling me this?" Kitty wondered. Life was becoming complicated, especially if you were ten years old. Kitty's mind replayed all the events of the trip: Oila's instructions that she should say that she was a Catholic, the Star of David and the word *Jude* painted on the windows of the Jewish shopkeepers. The synagogue abandoned. The despicable faces on the handbills with the exaggerated noses and the cruel words.

"That is why you did not want anyone to know I was Jewish? Because then they would hate me, too? Oh, Oila!" Kitty began to sob. "They hate all of us, don't they? Father? Bettina? Hanuš? Otto? Why, Oila? Why?"

The bell at the church in Stephanplatz began tolling for evening prayers.

"My dear Kitty," Oila replied. "I don't know." She was silent for a moment. "It is time to go home."

CHAPTER FIVE

Karel walked a few steps in front of Vlada on their way to the coffeehouse at the Hotel Veselka, blocking the strong blasts of icy March wind that whipped up from time to time. They passed an acquaintance of Karel, both men tipping their hat to each other in a good-natured greeting.

Vlada watched the interaction and grabbed the tweed fedora from his head hoping to tip it at the passing gentleman in a manner similar to his father's. But he was new to the etiquette of adulthood and too slow, and the man had already passed them by. Vlada's hat was new, a gift from his parents for his bar mitzvah, completed only the day before, and it felt like part of a costume for a role he was playing. He placed the hat back on his head, vowing to do better the next time, when a healthy gust of wind took the hat and lifted it from his head.

The hat fell onto the rough cobblestone street, and, carried along by another gust of wind, it tumbled down the street end over end behind him. Vlada turned and chased after it, finally catching up to it and stopping it with his foot. He looked around, picked the hat up, brushed it off against his new coat and ran to catch up to his father.

Karel continued walking on ahead, hiding a smile and pretending to be unaware of the comic scene that had just unfolded.

One day earlier at the flat, prior to leaving for Vlada's bar mitzvah at the synagogue, Karel had looked at Vlada, taking the measure of his son.

"Come here," his father motioned. There on the bed in his parents' bedroom sat a cardboard hat box. Karel removed the lid, revealing the grey tweed fedora, which he lifted out of a box and handed to his son with a flourish. "For my young man," his father's voice was low and gravelly.

Vlada put the hat on excitedly and turned to look at himself in the mirror that hung above his mother's vanity. His father stood behind him and put his hands on Vlada's shoulders. Vlada smiled at his reflection in the mirror. "It's a perfect fit, Tati. How did you know?" He looked at his father in the mirror then back at himself. "Do I look different, Tati? Older?" Vlada was thirteen, but today he felt taller and wiser, and more in command of his destiny.

Of Pardubice's twenty thousand inhabitants, barely five percent were Jewish. Vlada's family was one of that five percent and they belonged to the Pardubice Synagogue, an imposing stone building not far from the distillery with long, scalloped arches and windows, and Stars of David on the exterior. The family's religious observance was relaxed at best; his parents could be found in attendance at the synagogue on High Holy Days twice a year. As Karel liked to say, they were Czech first, Jewish second. Jewish customs were not central to the family's traditions and because of this, it was with great irritation that Vladimir participated in one hour of Jewish religion class after school on Saturdays.

Throughout the previous fall and winter, Vlada sat on a bench in the synagogue as the elder rabbi's voice droned on in his head. His mind wandered throughout each lesson, his attention focused on the things he would rather be doing like helping his father in the distillery, going to the bookstore, or riding his bike.

Vlada's daydreaming had not gone undetected. "Vlada, pay attention!" said the rabbi. "My dear boy. You must focus on this important task. The bar mitzvah ceremony is only a few months away." The task was to read a passage from the Torah, the Hebrew Bible. Vlada struggled to learn the prayers, while the other boys in the class seemed to master them with ease.

Christmas was fast approaching and with it winter vacation and Vlada had made little if any progress on his task. The rabbi realized time was running out for his daydreaming pupil to get up to speed and he devised a plan for Vlada's success, revealing it during the last class before the winter holiday.

"Memorize these, dear boy." The rabbi pressed a few sheets of paper into Vlada's hand. The rabbi had written out the prayers that Vlada would need to recite during the ceremony phonetically. All Vlada needed to do was memorize the words and he could successfully fake his way through the reading.

Karel insisted that Vlada bring the rabbi's notes with him to the mountains for winter vacation. Vlada's heart sunk. His success at the bar mitzvah meant the ruin of his winter vacation. Vlada had just been given the worst Christmas present ever.

Hermina sat with Vlada at the kitchen table of the tiny winter cottage on the mountaintop, encouraging him in his task of memorization, forgoing sunny days on the pristine ski slopes to help ensure Vlada's success. "You were able to recite the entire *Ballad of Charles IV* by Neruda for Babicka Emilie, Vlada. This should be easy for you." Hermina rewarded her son's progress with a slice of babkova or a cup of hot cocoa. Still Vlada struggled and stammered through the phrases for the entirety of the trip.

In March, the day of reckoning arrived. Sun streamed through the long windows of the synagogue, filling the huge interior with light, bouncing off the highly polished wooden cabinet that held the Torah. Vlada sat on a bench, his parents next to him, as his stomach roiled. Everyone stood as the Torah was placed on a podium in front of a raised platform. The rabbi motioned to Vlada to approach. He slowly made his way to the front of the synagogue, his legs feeling like lead. He thought he must look like one of Karel Capek's robots in a science fiction novel, woodenly marching toward his fate.

The prayers Vlada thought he had memorized became jumbled in his mind. "Is it *Baruch ata Adonai* or *Eleheinu, Melech haolam* that comes first?" Vlada stood behind the podium and looked out at his parents, his aunts, and uncles also in attendance, seated in the front rows of the synagogue. He was going to humiliate himself in front of everyone.

Vlada looked down at the Torah, figures scrolling across the page in a foreign text he would never comprehend. He closed his eyes, his hand damp with sweat and shaking as he picked up the *yad*. He moved the *yad* slowly from right to left across the page over the appointed text, reciting from memory. When he opened his eyes again, he saw the rabbi proudly smiling at him.

Karel stood up and recited a blessing in response, his voice carrying out over the large space. *"Baruch sheptarani mei-onsho shelazeh."* Vlada met his father's gaze. He had never heard his father speak Hebrew before and his pronunciation was perfect. Vlada found his mother in the front row, she wore her best suit, and her face was flushed with pride. I did it, he thought. He grinned broadly from his place behind the podium, his chin high, shoulders back, reveling in his accomplishment.

A small group of relatives had gathered outside the synagogue to congratulate Vlada. Uncle Jindrich shook his hand and pressed a fountain pen from his factory into Vlada's outstretched hand. Aunt Berta kissed him on both cheeks, and Uncle Max patted him on the back. When they returned to the flat, Karel took photographs of Vlada in his new hat and long pants out on the balcony, Vlada squinting in the bright sunshine. In some of the photos, he was allowed to hold Čigy by the leash. Vlada was not used to being the center of attention. He quite enjoyed the fuss.

As father and son approached the corner of Peace Avenue and Masaryk Square, the magnificent Hotel Veselka rose in front of them, occupying the entire corner of a prominent city block. The hotel had a storied history, and Vlada never tired of hearing his father tell of it. Karel's passion for the building had more to do with the hotel's famous visitors than its outward grandeur.

"Do you think T.G. liked the gingerbread, Vlada?" His father was referring to T.G. Masaryk, the first President of Czechoslovakia. Pardubice had a centuries-old tradition of baking the best gingerbread and the former president, his father's one true hero, was known to have been gifted the treat on at least one visit to the city.

"I hope he ate less of it than I did of the *koblihy* that one day, Tati." Father and son burst into laughter remembering the day Vlada had eaten himself sick with jam-filled carnival donuts.

In its heyday, the Hotel Veselka's grand ballroom had hosted concerts by Czechoslovakia's greatest composers, Bedrich Smetana and Antonin Dvorak. Vlada loved it when his parents played Smetana at home on the gramophone, the imagery of the composer's symphonic poem *Vltava* evoking the ebb and flow of the river near Prague. The hotel was also rumored to be the birthplace of the first Czech aviator, Jan Kaspar. It was *the* gathering place after the city's cultural and sporting events.

The family maid, Klara, often brought home gossip gleaned from her fellow domestic staff at the hotel. She informed Hermina of the epicurean delights fed to the throngs that gathered there after the Golden Helmet motorcycle races, meals created by the grand hotel's kitchen, served up by its first-rate staff.

"Madame," Klara told Hermina. "They tell me the buffet tables groaned under the weight of huge platters of goose liver risotto, caviar with lemon and Hungarian salami." Klara's words made Vlada's mouth water, even if only half of what she said were true.

Karel pushed open the door to the coffeehouse on the ground floor, allowing Vlada to enter first. Karel removed his hat and Vlada followed his father's example. On, off. On, off. Vlada thought the etiquette of wearing a fedora was going to take some getting used to. Maybe next time I will leave the hat at home, he thought.

Vlada had become accustomed to his father's coffeehouse habits. Karel typically socialized first, then settled in to read the newspaper in one of the comfortable leather chairs. In recent days, there was more talk and less reading. Conversations had grown heated when the discussion turned to Germany.

Karel removed his coat and Vlada could sense his father was lost in thought. "Can you believe, Vlada," his father began, "it was only last year that Lata Brandisová won the Velká Pardubická?" Lata was a female jockey who had ridden her mare, Norma, to victory over Germany the previous summer, defeating six SS officers who were entered in the decades' old race that had brough the small city acclaim.

Tensions had been running high between the two nations, and Vlada could remember hearing the roar of the crowd at the racetrack that day all the way from the distillery. The celebration over Lata's win spilled out onto the racecourse and then over to the hotel, where it continued for hours. Lata was a national hero whom his father feared no one would remember, her accomplishment a fading footnote, drowned out by the noise and braggadocio of the Nazi party.

"What a difference a year makes, eh, Vlada?" Vlada heard the melancholy in his father's question.

The memory of Lata's faded accomplishment put his father in a dark mood, which carried over to his conversation with some acquaintances whom he found sitting at the café's long, marble bar. "The Anschluss, this annexation of a sovereign nation, is just the beginning." Karel's voice rose slightly. "We cannot ignore the fact that we may be next." The other men glanced around warily to see if anyone outside their circle had overheard Karels' remarks.

"How has it come to pass that we can no longer speak openly about matters of such importance to the Czech nation?" Karel continued. Vlada watched as the men his father had been speaking to stood up and dispersed to other corners of the room.

"They must not have family in Austria, Tati," said Vlada, attempting a show of support. Vlada knew firsthand about the Anschluss. His mother's sister, Aunt Helena, lived in Austria. Grandfather Adolf had gone to live with Helena, on the outward assumption of assisting his daughter and son-in-law in their leather goods store. Knowing his father-in-law as Karel did, he doubted Adolf was anything more than an amusement for his sister-in-law's customers.

Grandfather Adolf's living arrangement was working fine until Hitler moved to annex Austria in the name of the Reich just weeks before. At the same moment Hermina watched with pride as her son made bar mitzvah, she waited for news about her father, a Jew who was no longer welcome in Hitler's Austria. Word arrived that Grandfather returned home to Czechoslovakia without incident and was safely ensconced at the home of his daughter, Ida, in Spálené Poříčí. The family was blissfully unaware that their interpretation of safety from that point forward was at its best intangible, at worst, elusive.

The coffeehouse was now bustling. Vlada sat cross legged, in his favorite leather chair, slightly bored, flipping distractedly through an issue of *Life Magazine*. He wished today was philatelic club, the one day each month when he and his father gathered with other local stamp collectors. Karel's stamp collection, begun before Vlada's birth, was colorful and diverse, with stamps of castles, city scenes of Prague, Karel's hero President Masaryk, and other notable figures. The collection's crowning glory was a commemorative stamp Karel had purchased honoring the tenth anniversary of the founding of Czechoslovakia.

After the Great War, the Czech government set up struggling Legionnaires who had helped build the fledgling nation in *traficka*, stores that sold tobacco and stamps, with the hope that they would succeed and prosper post-war. Vlada's father was inclined to give one of his fellow Legionnaires his financial support by purchasing stamps solely from him. In exchange, his former compatriot, a man named Marek, alerted the two collectors to the latest issues.

"Another beauty, Marek," said Karel, looking at a single stamp Marek had set out for him on a velvet background. "Thank you for bringing it to our attention. What do you say, Vlada? Shall we add it to the collection?" Vlada took the magnifying glass from his father and looked closely at the image. It was a beauty, indeed, an image of Vysehrad, a fort in Prague set high on a hill overlooking the Vltava River. Vlada drew in a breath. The detail in the small stamp using ink in shades of blue was stunning, even to Vlada's inexperienced eye. Vlada nodded his head enthusiastically. Karel gave his compatriot a wink and reached in his pocket for his wallet.

"Your collection is becoming quite valuable, Karel," Marek noted. Something in Marek's tone did not sit well with Vlada, the man's words ringing hollow. If Marek knew his father at all, he should know the monetary value of the collection mattered little to him. Vlada looked at Marek with suspicion, then felt guilty for thinking badly of his father's 'friend.'

The waiter rolled the patisserie cart up to where Vlada was seated, breaking him from his reverie. "Coffee? Pastry?" Vlada recognized the tall, thin man from their many visits. The shelves of the cart were filled with slices of layered cakes topped with chocolate ganache, cream puffs filled with whipped cream in frilled paper cups, and Vlada's favorite – profiteroles filled with coffee cream. Karel arrived to find his son perusing the treats on the cart.

"We have something waiting for us at home, but thank you, Josef," his father said to the man. "Let's head home, Vlada."

"*Babovka*." Vlada immediately recognized the sweet smell of his favorite cake, the scent of it wafted down the stairs of the flat to greet them after their walk home in the brisk March air. Karel had been right to decline the coffeehouse treats. Weekday breakfasts before school were simple affairs, usually a slice of bread with butter. On leisurely Sunday mornings one could often expect something special from his mother's kitchen. Today, Hermina had made Vlada's favorite cake in its signature round tin.

Vlada had watched his mother make babovka many times, sometimes even helping to mix the sweet batter. When time permitted, Hermina separated the cake batter into two equal portions, adding cocoa powder to one. She dotted the plain batter with the cocoa-infused batter, swirling them together with the tip of a knife. After the cake was baked and completely cooled, his mother tipped it out of the pan onto one of her best plates and dusted the top with powdered sugar. Waiting for the cake to cool was one of the hardest things Vlada had to endure in his young life.

The marbled chocolate version of the cake sat in the middle of the cloth-covered table, freshly baked, cooled and dusted with sugar. Hermina stood beside the table, her apron infused with the scent of sugar and butter, streaks of chocolate batter on it where she had wiped her hands.

Hermina smiled at Vlada's reaction to the treat. "Good afternoon, gentlemen." She hugged him to her, breathing in deeply. "Oh, you smell of fresh air. And how are my two men doing today?" Vlada nearly blushed at the thought of his mother calling him a man. It had been barely twenty-four hours since his bar mitzvah. "You are growing up too fast, Vlada." His mother squeezed him again and pulled out a chair at the table for him. She cut a thick slice of cake, put it on a plate and placed it in front of him.

When Hermina had finished eating her cake, she stood and went to the pánsky room. Vlada heard the tinkling of the piano, his cue to cut another slice of cake. He ate the second slice quickly, hiding the evidence. If his mother noticed, she never said a word.

The travails of the school year ended and Vlada looked to summer vacation as a respite from the growing tensions there. But the unease remained, it just changed form. A family tradition of gathering around the radio each evening for music and news become an unpleasant foray into fear and uncertainty. Vlada watched as his father tuned the radio to a broadcast out of Prague. Each night things seem to go from bad to worse.

The reports of the affairs of Germany and its Führer, Adolf Hitler, were like dark clouds rolling in before a storm. The air in the living room changed every time his voice came over the radio. Vlada watched as his mother stiffened at the harsh staccato of the Führer's delivery. One night it was just too much.

"Shut it off, Karel! Please," Hermina pleaded. Vlada's cheeks reddened, embarrassed by his mother's emotional outburst. She stood and went into the pánsky room. She closed the French doors behind her and played the piano for over an hour.

"What is Lebensraum, Tati?" Vlada had heard the word uttered by the Führer over the radio and seen it in newspaper headlines.

"It is colonialism, Vlada. Pure and simple," Karel replied. "They want to conquer and colonize us." His father had explained in simple terms Hitler's threats to forcefully take over the Sudetenland, the region of Czechoslovakia occupied primarily by ethnic Germans. In anticipation of German military aggression, the Czech government spent half its budget on border fortifications in Vlada's beloved Krkonoše mountains.

Karel patiently described how France had created the Maginot Line fortifications to deter an invasion by German forces. The Czechs consulted with the French military, making changes in their own defensive design. The hope was that the resulting structures would be impervious to an attack by German forces. Construction of the fortifications was rapid, even though the Czechs considered relations with France and Britain to be supportive and the risk of German invasion low. Ultimately, they were wrong on both counts.

In the fall, Karel received a telegram immediately ordering him to report for military training. It seemed the Czech government felt Hitler's rhetoric could not be ignored, so at forty-five years of age, Karel was called for duty in the Czech army to serve and protect his country against possible Nazi aggression.

Hermina was stoic, but Vlada could not accept the news of his father's conscription. "Tati, why you? Don't they know you are needed at the distillery?" Vlada tried not to sound childish.

"The nation needs me more, Vlada," his father replied, a defeated look on his face. In the days leading up to his father's departure, Vlada alternated between feelings of pride and fear. He looked at the framed photo of his father in the uniform of the Czech Legionnaire. When Vlada was younger, he had shown the photo to every friend who came to the flat, never once thinking his father would again wear any sort of uniform.

The fear of being separated from his father for the first time since his birth made Vlada physically ill. He trembled in bed at night. Hitler's voice from the nightly radio broadcasts echoed in his ears. Night after night, Vlada's dreams were filled with images of his father holding a rifle, the sound of gunfire and tanks crushing their way across his beloved white-capped Krkonoše mountains.

When the day arrived for Karel to report for military training exercises on the border of Poland near Ostrava, Vlada was in disbelief. It was a nightmare from which he could not wake.

"Vlada, we must prepare to leave as well," his mother told him. This was unexpected.

"Where are we going, Mami? Why do we have to leave?" Vlada felt like a child, not the young man who had just months earlier made bar mitzvah in his new fedora. His world was turning upside down. In just a few short weeks school was set to begin. "Mami, please. Let's stay at home where we can wait for Tati to return," Vlada pleaded.

"Vlada, I explained this to you. Tati wants us to go and stay with Aunt Berta and Uncle Max until he returns," his mother said, her voice betraying her own fear. "We must do as he asks." Hermina left no room for discussion. Berta was Karel's older sister. Fifteen years separated the siblings, making Berta, at sixty, feel more like a grandmother to Vlada than an aunt.

"Berta and Uncle Max are so old," Vladimir groaned. His opinion did not matter. They were going to live in Městec Králové with his old aunt and uncle whether he liked it or not.

It was barely an hour's travel by train to Aunt Berta's. Like so many train rides before, Vlada watched as a deep calm descended over his father after the train pulled away from the station. Karel gazed out the window of the train, lost in some unspoken daydream, the rhythmic clack-clack of the train casting a spell over him. Now and again, he turned to look at Vlada, mouth poised to speak, then turned to the window again. They passed the trip in silence.

Uncle Max was waiting to pick them up at the train station in the small village. Max's face was solemn as he walked toward his father and shook his hand. Neither man spoke which made Vlada's stomach drop. They drove in silence to the house. Aunt Berta and Uncle Max's house was modern, newer than the building that housed their flat at the distillery. Uncle Max's haberdashery shop was on the first floor, the family's living quarters were on the second. The business had a prime location on the corner of a busy block. Vlada entered the house first, his aunt barely pausing to greet him as she rushed to hug her younger brother.

"Karel," her voice was muffled, trying her best not to cry.

Vlada thought the house smelled different than the flat, like stale laundry and old people, but he kept his thoughts to himself. Berta showed Vlada to his cousin Rudolf's room. He put his bag down and sank down cheerlessly on the edge of the bed. Karel came in and sat down next to him.

"Vlada, this is only temporary." Karel put his arm around his son's shoulders, causing Vlada to feel even greater concern.

"How long, Tati?" Vlada was doing his best to be brave but the whole series of events was upsetting his predictable world. His father's gaze did not meet his. He knew his father wanted to say something hopeful, but he would rather not lie.

"Soon, Vlada. Soon," said Karel.

Uncle Max looked in on them and nodded to his brother-in-law. "I'm sorry but we really must go soon, Karel," Uncle Max's voice was husky and low. It was as if Vlada was seeing his uncle for the first time. He had never seen anyone so well dressed. His suit was a rich grey wool with pinstripes, and he wore a crisp white shirt and a paisley tie with shades of red running through it. His shoes were shined to perfection. The distraction was fleeting. Karel stood and gave Vlada one last hug.

After his father's departure, Vlada spent the last weeks of summer in a fog. Hermina enrolled Vlada in the local school that fall, where he struggled to pay attention, going through the motions, and not caring whether he fit in with the other students. He told himself it did not matter; he would not be here long. After weeks of watching her son struggle, Hermina arranged a surprise.

"We are going to Prague, Vlada," she said excitedly. The train ride took two hours. Everywhere on the train men were dressed in uniform which made Vlada miss his father even more. When they arrived in Prague they walked for blocks until they arrived in front of a cinema featuring a grand marquis that read *Snow White and the Seven Dwarfs*. His mother smiled and hugged him to her.

"Thank you, Mami," said Vlada. Hermina's eyes glistened. They entered the theater and sat in the dark, both barely able to pay attention to the sweet animation on the movie screen, consumed by the same thought: where in the world was their beloved father and husband at that moment? When would they see him again?

Six weeks passed. Vlada arrived home one day from school to find his father standing in Aunt Berta's living room. Karel was pale, thin, quiet.

Vlada did not know whether to approach his father or not.

"Tati?" Vlada felt awkward.

"We must go," his father said in an unfamiliar voice. Hermina had not been expecting him either and struggled to hide her shock at her husband's changed appearance.

"Pack your bag, Vlada," his mother instructed him as she rushed around the house gathering their things. They rode the train ride back to Pardubice in silence. Vlada dared not ask his father anything. He watched as Karel turned a postcard over and over in his hands. It was from Max. On one side was a photograph of Max, Berta, and their son Rudolf. On the other side was a handwritten note to Karel sent to encourage him during his recent military mobilization. Vlada felt bad that he had not written to his father while he was away.

They walked in the flat and Vlada breathed in its familiar scent. Čigy had been left in the care of Pan Zak and the dog bounded up the stairs, almost knocking Hermina over. It was good to be home. Vlada went to sleep that night in his own bed, comforted by his father's presence.

Vlada's slumber was deep and free from nightmares. But the return to normalcy was short-lived.

"Sit down, Vlada." His mother's face was pale as she motioned for her son to sit down at the kitchen table. The radio's volume was turned all the way up, blaring the news coming out of Prague. His father came into the kitchen holding the morning newspaper, his face filled with dread.

Karel's sudden release from military service had been revealed. To appease Hitler and prevent war, leaders from Germany, France, Italy, and Great Britain had met and signed over the Czech territories of the Sudetenland to Hitler. They were to be "lawfully" annexed by Germany on September 29, 1938. No representatives of the Czechoslovak government attended the meeting, yet they were being forced to accept the terms of the agreement or face Hitler in military battle alone. The newspaper headline screamed a quote from Czech Prime Minister Jan Syrovy: *We Are Abandoned.*

"What does it mean, Tati?" Vlada had so many questions.

"We have lost the border region to Germany, Vlada," Karel answered without looking at Vlada. His father's shoulders sagged, and he let out a long, low sigh.

"What about the fortifications?" Vlada had hoped to see the Germans try to cross the border in the mountains and get trapped and captured in the defenses the Czechs had worked so hard to create.

"The defenses are now in the hands of the Germans, Vlada," Karel spoke the words like a man in shock. "We are now in the hands of the Germans." Hermina walked into the dining room and turned the radio off.

CHAPTER FIVE

Kitty refused to walk on the sidewalk with Oila, instead dragging her rain boots through the puddles that formed on the edge of the curb in the street. Her legs were red, and they stung where the driving rain and frigid wind had found bare skin, from just above her knee socks to the hem of her wool coat. But Kitty barely noticed. Holding a large black umbrella, Oila walked next to Kitty on the sidewalk, sidestepping the puddles on the walk home from their weekly trip to the post office for Kitty's father.

It was Hanuš's thirteenth birthday. In a few weeks he would make his bar mitzvah. "Everything is about Hanuš right now," said Kitty. "I really don't think he will learn the prayers in time for his bar mitzvah. What do you think, Oila? He is clever but I just don't see him 'buckling down,' as Father would say." Kitty prattled on, stomping her feet in the puddles at the end of each sentence for emphasis, causing the reflection of a thin, bare tree to scatter in a thousand ripples.

Since his father's death in 1931, Karel sent money to his mother in Jesenice. It was a source of contention with Bettina, so Karel asked Kitty and Oila for their help with the weekly post. "Your grandmother can barely survive on my father's pension," Karel explained. "Because Grandpapa was the rabbi in a small community, he was often paid in eggs and goose liver, not korunas. It was not a particularly clever way to build up a nest egg." Oila laughed at Karel's play on words, but the joke was lost on Kitty.

The weather changed in an instant. Bright sun peeked through clouds that just moments ago had battered them with rain. Oila looked up, shielding her eyes with her hand. "Thank goodness for small things." Oila closed the umbrella, sat down on a bench at the entrance to the park and patted the spot next to her. "Sit with me, Kitty." The street was empty of pedestrians and vehicles. Oila turned to Kitty and held her hands in hers, her face solemn.

"Is this about Vienna again?" Kitty asked. Kitty had endured a series of nightmares featuring the awful caricatures on the handbills after they returned from their trip. It troubled her young mind, and no matter how hard she tried, she could not make sense of it. "I am Czech, and I am Jewish, and you are Austrian and Catholic, and we love each other. Why do people in Austria and Germany hate the Jews?" Kitty asked innocently. Oila did not have an answer for her.

"This is not about Vienna." Oila paused. A dog barked somewhere nearby. "My mother is not well, Kitty. I must go back to Austria."

Kitty turned to look at Oila, her eyes narrowed. "But you will be back soon? Right, Oila? Once she is well again?"

"I don't know, Kitty. She is terribly ill."

"When will you leave?" Kitty asked, her voice tight.

"I am afraid it will be soon. No later than the end of the month." Oila looked down at her hands in her lap.

Kitty's brow furrowed in concentration, mentally counting off the days they had left together. "That is fourteen days from now. Why didn't you tell me earlier?" Kitty's demand hovered between anger over Oila's perceived betrayal, and heartbreak. Kitty's face fell, her lip quivering.

"Your mother thought it best, *mein kleine*," said Oila. Kitty sat motionless on the bench next to Oila, blood pounding in her ears, anger at Bettina, and anger at Oila's mother, threatening to overwhelm her.

Oila stood up. "I am sorry, Kitty," said Oila, doing her best not to allow her voice to falter. "We will make the best of the time we have together. We always do." Oila had hoped to sound cheerful, but her voice betrayed her feelings. The clouds had all but disappeared and the sun warmed their backs on the return walk to the house. The only sound was that of their footsteps on the pavement.

"What a stupid woman! To think Oila's mother getting sick." Kitty found Hanuš later that afternoon in the backyard, kicking a ball in the damp grass. "Doesn't her mother know we need Oila here?" Kitty said, her irritation on full display.

Hanuš picked up the ball, and paused for a moment, studying Kitty. He sighed. "Kitty, you need to know the truth. Oila's mother is not ill. It is the Nazis. They are threatening to take over Austria. Oila cannot stay here much longer."

Kitty absorbed the news Hanuš had just delivered and stomped her foot in the grass. "It's the Nazis? Always the Nazis! First Papa's heart attack and now Oila! I hate the Nazis! I hate them!" Kitty pouted, her hands on her hips, her eyes darting helplessly as she decided whether to continue her emotional indictment.

Hanuš set the ball down in the grass, walked to where Kitty stood and whispered in her ear. "Kitty," he said firmly, "you must *never* talk about the Nazis like that again." He stepped back and was silent. Kitty considered what Hanuš had just said. She had never heard her brother speak that way before. Her lower lip trembled. She ran across the yard and up the back steps and into the house.

Kitty found Bettina in the kitchen supervising the last details of the evening meal, hovering over Cook while she attempted to decorate Hanuš's birthday cake.

Kitty cleared her throat. "Mother, please," Kitty pleaded. "You must do something to keep Oila here. Please."

Bettina had moved to the stove, and proceeded to dip a large spoon into the thick stew that simmered there. "Kitty, there is nothing to be done," Bettina replied, blowing on the spoon's rich contents. "Oila is fortunate she has the freedom to leave." She slurped from the spoon, signaling the conversation was over.

Kitty stared at her mother, her mouth open, waiting for a different response. Bettina continued. "Kitty, you are almost ten years old. You can easily survive from now on without a governess." At that moment, Hanuš entered the kitchen from the backyard. He sensed the tense mood and began to back out, but Bettina dropped the spoon and moved toward him, fussing over him. "There is my young man. My birthday boy. Thirteen!"

Kitty ran out of the kitchen. She ran straight to the parlor and sat down on the floor near her father's chair, pulling her knees up to her chest and rocking back and forth. Pavla padded into the room and nuzzled her arm. Kitty continued to stare straight ahead and rock, fat tears spilling down her cheeks. Pavla lowered himself onto the rug beside Kitty and sighed.

An hour or so later, Oila opened the door to the parlor and found Kitty in the same state. Oila shook her head. She lifted her forlorn charge up by the elbow and guided her to the dining room for dinner. Kitty sat down in her chair and looked around the table. She heard the animated voices of her family talking about the events of the day, laughing, eating, and smiling. The information arrived as if through a thick, gauzy filter. Kitty remained silent throughout the meal, mute while the family sang "Happy Birthday" to Hanuš. The slice of birthday cake Oila set in front of her went untouched.

The days before Oila's departure drifted by in a similar haze. Then time ran out. No more days stood between the sad day when Kitty had learned the news of Oila's impending departure and the actual leaving. Kitty awoke as if from the oblivion of her hospital stay, confused and angry she had wasted the last precious hours with her beloved Oila.

Kitty walked slowly down the stairs from her bedroom and found her family and the entire house staff, surrounded by a heavy silence, gathered near the front door to bid Oila goodbye. Oila stood awkwardly waiting for someone to speak, her discomfort at being the center of attention apparent as she clutched her purse and the strand of pearls around her neck, alternating nervously between the two.

"This feels like a funeral. Please do cheer up, everyone." Oila attempted to lighten the mood.

Bettina kissed Oila on both cheeks. "Godspeed, Oila," Bettina's lip trembled, and her voice shook. "You must write to us often." Hanuš stepped forward and shook Oila's hand, then turned and ran up the stairs and into his room, slamming the bedroom door. Oila hugged Cook, who brushed away a tear that threatened to escape her eye.

Karel broke the silence. "Let's go, then. We don't want to miss the train." With Uncle Erich in Prague, Karel had agreed to allow Kitty to ride along in the company car to the train station. A light drizzle of rain fell, and the only sound in the car was the rhythmic back and forth of the windshield wipers. At the train station, Oila walked haltingly to the platform, like a dying man to the gallows. Karel stood in the rain without an umbrella, his thick hair flat and pasted to his head.

He shook Oila's hand. "Thank you, Fraulein. For everything."

"I am sorry it ends like this, Karel." Oila dabbed at her nose with a handkerchief, her voice breaking.

"Say your goodbyes now, Kitty." Karel nodded to his daughter and walked off the platform to wait in the car.

Oila took Kitty's hands in hers. "Kitty, promise me you will do everything your parents tell you to do. They know best. I want you to be safe. We must make sure we see each other again someday." Kitty threw her arms around Oila's waist and buried her face in her coat. She began to sob, her body heaving in great waves. Oila grasped Kitty's arms from around her waist and gently pushed her away.

The icy rain mixed with Kitty's tears, coursing in shiny rivulets down her cheeks. Her eyes pleaded with Oila. "Don't go. Don't go, Oila. Please! Don't...leave... me...behind...." Kitty gulped for air between each word.

Oila stood helpless on the platform, the train whistle signaling its imminent departure. "Karel!" Oila shouted and Kitty's father came running back up onto the platform. His face fell at the full force of Kitty's despair. He gently held Kitty by the shoulders and slowly steered her backwards, widening the gap between her and her governess. Oila turned quickly and boarded the train. She found a seat by the window and managed a small wave.

The train jerked forward. Kitty ran in the rain outside the window where Oila sat, keeping up with the train. "I'm sorry, Oila. Yes, I promise! I promise, Oila!" Kitty stopped running as the train picked up speed. She turned, soaking wet, arms by her sides and looked at her father, her face twisting in pain. "Papa!"

The scene on the platform had attracted the attention of other passengers. Karel walked to where his daughter stood, anchored in place by her grief. "Come, Kitty," Karel said gently. Karel shielded Kitty from the prying eyes of the bystanders, and they walked together down the length of the platform, the freezing rain continuing to fall, the train whistling a last warning as it crossed over the town line and headed south.

Hanuš was right. In March, the newspaper headlines and radio broadcasts screamed the news of Germany's annexation of Austria. Karel held the newspaper out in front of him, struggling to hide his disgust. He read the headline aloud. "Austria 'joined' to Germany.'" My God, have they no shame."

Kitty moved through each day in a murky haze of sadness. One evening at dinner toward the end of the school year, Karel announced there would be no trip to Jesenice that summer.

"The political situation is unstable to say the least. It would be best if we stayed in Teplice."

Kitty ran the implications through her mind. No Aja. No acting out plays with the other children. No swimming. Jesenice might have been the tonic for Kitty's deep grief over the loss of Oila. Instead, summer dragged, one day melting into the next in its sameness. Daily, little things reminded Kitty of her governess, something as simple as a button that needed mending, or Cook making apple strudel stirred the loss of Oila back up to the surface.

But the first week of school approached and even Bettina hoped the change of routine would reignite Kitty's vanished zest for life. It did not go as expected. Hanuš arrived home first. He was in the kitchen eating an apple when Kitty ran in crying, red welts covering her arms, a thin layer of skin scraped from the heels of her hands.

"What happened?" Hanuš's concern boiled over into anger as she relayed the day's events.

"The German boys threw stones at Agata and me on the way home from school." Kitty winced as she washed the scrapes on her forearms and hands with soap and warm water. "One of them pushed me and I scraped my hands on the sidewalk. They called us dirty Jews! Why are we suffering for something we don't even take part in?" Kitty looked at Hanuš, waiting for an answer.

Hanuš's face was grim, determined. "It won't happen again, Kitty. We let our guard down and I am sorry. I will walk you to school from now on. Let's keep this between us though, shall we? Mama and Papa have enough to worry about."

The next morning, Kitty and Agata waited at the corner a few blocks from the school. They were soon joined by Hanuš and three of his Czech school friends.

"You girls," Hanuš instructed. "Get in the middle." Hanuš motioned to his friends to surround the two girls. Two boys, dressed in khaki uniforms that had become easily recognizable, approached their small party, with stones in their hands. The apparent leader, a tall boy with a sullen face, assessed the odds, sneered, and with a silent tilt of his head, commanded his subordinate to abort their plan.

"Not so brave with your stones now, are you?" Hanuš called after them and then slyly winked at Kitty.

Josef Meyer, Karel's employer, was noticeably absent from his office on the first floor of the villa. It had been weeks since he had come to work and even Kitty had noticed that her "uncle" had failed to make an appearance. Karel made repeated calls to the company's headquarters and had received no reply.

"I am going to see for myself what is going on," Kitty heard her father tell Bettina. Karel took the company car and drove off for Litoměřice, a large town a half hour south, where the Brüder-Willner headquarters was located. Bettina was surprised to see her husband return home a few short hours later. She greeted him at the door of the flat.

Karel took off his hat and shook his head, his face exhibiting concern. "All the equipment used for production is gone. Sold. The factory is empty." Kitty sat at the top of the staircase, listening to her parents' conversation, struggling to comprehend it. The man who had once treated Kitty like his own daughter had disappeared, leaving Karel with no source of employment and no income.

"We are going to have to be very careful," Karel cautioned Bettina, as he paced back and forth, sorting his thoughts. "We will have to live off our savings now. I will put everything else in a safe deposit box: cash, jewelry, insurance papers. The Nazis won't be able to get it there." Bettina clutched at the pearls around her neck.

"What did I tell you, Karel?" Bettina had listened to the news and had conversations with her friends. "It was foolish to think that we would not be affected." Bettina took hold of Karel's arm. "Let's leave now Karel. Let's go to America."

Karel regarded his wife, shock registering on his face at her drastic proposal. "You know I can't leave my mother and sisters alone." Kitty's grandmother Ludmila lived in Jesenice still with her two daughters, Eliška and Bedřiška.

Family lore had it that when Bedřiška was a child, the neighborhood boys teased her and put a tin drum on her head. Once on, her mother could not get it off. Kitty remembered hearing her grandmother tell the dramatic tale. Ever since that unfortunate incident, whenever Bedřiška was excited, she shook uncontrollably and made a peculiar whirring sound. Kitty had witnessed Bedriska's episodes and remembered guiltily feeling a mix of fascination and pity for her aunt.

"Karel, at least let us try to get Hanuš on the Kindertransport." Bettina's voice was fraught with desperation. Kitty sat, not moving at her post at the top of the stairs, her ears pricked up. "If we move quickly Hanuš could be on a train out of Czechoslovakia and on his way to safety in England." Kitty's eyes widened. It was bad enough that she had lost Oila, but to lose her brother, too? He had become her faithful protector.

"Bettina," Karel's voice was firm, final. "My mother says she will kill herself if we send Hanuš away alone." Kitty's parents were at an impasse and thus, they did nothing.

Kitty woke to the incessant buzzing of the doorbell. She caught a glimpse of her father in his dressing gown, running past her bedroom, his hair rumpled from sleep. Her eyelids drifted closed again when suddenly she felt someone shaking her by the shoulders.

"Kitty, wake up. Kitty!"

Still in a haze of sleep, Kitty responded dreamily. "Why, Oila? What is happening?"

"Kitty! Open your eyes! It is Mama! We must get you and Hanuš out of Teplice." Kitty's eyes opened to see Bettina moving quickly about her bedroom. She sat up, confused by the incongruous sight. Kitty's small suitcase sat open on a chair. Kitty watched Bettina grab small piles of clothing from Kitty's bureau and place them in the suitcase. When the suitcase was nearly overflowing, Bettina slammed it shut. Kitty heard the locks of the suitcase click in place. Bettina pointed to the clothes she had laid out on Kitty's bed – a dress, socks, and shoes.

"Get dressed," Bettina instructed. Kitty did not recognize the tone in her mother's voice.

Kitty sat up in bed, surveying the scene. "Where are we going, Mama? It's the middle of the night! What is happening?"

"Kitty, there is no time for questions. I will explain everything downstairs. Now, hurry!" Kitty obeyed her mother's strange request, kicking the bedsheets off and standing up. She looked down at the dress her mother had laid out for her. It was green plaid, with a white Peter Pan collar that Kitty thought made her look like a baby. It was her least favorite of all her dresses. She obediently changed out of her nightclothes and looked around the room. On her bureau sat a picture of Kitty and Oila taken in Vienna while on winter holiday. Kitty grabbed it, opened the suitcase, and tucked it inside.

Kitty stepped into the hallway in time to see Hanuš coming out of his room. "What's happening, Hanuš?" Her brother shrugged his shoulders. They walked sleepily down the stairs, suitcases in hand.

The entire household stood gathered in the dining room, which was dark save for a couple of tall, thin candles in the center of the table. The candles cast an eerie, flickering glow on the faces gathered there. "Why aren't the lights on?" Kitty asked. It was the middle of the night, and everyone wore their street clothes. In the wavering light, Kitty made out Uncle Erich seated at the table. "Uncle Erich. What are you doing here?" He smiled weakly at his niece.

Karel entered the dining room, and, to make matters even more irregular, the town Komisar, Marek Cipra, a Czech and an old friend of Karel's, followed behind. Kitty stepped nervously behind Hanuš. "Everyone please stay calm," Karel said, his voice was even, controlled, but his face was pale and his forehead bore a thin sheen of sweat despite the cool evening. "Marek. Please tell us what is happening."

The Komisar was a big man, tall with dark circles under his eyes. His uniform looked as if he had thrown it on in a hurry, and his boots were not properly tied. "I am here on unofficial business, Karel." He nodded at Bettina. "Frau Löwi."

"I don't suppose any of you heard the speech on the radio a few nights ago?" the Komisar inquired. "Hitler is accusing the Czech people of crimes against the German minority in our region. It doesn't matter that it is not true. What matters is that people believe it." The tension between Czech Jews and Sudeten Germans had been building, and the speech had accomplished its goal of arousing further division.

Kitty had heard Hitler's voice booming from the radio in the parlor where her father sat smoking his pipe, and she had run to find Bettina, begging her to make her father shut off the radio for fear the Führer's rhetoric might prompt another heart attack.

"I will get straight to the point. I have reliable information that the Sudeten branch of Nazis are planning a pogrom tonight against the town's Jews." The Komisar paused for a moment to let his words sink in. "Karel, it is not safe for you and your family here." Bettina breathed in sharply. "At the very least, I would get the children out of town now. My wife, Elsa, and my son Michal are outside. Hanuš and Kitty can travel with my wife to her parents' house in Dobřichovice until we can determine the outcome. There is a room for them there." The room was silent for a moment before it erupted in a chaotic tangle of voices.

"Karel," Bettina sought out her husband across the room. Karel took his wife's hands in his and a look passed between them. Hanuš tried to get his father's attention, repeatedly calling out to no avail. Kitty felt dizzy trying to keep track of the conversations. As the voices continued to rise and fall around her, she went to the table and sat down in her chair. She closed her eyes to shut out the competing voices. "If only Oila were here, she would know what to do." When she opened her eyes, the adults continued to speak over one another, and the conversation had gained urgency.

The Komisar nodded to Karel to take control of the situation. "The children need to leave at once," Karel said decisively. "Erich, you will take Hanuš and Kitty, along with Elsa and Michal, in your car to Elsa's family in Dobřichovice. Go back to Jesenice from there and check on Mother and our sisters."

"Where are we going, Father?" asked Hanuš.

Karel looked at his son. He spoke slowly and deliberately. "You and Kitty will go with Uncle Erich to the home of the Komisar's in-laws. Your mother and I need you to take care of Kitty. We will come to you as soon as we can." Hanuš stood up. His chest puffed slightly at the thought of overseeing his younger sister.

"Yes, Papa," said Hanuš. "You can count on me. Come, Kitty." Hanuš picked up his suitcase. "Goodbye, Mama." Bettina's eyes were wide, her hand over her mouth. She hugged Hanuš tightly to her. When it seemed like she might never let go, Hanuš extracted himself.

Karel handed Hanuš an envelope filled with cash. "Use this for food and anything else you need." He pressed it into his son's hand. The two shared a brief hug.

Kitty felt like her body was on fire. She remained seated at the table. She watched Uncle Erich pick up her suitcase and begin to move toward the front door of the flat. "What about Pavla?" Kitty's voice cracked. Everyone turned to look at Kitty where she sat alone, dwarfed by the long table, shadows flickering over her face in the candlelight. Upon hearing her name, the dog came out of the kitchen, her nails clicking against the polished floor of the foyer.

"Pavla will stay here with us for now, Kitty. You will see her again soon," replied Bettina. Kitty detected a cheery inflection in her mother's voice that belied the truth of the matter.

"That's what you said about Oila," shouted Kitty. "You are a liar. I hate you. I hate you!" Kitty leapt up from the table and ran to where the dog stood, oblivious to the drama around her.

Hanuš stepped toward Kitty. "Kitty, you heard the Komisar. It is dangerous here," Hanuš spoke with a mixture of pride and urgency. "We must leave at once. We will worry about Pavla later."

Kitty kneeled in front of the dog, who searched her worried face. "Oh, Pavla," Kitty cried, burying her face in Pavla's coat. She hugged the dog so hard it yelped. Karel leaned down and gently pulled Kitty away.

"Kitty, come with me." Her father led her into the parlor, the room where they had shared so many cherished moments together. Karel held out his arms, and Kitty walked toward him, sniffling, and sat, balancing herself on his knee. Kitty was taller now than Karel realized. Her long legs dangled down to the floor, her body trembling.

"My dear Kitty," her father began. "These are dangerous times. Unfortunately, they call for extraordinary measures. We will all be together again. This is only temporary." The smell of her father's cologne mixed with the sweet smell of his pipe tobacco soothed her. "You are the strongest young girl I know. It's not fair. I know. But it won't be forever." They sat for a moment together without speaking. Kitty wiped her tear-streaked cheeks with the back of her hand and let her father lead her back into the dining room.

Bettina was waiting for her, and Kitty saw an expression on her mother's face that was painful to witness. Her mother winced, and her shoulders fell heavily as if all the air had left her body as she opened her arms to Kitty. Kitty let go of her father's hand and ran to Bettina. Kitty breathed in deeply of her mother's perfume, so rare was it that she got this close. Bettina stroked Kitty's hair and they seemed fused together until Karel touched Bettina's elbow and she slowly released her grip on her daughter.

Uncle Erich and Hanuš went to Kitty and stood on either side of her. They took hold of her hands, walking her slowly but purposefully down the steps to the waiting car. They all stopped short, flinching, at the sound of a deafening crash nearby, followed by the sound of shattering glass. The acrid smell of smoke reached them, plumes rising in the sky off in the distance somewhere across town. Sirens came from separate locations, piercing the night. Dogs barked all over the neighborhood. Kitty stopped and turned to look at the house. She did not care about any of it: the house, her dolls, the piano. Her family was what mattered most: Oila, her father, Bettina, Pavla.

A woman stepped out of the front seat of the car. She was blond and well-dressed, a younger version of Bettina. "You must be Kitty," the woman said. "I am Elsa, and that," she pointed to a small boy much younger than Kitty curled up in a blanket in the back seat, "is Michal." The boy opened his eyes sleepily and then closed them again.

Elsa took Kitty by the hand and helped her into the car. Hanuš put the bags in the trunk and crawled in the back seat next to Kitty. The Komisar stood next to the car, helping his wife into the front passenger seat. He closed the car door and leaned in the window. "Be safe, darling."

The Komisar jerked his head in the direction of another crash, followed by the sound of men shouting, the voices echoing down the street. "Go. Now!" The Komisar instructed Uncle Erich. He rapped on the hood of the car, signaling urgency. Uncle Erich waved goodbye to Karel where he stood on the curb, and stepped on the gas, the car disappearing down the darkened street and into the night.

Dobřichovice was a two-hour drive by car under normal conditions. Uncle Erich drove cautiously, taking the car the long way around, along the outskirts of Prague, hoping to avoid detection. Hanuš fell asleep. Elsa spoke soothingly to Kitty from the front seat, but her attempts at comforting her were unsuccessful. Kitty sobbed the entire trip, staring straight ahead, unseeing, and inconsolable.

Light was just coming up on the horizon when they reached Dobřichovice. Spent from crying, Kitty had just begun to doze off as the strange band of travelers reached their destination. An elderly couple came out of a stately brick house on a tree lined street. Elsa hugged her parents and helped Kitty and Hanuš out of the car.

The elderly woman studied the Löwi children. "Welcome," she said, greeting Hanuš and Kitty kindly. They moved quickly and silently. Elsa picked up Michal, who was still sleeping, from the back seat.

Kitty watched the young mother with her son. "I know," Elsa said, smiling. "He is too big to carry. I tried telling him that."

They walked up the steps and entered the house. Kitty and Hanuš stood awkwardly in the foyer, taking in the chandelier and the elegant furnishings. Elsa's mother spoke to Hanuš and Kitty. "I have made up two beds in the attic for you. You will be safe here." She paused. "You are welcome to stay as long as is necessary."

Elsa handed Michal off to his grandfather. "I'll take them up, Mother." She reached for Kitty's hand and led her up one flight of stairs. She opened the door to the attic staircase, pulled the string attached to the light fixture, illuminating the stairs, and went up. Hanuš followed close behind.

The attic was large and littered with old furniture covered in sheets. It was clean and dry. Two makeshift beds made of blankets with floral coverlets and fluffy pillows beckoned the weary travelers.

Elsa turned to Kitty, who had not spoken a word since they left Teplice. "I used to love to play up here as a child," Elsa told her. Kitty sat down on one of the beds, pulled her knees up to her chest and began to rock back and forth. "There, there, my dear." The woman she had only just met kissed Kitty on the forehead. "Things will look better after you get some rest."

In the morning, sunlight streamed through the round window at one end of the attic, illuminating the dark corners where the light had not reached the night before. Kitty looked around at the strange surroundings, shock waves flowing over her.

This woman is truly kind, thought Kitty, but she knows nothing of my life. I have lost my Oila. I have lost Pavla. I have lost Bettina, and I don't know when I will see Father again. Kitty doubted very much that anything would look better again anytime soon.

CHAPTER SIX

VLADA MARCH 15, 1939
PARDUBICE, CZECHOSLOVAKIA/PROTECTORATE
OF BOHEMIA AND MORAVIA

Like so many mornings, Vlada stumbled bleary-eyed from his bed to the breakfast table. Hermina gave her son a peck on the cheek and tousled his hair. Vlada was fourteen and she considered herself lucky her small gestures of affection were still tolerated. Vlada sat down, his usual toast with butter arranged on a floral china plate. Steam rose from his teacup, and he dipped his toast in the hot liquid. Picking up the cup, he slurped down the remaining tea, leaving only crumbs behind.

The walk to school was the same as always. Vlada crossed the courtyard, walked up the steps and through the front doors of the school. Then, chaos greeted him. Teachers scurried in and out of their classrooms, some huddled in pairs in the hallway, speaking to each other in hushed tones. Students milled aimlessly in the hallways, and stranger still, no teachers or administrators reprimanded them for loitering. Vlada walked by the principal's office. He heard the low hum of a radio emanating from the room and lingered outside the door long enough to hear the announcer repeating the same phrase, barely audible over the static. "Please stand by. Please stand by."

Suddenly Jirka appeared in front of him "What is going on?" Vlada shrugged his shoulders. The bell rang and they walked quickly to one of the classrooms and took their seats. The professor at the front of the class was not their usual teacher and the man seemed lost, alternately fumbling through a stack of papers while he glanced at his watch.

Before the man could speak, the principal's voice came blaring over the school intercom. "Attention all students! Please listen carefully. School is cancelled for the rest of the day. Please take your belongings and exit the building immediately. Single file, in an orderly fashion, please. Thank you."

The principal's voice sounded nervous, hesitant. Vlada imagined him in his office with the bad guys from a Tom Mix movie holding a gun to his head and telling him to act normal. The man sounded anything but normal.

Students began standing up abruptly, knocking over chairs, some pushing their way to the door to get to their lockers. Vlada and Jirka looked at each other, and Vlada walked slowly to his locker, placing his pencils, books, and notepaper into his rucksack. The boy next to him tried to stuff handfuls of papers into his rucksack, but half of them cascaded to the floor. The main hallway was lined with a gauntlet of the school's professors, many of whom seemed torn between maintaining order and fleeing the building. A strange hush fell over the hallway as, one by one, the students took their cue from the somber adults.

The hallway filled with students, a stream of them flowing like the Vltava toward the front doors of the school. Vlada joined in and let the tide carry him toward the exit, Jirka having somehow appeared next to him. They smiled nervously at each other over their unexpected good fortune of being released from school early.

Professor Jicha stood with his arms crossed outside his classroom door, appearing strangely pleased with the events unfolding around him, his signature bowtie slightly askew. The Latin teacher's expression changed as Vlada, with Jirka beside him, passed by.

"*Störendes element,*" Professor Jicha said under his breath. "If it isn't the bad apples. Tch, tch, tch." The teacher shook his head. The German phrase translated into 'disturbing elements,' and Professor Jicha had taken to addressing them as such in recent months. Vlada's eyes narrowed, remembering that no matter how exceptional his grades were, the man's loathing for him had grown daily.

Jirka had tried to tell Vlada to stop trying but it was no use. "Wake up, Vlada!" Jirka told him. "You can get a perfect score on every exam. In his eyes, nothing can change the fact that you are a Jew."

The previous year, Jicha had kept his antisemitism, simmering just below the surface, in check. But after the Munich Agreement in the fall, he felt emboldened, his taunts erupting like Mount Vesuvius, spewing burning insults toward the two friends, the only Jews in the class. Vlada's cheeks burned with humiliation.

The boys continued the slow shuffle toward the front entrance of the school. The doors opened onto the street and the children spilled out of the building, down the front steps and into the blinding sunshine of a chilly winter day. The noise on the street was deafening. Sleek black cars, motorcycles with sidecars and machine guns, a parade of sinister vehicles bearing small flags with black swastikas, all assaulted the narrow street in front of the school, filling the air with menace. Nazi officers in uniforms spanning all levels of authority occupied the cars coming from the direction of the West, from Prague.

Jirka shouted to Vlada over the din. "What is going on?" Jirka dropped his rucksack on the steps, holding his hands to his ears to block out the jarring sound of the vehicle engines and the officers' brusque demands.

"Nazis," Vlada mouthed back. The two boys exited the courtyard and stood on the edge of the sidewalk. Vlada looked out over the cavalcade, fascinated by the powerful display. He spotted the double lightning bolt insignia on the collar of an officer in one of the vehicles. *Schutzstaffel.* Vlada had seen the insignia in photos in the newspaper but never on an actual person. From their rigid bearing and scowling expressions, Vlada knew these were not good men. Off in the distance, somewhere in the town, Vlada could hear voices singing, faint strains of the Czech national anthem. "Where is my homeland?" the voices cried out plaintively. The hair on the back of Vlada's neck stood on end.

Jirka picked up his things, gave Vlada a quick wave and ran off down the sidewalk. Vlada stood on the curb, mesmerized by the unexpected convoy, and waited for what seemed like an eternity for the motorcade to subside. A regiment of soldiers, guns slung over their left shoulders, their eyes obscured by their helmets, marched behind the last of the staff cars. The soldiers moved like one large organism, kicking their black boots high off the ground in perfect time. The stomping of their bootheels echoed off the cobblestone streets, filling Vlada with a rush of anxiety.

When the last soldier had passed, Vlada nervously stepped into the street and started walking. The streets were empty and quiet. The sky had clouded over, and flurries of snow appeared. For the first time Vlada felt the cold. He turned to look back at the school. He had no idea if he would ever go back. The Nazis were occupying Pardubice.

On the walk home, Vlada's thoughts travelled back to a day in early January. He had come in from playing outside and was shaking the snow from his hat and gloves. His parents sat unmoving at the kitchen table, listening to the radio, the jarring staccato of Hitler's voice an assault on their ears. Vlada's German was mediocre at best, but there was no mistaking the overall tone of the speech: Jews of Europe, beware.

His mother's face was white and drawn. "We have to leave, Karel." She stood up and began to pace, wringing her hands as she talked. "The Bergmans are gone, the Auerbachs, the Lieblitzs." All the families his mother identified attended the synagogue.

Karel looked directly at Hermina, studying her face. "Darling, but where will we go?" Karel's parents were deceased. He had no relatives anywhere else in Europe that might take them in. "And besides, why should we leave? How can I leave?"

"I don't care about us, Karel. Do something," Hermina implored. "Do it for Vlada!"

Karel remained at the table, holding his head in his hands, and the awkward tension that permeated the room left Vlada feeling uncertain and on edge. His parents were fighting over him, and Vlada's cheeks flushed with shame. They think I am still a child, thought Vlada angrily. He grabbed his coat from the door hook and ran down the stairs.

On Sunday, Karel informed his son he was going to the coffee shop. Alone. Vlada was hurt not to be included. It was one of the simple pleasures he and his father still enjoyed.

Later, Karel returned with promising news. "I spoke with some of the men at the coffee shop. Visas to most countries are limited. We will need a sponsor." He showed Hermina a list of agencies he needed to contact. "Darling, I feel hopeful that we can find a sponsor and assemble the necessary documentation."

His parents' conversation sounded thoughtful and rational, and Vlada's shoulders let go of the tension. Things were returning to normal.

"But why the United States, Tati? Why not Switzerland? Or better yet, France"? Vlada knew the Nazis had already taken over Austria. Grandfather Adolf had been living in Vienna with his daughter, Helen, when it happened, forcing his return to Czechoslovakia after the Anschluss. Still, Vlada thought there must be other countries in Europe that would take them in.

"I know it is confusing, Vlada," his father began. "But I have been advised by men whose opinion I trust that it would be best to leave the continent." His parents exchanged a look that meant the conversation was over. Again, Vlada felt the flush of heat on his face as his parents once again treated him like a child.

That morning, on the way to school, Vlada confided in Jirka. "My parents are contacting agencies and sending letters to anyone with the last name "Munk" in America so we can emigrate to the United States."

"The United States?" Jirka replied. "I am sorry, my friend, but it sounds like a longshot. I think you are stuck here with me and the rest of the Jews!" Jirka laughed and punched Vlada in the arm.

A few weeks after the letter writing campaign, Vlada returned home from school to an empty flat. He heard rustling in the pánsky and walked in to find his mother sitting at the piano, straightening her sheet music, Čigy curled up on the floor by her feet. "Did something happen, Mami?"

"Tati had a meeting," Hermina replied, avoiding her son's gaze, studying the creases in her hands. "The search for a sponsor has failed, Vlada. All that work by your father. For nothing." Hermina breathed deeply. "I was foolish to believe we might get an offer from some caring Jewish family with the same surname in America. But no one wrote back."

Vlada's cheeks reddened. No further explanation was necessary. It was simple. No one wanted them.

"Your father…has had another idea," Hermina tried to make her voice sound cheerful, but it came out sounding forced. "He is joining in a business venture with some other men." Vlada did not like the idea but kept his thoughts to himself.

A few nights later, during dinner, a sharp knock at the door made Hermina jump. Karel rose slowly from his seat at the table, placing his napkin purposefully on the table. He opened the door, and Vlada saw his father stiffen.

Karel spoke in a polite manner, but Vlada could tell by his father's rigid posture that he was not pleased. "Mr. Hlavac, I wasn't expecting you." Karel held the door halfway open, keeping the man on the threshold outside.

"Sorry to interrupt, Karel," a gruff voice replied. "It is something of an urgent matter." The man pushed past his father and inserted himself into the flat. Vlada felt an instant dislike for the man. His suit was cheap, made of shiny fabric, not like the ones Vlada's father wore, and his black hair was greased back. He reminded Vlada of a villain from one of the Tom Mix movies.

"This opportunity is not going to come by again, Karel," the man said. He spoke fast, his hands fidgeting with the brim of his hat. Hermina said later that the man lacked "social graces." Grandfather Adolf would have called the man at the door "silver-tongued." Vlada felt his body tighten in knots as his father ushered the man into the pánsky room and closed the doors.

Vlada and his mother overheard his father and Mr. Hlavac's exchange, low rumblings punctuated with a rise in tone when questions were posed. "This is your last chance, Karel. Take it or leave it." Karel's reply was low and inaudible, but it sounded to Vlada like his father was deferring to the man. Whatever help the man was offering, Vlada was sure there was a very big catch. The man mentioned something about Ecuador. Vlada would have to look it up on a map.

"Good, Karel. You've made the right decision. Everyone else has paid in. Once you get the money from the bank in the morning, I'll go on ahead and lay the groundwork." The doors to the pánsky room opened and the two men walked to the kitchen. Vlada looked up from the book he pretended to flip through, and noticed the man smelled of cigar smoke.

"Good night," said Mr. Hlavac, awkwardly tipping his hat to Hermina, and ignoring Vlada completely. No one spoke as they listened to the man's receding footsteps. When he was gone, Hermina sat at the table to collect herself.

"Karel! That man!" Hermina looked beseechingly at her husband for an explanation.

"I have it on good authority that he can help us, darling. He has the money for all the permits to start a business in South America. Once it is established, we can apply for visas, since I will be part owner. Then we can safely leave," his father said the words like an actor would recite lines in a play, as if repeated enough, they would convey some truth.

"Leave for where, Tati?" Vlada asked, confused. His father had a job. In what world did his father have to form a partnership with the likes of the man who had just left?

"Ecuador," his father replied, his voice betraying his distress. Karel felt like there was a noose tightening around his neck. Hermina and Vlada were looking to him for a solution and he was running out of opportunities for his family's safe departure. Against his better judgment, he gave the man an undisclosed sum. He never saw Mr. Hlavac again.

Hermina spoke tentatively to her husband, aware of the pressure he was putting on himself to keep the family safe. "Karel, did you hear about the Novaks? They sent their daughter to England." They sat at the dining room table having coffee after dinner. Karel looked down, fiddling with the cuff of his suitcoat. He found it hard to look at his wife after losing a large sum of the family's savings under the guise of a South American business venture.

Karel sighed. "I will talk to the Novaks, darling." His voice was resigned, his shoulders hunched. The spate of violence against Jews, and the destruction of Jewish homes and businesses, had prompted a public outcry in Britain, prompting them to allow refugee children to enter the country unaccompanied by their parents.

"What about the *Zentralstelle Fuer Juedische Auswanderung*?" Hermina asked. Karel shook his head at his wife's naivete. "It's a sham," he told her. The Nazis had established the Centre for Jewish Emigration in Prague under the guise of aiding Jews to legally emigrate from the republic. But there was one caveat. All the individual's belongings were to be left behind; all financial holdings signed over to the Reich. Some of their friends had given up everything they owned to leave the country.

The solutions his wife was suggesting were tenuous; the window was rapidly closing on the Kindertransport. Even if Karel were to arrange safe passage to Britain for their son, when the time came to put him on the train, Hermina would never let Vlada go. That evening, the pained look on Karel's face conveyed what he dared not say. The family was stuck in Pardubice to ride out whatever lay ahead.

The Nazis had marched through Pardubice, occupying the border region. Then, as if nothing had happened, Vlada returned to school. But things were different. Some of his Jewish schoolmates' parents had lost their jobs. One had committed suicide. The Gestapo had expelled business owners in the center of town, taking over the Jewish storefronts, and setting up their headquarters in the post office. The Czech police in Pardubice now reported to the Gestapo.

Vlada gathered his things for school and placed them in his rucksack under his mother's watchful eye.

"Our teacher told us that we live in the Protectorate of Bohemia and Moravia now, Mami. I don't understand. How can the Nazis change the name of Czechoslovakia?"

Hermina did not answer the question. She was nervous, on edge, and hugged Vlada a little too long, forcing him to extract himself from her embrace.

"Be safe, Vlada," his mother cautioned, nervously twisting her apron.

"Mami, please. I am fourteen now." He would not say it out loud, but he found the presence of the Nazis fascinating: their sleek black cars, the tanks rumbling through the streets of town. Vlada walked to school alone, passing abandoned houses where Czech Jews had once lived, and businesses 'bought' by the Germans from Jewish shopkeepers, some of their windows permanently shuttered.

Vlada looked around the half-full lunchroom on the last day of school before summer vacation. The girl he had a crush on all year, the one who wore her long, brown hair in two braids, had stopped attending school after the Nazis occupied the town. Vlada heard from Jirka that her family had emigrated to Palestine.

Vlada had always liked school. Not anymore. The teachers had changed. His friends had changed. Everything had changed.

CHAPTER
SIX

KITTY 1938 -1939
DOBŘICHOVICE, CZECHOSLOVAKIA/
PROTECTORATE OF BOHEMIA AND MORAVIA

Hanuš awoke in the makeshift bed on the attic floor and immediately reached for the thick packet of money his father had handed him during the nerve-wracking events of the previous night. He counted the bills and coins as Kitty began to stir on the floor next to him. She stretched and wiped at the crust that had formed in the corners of her rheumy eyes, remnants of the previous night's tears.

"Well," Hanuš announced to Kitty matter-of-factly, "we've got enough here to do anything we want, for a long while." Kitty looked at her brother, her mouth open, incredulous at his insensitivity, as a fresh wave of tears welled up in her eyes. They heard footsteps tiptoeing slowly up the attic stairs, and Kitty quickly wiped her eyes, waiting for the visitor to reveal themselves. A small head with tousled brown hair crested the stairs.

"Good morning," a tiny voice said. It was Michal, the son of Elsa and the Komisar, still wearing his pajamas and carrying a small stuffed bear. The arrival of the little boy and his charming greeting caught Kitty and

Hanuš off guard, and Kitty smiled weakly at the child. Heavier footsteps followed quickly on the stairs as Elsa caught up.

"Michal," Elsa took her son's hand and turned to Kitty and Hanuš. "I hope he didn't wake you."

Hanuš shook his head in response. Kitty stood up, clutching one of the blankets in her hands and fretting at the edges as she cleared her throat to speak.

"When will our parents be here?" Kitty stared intently at Elsa, awaiting her response. The sweetness of the previous moment had vanished.

Elsa moved toward Kitty and gently put her hands on Kitty's shoulders. Elsa felt Kitty trembling, her eyes wide and dilated. "I don't know, Kitty," Elsa spoke slowly. She recognized the symptoms of shock in Kitty's behavior and did her best to remain calm.

"I will let you both know the minute I hear any news. There was no mention of school, so you have the day to yourselves," Elsa paused for a moment, her hands lingering on Kitty's shoulders, inspecting the faces of her two unanticipated charges. "You are safe here in Dobřichovice. My husband thinks the Germans will be happy with the Sudetenland and will leave us alone."

Kitty took a step back, forcing Elsa to release her grip on Kitty's shoulders. Elsa continued. "There is breakfast downstairs in the kitchen when you are ready. You can wash up in the bathroom on the second floor." Elsa took Michal by the hand, turning to walk down the stairs.

Michal turned to Hanuš and Kitty, waving to them. "Bye-bye." His voice was disarming in its innocence and Kitty sighed deeply, her shoulders relaxing slightly. Elsa's hands on her shoulders had provided Kitty with unexpected comfort, the warmth and proximity of this woman she barely knew easing Kitty's anxiety if only for a moment.

When they were alone again, Hanuš turned to Kitty, grinning broadly. "Did you hear that, Kitty? No school!" Hanuš shook his head, puzzling over the conditions of their good fortune. Kitty did not share her brother's enthusiasm; her thoughts turned to her father, and Pavla, and Bettina, wondering what they were doing and if they were safe. But Hanuš's eagerness to make the most of the new circumstances proved difficult to ignore, and Kitty felt she had no choice but to reluctantly follow along.

The pair were unlikely companions, having spent little time together by choice, now thrust together for reasons beyond their control. The siblings dressed and descended the attic stairs. A grey striped cat sat at the bottom of the attic staircase, mewing loudly, confused by the new residents. Kitty thought of Pavla, and her heart ached for her sweet mutt.

It was later than they thought, and they had missed breakfast with the family. Toast and jam greeted Hanuš and Kitty's belated arrival in the kitchen downstairs. However, Hanuš didn't dawdle when, still chewing his last piece of toast, he ran back up to the attic, peeling off a few bills from the bundle and putting them in his pocket.

They stepped out the front door of the house with no set plan in place; Hanuš was in search of adventure and fun, while Kitty hoped to find one small thing that felt familiar. Hanuš led the way down the unfamiliar street and Kitty followed, her head down, pondering what Elsa meant when she said that they were safe here in Dobřichovice. Did that mean they were never going to be safe in Teplice again?

The first few days at the house were a blur; Kitty and Hanuš took their morning meals with Elsa, Michal, and Elsa's parents in the dining room of the house, then left the house for the day, walking about the town, Kitty lagging behind Hanuš as he walked in and out of the shops, peering at menus in the windows of the town's small cafés.

Cook was from Austria, and they had rarely eaten traditional Czech food. Hanuš selected each lunch spot carefully, and he reveled in the choices. Kitty watched as her brother tried all manner of dishes they had never had before, one day nearly licking a plate of *Svíčková na smetaně* clean. Kitty, on the other hand, had lost her appetite. She sat across from Hanuš as he heartily devoured a helping of schnitzel or mincemeat or pork while all she could do was think of Cook, which made her think of Oila... which made her miss her parents, round and round in an endless loop of sorrow and longing. In the evening, they returned to the house and sat down for supper with the family, retreating to the attic quarters after the meal was finished. They were boarders, not family, even if their lodging was free.

Communications from Bettina and Karel were sparse at first, delivered to Hanuš and Kitty through Elsa. "Your parents are trying to find passage for you out of the country to America," Elsa explained. "Your mother has gone to Prague to find your grandmother an apartment and your father has remained in Teplice."

Kitty frowned at the second piece of news. She pictured her father, alone, at the house in Teplice, and choked back tears. "They are both safe and in good health and they will come to visit soon," Elsa added, sensing Kitty's concern.

Kitty's face lit up. "When Elsa, when?"

"Soon, Kitty," Elsa replied.

Kitty perked up upon hearing the news of her parents' impending visit. A few days passed and Kitty and Hanuš continued with their routine, wandering Dobřichovice after breakfast, discovering a new café for lunch, and returning to their attic room for a nap. Upon returning from their excursion one afternoon, Hanuš opened the door to the house, and was surprised to see his parents in the sitting room sipping tea and talking with Elsa. Kitty ran to her father, gleefully shouting his name. Karel barely had time to set down his teacup before Kitty collided into him.

A huge grin spread over Hanuš's face at the sight of his mother. He greeted her with a hug, then pulled away, standing up tall and puffing out his chest, hoping he looked the part of the man of the family with his father in absentia.

Kitty stepped away from her father to look at her mother, her knees wobbling with relief at the sight of her. She wanted to speak, but nothing came out, so she walked unsteadily to where Bettina now stood and leaned against her. Bettina drew in a breath, then let out a long sigh, putting one arm around Kitty and stroking her hair. When Kitty pulled away, she saw that her mother looked tired; her cheeks sagged and there were dark circles under her eyes. Her skirt was wrinkled. And her shoes bore the dust of their journey. The weeks away from her children had been hard on her, too.

"Your mother was able to secure a ticket on a boat heading to the United States. She did not require an affidavit because she is an American citizen, but it will be impossible to secure tickets for the rest of us," their father explained wearily. Kitty looked at Bettina, her face questioning the news. Bettina hung her head, her shoulders slumping like a marionette collapsing in a heap on a stage.

"I won't go alone," Bettina said in a low voice. "I won't leave you." She looked up and her eyes met Hanuš's and then Kitty's. "I will give the ticket to Uncle Willie." Willie was Bettina's brother. His wife, Anna, was a Gentile, and they had a daughter, Eva, a year younger than Kitty. Bettina looked at the others in the room for their reaction. Kitty stared at her mother intently, a satisfied smile spreading across her face.

Kitty did not want to move to America. Czechoslovakia was her home and nothing the Germans did could change that. She thought this was the most unselfish act her mother had ever made.

Kitty's mind wandered back to earlier events at the villa in Teplice. She recalled how conversations during the family lunch had begun to take on a more serious tone, her mother leading the charge.

"Is it safe, Karel? Will Hitler get away with it?" She pressed her husband about the shocking new laws against Jews in Germany and how he thought they might affect the Jewish people of Teplice. She had heard things in discussions with her women friends, bad things. "Should we stay, Karel, or should we leave?" It was rare for Bettina to seek her husband's counsel.

Karel hesitated before answering, his mind racing, eyes darting as he contemplated the ramifications of leaving. "It's a moot point," he replied. "I can't leave my mother behind."

Bettina frowned at her husband's response. "I have been told that Jews are losing their jobs, Karel. That people are fleeing the border regions." Kitty remembered it was the most impassioned speech she had ever heard her mother give. Bettina crossed her arms, frustrated, demanding an answer.

As it turned out, her mother was right to be concerned. Jewish families in their community had already begun to suffer huge financial losses as Jewish men lost their jobs and had difficulty finding new employment. Their wives trusted that the community would support them, and women who had formerly been of means found themselves knocking on their neighbors' doors, selling baskets of homemade soaps to keep their households going. Bettina bought every single item that was offered, filling drawer upon drawer in the house with soap – round ones, square ones, in pastel blue, pink, and yellow, some scented, some not. "They have so little, Karel, and we have so much."

Kitty had looked on, astonished, as Bettina and her bridge partners began collecting clothing and distributing it to the newly disadvantaged. Kitty's favorite dresses and play clothes, those that no longer fit her, were carried in baskets out the door for the cause. Kitty remembered having mixed feelings about her mother's philanthropy; she felt proud of Bettina's generosity but slightly jealous over her interest in these children who were not her own.

One morning at breakfast in Teplice, Kitty recalled Bettina announcing her latest act of benevolence. "You are all to choose a child whose parent has lost their job and invite that child home for lunch with you," she instructed Kitty, Hanuš, and Otto. The children looked disbelievingly at each other across the dining room table. "Those children will be welcome here every day."

Kitty invited Lisa Lotte, a shy girl from her class to come to the Löwi household for lunch. Hanuš invited a rude boy who had the annoying habit of removing the caraway seeds from every food he was served, piling the seeds on the edge of his plate. The lunch guests were always sent home with leftovers –stew, or spaetzle, sometimes even strudel – right up until the day the family was forced to leave Teplice. Kitty wondered what had become of little Lisa. The memory of those days made her yearn for her old life in the villa.

The reverie of Teplice receded into memory, vanishing like a wisp of smoke, and slowly Kitty came back to the conversation at Elsa's. "So, we are staying, then?"

"Yes, Kitty." Her father stood and reached for his hat. "Bettina, we must be going."

"What? So soon?" Kitty grabbed her father by the arm, her voice high and shaky.

"Kitty," said Bettina in a calm voice. "I am going back to Prague. In two weeks' time, I will return for you."

Hanuš had been quiet until then. "What about the house in Teplice?" He was enjoying his newfound freedom, but he had assumed things would return to normal soon.

His parents looked knowingly at each other but neither of them spoke. Elsa tentatively entered the room; aware she was interrupting an awkward moment. "My husband is on his way to pick you up," said

Elsa to Karel and Bettina. Elsa's eyes met Kitty's, and she smiled weakly, the room filled with the silence of broken promises. When Kitty did not return her smile, Elsa turned, head down, and slowly led the family through the hallway to the front door.

Karel and Bettina stood in the open doorway, Bettina biting her lip; Hanuš and Kitty shuffling along behind them. Kitty buried her head in her mother's jacket, breathing in deeply, hoping to preserve the smell of her until they saw each other again. Bettina hugged Kitty to her, her eyes staring forward, resolute. Karel and Hanuš shook hands. Hanuš attempted to stand taller, but the weight of the moment held him down.

Karel knelt to be on Kitty's level, looking directly in her eyes. Kitty kissed him quickly on the cheek and ran up the stairs, choking back tears. There were only so many goodbyes she could endure.

Bettina led Kitty into the small one-bedroom apartment in Prague occupied by her mother-in-law. A pungent smell of old people and vinegar greeted Kitty, and she pinched her nose as she entered the apartment; it was a combination befitting the new phase of purgatory the family had entered. Kitty had never seen Grandmother Ludmila anywhere other than the house in Jesenice. But now Jesenice, the family's beloved country paradise, was lost to them, quite possibly forever, all because it fell squarely within the Sudeten region. The thought of the Germans in the villa made Kitty's skin crawl.

The apartment was small and sparsely furnished, all the lovely family heirlooms – the cobalt-blue Bohemian crystal, her father's walnut writing desk – left behind in the villa. It had been difficult to find an apartment in Prague following the mass influx of Jewish residents from the border region.

Grandmother Ludmila was a large woman and when she spoke, Kitty's father paid attention. Kitty did not know whether to thank her or be angry that she had prevented Karel from sending Hanuš to England with the Kindertransport.

Instead, Hanuš had been sent to live with their grandfather in another part of Prague, and although it pained Kitty to admit it, she missed him. She had seen a different side of Hanuš during their time in Dobřichovice; her brother, it turned out, was independent, kind, generous, and adventurous away from the confines of home, and she liked that version of him very much.

Bettina left Kitty behind in the apartment in Prague every day. She still held out hope for a passage out of Czechoslovakia and spent hours each day chasing down leads, hoping to use her American citizenship as leverage in search of an exit strategy for the family. Kitty loathed the long days at the apartment and felt imprisoned. She loved her grandmother, but she was old and ill, and Kitty found herself restless and bored. Eventually, Bettina permitted Kitty to travel to her grandfather's apartment a few blocks away, where she could spend time with Hanuš and Bettina's sister Rose, who was their father's caretaker.

Hanuš opened the door of Grandfather's apartment when Kitty knocked. The two stood and looked at each other, grinning madly, happier than ever to see each other, both feeling too awkward to hug.

Grandfather was in the small kitchen, cooking, and motioned for Kitty to come to him. He had raised three daughters and he loved spoiling Kitty, allowing her free reign to run a finger puppet over imaginary roads all around his bald head. Kitty and Hanuš set the table while their grandfather finished cooking. The meat in the cast iron pan had a sharp smell, rather like the time the icebox at the house in Teplice had ceased working, forcing Cook to discard pounds of spoiled stew meat. Kitty breathed in deeply and coughed, regretting her decision to visit. The other apartment might not have Hanuš, but the cooking was better.

In the kitchen, they gathered at the small wooden table, Hanuš, Kitty and Grandfather, as the old man doled out portions of a brown slab onto each plate. Kitty and Hanuš shared a look and then Hanuš sliced into the mound and shoved a forkful into his mouth. Kitty attempted to cut the meat into slices but found it unyielding to the sharpest part of the knife. She bit off a piece, chewed quickly and swallowed, unable to finish the serving that sat on her plate. Rose had gone to visit a friend and Kitty understood why.

An hour or so later, Hanuš and Kitty were sitting on the couch in the living room playing a game of cards when Kitty was struck with a wave of stomach cramps. She jumped up and ran to the bathroom. Twenty minutes later when she had still not come out, Hanuš knocked quietly. He could hear Kitty groaning on the other side of the door. It was Kitty's last meal at Grandfather's apartment.

It took weeks for Kitty to regain her appetite. When she was finally able to eat normally, Hanuš told Kitty he had a surprise. He led his sister through a maze of city blocks to a restaurant with a simple sign on the exterior that read 'Automat.' They walked inside and Kitty's mouth fell open in amazement. One whole wall of the restaurant was covered in gleaming steel, with tiny little glass doored compartments set into it that held pre-made sandwiches, soups, slices of cake and pie. Shiny metal stools lined polished counters, and the room teemed with customers, many drinking liters of beer.

Hanuš tried to pry open one of the compartments, but it would not budge. They watched as another customer selected a compartment containing a slice of cherry pie, inserted a coin in the slot, turned the knob and—pop! —the window opened. The man pulled out the piece of pie, a perfect dollop of whipped cream on top, and carried it to a small table.

The food in the compartments was cheap and delicious, and without hesitation, Kitty and Hanuš chose *chlebicky*, an open-faced sandwich with meat and cheese, and strudel for dessert.

After the first excursion to the Automat, Hanuš came to Grandmother Ludmila's regularly. He picked up Kitty and they walked the streets of Prague together, eating at the coin-operated restaurant. Later they bought tickets to a movie and sat in the dark theatre watching the adventures of Tom Mix, Tom Shark, and Charlie Chan. Kitty would have preferred to watch a Shirley Temple or Mary Pickford film or perhaps Fred Astaire and Ginger Rogers, but she usually gave in to Hanuš's preferences.

On a grey day in November, Kitty and Hanuš walked the route they knew by heart on their way to the movie theatre. They passed a newsstand, every inch of the exterior covered with newspapers, the headlines heavily pronounced in bold typeface: Nazis Smash, Loot and Burn Synagogues. One image caught Kitty's eye; it was of the synagogue in Vienna, she was sure of it. She and Oila had passed it on their holiday. She clutched at the collar of her coat and stood in front of the newsstand, immobile.

Hanuš stopped next to her, looking up at the glaring headlines, images of synagogues and storefronts on fire, broken glass everywhere. "Let's go, Kitty." He took Kitty by the elbow and guided her the rest of the way to the theatre. Kitty sat in the middle row of the theatre and thought of Oila and of Otto. She held her hand over her heart and knew somehow that Oila, who was not Jewish, was safe. She was thankful that Otto had missed the terrifying pogrom in Teplice and saddened, too, that he had to leave his home and the beauty of Jesenice for a small apartment in Prague.

Hanuš and Kitty lost themselves in the images projected onto the movie screen. They stayed for a double feature and then walked through the streets of Prague by the light of the streetlamps. Kitty felt a thrill, a mix of fear and excitement. They arrived back at the apartment to find Bettina furious. She had seen the headlines and feared for her children's safety even though the ugly events had taken place in Germany and Austria.

"I thought someone had taken you." Her breathing was shallow, and she was close to hyperventilating.

"Who would take us, Mother?" Hanuš joked. Bettina did not laugh. She did not revoke their privileges but instructed them to never again be out after dark.

Hanuš and Kitty were on their own. Although the world was a mixed-up mess, the siblings reveled in their newfound freedom. Kitty lived her life between three households: their maternal grandfather and paternal grandmother in Prague, and Elsa and the Komisar's house in Dobřichovice, but at least she was not alone. Other people she loved had to give up their homes and were on the move as well.

Life continued that way for months, the family traveling between Prague and Dobřichovice, with schooling put on hold. Then, in March, without so much as a shot fired, Czechoslovakia became the Protectorate of Bohemia and Moravia. The Munich Agreement puzzled Kitty, but during the evening, when she feigned sleep, she overheard her parents talking at the kitchen table.

"Can the Nazis get away with it, Karel?" The distress in Bettina's voice frightened Kitty.

"They already have, mein Schatz." Her father's tone was resigned at first. "Hitler wasn't happy with just the border regions." Kitty heard her father's voice grow louder, agitated. "He won't be satisfied with Austria and the whole of Czechoslovakia. It is not going to stop here."

Kitty wanted to get up and soothe her father; when he sounded distressed, she, in turn, became more anxious. Her father had suffered his first heart attack during one of Hitler's speeches threatening the Jewish people. She knew he had to keep his anger in check. But she lay frozen on the couch.

"Karel, calm down, please," Bettina pleaded. He breathed deeply and let out a long, dejected sigh.

"We must leave the city. That much is certain."

Kitty rolled over on the couch, turning her back toward her parents as waves of sadness washed over her. She held her breath and tried not to cry. Children were not allowed to make decisions. Neither Kitty nor Hanuš ever expressed their wants, they never complained. It was clear her parents carried the burden of everything.

Kitty had begun to adjust to life in Prague. She liked it here. If they moved again there would be no more strudel from the Automat, no more Charlie Chan at the movie theatre.

In the morning, Bettina announced that her cousin had a summer cottage in Dobřichovice and had offered it to the family – two rooms with no running water. If they were to leave Prague, it was their only option. Kitty did not ask how long they would have to stay there. She did not want to know the answer.

CHAPTER SEVEN

The Nazis issued a decree banning Jews from owning radios and "German Army attacks Poland!" was the last news broadcast the family heard before theirs was confiscated. Vlada had to give the Nazis credit. He was impressed with how swiftly they were moving, though he dared not say so aloud.

Vlada recalled his father going to the sideboard where the large, brown radio had sat since its purchase. Now, Karel unplugged the radio and began wiping it down with a cloth. "You're cleaning it for them, Karel?" Distraught over the radio's confiscation, Hermina ran to the bedroom and closed the door. The radio had been their lifeline to the outside world and for years before that, a repository from which emanated beautiful music from the nation's orchestras and fabulous stories from the best writers of their time. Suddenly that was over.

Vlada thought things would be better without the radio in the flat. His mother reacted so viscerally to each news report he would rather his father decided what news to give her now, if any. His father tasked Vlada with returning the radio to the *Oberlandrat*, the German District

Administrator's office in the former post office. Karel placed the radio on a cart and Vlada set off, pulling the cart behind him.

When he approached the building, Vlada looked up at the massive pillars marking the entrance, having passed through them many times with Hermina to post a letter to his grandparents or to his mother's sisters. The once friendly landmark had been commandeered by German officials after the occupation, and flags with swastikas flapped in the cool autumn breeze. He sighed. He looked up at the window boxes that lined the second story. The greenery that had once filled them was dead now. The Nazis had managed to kill everything and make it look ugly in such a short time.

Vlada stiffened slightly at the knowledge that he was about to enter a building filled with Gestapo. Rumor had it there were at least twenty of them stationed in the town. He opened the heavy brass door, lifted the radio from the cart, and entered the building. He ascended the worn stone stairs to the office, struggling with the bulky radio. They've redecorated, thought Vlada. Another giant flag bearing a swastika hung behind the desk of the office on the second floor. The officer behind the desk was young, in his early twenties. He spoke to Vlada in German, not bothering to glance up from what he was doing.

"Set the radio on the counter," the officer instructed. Vlada did as he was told.

"Name?" The man stared at a ledger on the desk, his hand poised to write.

"Munk. Karel Munk." The officer wrote in the ledger and then tore off a receipt and handed it to Vlada, never making eye contact. With that, Vlada was dismissed. All common courtesy had been abandoned. No pleasantries. No please, thank you, or good day. Vlada felt like the invisible man of the H.G. Wells science fiction novel.

Vlada exited the building, nearly bumping into the father of a younger boy from school, whose family were also members of the synagogue. The man held a radio in his arms. His eyes met Vlada's, then he quickly looked away, ashamed. Vlada had heard the phrase "misery loves company." This was not the kind of misery anyone felt good about sharing.

After declaring war on Poland the previous fall, Hitler was brazen. He swatted away the olive branch extended by Neville Chamberlain, the British Prime Minister, as if it were a pesky fly, forcing Britain and France to declare war against Germany. That further angered the Führer, and in the spring of 1940, German forces moved with audacity, assaulting everything in their path. Holland surrendered, along with Luxembourg and Belgium. Norway and Denmark capitulated. Then France. France! The German army rolled over once-sovereign countries with precision, systematically crushing any resistance.

At the end of June, all Jewish children were expelled from public schools, forcing Vlada's thoughts away from the Nazi's tactical prowess to his own future. He liked school, or at least he had before the occupation. What would life look like without the predictability of the school year, punctuated by summer and winter recesses? Walking home on the final day of his middle school education, Vlada's thoughts turned to summer vacations past, spent hiking in the beautiful Krkonoše mountains, of his cousin, Mirek, who always joined them for the summer trip, of the family's favorite restaurants there. His father had informed him that there would be no summer vacation. Vlada would have to settle for time spent at his father's camp in Polabiny, and if he was lucky, he might be allowed to attend the scouting camp jamboree in mid-summer.

The following day, Vlada and Jirka bicycled to Karel's tiny cottage on the marsh. It was a poor substitute for the mountains Vlada cherished in any season. Karel was expecting them, an array of fishing rods and jars of bait and hooks arranged on a rough table outside the cabin. Karel placed a rum-soaked ball of bread – prepared by Hermina – on a fishhook and walked to the water's edge. He mounted the long skiff, casting his line out over the water. Vlada watched his father's body relax, his shoulders loosen, his face reflecting calm.

Vlada followed his father's example, casting his line over the water and waiting. Jirka sat at the water's edge, throwing sticks into the calm water. Vlada gently tugged at the pole. "I think I've got one, Tati."

"Shhhhh." Karel put his finger to his lips. "Fishing for carp is most successful when the fisherman is quiet." Vlada began reeling in the line slowly. A good-sized fish broke through the water, struggling wildly to free itself from the hook. Čigy barked his congratulations, running back and forth along the edge of the shore, effectively scaring away any other fish within earshot for the next few hours. Vlada landed the fish in the skiff, conflicting feelings of pride and sadness running through him as they prepared the fish to be scaled, gutted, and cooked.

Since the occupation, Jews were no longer permitted to run businesses and Jirka's parents' grocery store had been taken from them. Karel was fortunate; a German treuhänder, or trustee, had been assigned to oversee the distillery. The treuhänder, a gruff, uneducated man, wanted nothing to do with the day-to-day running of the business. He spent his days eating and picking his teeth, rarely intervening in the factory's daily operations, leaving Karel to do as he knew best. Still, the treuhänder's presence on the property was unsettling.

Today Vlada was alone in the flat except for Čigy, who barely acknowledged his presence from a spot on the rug in front of the kitchen sink, where he waited patiently for Hermina to come home. The dog let out a deep sigh.

Vlada looked around the flat. Everything looked the same on the surface, yet underneath was wave after wave of uncertainty, tossing their once-predictable life like a boat at sea. Vlada had seen a change come over his mother since Karel's inability to find the family safe passage to emigrate. Many families had tried to escape and failed, only to try again. But Hermina had not regained her usual optimism. Her brightness had dimmed. She existed in perpetual dusk.

Vlada blamed the Nazis. Each decree came quickly on the heels of another and visibly weakened her leaving no time for recovery. Jews were excluded from all kinds of professional associations. Jews could not be civil servants. They were not allowed to leave their houses after 8 p.m. They were banned from traveling unless they obtained permission from the local German authorities. If they did travel, they were only allowed in special compartments. They were not allowed to change their place of residence without permission. Voting rights were revoked. Jews were excluded from attendance at public events, the theatre, movies.

"The world has deserted us, Karel," he heard his mother say. By "us" she meant not just their family, but the whole Jewish race. After the declaration of war on Poland, the Nazis instituted wartime food rationing and Jews were given different ration coupons than non-Jewish Czechs. Hermina had always expressed her love for her family by making their favorite foods or surprising them with special treats. The family's ability to purchase sugar, butter, meat, and milk were now restricted; the Nazis controlled what she fed her family, how much, and when she purchased it.

Jews were only allowed to shop for food during certain hours of the day, from 3 to 5 p.m., when the lines were the longest and basic items were sold out. The trip was compounded by having to navigate streets and intersections that were now designated as off-limits to Jews whether on foot or by vehicle. After years of habit, Hermina often found herself on the edge of the park, which she had always crossed to get to the grocer.

A sign at one entrance issued a cold warning: *Für Juden verboten* (No Jews allowed.) Jews could be fined or worse for entering the park or crossing the wrong street. Filled with doubt about whether a particular street was passable, Hermina succumbed to a deep fear of retribution, and opted for the longest, safest route. A trip that used to take her one hour now often took three.

As Christians, Milan Hasek's family had retained ownership of their family grocery store. Hermina stood dutifully in line at the store and watched non-Jews ahead of her present coupons for items she wanted but could not purchase. Her chin quivered as she fought back tears. Mr. Hasek motioned to Hermina to his queue, asking after Vlada while filling her order, secretly slipping items for which she had no coupons — meat, coffee, eggs — into the bottom of her bags. Mr. Hasek did so at great risk to himself and his family. After arriving home and finding the contraband items, on her next visit to the store, Hermina protested.

"I cannot possibly take these things!" Hermina leaned over the counter, stressing each syllable of every word with a loud whisper.

"Take it, Hermina," Mr. Hasek insisted. "There may come a day when I am no longer able to do it."

Vlada could not bear for his mother to face the weekly humiliation that buying food had become under the Nazis. "Mami, I will stand in line and get the rations," Vlada insisted.

Hermina would not hear of it. "No, Vlada," she said firmly. "You have your studies." Her son's education was the only thing she prayed would stay out of the Nazi purview. Vlada watched her crumble when she heard the news that Jews had been expelled from school. He recalled the phrase his grandfather Adolf liked to use: The straw that broke the camel's back. He understood the metaphor now.

Vlada sat at the kitchen table. It was almost five o'clock. His mother would be home soon from shopping. It was officially the beginning of summer and before the occupation, that meant time spent with his mother at another favorite summer place: the tennis club. Vlada shot Čigy a look. No more tennis club for you.

After the litany of checks on their freedom, Hermina hoped that something as simple as a gathering place for sport would remain off the Gestapo's radar. She had insisted that Vlada walk to the tennis club with her, hoping to find their membership was still valid. Karel had been reticent about the trip, sensing his wife's fragile state, her frequent sighs, her hunched shoulders. He caught Vlada's eye for a moment, wanting to protect them both.

A short while later, mother and son were standing in front of the gate that led into the tennis club. The loathsome sign that had become all too familiar hung above it. *Für Juden verboten*. To the right of the entrance, a piece of paper was tacked to the door, flapping in the breeze. Hermina held it down and read the words at the top in large letters: **Membership Revoked**. Below the words on the sign was a long list of names, and tracing her finger down the paper, she read the names in alphabetical order: Munk, Hermina. Munk, Vlada.

Inside the gate, their non-Jewish friends walked by, wearing crisp white outfits, tennis rackets balanced on their shoulders, laughing, talking. A boy in Vlada's class walked by slowly, bouncing a bright white tennis ball on his racket. A friend of Hermina's noticed them standing outside. She raised her hand to wave and then thought better of it. "Let's go, Mami." Vlada felt anger rise in him, and he clenched his fists. His anger would soon require an outlet, a release from the uncertainty and rage rising inside him.

Hermina likened the restrictions to the stars in the heavens, each small freedom was a star darkened forever. A few days later, the sky darkened further. Karel was at the distillery and Hermina had just returned shopping when there was a sharp rap on the door. Vlada braced himself as his mother slowly approached the door. Two Gestapo officers stood on the landing. They were tall and wore civilian clothes, but there was no mistaking them.

"What can I do for you, gentlemen?" His mother's voice was shaking, as her hands nervously twisted the hem of her apron. Čigy rose from his place by the sink and stood behind Hermina, growling.

"We have it on good authority that there is something of great value here. We would like to evaluate it," one of the men said in German. There were footsteps rushing up the stairs at that moment. The machinist had seen the long, black vehicle in the factory yard and alerted Karel, who entered the flat.

"What is it that we can do for you gentlemen?" He spoke politely, his voice tight, controlling his outrage at the intrusion.

"It seems there is a certain stamp collection that may have a value above the allowable limit, Herr Munk. We would like to take the album back with us to headquarters for evaluation. If we are mistaken, it will most certainly be returned," the officer made the request sound reasonable. Vlada knew better.

Karel hesitated for a moment. Hermina sat down in one of the chairs by the table, and motioned Čigy to her side. When Vlada thought he could barely stand another second, his father spoke.

"That seems reasonable. Vlada, would you be so kind as to get the stamp collection for these gentlemen?" Vlada knew exactly where the album was. He had looked through it a few days earlier. As if through mud to the pánsky room he walked; the album was right where he had left it on the settee. He picked it up like it was a bomb, walked back to the landing and handed it to his father.

"Ah, yes. There it is. Here you go, gentlemen. We look forward to its return." Karel casually handed it to the officer.

"Thank you, Herr Munk, for being so cooperative. Good day," the officer replied, clicking his heels together. The officer turned abruptly, the cherished album tucked under his arm, the other man following behind. Vlada looked at the open door, wondering how anyone could be so polite and instill such terror at the same time. Karel closed the door and went to Hermina where she sat, motionless, putting his arm around her.

"Why, Tati? How did they know about it?" Vlada knew the answer before he finished the question. There was only one person who could have known about the collection.

"I'm sorry, Vlada. There is no honor now," Karel shook his head. The former Czech Legionnaire whom his father had supported out of the kindness of his heart had thrown away the comrade code of conduct to ingratiate himself with the Nazis.

Vlada could not let the incident of the stamp collection go unchallenged. It gnawed at him; it was one of the few tangible things he and his father shared, and he wanted it back. He could think of nothing else for days. One afternoon, he left the flat without telling Hermina where he was going. He walked to the post office, climbed the stairs to the second floor and strode into the Gestapo office with his head held high. "I was told my stamp collection would be returned if its value was under the allowable amount. I know that to be the case, so I have come to pick it up."

The officer at the desk looked at Vlada for a moment, momentarily shocked at his forceful demeanor. Vlada watched as the man's face changed, his lip curled, his mouth twisting into a sneer. The officer started to laugh. He turned to another young officer who sat at a desk behind him, typing feverishly. "Did you hear that, Kurt? This Jew wants his stamp collection back." The man named Kurt looked at Vlada. Vlada saw a flash of sympathy in the man's eyes, then, a dark shadow fell over his face, turning it to stone and he too began laughing.

A phone rang somewhere in the office. The shrill sound startled Vlada. He turned and ran down the stairs, pushing past an older couple on their way into the building. He ran down the street until he could not run anymore. A grey truck rumbled by in the direction of the old post office, where Vlada pictured the German soldiers were still laughing at him. He leaned against a building, his chest heaving, tears of anger and humiliation running down his cheeks. He never told his parents about the trip.

In the middle of the summer, there was a flurry of activity at the flat as Vlada prepared to leave for the annual Junák scout camping trip. He carefully packed his rucksack with two weeks' worth of clothing – pajamas, swim shorts, a second scouting uniform, two books, and a flashlight – taking great pride in his membership in the national organization with over seventy thousand scouts in its contingent.

Hermina fussed with the dark brown neckerchief of the uniform. She had tied it more times than Vlada could remember. But something was different this time. His mother looked him in the eyes as she took both ends of the dark brown cloth and inserted them into the slide. She pushed the slide up past the point of comfort, pretending to choke him.

"Mami!" Vlada sputtered, playing his part, pretending he could not breathe. They both laughed like they had so many times before, but this time their laughter sounded hollow, and it trailed off.

"Let's take a photo before you go, Vlada. Karel, come here, please." Hermina summoned her husband, the official family photographer, out onto the balcony.

"Wait, Tati! My hat," said Vlada, motioning for his father to stop. His favorite part of the scouting uniform was the campaign hat, made of brown felt with deep indentations. He placed it on his head, the chin strap dangling jauntily. "Now I am officially a scout!"

Vlada ran back inside and grabbed Čigy by his leash, positioning the uncooperative mutt in front of him for the photo, knitting one hand into the dog's wiry fur, pulling him up by the leash with the other. Wearing the scout uniform filled Vlada with pride, and he held Cigy confidently, his legs planted firmly apart, shoulders back. Karel snapped the photo. Neither of them knew that both the dog and the camera would be the next possessions forbidden to them as Jews.

"This is a special summer camp, Tati. First, we are going to fish and then we are going to clean the fish, and the older boys will cook them for our dinner," Vlada rambled on in an excited state. "We will raise the tents first, of course, in case there is bad weather. And then at night, we will take shifts guarding the camp." His parents exchanged concerned looks.

"Things are different now, Vlada," said his father, referring to the Nazi occupation.

"I know, Tati," said Vlada, impatiently. "But camp may be the same."

Hermina accompanied Vlada to the bus depot, where most of the scouts had already boarded the bus that would take them to the scout jamboree in Zeliv. "Be safe, Vlada." Hermina always said, her voice husky. She swept Vlada into her arms, holding him tightly, clutching him to her bosom, and inhaled sharply.

"Let go, Mami! You're squeezing too hard!" Vlada did not want to be teased by the other boys when he got on the bus, but he also did not want to hurt her feelings by pushing her away.

Vlada recalled the first year he had gone to the summer encampment. He was nine years old. His mother could barely release him from her embrace and into the custody of the bus driver. Some of the other scouts had facial hair already, and they teased Vlada about hugging his mother. He puffed his chest out. He would prove to them he was not a baby anymore. When the bus pulled away, Vlada pretended not to see his mother waving goodbye.

Later that week, Vlada was happily surprised when his parents "accidentally" came to the same town where the scouts were making a day trip. He glanced around to see who might be watching him, and then ran to his mother, almost knocking her down when he crashed into her.

"My Vlada!" She laughed, hugging him, and kissed the top of his head as Karel looked on, smiling. Vlada breathed in deeply. His mother was wearing a familiar dress, blue seersucker with white stripes. He had missed her. After being away from home for three days, he did not want to let her go.

The bus ride to the scout camp in Zeliv in southern Bohemia took two hours. Jirka knocked Vlada's campaign hat off his head while he reached for his rucksack. "Here," Jirka said, and presented Vlada with a book. It was a scout book used to identify animal prints one might find in the forest.

"Jirka, I have been tracing the animal prints for weeks." Vlada took scraps of paper out of his rucksack proudly, marked "Bear," "Wolf," and "Pheasant," with drawings of each animal's paw print.

"Maybe we will see some wild things out in the woods this time, Vlada. Do you have a tracing in there of a German soldier?"

Vlada shot his friend a look. Vlada's parents had warned him not to talk about the occupiers in public, and here was Jirka, going one step too far.

As the bus reached camp, the boys cheered loudly, and Vlada and Jirka jockeyed for position at the window. The boys got out and marched to the encampment, and soon spied the copper turrets of the Zeliv monastery. Vlada hoped he would see Father Paul, a member of the

Premonstratensians, who lived in the monastery with other clerics. Father Paul and Vlada shared a love of books, which made Jirka a bit jealous.

The boys continued marching past the complex of buildings that made up the monastery and arrived at the campsite to find it buzzing with activity; scout leaders swung hammers, assembling the wooden bases over which the tent canvases would stretch, and older scouts stacked wood near the fire pits that would be used for cooking and later that evening, a campfire. Vlada spotted their scout leader, a tall, thin man with kind brown eyes. They were accustomed to being greeted with enthusiasm, but today he stiffly approached Vlada and Jirka, speaking in a dull, methodical tone.

"You boys are to set up over there on the end. We are taking a risk just having you here. The farmer who rents the land asked if any Jewish boys would take part this year. We cannot have the higher-ups know that we allowed you to participate. You will have to leave before the final jamboree." The speech sounded rehearsed, and awkward. "I am sure you boys understand," he added. But before either boy could reply, the scout leader turned his back to resume his hammering.

Vlada's parents had warned him things might be different this year. But the scout leader's stilted speech, informing the boys they were to leave before the final jamboree, was unexpected. Vlada and Jirka walked to the end of the row of wooden boxes, avoiding eye contact, both slightly embarrassed and disappointed, dropped their things, and quickly began raising the canvas cover as storm clouds threatened overhead.

They laced the tent shut with string at the grommets to keep the rain out. "Hey, after this is done let's race to the river and catch some fish," said Jirka, trying to sound enthusiastic. "It's a perfect day for it," Jirka continued, his shoulders falling, no longer able to hide his sadness. "We'll show them!"

A light drizzle started as they gathered their fishing poles. Vlada reached into his rucksack and pulled out the rum-soaked balls of bread which worked so well attracting the carp in Polabiny. Jirka laughed at the memory of the fish getting drunk off their bait. The tension from moments earlier dissipated, and the boys mindlessly kicked rocks as they wandered to the brook.

Darkness descended over the tents, and around the campfire the scouts' clear voices rose in unison as they sang scouting songs. The day's adventures concluded in the tent where Vlada tossed and turned, listening to Jirka's measured breathing next to him.

His parents were right. Things were different this year. There had been no summer vacation to Krkonoše with his cousin Mirek. No tram up the mountain, singing silly songs as they marched back down, no delicious meal in their favorite restaurants. No tennis club. And now this, the punishing words of the scoutmaster warning them they weren't welcome. The crackling of the campfire was the last sound Vlada heard before drifting off to sleep.

In the morning, Vlada went to the scout leader and informed him that he would like to earn the highly coveted Eagle Feather badge. Vlada had not told his parents, or even Jirka, that he was going to attempt to earn it; he wanted it to be a surprise. If the medal was indeed conferred upon him, Vlada knew exactly where he would put it: right beside his father's Czech Legion medals in the china cabinet.

Jirka sat in the tent reading the scout handbook, reviewing the badge's requirements. "'Number one: The scout must not speak for an entire day.' Already, Vlada you are done for!" Vlada did not respond, shaking his head in reply. As Vlada began his attempt at the medal, Jirka taunted him. "You'll never do it," he scoffed. "It's too hard."

The second requirement proved more challenging. Vlada was to sleep outside for the whole night. He was allowed the use of his blanket and his rucksack for a pillow. That evening the sky was clear, but the ground was slightly damp from the previous day's drizzle. One other camper slept outside that night, another boy desiring the Eagle Feather badge. The other boy was older, and he ignored Vlada's wave, an attempt at solidarity in pursuit of a common objective. When Vlada finally fell asleep, it was fitful.

Morning broke, a light dew covering the grass, dampening the blankets. A fire crackled in the pit. Vlada stretched. He had completed two out of the three conditions. Today was the final challenge. No food must pass through his lips the entire day. When that was done, he would be awarded the most prestigious of badges.

"I am impressed, Vlada," Jirka looked at his friend, shaking his head in surprise. "I think you might be able to do this after all."

That evening, the campers sat around the fire and ate sweets, a gift from the monks at the monastery. Vlada watched as his fellow scouts ate, envying every bite. His mouth watered and his belly ached with hunger pangs. Finally, he could stand it no longer. He reached his hand into the box of sweets and pulled out a piece of shortbread, popping it in his mouth. The minute he bit down, he groaned. He had failed. Failed himself and failed to bring home something that would have made his parents proud.

The following morning, Father Paul approached the encampment from the monastery, the starched white robes of his habit standing out against the backdrop of trees, the wide belt around his waist blowing behind him in the breeze. The cleric was greeted by the scouts shouting his name, and he found himself quickly engulfed in a swarm of brown uniforms, everyone vying for his attention.

"We went fishing, Father Paul!"

"I made the fire last night, Father Paul!"

"Father Paul, won't you stay for dinner tonight?"

The monk smiled and laughed. He was in his thirties, prematurely bald, like Vlada's father, with a round face and a ready smile. Jirka quickly found the sulking Vlada sitting cross-legged in front of the tent, to alert him of Father Paul's arrival.

Father Paul suggested a game of volleyball to the boys and when he walked out onto the field, he noticed Vlada sitting alone in his tent. He waved to Vlada, the long sleeves of his robe flapping in the summer breeze. "Why the long face, Vlada?" A volleyball net had been set up in an open field, and Father Paul began unbuttoning his cape. Underneath his starched white habit, he wore an athletic singlet and shorts. He laughed as some of the boys' jaws dropped at his transformation from cleric to athlete.

Vlada walked over and hovered on the sidelines as the scouts formed into teams on either side of the volleyball net. Father Paul served, the leather ball made a resounding thwack against his palm, and the match began. It was a lively game, the older scouts diving, staining their uniforms with grass, and spiking the ball whenever possible, peals of laughter ringing out, the camaraderie between the scouts and a favored monk evident. The dinner bell rang, and groans rose from the boys as they said goodbye to the cleric and ran to wash before dinner. Father Paul donned his habit again, which he had carefully placed on a blanket before the match. He knotted the belt over his robes and prepared to leave.

"Come and see me later, Vlada."

After dinner, Vlada slipped off to the monastery. He had been in the Church of the Nativity of the Virgin Mary before, but its beauty amazed him every time. "It is so different from the synagogue back home," he had told Father Paul, looking up at the pristine white walls, the tall, vaulted ceilings, and iconic paintings and statuary in gilded frames. It was a peaceful retreat after the bedlam of the camp.

"Now, Vlada. Tell me, how are things?" Father Paul and Vlada walked down the center aisle of the church and turned into a large common room off the sanctuary. Alone with Father Paul in the hushed silence of the church, the skulking Vlada relaxed. He felt at ease around the Premonstrat.

"I told you about my father's medals from the Czech Legion," began Vlada. The cleric nodded. "I was foolish to hope I could bring home a medal of my own." It felt good to share his disappointment with Father Paul about his failed quest for the Eagle Feather badge. Vlada wondered if that was what confession felt like for Christians.

"Vlada, sometimes our goals are delayed a bit, for reasons we simply cannot control. I wanted to go to university, but my family did not have the money. So, I did the next best thing." Father Paul gestured at his surroundings. "I came here, where I can do what I love, work with rare books. Someday I hope to complete my education, but until then, this is an excellent compromise." Father Paul sighed, calmly folding his hands in his lap. "And Vlada, I can assure you that your parents do not need you to bring home a medal to be proud of you. These are difficult times, and you are doing well."

Vlada felt like a grown-up; Father Paul had shared something with him in confidence. He had often wondered why someone as smart as Father Paul had joined the Premonstrates, but he had been too shy to ask.

"Now, tell me Vlada," Father Paul asked, moving on to their favorite topic, "what books are you reading?"

Chapter Seven

KITTY FALL 1940-1941
DOBŘICHOVICE/PROTECTORATE OF
BOHEMIA AND MORAVIA

Kitty looked around the main room of the flat on Raisova Street, wiping her hands on her apron. Sunlight streamed through the window overlooking the small backyard. Kitty could see the morning laundry billowing in the autumn breeze on a makeshift clothesline. The sun filtered through the trees, dappling the sheets with speckled sunshine, triggering a memory of the house in Teplice. The moment seemed frozen in time: Cook standing at the stove, stirring a stew of some sort, wearing her trademark apron; Oila leaning against the kitchen table, holding a cup of hot tea, gossiping with Cook about a mutual acquaintance.

Kitty blinked and the image vanished, leaving a momentary heaviness behind. She shook her head, hoping to ward off any lingering melancholy, vigorously stirring the soup in the large pot in front of her on the stove. She lifted the spoon to her lips, blew on it, and tasted it. Not bad, considering the rations they were getting these days. There was no meat in the soup, but Kitty had made stock from the last piece of brisket, boiling it to impart the faintest hint of it into the water for the barley and root vegetable medley. Cook would be proud of her. Oila would be, too. She wondered what they were doing right now, both having returned home to Austria.

It had been almost three years since the Löwis fled the villa on Masaryk Street in the middle of the night, escaping the pogrom and evil acts perpetrated that night by men who had once been their neighbors. Kitty had left behind her beloved Pavla and the only home she had ever known. The months of uncertainty left Kitty feeling dizzy. She felt like a yo-yo, pushed and pulled repeatedly between her grandmother and grandfather's apartments in Prague, and Elsa's parents' home in Dobřichovice.

The offer from Bettina's cousin of the flat on Raisova Street had been the family's only option, a safe, but seemingly temporary waystation in uncertain times. Kitty recalled the bumpy first weeks and months there. Karel had arrived at the small flat with items he had salvaged from the villa in Teplice – bedding, a few dishes and cooking utensils and the Blaupunkt radio. Kitty would happily have done without the last item. The radio had started out as a fascinating addition to the household, and Kitty treasured the early moments she shared with her father in the parlor back in Teplice, sitting on the carpet at his feet, listening to story programs together, the little light blinking inside, connecting them to the wide world outside the small town. The memories turned frightening after that; she remembered her father's first heart attack, the way he had gripped his arm and sunk to the floor, directly linked to the news emanating out of the once benign appliance.

In the first few days after their arrival at the small house, Kitty watched her mother walk from one room to the other of their new quarters, disoriented, adrift. There were no housemaids to call on, nor could she rely on Cook. There was barely room enough for the family of four in the flat and her father had made it abundantly clear they could not afford to pay for any outside help.

Bettina was completely lost. She had never sewn a button, never cooked a meal, never ironed clothing. Kitty could hear Oila's voice in her ear: *Mach vas.* Do something. It was as if Oila's lesson to always be doing something constructive had somehow prepared Kitty for this moment.

Kitty had taken it upon herself to set up the kitchen: she placed the dishes, some of which had chipped in transport, in the cabinets with the cooking utensils. Cook's precious kitchen belongings were left behind in haste and confusion. She put away the heavy cast iron skillet, perfectly seasoned, and the stock pot with its bottom kissed by the fire of the stove, in places she knew would be handy. She conjured images of Cook's kitchen, organized and functional, and began stocking hers with the same basic items – flour, margarine, salt, potatoes – purchased with the family's food ration coupons. Bettina stepped back and watched her daughter assume control of the household, filling the void in the face of Bettina's inability to do so.

Kitty opened and closed the cupboards in the kitchen, taking a quick inventory of the foodstuffs. "Try to get some lard," Kitty instructed her mother, as Bettina prepared to go food shopping for the family, ration coupons in hand. Bettina was not resentful of Kitty's orders; rather, she felt the opposite. She was relieved that someone was running the ship, and for Kitty, it was fun managing the household. Her father told her she was an angel, and Kitty gladly accepted the halo. That was in May of 1939. Kitty was ten years old.

In the fall of that first year in Dobřichovice, Bettina made an announcement. "Kitty, you are going to return to school." The news was met with mixed enthusiasm: Karel smiled, pleased at Bettina's disclosure. But Kitty was indignant.

"Who will cook supper and keep the house clean?" Kitty's question was rhetorical. She had made herself indispensable, confidently managing the household's daily chores and affairs. Not to mention, Kitty and school had a checkered history. From the year she had missed with appendicitis to the German boys throwing rocks, there were few moments of enjoyment in her short educational career.

"We will make do, Kitty," Karel replied. "You have been out of school for over a year. This is good news."

The school in Dobřichovice had been requisitioned by the German army after the occupation. A Nazi flag flew from the flagpole schoolchildren had gathered around just the previous year. Kitty walked with Hanuš to their new school following instructions Bettina had given them. The directions ended in front of a tavern.

"This is it," said Hanuš. He walked inside, Kitty following behind. The tavern smelled of beer and sausage, prompting Kitty's stomach to growl. In a far corner of the tavern, a man sat surrounded by a few children around Hanuš's age.

"Welcome," the man greeted Kitty and Hanuš. He had a beard and was dressed in a dark shirt and pants, a small brimless hat perched on the back of his head. The man scanned the siblings' faces, and a look of understanding spread across his face. He smiled.

"You were expecting school? This is *schule*," the man chuckled under his breath. "I guess your mother did not tell you that part. I am Mr. Abrams. Why don't you both take a seat?"

Kitty and Hanuš looked at each other. A young girl with dark, deepset eyes made room for Kitty on a bench, and Kitty sat down beside her. "*Schule*," Mr. Abrams explained, "is a reference to the synagogue as a place of learning. But going to the synagogue is not possible since that is yet another building the Germans have commandeered for their purposes." He stopped for a moment, glancing around the room, regretting his choice of words. "There are several other schools of this kind, and we operate under one principal. The tavern owner has kindly agreed to allow lessons to be taught here for a small group of students. This 'class' meets weekly; I give you assignments and you complete them at home. Understood?" Kitty and Hanuš nodded, and Mr. Abrams launched into the first lesson.

Mr. Abrams was strict, but kind. Kitty learned to arrive at the tavern with every assignment completed. She liked the life lessons best: Never shy away from conflict. Never seek publicity for what you do. Love accepts all of someone's traits, good and bad. Kitty had to rely on the last lesson a lot. She did not tell Mr. Abrams that they reminded her of things she had learned from Oila.

The work was challenging; sometimes Mr. Abrams used Hebrew words: *Machloket, Minhag* and *chavruta,* which meant learning partner. Otto would have been her learning partner, Kitty was sure of it. She swore Mr. Abrams spoke in a lower voice when he recited the Hebrew words, but Hanuš disagreed. Kitty accepted his objection; it was acceptable behavior according to the life lessons. Kitty had never known school to be this difficult or interesting.

In the spring of 1940, Mr. Abrams informed Kitty that she had completed the sixth grade. "Well done, Kitty," he said, smiling and handing her the report card with her scores in each subject for the year. "See you in the fall."

Kitty rushed back to Raisova Street, gripping the report card in her sweaty hand. Karel sat in a chair in the main room of the house, and Kitty eagerly handed her father the envelope without looking at it first.

Karel removed the card from the envelope, slowly scanning it up and down, the corners of his mouth edging upward. "This is excellent, Kitty," he looked at her, shaking his head and watching her closely. "This deserves a reward." He stood and went into the bedroom, returning a moment later with a coin. He dropped it into Kitty's palm, closing her fingers around it. "Shhh," he winked conspiratorially. "It will be our secret." Kitty hugged her father tightly, and grinned.

Kitty hummed happily in the kitchen that summer, resuming control of the household. She tried to recreate Cook's favorite family recipes, like spaetzle and goulash, embracing the challenges wrought by ration coupons and shortages. She measured flour for biscuits, adding mashed potatoes to the mixture when flour was in short supply. One afternoon, Bettina returned from waiting for hours in the food queue, sweating and angry. "They ran out of meat right before I had my turn," Bettina complained.

Kitty looked at her mother, wearing a plain dress with practical walking shoes, dabbing the sweat from her brow with a handkerchief. There was a time when the sight of her mother like this might have filled Kitty with a perverse pleasure, but that time had passed. They had not grown close since the move from Teplice, but they had come to an unspoken understanding, a slightly begrudging mutual appreciation. Her mother routinely expressed her gratitude to her daughter for managing the household, and Kitty appreciated the freedom Bettina gave her to make decisions like a grownup.

"It's okay," Kitty replied. "I can make do."

As the end of the summer of 1940 approached, the principal of the school came to the house on Raisova Street. He stood in the doorway, his hat in his hands, his brow furrowed. "I have information, Karel, that

I feel I must pass along. May I come in?" He looked around nervously and stepped inside the house. "I have been instructed to allow the Jewish students to attend the first day of classes next month and then I am to send them home in shame," he hung his head. "From this fall forward, Jewish students will be expelled from all schools. Please just keep your children at home so they don't have to experience this indignity." The principal continued talking, but Kitty had stopped listening.

The *schule* had been her best, most favorite year of school ever. Kitty had been so proud of herself, completing the challenging lessons on time and receiving excellent grades from Mr. Abrams. And then there was the bonus of her father's pride and the secret reward. Kitty thought she and school had reached an agreement, that they were now on good terms. But her comfort and success at school had been too good to be true. The principal, however, offered Karel a consolation prize, that he would help Kitty with lessons should her parents choose to continue her education at home. It was an offer that would put him at great risk of retribution with the Germans.

Karel was quiet for a moment. He avoided Kitty's gaze. "Thank you for your kind offer. We could never ask you to jeopardize yourself in that way," Karel continued. "If it is math, I could help her myself." Turning away from the men, Kitty walked to the kitchen.

That winter, thick flakes swirled outside the window of the flat on Raisova Street, accumulating on the street and the front yard, causing panic to well up inside Kitty. She had always been entranced by the beauty of falling snow, but now, because of the Nazis, she had come to look upon each glistening snowflake with dread.

Since the occupation, Jews were expected to shovel the streets after every snowstorm, and Kitty braced herself for the inevitable knock on the door. The Germans sent Czech guards to each house, ordering the Jewish families out into the street with whatever implements they had at their disposal; no one was discharged from the task, no matter what their age or health conditions.

It was not uncommon to see young and old alike struggling with shovels full of heavy snow and ice in the early morning hours. Jews found idle were reprimanded and threatened with reduced food ration coupons or deportation.

Kitty looked at her father, dozing in a chair in the main room, breathing deeply, oblivious to the fact that the Germans didn't give a moment's thought to his health. Not long after Kitty's education ended, Karel suffered his second heart attack. The family was sitting down for supper and Bettina was complimenting Kitty on the stew she had made.

"I don't know how you do it, Kitty," her mother said. "Making stew out of thin air." The ration coupons seemed to afford them less and less every week yet still somehow, Kitty managed to create something out of nothing. Kitty was proud of herself for her ingenuity in the kitchen. She was just about to explain how she had thickened the stew with mashed potatoes when her father interrupted.

Karel shook his head. "She should be in school, not in the kitchen," he exclaimed, a flush of splotchy color spreading over his face and neck. He was agitated more frequently of late, and the same topics were the source each time: Kitty's education or current lack thereof and the endless Nazi decrees, including the confiscation of the radio, that impacted the lives of Jews in the Protectorate almost daily.

"Karel, calm yourself," said Bettina, as she stood up. Karel clutched his arm and began to slide down in the wooden chair; Bettina guided him slowly to the floor. Kitty ran to her father's side. His eyes were closed tightly, his face grimacing in pain.

"Can't we do something?" she cried, looking at Bettina. Bettina shook her head.

"Hanuš, help me get him into the bed," Bettina instructed. "All we can do is make him comfortable. There is no medicine and no doctor who will see him." Hanuš and Bettina lifted Karel gently to his feet, each gripping his elbow as he shuffled, his breathing shallow, to the bedroom.

Kitty returned to the table, great sobs shaking her shoulders, inhaling in jagged gulps. When Karel was settled in the bedroom, Bettina came back out to find Kitty, her face tearstained and crestfallen.

"It's my fault," Kitty cried, another wave of sobs washing over her.

"Kitty, that is not true," Bettina said, comfortingly. "Your father is not a well man and the conditions under which we are living are challenging for those in the best of health." Kitty looked at the half-eaten dinner on the table, moments earlier a source of pride, now a reminder of her father's tenuous health. She picked up the bowls and carried them into the kitchen.

Karel had been slow to recover from the second heart attack, spending more and more time in bed. When he did rise, he was dizzy and unstable on his feet. He was in no way capable of lifting a shovel full of snow. Shouting could be heard in the streets outside as the Czech police came closer to the house. Kitty stiffened at the sound.

"Papa cannot shovel, Hanuš. His heart cannot take it. What are we to do?" Kitty pleaded with her brother to come up with a plan.

"We will get him out into the street," Hanuš instructed. "We will form a circle around him. Even though he is a bit taller, his body will be hidden. He must walk for as long as it takes us to finish our section." They were taking a chance, putting their father's health and the family's credibility at risk. But it was worth a try.

Kitty looked at her brother with admiration, smiling slightly. The plan reminded Kitty of the way the older boys had protected her and Agata from the stone-throwing German youth on the way to school in another town, a lifetime ago. It seemed that every day was spent trying to find ways to protect someone in the family from the latest Nazi decree.

In the summer of 1941, not long after Kitty turned thirteen, she became a mercenary, engaging in underground activity. It seemed a normal extension of her responsibilities.

On a dazzling summer day Kitty stepped out the back door to check the clothes drying on the clothesline. The air smelled of honeysuckle and Kitty could almost imagine that the world was not at war. She was walking back up the simple wooden stairs when something caught her eye. There, under a budding shrub, was a small package wrapped in brown paper. Kitty looked around, unsure of how it had arrived there, suspicious of its origin. She picked it up and ran up the stairs into the house.

Karel sat in his chair in the main room and Kitty approached her father, holding out the package. Before she could speak, her father took it from her hand.

"Where did you find this?" Karel spoke in a low voice, so Kitty responded in a similar fashion.

"By the back door," she whispered. Karel unwrapped the brown paper, the newspaper's headline revealing an anti-German sentiment that shocked Kitty. Her eyes grew wide.

Karel cleared his throat and reached for his daughter's hand. "Kitty, let's keep this between us." Her father still spoke in a whisper, even though no one was nearby. Kitty nodded. She loved secrets and considered herself very good at keeping them. "I may have to ask you a favor, Kitty. I would do it myself, but I am not well, so the task may fall to you."

Kitty was even more intrigued now and her ears perked up at her father's unusual request. Hanuš walked in the room at that moment and Kitty expected her father to hide the newspaper, but he left it in plain sight. Hanuš looked at Kitty sternly.

"Kitty, you mustn't tell anyone," Hanuš cautioned Kitty. He shook his head, acting very grown-up, and walked across the room, taking the paper from his father. He unfolded it and began reading the front page. Kitty was disappointed and she smiled bitterly. Of course, Hanuš knew already.

"When you are done, wrap it up and give the package to Kitty," her father instructed. "She will attract less suspicion than you, Hanuš." Hanuš nodded. Kitty went into the kitchen and started chopping potatoes. She loved this game of cat and mouse and could not wait for further instructions on her role.

Hanuš found Kitty in the kitchen. The newspaper had been returned to its original condition, wrapped in brown paper the same way Kitty had found it. Hanuš handed her the package.

"Grab a jacket, put it on, and tuck this inside so it is well hidden," Hanuš told her, looking Kitty directly in the eye. "Run across the street to the neighbor's house and knock on the door. Give him the package and come directly home. Do you understand?"

Kitty grabbed a sweater from the hooks near the front door, tucked the package inside it under her arm and walked out the front door. She stood on the stoop, scanning the street. She was not scared, rather she felt a strength welling up with her to protect her family's ability to obtain the truth, whatever form it took. Up the block she saw a man walking his dog. She determined he was not a threat and walked confidently to the house on the other side of the street.

You must act like you are supposed to be here, thought Kitty. She knocked boldly on the door, her heart pounding inside her chest. Seconds passed and that was all she needed for doubt to creep in. She brushed it away. There was a resistance happening and there were people that needed to know the Nazis movements. She was acting on her family's behalf and that gave her strength and confidence. But a minute had passed, and she shifted from one foot to the other. What if the second drop off had been compromised. Should she start to back away?

She was about to knock again when the door opened. The face that appeared was tense, and the man in the doorway eyed Kitty suspiciously. He reached out his hand for the package and, without a word being spoken, took the package and closed the door.

This was Kitty's first underground activity, her first antigovernment act. Kitty stood on the front stoop of the house, catching her breath. She felt exhilarated, wondering, hoping she might go underground again.

Chapter Eight

VLADA 1941-1942
PARDUBICE, PROTECTORATE OF
BOHEMIA AND MORAVIA

Vlada boarded the train bound for Přelouč at seven every morning for his shift at the sugar beet refinery. The director, Dr. Vocu, was a chemist and a friend of Karel's. The two men had entered a barter, a condition of Vlada's employment: each day Vlada boarded the train carrying a demijohn filled with alcohol from the distillery in exchange for sugar from the refinery; sugar was the more precious of the two, having become impossible to obtain under Nazi rationing.

It seemed a fair deal except that each morning every train car was full of German soldiers on their way to work, passing the time playing cards and talking. Vlada's private German lessons in the Krkonoše might have ruined his summer vacation, but they were paying off now. Vlada understood every word the soldiers said.

Untermenschen. Subhuman. *Ratte.* Rat. Vlada sat barely moving in the train car, attempting to make himself invisible, hiding the demijohn of alcohol as best he could and dripping with sweat for fear the soldiers might notice the contraband in between insults aimed at the Jews.

Vlada juggled the job at the refinery with his studies. Jirka Friedmann's father, Martin, had found a way for the two boys to continue their education after the Nazis expelled all the Jews from school.

Karel had been skeptical when the idea was first presented. "There is a school for Jewish students that has remained open, Karel," Martin told him. "There is only one problem: it is five hours away by train. In Brno." It was an impossible plan to execute, but Martin had pressed the teachers at the school, and a solution revealed itself. "The boys will be assigned a student at school in Brno who will share their class notes with them," explained Martin.

Vlada and Jirka became long-distance students of the Jewish reform gymnasium in Brno that fall. A notebook arrived weekly, the boys greeting it as if it were a Christmas present. They pored over the notebook's contents, the meticulous notations covering a variety of subjects. They searched for clues as to the personality and temperament of the student who created it.

"Do you think this person is the smartest student in the class?" Jirka guessed it might be a girl.

Karel tutored the boys in French. The provisional system of educating the boys was a far cry from being in the classroom. Everyone did their best.

Karel prepared Vlada and Jirka for the upcoming midterm exams; the boys would need to travel to Brno to take the exams in person. Jews were not allowed to travel except with special permission. Karel was forced to stand, hat in hand, in front of the local Gestapo, to beseech them on his son's behalf for permission to travel for the exam. The officer made Karel wait an hour, under the guise of showing the request to a superior. When the man handed Karel the signed permission, he could feel the man's disdain.

A few days later, Vlada and Jirka boarded the train to Brno; Jirka spent his time reviewing his notes. Vlada had difficulty concentrating and he looked out the window at the passing scenery, agitated, shifting in his seat.

The train's route crossed into territory not occupied by the Germans and then wound back into the Protectorate, the Germans arranging for the train doors to lock during the transition out of occupied territory in case anyone thought they could escape. Vlada shook his head, marveling at the Nazis and their foolish rules.

In Brno, the boys struggled through the exams. The notes their counterpart had sent were no match for a flesh-and-blood professor. When they returned home, Vlada checked the post daily, awaiting the arrival of his final grades. When the envelope containing his grades finally arrived, Vlada opened it warily. It was rumored that Dr. Schoen, the rabbi in charge of the Jewish religion exam, was a harsh grader. Jirka received a *D*; Vlada received a failing grade.

"I guess I am no longer a Jew." Vlada was not joking. He seethed with anger that, given the circumstances, the rabbi had not seen fit to give Vlada a passing grade. Two months later the Nazis shut down the Jewish school in Brno before the completion of the spring semester.

It was the end of February, the twenty-seventh, to be exact. Under normal circumstances, Vlada would have been excited for his birthday. These were not normal circumstances.

"Sixteen." Hermina sighed deeply. "Where did the time go, my sweet Vlada?" Hermina smiled at the young man in front of her. It was a bittersweet milestone. The Nazis had decreed that every healthy person sixteen years or older must register to work. If work was not obtained, there would be no food ration coupons. Worse yet, any individuals who did not comply ran the risk of being sent to a hard labor camp.

A light dusting of snow had fallen overnight, sheltering the city beneath a downy blanket. Hermina handed Vlada his coat. He left the flat, dragging his feet in the fresh snow as he walked to the old post office to register for work with the German authorities. His thoughts turned to the war. The Germans were using U-boats in the Atlantic. And they were fighting on another front in Africa. He was impressed by the German forces and their accomplishments. But he was now old enough to be careful to whom he expressed his thoughts on the matter.

The wind blew, picking up the fluffy snow and sending it spinning in squalls across the quiet streets. He walked past the house of a former schoolmate. His thoughts turned to school. And girls. It was tough meeting girls now that he was no longer able to attend classes.

Isolation had prompted a handful of Jewish families from the synagogue to meet in various apartments over the winter. Beleaguered and anxious, the families sought comfort in friendly faces and exchanged news of the world outside Pardubice. One afternoon, Vlada reluctantly accompanied his parents to the well-appointed flat of a lawyer and his family. Vlada was pleasantly surprised to see a beautiful girl there. Nora Kafkova was younger than Vlada by two years.

"Don't worry," Jirka told him. "She already has a crush on you."

Thoughts of Nora kept Vlada's mind pleasantly occupied as he walked to the post office. He loved that even in winter she wore thin, cap-sleeved shirts. If he stood to one side of her, he could sometimes catch a glimpse of her tiny breasts. But the strict curfew imposed by the Nazis made it impossible to spend time alone with her.

Lost in his reverie of Nora, Vlada was shocked back to reality when he found himself standing in front of the post office. He breathed in deeply, pushed open the door to the building and stepped inside.

When he returned to the flat, Vlada handed his father the slip of paper that held instructions to Vlada's first work assignment: a barrack on the outskirts of town that once housed Czech soldiers and was now being used by the German army.

"It's disgraceful," Karel said, outraged. "The men who fought for Czech independence once lived there and now it is filled with Nazis."

Hermina removed herself from the conversation to the kitchen. In the past, cooking had helped ease her anxiety. Now, it only made things worse, the severe rationing forcing her to modify every dish she made. Each meal required her to dig deeper and deeper into a well of creativity to create something palatable. The small amount of sugar they received from the beet factory was not enough to make her family's favorite dessert, and there was rarely any meat for stew. What had once been one of her favorite tasks had become a source of bitterness.

She dropped the ladle down to the bottom of the stew pot where the paltry bits of meat and vegetables were lodged. If not for Mr. Hasek's continued generosity, the ladle would most certainly have come up empty. She spooned a portion of the stew into a jar for Vlada to take with him for lunch on his first day of work.

"This should get you through the day, Vlada." She forced a smile as she handed him the lunch sack that contained the stew and a thermos of watered-down coffee.

Vlada took the bag. "Mami, Tati," Vlada said, pausing for a moment at the door of the flat. "It is going to be okay." He said the words intending to comfort them. The knot in the pit of his stomach told him otherwise.

Vlada could see his breath as he walked briskly through the empty streets of Pardubice. He pictured himself in the peaceful quiet of Szezka, at the top of the mountain where only the bold or foolhardy began their trek. The quiet was deafening, and the journey tinged with danger in both places.

I feel like *Adam the Creator*, Vlada mused. *Adam the Creator* was the hero of Karl Capek's novel, whose hopes to destroy a bad world and replace it with a good one mistakenly leaves him as the only survivor. The sky brightened as he walked; clouds in the distance appeared as if on fire, glowing fuchsia and orange. Vlada thought of the old saying: "Red sky at night, shepherd's delight. Red sky in the morning, shepherd's warning." He hoped it was not an omen.

He reached the barrack and timidly knocked on the door, his whole body tense. Minutes passed before the door swung open and Vlada was greeted with a familiar smile.

"What took you so long, Vlada?" Jirka clapped Vlada roundly on the shoulder. "Come in! Come in! I'll show you around." Vlada, finally able to relax a bit, loudly exhaled.

Vlada followed his friend past rows of bunk beds, spread out in neat rows across the large room. At one end was a small office where a young German officer sat behind a plain metal desk. The man's green wool uniform was formfitting, and he wore a wide black leather belt cinched tightly at his waist. Vlada did not recognize the rank indicated by his epaulets but guessed lieutenant. The man's face was thin, his forehead topped with a prominent widow's peak.

"Lieutenant Weber. This is Vlada Munk," Jirka spoke in German.

Vlada could not recall hearing his friend speak in such a formal tone.

"Herr Munk," the man replied. "Follow me." They walked in silence behind the lieutenant, Jirka making faces at Vlada, then down a flight of stairs to the boiler room where a large coal-burning furnace took up one corner. It clanked and moaned, the metal expanding and contracting as the fire burned inside. Metal doors that led to the outside were used for the delivery of coal, the pile at the base of the coal chute as big as the one in the factory yard.

"I will demonstrate how to properly shovel the coal," Weber said. "If you follow my instructions, you will remain free from injury." The two boys looked at each other. Weber grabbed one of two shovels leaning against the wall and planted his feet shoulder width apart, his left shoulder perpendicular to the furnace. He shifted his weight onto his back foot, knees bent, and drove the shovel into the pile of coal. Rocking forward onto his front foot, he fed the black rocks into the open mouth of the furnace.

"Okay? Now it is your turn." Weber handed the shovel to Vlada, who took it awkwardly. He planted his feet like the officer had demonstrated, leaning back on his right leg, and scooped up the coal. Then he lunged forward onto his left leg, propelling the coal off the shovel and into the furnace. When Weber did not respond, Vlada did it again. Sweat began to drip down Vlada's face from the exertion and the heat pouring out of the furnace.

"Excellent! You and Herr Friedman will work in shifts," Weber said. With that, he walked away and left them alone in the basement.

Jirka picked up the other shovel. "He's not such a bad guy," said Jirka, "for a German." He bowed to Vlada, gesturing to the pile of coal. "After you."

The two friends spent the rest of the winter shoveling coal in the manner Weber had taught them. Some days, Weber lingered in the basement, a German among Jews. He desired their company, their easy laughter, but he was their overseer, duty-bound to stay removed, remote. So the only thing the boys felt in his presence was the intensity of his loneliness.

"The look on Weber's face today," Jirka shook his head as he and Vlada walked home. "It reminds me of being in the second class when we wanted the older boys to play with us."

"He is an intruder, an invader," Vlada said firmly. "He comes across as a gentleman, but he is a Nazi, Jirka. He is not our friend." When the weather warmed the boys were assigned to sweep and clean the barrack, a welcome respite from ending each day covered in coal dust.

On a warm summer Sunday in June, the news that the German army had launched a surprise attack against the Soviet Union, its ally in the war against Poland, quickly spread. Vlada was outraged.

"Hitler has violated all codes of ethical combat," Vlada spoke under his breath to Jirka. "We already knew he was evil but now he is a traitor."

"Keep your voice down, Vlada," Jirka cautioned. "We are not among friends." The easy manner they had with their German manager quickly vanished. They found Weber guilty by association.

The awkwardness between Vlada, Jirka, and Weber was compounded in the fall when Hitler appointed Reinhard Heydrich as Deputy Reich Protector of the Protectorate. Heydrich's first act as Reich Protector was to decree that all Jews over the age of six were to be publicly marked with the yellow star of David.

Vlada and Jirka arrived at the barrack, the presence of the yellow stars on their jackets prompting a perceptible shift; Weber did not meet their gaze. The divide between oppressor and captive had grown too wide.

News spread in the town that František Černý, the manager of Jiskra, a cooperative of machinists and tool makers, had received a contract to produce radio receivers, and approval from the Germans to hire Jews as cheap labor once a separate barrack was completed to house them.

"Jirka is going to try to get me a job wiring radio receivers once Černý's barrack is completed," Vlada reported to his parents. Hermina let out an audible gasp of relief. "Or should I stay and work for the Germans a little longer?" They laughed together, a rare moment of levity in increasingly tense times.

The Černý radio cooperative was housed in a collection of barracks across the bridge on the corner of Národních Hrdinů Street. Vlada stood outside the entrance on his first day. The building was brand new, Černý having constructed the new barrack to segregate the lower-paid Jewish workers from their non-Jewish counterparts.

A man greeted Vlada, introducing himself as Jakub. Jakub wore a jacket, white shirt, and a tie; a yellow star was sewn over the pocket of his jacket. Vlada's shoulders relaxed. He much preferred working for someone wearing the yellow star than someone with the lightning bolts of the German SS on their collar.

"Good morning, Vlada," said Jakub. "Let me show you where you will be working." Jakub led the way and Vlada followed, taking in his surroundings as he walked. The inside of the barrack was one large, open workroom with high ceilings and large wooden beams. A few offices occupied one corner.

They walked the length of the assembly line, passing a section where blue flames glowed from the acetylene torches workers used to attach pieces to the circuit boards. Vlada recognized the smell of the molten solder from his days helping his father in the laboratory at the distillery. He was surprised to see almost as many young women as there were men working the line. The women wore aprons to protect their dresses from grease and the slivers of metal used for soldering.

They stopped in front of a work bench at the end of the assembly line. "You will perform the final stage in the process here: tuning the radios. Mr. Černý will be here in a moment to show you the correct procedure. Have a seat."

Vlada sat on a stool at the end of the tuning table. An older man nodded a greeting and went back to what he was doing. Vlada looked around, certain the Jews at Černý's factory were being paid less than their non-Jewish counterparts. But the fact that no Germans were breathing down his neck made the cut in pay worthwhile. And there were girls here.

A few minutes later, Černý arrived. He was a short man with a thick shock of dark hair and a mustache. "Welcome. Have you ever done this type of work before?" Vlada shook his head. "All right, then. Let me show you how it's done." Černý tucked his tie into his shirt halfway down between two buttons and sat on the bench in front of the receiver. "Watch closely," he said. He moved the dial, the machine humming and scratching until it hit upon a clear signal. "There. When you find this spot on the dial, you've got it."

The work was easy but boring. Within weeks Vlada realized that he could tune a finished radio receiver to a BBC news broadcast in Czech from his workstation. It was a crime punishable by jail or sentencing to a labor camp, and his palms were damp with sweat as he turned the radio dial. But it was worth the risk. No one had kept a radio after the ban; it was too risky. Everything his father heard lately about the outside world was unsubstantiated gossip. Vlada wanted to hear the truth. Unfortunately, the news was not good. The Germans were winning the war.

One cold December afternoon, Vlada glanced at the clock at the far end of the room and stopped what he was doing. He spun the receiver of the radio on his bench, tuning in just in time to hear the theme song from Beethoven's Ninth Symphony, signaling the beginning of the BBC broadcast. A handful of other workers on the assembly line heard the music. They stopped what they were doing and gathered around the radio at Vlada's workstation.

"Lukas! Anna! Stand guard." Vlada's partner in crime, Jirka, instructed his friends to stay by the windows and give a warning sign if they saw someone approaching. A hush fell over the small group.

"December 11, 1941," the announcer's voice crackled over the radio. "The United States has declared war on Germany and Japan." A loud murmur erupted from the group.

"Did he say what I think he just said?"

"Should we celebrate?"

"What does it mean?"

"Shhh!" One of the girls cautioned over the din. When the news broadcast ended, Černý appeared. He was aware of the group's clandestine activities and he chose to look the other way at great risk to himself. A simple denunciation and the Gestapo would descend upon him. The look on his face made it clear that he was similarly shocked by what they had just heard.

"All right, now. Please make sure everything is in order and that all radios are tuned to the proper domestic wavelengths," he instructed. The young workers filed out of the building, whispering amongst themselves.

Vlada ran all the way home in the fading evening light. The streets of Pardubice were alive with activity, people standing on street corners talking animatedly and car headlights moving swiftly in all directions. The news that the United States had entered the war arrived home before Vlada did, along with news of a more personal nature, none of it good.

Vlada found his parents seated at the kitchen table. A long thin candle burned in the center, Hermina's face grim in the flickering light. His mother sat staring straight ahead, her breathing shallow, shoulders heaving up and down as if she might cry at any time. Vlada wondered how long they had been sitting there.

"Mami? Tati? What is it? Is it about the Americans and the war?" Vlada asked.

"Sit down, Vlada" his father spoke quietly. He breathed in deeply and continued. "Your cousin, Hana, and her husband, Leo, have been sent to that resettlement camp, the one in Terezin. They were put on a train yesterday." Hermina held the crumpled letter from her sister, Kamila, in her hand, refusing to part with it. Vlada sat down. Just weeks before Karel had received word that his sister, Rudolfina, and her husband, had been forcibly put on a train to Minsk.

"I thought you said the camp was for German Jews, Tati?" Vlada said, confused. "Why are they sending Czech Jews there?"

"Don't you see? They can do whatever they want," cried Hermina. "Our family is disappearing and there is nothing we can do about it."

Each new year had always brought such promise, yet here they were just weeks into 1942 and the good moments were impossible to identify, if they existed at all, as the moments of darkness kept piling up and overshadowing them.

A letter arrived from Babicka Emilie bringing more bad news: Hermina's sister, Ida, and her family, were the latest deportees to Terezin. Ida had divorced her husband Rudolf, the good-for-nothing mentioned in her mother's diary, and married a man named Arthur. In a strange twist of fate, Rudolf, their daughter Marie, and Marie's husband, were instructed to board a train to Terezin on January 18, 1942. Eight days later, Ida, her second husband, Arthur, and daughter, Jindriska, were forced aboard another train to the same location. Ida had another companion on the train to the camp: her father, Grandfather Adolf. He was eighty-five years old.

"Why is this happening?" his mother lamented. Vlada and his father looked at each other. The image of Grandfather Adolf boarding a train at his age was worrisome for the whole family, and Terezin was a mystery, an enigma.

"We have no reason to worry unnecessarily," Karel cautioned.

Hermina greeted each delivery of the post and each knock at the door with dread. A week before Vlada's seventeenth birthday in February, a letter arrived from Hermina's sister, Anna. His mother refused to open it, as if doing so would ward off more bad news. Karel took the envelope gently from her hands and read it aloud. It was as they suspected. Anna and her husband, Robert Eisner, along with their children, Vera and Mirek were being deported. The Eisners were going to Terezin.

Vlada's first thought was for his beautiful cousin, Vera, the one on whom he had a wicked schoolboy crush. Vera had converted to Catholicism the previous year, an act that Vlada questioned. Vlada's thoughts then turned to Vera's brother, Mirek. "Maybe Mirek will write, Tati." His father looked unconvinced.

Hermina spent more and more time alone in the pánsky room. The maid had left long ago, and Hermina grew accustomed to carrying out the bulk of the household chores. At first, she mended clothing or the occasional bed sheet, but as the winter wore on, she spent more time in the room sitting idle. Vlada often came upon her staring out the window onto the street outside.

In March, all communication regarding Aunt Rudolfina's whereabouts dried up completely. One evening not long after, Karel pulled Vlada aside. He followed his father down the stairs and out to the factory yard. It was almost dark. Karel grabbed two large burlap bags and a shovel from a hiding place near the train car. He handed one of the bags to his son. "Hold this open, Vlada." Vlada did as he was told, watching his father stoop in the semidarkness to fill the shovel with coal, then struggle to deposit the overloaded blade of coal into the bag.

"Tati," Vlada said. "Allow me." He took the shovel from his father, and they traded places. Using the shoveling method he had learned from Lieutenant Weber, Vlada filled the first bag with ease. Karel looked on, shaking his head, impressed with Vlada's skill with the shovel. When the second bag was full, the two men lugged the bags a few short blocks under cover of night to the home of Karel's friend who lived nearby.

The man greeted them, motioning them to quickly descend the cement steps down to a low-ceilinged basement. Vlada emptied the contents of the bags onto an existing pile of coal while Karel spoke in low tones with his friend. Clouds of coal dust billowed up into Vlada's face. As weeks passed, the pile of coal in the basement grew while the pile in the factory yard appeared unchanged. At the end of each evening, Vlada was covered in gritty black film; he felt like a chimney sweep.

"This is just in case, Vlada," his father said to him one evening on the way home from dropping off two more bags of coal.

"Just in case of what?" Vlada wondered — but dared not ask.

Amidst the uncertainty and fear of deportations, Vlada buried himself in a predictable routine. Work. Friends. Home before curfew.

A core group of Černý's Jewish factory workers continued to gather around Vlada's radio at the appointed time. The latest news from the BBC reported the German Luftwaffe were bombing provincial towns in England, the Royal Air Force (RAF) responding by bombing locations in northern Germany. Each RAF victory filled Vlada with excitement. One afternoon he caught one of the girls, Vera, laughing at his enthusiasm.

"You certainly are rooting for the RAF," Vera said, her voice was lovely and lilting. Her dark brown hair was long and parted in the middle. She had full eyebrows and her brown eyes shone when she laughed. When it rained, she covered her head with a scarf, making her look even more charming. She was a year older than Vlada. Vlada completely forgot about Nora.

One particularly warm spring day, a few of the factory workers went for a swim in the Labe River after work. The young people ran down to the banks of the river. Following a dare, the boys stripped behind a large hedge. They left their clothes on the riverbank and splashed headlong naked into the cool running stream. The girls, including Vera, undressed cautiously behind a stand of trees.

"Turn around," one of the girls shouted to the boys splashing in the water. "We are coming in!" The boys obediently turned their backs to the shore. They could hear the squeals of laughter as the girls ran the short length of grass to the river's edge and ran in, splashing in the cool water. Vlada turned around to find all the girls submerged up to their necks. When Vlada swam close to Vera, she splashed at him, keeping him at bay.

The air began to cool. One by one the swimmers exited the water and ran up the shore. Dripping wet and shivering, Vlada dashed up the hill to where he had left his clothes and quickly put them on. Up the hill he caught sight of Vera on her hands and knees, frantically patting down the grass behind a stand of trees.

Vlada walked up to her. "What is it? What's wrong?" Tears spilled onto her cheeks. She lowered her eyes to hide that she was crying. When she stood up her dilemma became embarrassingly clear.

She had thrown her dress on over her still wet body, and she wore nothing underneath.

"Someone has stolen my underwear!" Vera cried.

Vlada began searching the grass behind the trees for any sign of her undergarments. "This must be a prank."

"None of our friends would do such a thing," Vera cried. "Someone was watching and did this on purpose!" She was mortified – beautiful and horribly embarrassed.

"Let's go to the police station. A crime has been committed and you need to report it," Vlada offered. Somewhere in this humiliating event he saw a chance to be Vera's hero. "I will go with you."

"You would do that for me?" Vera asked Vlada through her tears. Vera sat on the grass, shivering. It was getting darker. The air was growing colder, and the rest of their friends had left for home.

"Of course. Let's go, now." Vlada reached for her hand and helped her up. He saw himself as a modern-day D'Artagnan. He would get justice for Vera, and she would find a way to reward him. They walked a few blocks to the Czech police station; the air inside the building was warm and unmoving. The guard on duty had his boots up on the desk, a rickety fan blowing warm air trained on him. He stood up, looking at the unlikely duo and grinned.

"What have we here?" the guard asked, looking Vera up and down in an ungentlemanly fashion, particularly offensive for an officer of the law.

"We are here to report a crime." Vlada spoke for Vera, who had turned away from the officer.

"Hey, Yan! Tomas! Come quickly! A crime has been committed!" The man laughed, shouting toward the back of the room. Two more police officers came to the front desk. They looked at the pair of soaking wet teenagers, and one of the men began to laugh.

Vlada turned to look at Vera. Her cheeks were bright red. She had turned to face him now and he could see that the white fabric of her dress was wet in spots, making it virtually see-through. "Let's go, Vlada. Please," she pleaded under her breath.

"Let's go, Vlada – please," one of the guards imitated her. Vera stood near Vlada, hair dripping, breasts visible beneath the dress where it clung to her no matter how she tried to keep it from sticking. Vlada moved to position himself in front of her. The laughter turned to lewd snickering and Vlada felt a subtle shift in the room, his body tensing as the mood of the guards segued from amusement to thinly veiled hostility.

"Stupid Jew. Go home with your girlfriend, Casanova." Two of the guards burst into another round of laughter. Vlada felt small and foolish and angry. He grabbed Vera's hand and led her out of the station and down the front steps.

"I'm sorry, Vera," Vlada said. "Let me walk you home."

"I'll be fine, Vlada. Thank you for trying. Good night," she said as she walked away from him, her head down. They never spoke again.

CHAPTER EIGHT

Kitty stood on her tiptoes on top of the bureau in the bedroom of the flat and reached for the sewing kit that sat on a high shelf. She could not understand why Bettina insisted on putting it in such an inconvenient spot. As she was about to jump down, she saw a flash of movement out the bedroom window, in the tall grass of the yard behind the house. It was Hanuš. Kitty watched as her brother cut large swaths of the tall grass with a pair of garden trimmers, throwing the grass on top of a growing pile. She set the sewing kit down on the bed and went out the back door to investigate.

"Hanuš!" Her brother turned around quickly, a guilty look on his face.

"You mustn't tell Mama or Papa, Kitty." The look on his face was concerning, forcing Kitty to nod in complicity. Kitty had proved her mettle smuggling the communist newspaper to the neighbor, and ever since then, the siblings had been in détente.

"Now what is it? What am I not to tell them?" Kitty tried to peer over Hanuš's shoulder to see the nature of his clandestine activity.

Hanuš spoke quickly, his words tumbling out in a rush. "I am glad Heydrich is dead but now I think I might be in trouble. I refused to turn my bicycle in to the Gestapo because I would rather die than give it to them." It was a warm summer day and there was a light film of sweat on his face. "Now they are searching for the bicycle that was used by one of Heydrich's assassins and they are going to find out that I kept mine." He stepped aside, revealing the bicycle in question, half hidden now underneath the grass clippings.

Kitty was glad that Reinhard Heydrich, the evil SS Reich Protector of the Protectorate, the man responsible for branding Jews with the yellow star and a trusted comrade of the Führer, had been assassinated. But the sight of the bicycle came as a shock; she had overheard her parents talking about the search for Heydrich's assassins, one of whom had fled the scene of the attack on a bicycle.

"Oh, Hanuš." Kitty sympathized with her brother. That morning at breakfast Kitty had been pointing out the Nazis and their flawed logic. "Decree. Decree. Decree. We turned in our radios, then our cameras, then our bicycles and our pets. Now it is martial law. Why are the Germans punishing us? We didn't kill him."

"Kitty! Karel, tell her she mustn't talk like that." Her mother dabbed at the sweat on her brow with a handkerchief.

"All Czech Jews are guilty in their eyes, Kitty." Her father's voice trailed off, his shoulders slumping. He looked worn out and hopeless.

Now, Kitty looked at her brother with a mix of surprise and pride. "Well, you can't leave the bicycle there. You'll get all of us in trouble." Hanuš's face was set in grim determination. "I know that look of yours, Hanuš. Please be careful."

Every morning after Hanuš's confession, Kitty walked into the yard and kicked at the piles of grass for signs of the bicycle; each day it remained in the family's possession meant another day Hanuš, and the whole family, were at risk. On the fifth morning, the bicycle was gone.

"Finally, Hanuš." Kitty breathed a sigh of relief and sat down in the grass. She lay down on her back, smoothing her dress over her legs, looking up at the deep blue of the early summer sky, dotted here and there with wispy clouds. If Otto were here, they would tell each other what shapes they saw in the clouds. Kitty thought Otto was always the more creative one.

"Look, there," Otto would say. "The sky peeking through the clouds is in the shape of a heart." They would turn their faces to each other, the grass tickling Kitty's cheek. Pavla would jump on her, licking Kitty's face, and then Oila would call them both for breakfast.

Kitty closed her eyes. There was no sound, no Otto or Pavla or Oila. They were all gone away. Kitty rarely cried and when she did it was only for her father. Today the tears would not be held back; they came in a deluge.

Bettina saw Kitty lying on the grass wearing one of her few good dresses. "What on earth are you doing, Kitty? Come back inside."

"Yes, Mother." Kitty sat up and wiped her cheeks. She cheered herself with the thought that the bicycle was gone. Hanuš was safe and the incident was over.

"Have they nothing better to do?" Karel snapped, his face reddening as he tossed the newspaper on the table. "There is an investigation underway for a bicycle involved in the attentat on Heydrich. It seems it was sold in Teplice. The Gestapo has a description of it, and they are searching the registry to see if it was returned." He threw his hands in the air at the absurdity of it.

Kitty and Hanuš locked eyes in panic. They excused themselves from the table and Kitty motioned for Hanuš to follow her into the front room. "Where is it?" she whispered. Hanuš shifted from one foot to the other, looking at the floor, rattled by the mention of the search.

"I am not going to tell you who I gave it to. I don't want you to be involved." Hanuš stuffed his hands in his pockets defiantly.

"Is it safely hidden?" Kitty pressed him, leaning in closer and whispering loudly.

"Yes, I think so." Hanuš looked away, signaling an end to the conversation.

The following day Czech police in uniform arrived at the house. Hanuš and Kitty hid in the front room, listening through the door. "Frau Löwi, we have word that a bicycle registered in Teplice belonged to this household. It was never turned in to the Gestapo. May I ask why that is?"

Kitty looked at Hanuš. He took a deep breath and shocked Kitty by opening the door and walking toward his mother and the men.

"Hanuš?" Bettina searched her son's eyes for an explanation. Kitty held her breath.

"The bicycle was broken, Mother. I had an accident with it. I didn't want to tell you. It was damaged beyond repair. It wasn't worth anything, so I brought it to the junk yard," Hanuš explained politely. "Wasn't that the right thing to do?"

"Now you have made extra work for us, boy," one of the Czech guards said angrily. "You will have to go there and show it to us." He glared at Hanuš.

The other officer shook his head. "Let it go, Martin. He is just a kid. Thank you, Frau Löwi. We will put it in our report."

Bettina closed the front door. She turned to look at her son, her hand covering her mouth, then grabbed him and hugged him tightly. Hanuš allowed his mother a moment before pulling away.

The following morning, Bettina stood at the door to the apartment wearing her best suit. Outside the day was quickly warming, the sun casting its radiant heat on every sidewalk, building and car. She soon discovered she was overdressed. Kitty marveled at how her mother managed to show no signs of wilting. Her hat was tilted to one side, and she had added a wave to her hair. If not for the yellow star sewn over her left breast pocket, she might have been headed out for an afternoon of shopping.

With a brisk wave, Bettina announced she was off to meet the new *Oberlandrat* for foreign affairs. When she was gone, Kitty found Hanuš in his room. The incident with the Czech police had put him in a dark mood.

"What do you think is happening, Hanuš?" Kitty asked, hoping to distract him from his brush with the authorities.

"All I know is that she was summoned to the office. She makes it seem like it is a social call," said Hanuš, wryly.

Hanuš and Kitty's concern was soothed when Bettina arrived home, breathless. Kitty could not tell if her mother was terrified or elated. "We are to appear as a family tomorrow before the *Oberlandrat*."

Karel walked slowly from the front room. "What do they want with us, Bettina?" Kitty went to her father and held his hand as they all waited for Bettina to reply.

"I told the *Oberlandrat* how the Czech Police used to bang on the door at all hours to make us shovel snow and clean the streets. I told him we were forced to flee Teplice to escape the 'disturbances' and separated from the children for months. Frankly, I think he was quite shocked and irritated when he heard about the treatment I had received as an American citizen. He was most sympathetic." She removed her hat, seeming quite pleased with herself. "He could not believe I had not left for America when I had the chance." Bettina's words hung in the air, their implication impossible to ignore.

"Bettina. No one forced you to give your ticket to Willie," Karel clarified.

"Karel, you know it was not as simple as that." Bettina's tone turned bitter, she turned her back to him and removed her jacket. Kitty squeezed her father's hand, limp in hers, and damp and clammy.

She turned to face them. "Ten o'clock. Tomorrow. We shall go as a family." Everyone seemed to hold their breath for a moment; the clicking of Bettina's heels was the only sound echoing in the empty room.

Bettina paused, pinching Kitty's cheeks to put some color in them before they entered the *Oberlandrat* office. Nazi flags flew outside, directly above their heads. The building, now filled with German officers, had once been the local Czech school. The secretary at the desk had golden hair, perfectly coiffed, and her ivory silk shirt was tied with a bow at the neck. She looked first at the yellow star on their clothing and then at their faces.

"Come this way." The secretary directed them to a small room. Kitty sat down, shifting impatiently in her chair. The woman returned shortly after. "The *Oberlandrat* will see you now."

The man they had come to see had his back to them as they entered the room. He was tall, with light brown hair. When he turned to face them, Kitty was shocked to see he had such a pleasant face. One side of his uniform was thick with ribbons. A cross and two badges decorated his left pocket and gold braids hung from the epaulet on his right shoulder which draped across the right pocket, disappearing inside his jacket. His hat sat, crisp and elegant, on the desk. He was higher up in the chain of command than Bettina had let on.

"Good afternoon. I have already spoken with Frau Löwi so I will be brief." The man looked at each of them standing at attention in a line in front of him. He walked up to Bettina. Something flashed in his hand, catching Kitty's eye. Kitty gasped when she saw the man remove a knife with a long, thin blade from its sheath. He grabbed hold of the lapel of Bettina's jacket with his left hand. Kitty opened her mouth to scream.

"From now on..." The man paused and then slid the knife underneath the yellow star, ripping at the stitches that held it to Bettina's coat. "You are no longer..." He cut away another side of the star. "Jews potentially subject to deportation." With a flourish, he cut the last remaining stitches. The fabric star fell from her jacket onto the floor in front of her. "You are American citizens with temporary passports. If anyone should ask to see your papers you are to tell them that you are under the protection of the Foreign Office Police." Bettina's chest heaved in and out, but she did not speak.

Hanuš stood next to Bettina. He flinched at the cut of the first thread, staring straight ahead until the yellow star fell, too, from his tweed jacket. Karel was next, and he teetered unsteadily as the *Oberlandrat* cut off his star with surgical precision. Kitty was last. She stood, immovable, as the knife slipped the stitches. When the man was finished, he took the star and put it in her hand. "A souvenir, young lady."

The Löwi family was dismissed from the office and quickly left the building. Stepping out into the sunshine, Kitty looked down at her sweater where the star had been. She touched the spot, the color of her sweater a brighter shade of blue underneath, a faint outline left behind by the thread that had held it there. Kitty felt naked without it. They walked a block in silence, and finally Karel spoke. "That man is mad. They won't honor his fake passports. We are breaking the law right now walking in public without the yellow star, and he won't be able to save us."

"Karel. His methods are unorthodox, but we have been given a gift." Bettina walked with newfound confidence down the street toward the villa. Hanuš and Kitty slowed their pace, falling behind their parents.

"Doesn't she realize the fabric is darker where the star has been all these many months? We need to get home and change our clothes," Kitty whispered to her brother, wanting to run the rest of the way home but afraid to call attention to herself.

Within days the *Oberlandrat's* bizarre actions made sense. Hanuš came back from a trip to the grocer. Kitty met him at the door and saw that he was shaking. "You are as white as a sheet. What is it? What has happened, Hanuš?"

"I just passed the train station. All the families are being transported to Prague and from there to somewhere else. At least the Jewish families, that is. Their houses are empty." Bettina and Karel walked in as Hanuš was speaking. He looked at his mother, his voice lowered to a whisper. "Everyone is gone. They are all gone."

"I think the *Oberlandrat* may have saved us from deportation," Bettina said smugly, the situation confirming that her connection had proven valuable. Her hand reached for the spot the yellow star had occupied on her jacket and flitted away.

Kitty pulled back the curtains in the front window of the apartment. The streets looked empty, filled with an eerie stillness. "Kitty, move away from the window," Bettina snapped.

Kitty felt guilty. "We are Jews, too. Now we are imposters. How long will it be before someone finds out?"

Kitty recalled summer days playing school outdoors in Jesenice; Kitty was the teacher, and her students were Hanuš, her cousins, Otto and Frankie, and her best friend, Aja.

Aja barely took her eyes off Frankie, causing her to miss the better part of Kitty's history lesson. All the girls had a crush on Kitty's cousin Frankie, and Aja was no exception. Now that he was older, he preferred to be called by his given name, Frantisek.

"Aja, pay attention!" That day Kitty's ragtag class proved themselves to be very poor students indeed.

Kitty pulled Aja aside. "I don't understand you, Aja. I know Frankie is handsome, but he is too old for you." Kitty left out that she had overheard Frankie talking badly about his little brother Otto, his cousins, and his friends.

"They bore me to no end with their childish games," Frankie had uttered. Kitty did not feel slighted in the least, but she knew Aja would.

Besides, thought Kitty, if anyone could benefit from a little summer school, it would be Frankie. She knew it was unkind to say such things, but he had started it.

After the Nazi occupation, the Löwi's no longer traveled to Jesenice. Aunt Flora, Bettina's sister, had moved to Prague with her husband, Otto, and Frankie. It was preferable to staying in the German occupied border regions. Of course, in retrospect no one knew at the time that soon the whole of Czechoslovakia would be swallowed up by the Nazis. Flora's weekly letters kept the Löwis up to date on the family's activities. The previous fall, a letter had brought unsettling news. "Frankie has been called into the service of Lina Heydrich."

Bettina put the letter down for a moment allowing the news to sink in: her nephew was working for the wife of the new SS Reich Protector, the man who since his appointment last September had made the lives of all Czech Jews barely tolerable with a string of endless rationing, decrees, and regulations, each one more stifling than the last.

Kitty noticed the color drain from her mother's face. "Mama, you look as though you've just seen a ghost."

Bettina had heard through wartime gossip that the wife of Hitler's right-hand man had taken up residence at Panenské Břežany, a manor house outside of Prague. The castle's previous owner, Adele Bloch-Bauer, was a patron and close friend of the great artist Gustav Klimt. Bloch-Bauer had passed, and the estate, including her possessions, had been confiscated by the Nazis after the occupation, including Klimt's portrait of Bloch-Bauer, *The Lady in Gold*.

The letter continued. "Lina Heydrich thinks of herself as some new breed of royalty. She is in the process of reconstructing the lower castle and gardens using Jewish prisoners, my son Frantisek included, as laborers. She demands complete obedience. They are to look at the ground in her presence. If they look her in the eye the workers are subjected to face whippings." Flora, who had never been religious, closed her letter. "I have already said too much. Pray for him."

Hanuš had relayed the news to Kitty. "Poor Frankie." Kitty put her hands to her face. She was consumed with guilt over her unfavorable thoughts regarding her older cousin. Hanuš continued. "As Papa always says, 'Keep your friends close, and your enemies closer.'"

The summer day when Karel gathered Kitty and Hanuš in the main room of the house for a serious talk they were right to be worried. "We have no idea how far Hitler and the SS will take their retribution for the death of Heydrich. Those poor souls in Lidice. Women and children. And now the deportations. Stay inside. I beg of you. We don't want to attract attention to ourselves." He looked down at his jacket, at the spot where the yellow star had been removed during their visit to the *Oberlandrat*.

Kitty and Hanuš looked at each other. "What about Frankie, Father? Is he still working for Frau Heydrich in Prague?"

"We don't know for certain, Hanuš. Your mother has not heard from Aunt Flora in quite some time."

Kitty continued to worry about Frankie, but her dear Otto was also on her mind, and her father's, too, no doubt. But Kitty had no time to lay about.

A few months passed after Heydrich's assassination; the ghastly spate of retributions was followed by an eerie quiet. Kitty continued to oversee the household, and there was always something to do. Today she busied herself in the kitchen, seasoning the soup on the stove, and setting out the bowls for serving. A loud thud rattled the bowls where they sat on the counter.

Kitty ran to the front room to find her father collapsed on the floor, his face pale, his breath coming in deep, ragged gulps. Bettina sat slumped down over Karel, a letter lay crumpled on the rug. "What is it? Father? Mother?" Kitty shouted for Hanuš. When he did not appear, she ran to find him. She moved as if through mud, her limbs heavy as if in a dream, running to each small room, calling his name. She found him sitting on the back steps. "Come quickly. It's something awful."

When Hanuš and Kitty returned to the front room, Bettina was weeping, her face anguished and drawn. "This can't be happening," she cried. She had managed to lift Karel back into his chair; she knelt in front of him, grasping his hands in hers.

Hanuš picked the letter up from the floor and read it aloud. "...regret to inform you of the deaths of Karel Polesi, Flora Polesi, Frantisek Polesi and Otto Polesi at Riga, Latvia."

Bettina made a muffled cry. "Flora. The boys. All of them."

Karel muttered. "Otto. My Otto." Karel clutched his chest. Kitty's cousin had been like a second son to him.

"Papa your heart. You must be careful." Kitty moved to stand by him, as Karel's breathing worsened. "He is having another heart attack. Hanuš, fetch the doctor." Kitty helped her father take off his coat. She felt a pang of guilt. She was so caught up in the bicycle fiasco with Hanuš she had given no thought to Frankie. Just a few months earlier he had turned twenty-one. He was a grownup now, he could take care of himself, right? But it was wartime. Nothing was as it should be.

It was unlikely the doctor would be able to offer any help. Kitty watched as her mother got up and walked slowly out of the room. She had no ill feeling for her at that moment. Kitty could not imagine losing Hanuš, and unthinkably, Bettina had just lost her sister. Kitty comforted her father, covering him with a blanket. What they all needed was a break from fear and grief, but the only thing Kitty could offer was rest and soup.

In the days that followed, Karel slowly pieced together the events that led to the family's murder. "Frankie was fired from Frau Heydrich's estate along with all the other young Jews. She held all of them responsible for her husband's death. The thought of him working at that beautiful palace for that hateful woman!" Karel stopped, holding his head in his hands. He spoke to the room, a far-off look in his eyes. "The neighbor said that when Frantisek arrived back in Prague, the whole family was put on what they are calling the "stuttering transport" from Prague. It was called Aaw." Karel's face contorted in anguish, and he covered his face with hand, choking out his words. "The train stopped at Terezin. They held them there for two weeks. Two weeks! Then were sent North. They said no one survived." Her father let out an anguished cry.

Kitty was at a loss to declare whose grief was deepest. Her mother had lost her sister and her nephews. Her father had lost Otto, his kinder, gentler 'son.' Both of her parents were so firmly enveloped in their own sadness, there was no one to comfort Kitty in the loss of her best friend and confidante, her constant companion, the boy she had promised to marry if no proper offers were received. Her Otto. She lay in her bed at night and pictured Otto's smiling face, the two of them staring up at the clouds, the grass tickling their cheeks. Kitty cried herself to sleep, and that night, a wounded bird appeared in her dreams.

CHAPTER NINE

VLADA MAY – DECEMBER 1942
PARDUBICE, PROTECTORATE OF
BOHEMIA AND MORAVIA

After three years under occupation, Vlada had developed a keen insight into the German machinations. Just a few years earlier he had been impressed with the Nazis' tactical prowess. Now, at the age of seventeen, he could see there were chinks in the Nazi armor. They were getting sloppy and making bad decisions. Vlada hoped their desperate acts were the first signs that an end, to the occupation and the war, was a real possibility. That hope was short-lived.

In late May, the headlines of the underground newspaper had screamed the news: *Attentat!* The news that Heydrich had died of sepsis came a week later in the form of martial law. The search for the assassins became a vengeful bloodbath, with Hitler vowing to catch the perpetrators and avenge Heydrich's death. Anyone rumored to have approved of the *attentat* was to be shot immediately. Word reached Pardubice of the destruction of the village of Lidice, where a few of the residents were thought to have played a role in the assassination plot.

"It was a bloodbath," Karel's voice was hoarse as he recounted the events. "The *Sicherheitspolizei*, the Security Police, surrounded the

village, rounding up and shooting every man over fifteen years of age."
Hermina gasped. She went to Vlada and put her hand on his shoulder.
Vlada could feel her trembling. "The town was razed, the women and
children sent to separate camps." Hermina slumped into one of the
kitchen chairs. The three sat in silence, digesting the horrific news.

"Do not go outside, Vlada," his father warned. "There are
spies everywhere."

During the week Karel forged ahead with business at the factory as it
limped along amid shortages and delays caused by the war. Sunday was
the most difficult day to pretend life had any semblance of normalcy.
The coffeehouse was now off limits to Jews: there was no philately
group, and no stamp collection for that matter. Still, Vlada could not
contain his shock at his father's suggestion one Sunday. "Let's develop
some photos today, Vlada," said Karel.

"Are you sure about that, Tati?" His father typically followed the rules,
rarely coloring outside the lines. It was not Vlada's habit to question his
father, but he was doubtful that this whim to retrieve the camera from
its hiding spot and develop a roll of old film was a good idea. The Nazis
were going to lose the war. Why jeopardize the family's relative safety
over a few old photographs?

"They took our radios so no one would be informed if their offenses
were met with resistance or, worse yet, failure. They took our cameras
for fear we might record their crimes," said Hermina. "Shouldn't we
leave well enough alone Karel?" His mother spoke words Vlada had
dared not.

Hermina had pleaded with Karel to turn over the camera when
they first heard the Nazi decree to confiscate them some months back.
"Please, Karel, just give it to them." She did not want to tempt fate
with the Germans. But Karel set his chin in a grim line and refused to
surrender it.

"I don't care if I ever use the camera again," Karel said adamantly.
Vlada knew his father was acting on principle, but his small act of
defiance had caused his mother to feel scared and vulnerable.

Today, his father would not be deterred. "Prepare the bathroom and
fetch the remainder of the chemicals, Vlada." His father's tone left no
room for objection. Vlada cordoned off the bathroom with a bed sheet,

transforming it into a makeshift darkroom as they had done so many times before. His hand trembled as he reached up and swapped out the incandescent bulb for the red one that would preserve the developing images on the paper.

What had once been a hobby for father and son was now a clandestine activity, an offense punishable in ways Vlada could not begin to imagine. The excitement that had filled Vlada years ago was absent today. Lingering for a moment in the bulb's red glow, the room looked awash in blood.

Karel slowly poured the developing solution into one of the trays. "Hurry, Tati!" Vlada knew each stage of the process was carefully timed, but his anxiety got the better of him. When he was young, he could barely wait for the images to reveal themselves; every step of the process filled his childhood self with wonder.

Father and son worked in silence, the ding of the timer signaling each next step. The film sat in the developer. *Ding!* Karel applied the stop bath. *Ding!* He then applied the fixer. *Ding!* Vlada was on edge, jumping at each ding of the timer. He had a flashback to a story his father had told him about a colleague who had also shared his love of photography with his young son. One day while father and son were in the darkroom, the little boy took the measuring cup filled with milky white developer and drank it, doing irreparable damage to his esophagus. Vlada hoped the memory of the ghastly accident was not a portent of things to come.

Karel reached out in the crimson semi-darkness, putting his hand on Vlada's shoulder. Vlada could not make out his father's face, but he heard his breathing change.

"Oh, Vlada," said Karel, choking back emotion.

Memories came flooding back as the negatives floated upwards in the syrupy liquid, slowly revealing their images. Vlada holding Čigy by his leash. Vlada's bar mitzvah. Vlada in his scouting uniform on his way to the Junak. Karel on the balcony of the flat at the distillery, reading a book, looking relaxed and happy. It was a lifetime ago. Before the Nazis. Before the yellow star. Before. Vlada looked away.

It was difficult to escape the fallout from Heydrich's assassination. Early one morning, Vlada and Karel sat at the kitchen table nursing weak coffee and dry toast when they heard a knock on the door. Vlada had a flashback to the German officers who had come for the stamp collection. Karel stood up, slowly walked to the door, and opened it, while Vlada held his breath.

Karel's shoulders relaxed. "Ah. Come in, Josef," said Karel. Josef was the director of the distillery. His visits to the flat were rare. Vlada nodded a greeting and then crossed to the dining room, closing the door behind him as the men began speaking in low voices.

"I'm sorry, Karel," Vlada heard Josef say. It was followed by the click of the door to the flat as it closed behind the director. Karel opened the door to the dining room, and Vlada could tell from his father's face that it was bad news.

"What is wrong, Tati? What did he say?" asked Vlada. Hermina walked tentatively out of the pánsky room.

"The director has looked out for us," Karel began slowly, avoiding eye contact with both Hermina and Vlada. "He kept me as head chemist for as long as he could even under the German *treuhänder*." His father drew in a breath before continuing. "Now it is over. This" — he looked around the room at the flat they called home — is over. I am sorry, Hermina." Karel had lost his job, and with it, the flat. They were casualties of the *attentat*. In minutes, they had become homeless. Hermina sat down at the kitchen table, head in her hands, and absorbed the implications of the news.

"We must move. Quickly," said Karel.

"Where, Karel?" Hermina looked up, her eyes searching his. The desperation in her voice startled Vlada. "This is our home."

"Darling," he sat down at the table. He took Hermina's hands in his and explained his plan to her in a gentle voice. "I have secured living quarters for us in the event of just such a circumstance. An attic apartment in the home of a friend, across the river in Bílé Předmésti. It has two small rooms — a large kitchen with space enough for Vlada to sleep and one bedroom. There is a toilet, but we will have to bathe elsewhere."

Vlada shook his head. He was angry at himself for not realizing what those trips laden with bags of coal had meant at the time. His father was not a fool. Of course, he had planned for just such an outcome. The family would use the supply of coal they had poached from the factory yard to heat the water at the other house when they needed to wash. It was what his father meant by 'Just in case.'

"Darling, we are going to need you to help now," Karel gently lifted his wife from her seat. "We will bring with us only what we absolutely need." His father paused for a moment then added, "We should consider ourselves lucky there is a place waiting for us."

If this was luck, Vlada hated to see the alternative.

The days that followed were a blur of activity as they quickly and methodically set about emptying the flat of the family's possessions, items they had come to treasure over the years since Vlada's birth. The carpets Hermina had made by hand were rolled up. The china cabinet was relieved of Hermina's crystal collection and Karel's Legion medals. Everything that was not necessary for daily life was destined for the homes of friends and acquaintances, non-Jews, for safekeeping.

Hermina sat at the kitchen table with a piece of paper checking off each item. Rugs to the Fialas. China place settings to the Horaks. Books to the Boceks.

Karel slipped on his overcoat. "Keep an eye on your mother," his father instructed, nodding to Vlada. "I need to go to the distillery to see Josef about another matter."

Vlada watched as Hermina emptied the bookshelves in a fog, taking his favorite book, *Babicka*, down from the shelf, opening it and running her fingers across the illustrations on each page. Tears welled up in her eyes. She caught Vlada watching her, closed the book and put it in a box, wiping her face with the back of her hand.

"Until after the war, darling," she said, convincing no one. They had no room for childhood playthings where they were going.

The next day was clear, with bright blue skies and an absence of clouds. Inside the house a storm was brewing as three burly men arrived at the flat to remove the piano.

"It will be moved to the Fridrich's house down the street, darling," Karel explained. He spoke to his wife gently, her eyes barely registering comprehension.

The men climbed the stairs and followed Vlada to the pánsky room, but Hermina arrived there first. She opened the piano bench and took out a few pages of sheet music, closed the bench and placed the pages on the piano. She sat down and lifted the fallboard, allowing her fingers to hover over the keys.

"A performance, Mami? Now?" Vlada asked nervously. One of the men shot him a confused look. Vlada shook his head, shrugging his shoulders in response.

Hermina began to play. It was a lullaby Vlada remembered from childhood, the familiar, lilting melody filling the apartment. His mother closed her eyes as she often did when playing, her body swaying gently in time to the music. A few minutes later the song ended abruptly. Vlada stepped toward Hermina to help her from the bench, but she hurriedly swapped out one page of sheet music for another, plunging herself into a lively piece by Smetana.

She played as if in a feverish state, rocking and trembling, the cords in her neck visible as the music built to a crescendo. Her dark hair fell from the neat bun she had pinned behind her ears, strands falling in front of her face and eyes as she pounded on the piano keys, her arms flailing, whipping herself into an agitated state.

Vlada heard footsteps and turned to see his father running into the room just as the music became discordant. The movers stood speechless as Karel gently took his wife's hands in his, preventing her from playing. Hermina looked around, embarrassed, as if she had awakened from a dream. The moving men nudged each other, breaking out in awkward applause. Hermina stood up from the bench, leaning on Karel as he walked her out of the room. Vlada stood frozen in the doorway.

The men looked at each other and then descended upon the piano, wrapping it in heavy blankets. They pushed the piano across the flat and with great effort made their way down the flight of stairs, huffing and cursing at every step. Vlada winced as he heard the piano bump noisily down the last remaining stairs, landing at the bottom with a forceful thud.

Vlada was glad to see it go.

The morning after the piano incident, Karel stood near the front door of the flat in his raincoat. In his hand he held the sleek, Swiss-made Hermès Baby typewriter, carefully packed into its case. When Vlada was young, he loved watching his father change the ribbon out for a fresh one each time the type grew faint. He loved the clacking sound the keys made against the roller.

"Care for a walk, Vlada?" his father asked. Vlada reached for his coat and an umbrella. The route they took was familiar, the sky dampening the day with light rain. Soon they arrived at the door of Vlada's Latin tutor, Frantisek Klout. Karel knocked.

"Karel. Vlada. Come in, quickly," said Frantisek. He moved aside to let them into his small bachelor flat, closing the door quickly behind them. Karel placed the typewriter on a table.

"I am sorry, Karel. I will take good care of it and return it when this is all over. *'Luctor et emergo'* — I struggle and overcome — Vlada." He smiled weakly at Vlada.

Vlada did not need the words translated. But he wondered if they stemmed more from his teacher's love of Latin, or his penchant for Communism. Vlada cast one last look at the familiar grey typewriter before they were ushered out the door into the pouring rain.

"Vlada, today we will go the house of Jaroslav Grus," said Karel. Karel and the artist had served together in the Czech Legion. Barely a year apart in age, they had taken very different paths after the war, Grus making a name for himself as a painter while Karel studied chemistry. It seemed fitting that Grus had agreed to look after the Munk's collection of his own work during the family's move. Following his friend's instructions, Karel cut the paintings out of their frames, carefully rolling the canvases in newsprint, and placed them in bags.

Vlada and Karel crossed the bridge over the river, then veered right toward the artist's villa, Vlada enjoying the intrigue of taking side streets to stay out of the way of Czech guards or the Gestapo who could be anywhere at any time. His father did not feel the same.

"We are traveling with contraband, Vlada," Karel said, glancing about nervously. Anything of value had been confiscated by the Germans, the paintings having somehow gone unnoticed, and Karel wanted to get them to the villa on Sakarova Street without incident. Vlada wondered what was more important to his father – preserving the work of his compatriot or keeping it out of the hands of the Nazis.

They arrived in front of the painter's house; it was a large building with smooth, pale yellow stone walls topped with terracotta tiles. His father knocked and the door was opened by the painter himself. So, this is the famous Jaroslav Grus, thought Vlada, studying his father's friend. Grus's head was round and devoid of hair; unlike his father's naturally bald pate, Grus appeared to have shaved his to similar effect. He wore glasses with thick, black frames and there were dark circles under his eyes. The house smelled of oil paint and turpentine.

"Don't blame me, Karel," his friend pleaded awkwardly in the foyer of the villa. "I will be safer this way. If they search the house, they will believe I am a new wave of Czech." Karel looked at Grus, puzzled by his friend's greeting. As they moved deeper into the grand foyer, the reason for his compatriot's apology was revealed. A white marble bust of Hitler in military garb sat in the entryway. Karel was silent. Vlada watched his father hand the bags containing the paintings to his friend. The two men had once been on a train crossing Siberia, fighting side by side for the future of the Czech people. Now here they stood, one man abandoned, the other abandoning his principles.

"Come, Vlada," his father turned and walked out the front door. When they were a few blocks away, Karel broke his silence. "The Germans will never search his house," Karel said angrily as they made their way from the sumptuous villa back to the now almost empty flat on Palackeho Street. "The statue is not for them."

Months had passed since Vlada took his final look around the flat on Palackeho Street. He had stood in the doorway, saddened by what he saw: the curtain under the sink pulled to the side revealing nothing underneath, one cabinet door open, the shelves, once filled with all manner of goods and sundry, now empty.

"It is as if no one ever lived here, as if no one ever filled this place with love and warmth and laughter," his mother said. "It is as if we were never here."

The family's new quarters in the attic apartment were cramped, putting a strain on everyone. Vlada preferred to be out of the flat whenever possible, and after his parents were notified of the family's impending deportation to Terezin, Vlada became a bit careless.

Tonight, he had stayed a little too late in town. With a girl. It was past curfew as he made his way through the park that led to the apartment.

He was violating two strictly enforced rules against the Jews: crossing the park and being out after curfew.

It had been worth the risk, Vlada thought, smiling to himself. Suddenly shouts could be heard coming from the direction of the park. A man a few years Vlada's senior was running toward him. He looked familiar, but Vlada was focused on getting home, the flat coming into view up ahead.

The man shouted as he closed in on Vlada. "What are you doing out past your curfew, Jew? Don't you know it is after eight?"

Now Vlada remembered where he had seen the man; he was loitering around the Gestapo office when Vlada turned over the family's radio a while back. Vlada had heard talk of Czechs who were in league with the German officers, turning in Czech Jews, even their own friends and neighbors for minor offenses, to curry favor with the Gestapo. Like that Legionnaire 'friend' of Tati's.

"Hey, you, there! Jew! Quit daydreaming and give me your identity card. I am reporting you!" Vlada broke into a run, trying to sidestep the man, who was just a few yards in front of him now. The tip of Vlada's shoe caught the curb, sending him sprawling across the sidewalk; immediately he felt the pain of the heels of his hands scraping against the rough pavement.

No sooner had he come to a stop than the man was on top of him. "Give me your ID card, Jew! You are in for it now." The man spat out the words. Their faces were within inches of each other, so close that Vlada could see the straw-colored fuzz on his enemy's upper lip, damp with sweat as his fist hovered over Vlada's face.

Vlada reached inside his pocket and handed his identification card to the man. The man snatched it and ran off into the darkness, leaving Vlada to walk up the stairs to the attic, his head hung low, arms hanging at his sides. He slumped in a chair.

Hermina rose from bed. She cried out when she saw Vlada's bloodied hands. Karel came out, leaning in the doorway, awaiting an explanation. Vlada relayed what had occurred while his mother dabbed at the scrapes on his hands with a warm cloth. His father's face tightened.

"We will deal with this in the morning," his father said. He returned to bed, leaving Vlada alone to endure a sleepless night.

In the morning Karel dressed in one of his best suits. "Get dressed," Karel told Vlada. Hermina had pressed a shirt and pants for Vlada, and he dressed quickly. Father and son walked in silence to the police station. Vlada knew it was best not to ask questions.

"I would like to speak to the Chief of Police. My name is Karel Munk," his father said to the clerk at the desk. After a few minutes, the door to the office opened.

"Mr. Munk, the Chief will see you now," the clerk ushered him into the office. Karel motioned for Vlada to stay seated, the door closing behind him. The only sound was the ticking of the clock and the occasional clatter of the typewriter. Vlada shifted in his seat, sweating. When Karel walked out of the office minutes later, Vlada flinched. Their eyes met and the stern look from his father's worn-out face marked a clear instruction to stay silent. Karel motioned for Vlada to get up; Vlada obeyed, walking stiffly out of the office.

Once they were outside the building, Karel turned to Vlada and spoke. "You are lucky, Vlada. The chief was an old friend of mine from the Czech Legion. It turns out for some of us, those old relationships hold more weight than the rule of the Nazis. He took a risk doing this for me." Karel handed Vlada his identification card, shaking his head. Vlada's face reddened with shame. He was wrong. The evening had not been worth it. He had embarrassed his parents and humiliated himself. The two men walked the rest of the way home in silence.

The end of summer approached, bringing with it the Nazis most agonizing decree: Jews were forbidden the right to own house pets; all dogs, cats, and other domestic animals in Jewish homes were to be turned in to the authorities to be auctioned in the city marketplace. Any animals that were not sold at auction were to be destroyed.

"I have no choice, Hermina," Karel's voice broke as he spoke through the bedroom door. He loved the dog, too, and he hung his head in shame and heartbreak at the task he was being forced to carry out. "I cannot delay it any longer, darling."

Karel reached for Čigy's leash hesitantly and Čigy began to jump excitedly. Karel turned away from the dog for a moment, shaking his head and attempting to compose himself. He slipped the leash around Čigy's neck, and kneeled in front of the dog, their eyes locking in the familiar way of master and cherished family pet. Karel scratched the top of the dog's head, and Čigy leaned in, lazily licking Karel's hand with his eyes closed. Theirs was a relationship built on pure trust, and Karel was about to betray it. Čigy excitedly led Karel down the stairs while Hermina remained in the bedroom unable to say goodbye.

The day the animals were to be auctioned, Vlada could hear the din all the way from the Černý building. There was a hush over the workplace and some of the girls were crying. At the end of the workday, Vlada took the steps to the attic apartment slowly, afraid for his mother's condition after the loss of the family pet.

He opened the door to find two women talking; his mother stood in the middle of the apartment with Aunt Mary, the Christian widow of Karel's eldest brother, Sigmund Munk. In her hand Aunt Mary held a leash with Čigy on the other end.

Aunt Mary was seldom heard from, but somehow word had reached her about the family's dilemma with the dog. Mary attended the auction and raised her hand to bid on Čigy, the lone bidder for the dog at the heartbreaking event. She had come straight from the auction to the apartment to show Hermina that he was safe.

"He can live with me for as long as is necessary, dear. Don't fret," Mary comforted Hermina, while Hermina, relief washing over her, affectionately nuzzled Čigy.

A few days after the auction, Karel heard scratching at the door of the attic apartment. He walked cautiously down the stairs and opened it to find Čigy, panting, no sign of Aunt Mary anywhere. The dog ran past Karel, bounding up the stairs, and jumped into Hermina's lap, excitedly wagging his tail as he licked her face. Twenty minutes later, Mary arrived, holding the leash.

"I knew I would find him here," said Mary. "He sits by the door to my flat, refusing to eat or acknowledge that I saved him. He waited for just the right moment and ran." Despite Mary's role in saving his life, Čigy remained hopelessly devoted to Hermina.

"Karel, please," Hermina begged her husband to let the dog stay, holding Čigy's face in her hands.

"The city is full of informers, my dear. I have heard that an unexpected search and discovery of the dog might result in a sentence of hard labor," Karel warned. Hermina recognized the inevitable, and the best she could hope was for Čigy to be safe with Aunt Mary. Karel took Čigy by the leash.

"Come, Mary. I will walk you both home," he said. In the weeks that passed, the dog completed a few more successful escapes. Each time, Karel led the dog back across the river, returning him to his new owner. Eventually, Čigy finally stopped coming around.

Vlada could barely contain his excitement; after all this time under German occupation, something was finally happening. It was December and, in a few days, he and his parents would board the train to Terezin, the Jewish settlement camp created by the Nazis northwest of Prague. Vlada pictured the camp as a world free of the limits imposed by the German occupiers, a place where they could live a normal life again.

"I won't be forbidden to walk in the park. I won't have to walk in the street. I won't be jumped for being out after curfew." Vlada spelled out the possibilities to his mother as he shuddered at the memory of being hunted down and turned in to the authorities. He followed Hermina around the attic apartment, acting like a child half his age, hounding her with a barrage of questions.

"What do you think will be the first thing we do when we get there, Mami? Do you think we will see Aunt Berta? Where do you think we will live?"

"I don't know, Vlada," his mother answered curtly. Vlada was puzzled why his parents did not share his enthusiasm for the upcoming adventure. They both moved as if through mud, their legs and arms heavy with uncertainty and fatigue.

Hermina and Karel had received notice of the family's deportation months ago. Vlada began packing his things right away, eager for a new journey, a new place that held promise, Vlada thought, or at least safety and stability. His mother, on the other hand, slipped immediately into denial.

"Pardubice is the only place we have truly ever called home," she lamented. She could not bear to begin preparing her family to leave.

"She has buried her head in the sand, Vlada," Karel said. "She is hoping for a miracle that will allow us to stay. It won't happen."

Hermina moved about the kitchen in a fog. Gone was the organized woman who had checked things off her list at the old flat. "Please, Vlada, no more questions," she insisted. "Can't you see I am trying to pack?"

Vlada looked over the odd mix of supplies strewn about the kitchen table. Measuring cups, toiletries, matches, books, clothing, family photos, a few simple tools. The mismatched collection of goods spread from the table onto the counters and kitchen chairs, threatening to take over the family's small living space. Only the most necessary of items had been transferred from the flat to the attic apartment, and from those remaining possessions, Hermina was tasked with whittling their belongings down even further to 50 kilos, a little over one hundred pounds, the amount allowed by the Nazis per suitcase.

If there was a method to her madness, only Hermina knew what it was. For every item she placed with certainty in the pile to be packed, one or two others were removed. She meticulously laid out items of clothing, only to swap a dress for a sweater and then put the dress back in the pile. She continued along in this manner for hours. The next morning, three suitcases sat on the floor near the table, stacked one on top of the other. She lifted the first suitcase onto the table and wrote Vlada's formal name on the side: *Vladimir*. She opened the suitcase and sighed.

Vlada watched as his mother lapsed into silence. She had always been vibrant, cheerful, adventurous. The German occupation had taken a toll on her, and on his parent's relationship. Over the past few months, their once gentle gazes and absent touches had been replaced by staccato bursts of communication of necessary information followed by long periods of silence. Having surrendered their radio to the Nazis, there was no background noise to fill the stillness that hung in the air like a living thing.

Of Hermina's seven siblings, three had already been sent to Terezin with their families. News that her father, Grandfather Adolf, had died at the camp one month ago had only just reached her, unraveling her even more. Karel's sister, Rudolfina, and her husband had been sent to Minsk the previous fall. A few months ago, they stopped returning Karel's letters. Karel's brother Max and his wife were sent first to Terezin and then on to Piaski in Poland. Since the move he had also not heard from them.

By day's end each of the family member's bulging bags had been placed near the door, where they were to be brought to the station for loading onto the train. In two days, the family was to report to the Obchodni Akademie directly across from the train station. There, Karel, Hermina and Vlada would be processed and transported to Terezin.

Vlada looked out the attic apartment window in time to see a bird alight on the branch of a tree in the yard. A train whistle blew off in the distance, startling the bird. It flew away as quickly as it had come.

CHAPTER NINE

KITTY FALL 1942 - FEB 1943
PRAGUE, PROTECTORATE OF
BOHEMIA AND MORAVIA

Hanuš was the first one to hear the doors of the car slam outside the house on Raisova Street. He pulled the curtain back and watched as two officers from the Foreign Police emerged from a sleek, black vehicle and made their way up the sidewalk. It was late September, and the streets of Dobřichovice appeared empty but for the fallen leaves scuttling down the street in the gusty wind.

"Papa! Mama! Police." Karel came out of the bedroom, tying the belt on his bathrobe, his hair disheveled. He gathered the family in the foyer and stood with his arms around Bettina and Kitty. Hanuš opened the front door.

The man spoke directly to Bettina. "Frau Löwi. The German government has made an agreement to exchange American citizens in German-occupied regions for German citizens who are being held in the United States. The *Oberlandrat* sent us to inform you of this news."

Bettina shrugged her husband's arm from her shoulder and stepped forward. "Why, this is wonderful news! What happens next?"

The older of the two officers bristled at Bettina's familiarity. Kitty's cheeks reddened, embarrassed for her mother, her brash American side showing itself in the moment.

"We will transport you to Prague and you will wait there for further instructions. Report to the office of the Foreign Police tomorrow morning at eight." The officer did not tip his hat or wish them a good day. He turned on his heel and the younger man turned and followed him back down to the waiting vehicle.

Bettina closed the door and turned to face the family. "Karel, it is happening. We are going to the United States! I told you to have faith." Kitty and Hanuš looked at each other in disbelief. "We must all pack at once." Bettina walked away, leaving the rest of the family by the door in stunned silence.

"Is it true, Papa, or is it a trick?" Kitty was fragile after losing Otto, as was her father. The last thing they needed was false hope. Karel put his hand on the shoulder of each of his children. There were tears in his eyes and his voice wavered as he spoke.

"I did not believe this would amount to anything. But, yes, Kitty, I do believe it is true. You are both going to be safe." A feeble smile crossed his face. "I am so very happy I was wrong."

The Löwis made their way through the streets of Prague, lugging their suitcases behind them, to the hotel where the Foreign Office Police had instructed them to wait for further information about the exchange. Prague was bustling, its bridges and buildings untouched by bombs, the streets filled with German officers in uniform and well-dressed people living seemingly normal lives.

They passed block after block of baroque and gothic structures, ornate buildings with tiny wrought iron balconies and balustrades, copper domes and spires that stretched heavenward. Kitty could not look at the beauty of the city's architectural details without a pang of sadness for her time in Vienna with Oila.

The family's progress through the streets of the city was slow, and as they crossed one of the cobblestone bridges over the Charles River, the sun fell below the buildings, casting the city in a golden glow. SS soldiers in their intimidating black uniforms stood at attention on street corners, ruining what might almost have felt like a pleasant family holiday.

They were close to the hotel when Bettina stopped abruptly. She looked again at the piece of paper the police had given to her in Dobricoviche. "This seems to be the correct address?" Bettina wavered uncertainly, as she confirmed that the name on the piece of paper matched the sign that hung from a metal bar over the sidewalk above them. The paint had been scraped away but the shadow indicating 'One-Hour Rates Available' was still visible. Broken glass was scattered on the sidewalk near the building.

"What does it mean 'One-Hour Rates Available,' Mother?" Kitty asked. Karel choked back a laugh, and Hanuš snickered. Bettina ignored Kitty's question.

They entered the lobby of the hotel and were immediately met with an offensive smell. Kitty pinched her nose but knew not to comment. She craned her neck at the high ceilings and tall pillars in the lobby, massive chandeliers hanging from an intricate coffered ceiling. Fancy couches dotted the large room, many with worn upholstery.

"Well, it must have been something in its day." Bettina breezed over the obvious shortcomings of their accommodations, continuing her cheerful banter as Karel made his way to the front desk. He returned with their room keys to hear Bettina still prattling on. "Isn't it nice to be in the city again?" Hanuš rolled his eyes and whispered to Kitty. "You would think we were on a family vacation, not refugees fleeing to safety in America."

The hotel was the worst and the best place Kitty had ever seen, and she loved it. They walked together up the grand staircase and found their room, Kitty and Hanuš quickly unpacking, running back down the stairs to the lobby to explore. Kitty could not believe her eyes. The place must have been grand. The paint on the walls was peeling in places, and the intricate pattern on the Oriental carpets had worn thin from years of traffic. Light bulbs were missing from the crystal chandeliers.

A crowd had gathered in one corner of the enormous lobby. Kitty and Hanuš heard music playing and worked their way to the front to see what the fuss was about. Three Black men in dark suits played a rollicking tune as people in the crowd danced and clapped. One man played an upright bass, another sat behind a set of drums and another man played a trumpet. Kitty's eyes grew wide with amazement, she could not take her eyes off the drummer, thrilled each time the cymbals crashed rhythmically.

Two women next to her were speaking English, the bottom of their dresses trimmed with fringe. The bass player and the horn player finished their part and the drummer, who wore a dark bowler hat, launched into a solo that built to a crescendo with a final crash of the cymbals. The crowd clapped and someone whistled.

Kitty had never seen a Black person before, except in the American movies she and Hanuš watched in the early days in Dobřichovice.

"Oh, Hanuš. This is so much fun!" The crowd began to thin and the drummer stood up from behind the drums and smiled at Kitty, emboldening her to approach him.

"*Dobrý den!*" The man greeted Kitty in perfect Czech but with the oddest accent. "Hello, young lady. What brings you here? Are you headed for the U S of A, too?"

Kitty nodded.

"Me, too. I can't wait to get home and have some of my aunt's pecan pie. I'm from Louisiana. You probably don't even know where that is." The food the man could not wait to eat had no comparable word in Czech, so he said the words in English. Kitty loved listening to him talk.

"Let me tell you. I came to Czechoslovakia in 1934. Some friends from America told me they were making good money playing music in Paris." He pronounced the French city "Paree." "Then the Czechs caught on to the big band sound and I went where they went." He continued to explain how he played as a drummer in one of the best bars in Prague. It was a successful way to make a living until the war. Now the city was filled with German officers. "I love it here, but I don't love the Germans. Not one bit. They are neither fans of my music nor my skin color. I am happy to be going back home. Name's Arthur, but you can call me Artie. What's yours?"

"I am Kitty, and this is Hanuš. Our mother is an American citizen." Kitty felt important and she stood taller, the conversation with a grownup encouraging her.

"Well, I would say that is a lucky break, young lady. There are lots of other folks here that were born in America. Look over there, that lady is married to an American, and she can't wait to get out of here. We are all just waiting for the word. We are all in the same boat."

So this is what solidarity felt like, thought Kitty. She had felt so alone, first as a Jew under German occupation, then as an imposter when they were stripped of the yellow star. Now she was a part of something. She had never appreciated her mother's citizenship more than at this moment.

Kitty looked around at the people milling about in the lobby. To some it might have seemed a way station for lost souls. To her, it was filled with the most interesting, well-dressed people, mostly Americans trapped in a country that was not their home, hoping to get back to the place that was.

If this was what Americans were like in her country, she couldn't wait to see them at home. She was sure it must be the most exciting place in the world – without the Germans, of course.

Weeks at the hotel stretched into a month, and Kitty wondered why they had not visited Grandmother Ludmila. Karel's mother, Ludmila, lived in an apartment in Prague; Kitty had spent time there in the weeks and months after the pogrom. Those had been uncertain times, and Kitty had been comforted by her grandmother's practicality, the neat, clean surroundings and her daily routines.

Bettina rarely left the hotel. "We don't want to jinx our good luck, Kitty. What if we are off somewhere and they come looking for us for the exchange? We need to stay put." Her mother's response was curt and Kitty could tell her mother was tense. She did not like Bettina's answer; now she, too, was nervous. Hanuš and Kitty had started to doubt the plan hatched at the *Oberlandrat* office would come to fruition, but they agreed to keep the thought to themselves.

The Foreign Office Police arrived at the hotel a few days later. A uniformed officer knocked on the door of the Löwis' hotel room. Bettina opened it and let the two men in. The man hesitated before speaking, regarding the family members' anxious faces. "The authorities were unable to establish the legitimacy of the papers you have in your possession. The only one that is valid is for Frau Löwi." The man spoke directly to Bettina. "We can send you alone to America, but your family will not be able to join you. Everyone else must return to Dobřichovice at once."

"I see. Thank you." Bettina showed the men out and closed the door, her hand lingering against it, her back to her family. She turned around and looked first at Hanuš, and then at Kitty. She sat down on the edge of the bed and began wringing her hands.

Karel opened the door and motioned for the children to go downstairs. "Kitty. Hanuš. Leave us alone for a moment." Hanuš and Kitty stood in the hallway outside the door long enough to hear their mother let out a guttural howl. "My babies! Karel, I can't protect my babies."

"It's not your fault, darling. Bastards!" Their father's outburst sent Kitty and Hanuš running down the hallway toward the stairs. Kitty could hear music playing in the lobby. She stopped at the top of the stairs and turned to Hanuš. They exchanged a glance, a knowing look acknowledging that they would never be in this place ever again.

Hanuš grabbed Kitty's hand, pulling her down the stairs, Kitty running her hand along the faded flocked wallpaper, following the sound of the music to the lobby where the other people around them still held out hope.

The Löwi family traveled from Prague back to Dobřichovice, the yellow star painfully absent from their clothing. Kitty's parents had discussed it and thought the family had the best chance of avoiding deportation if they kept up the ruse. They walked from the train station to the house on Raisova Street, dragging their suitcases behind them, Bettina hanging her head. Hanuš and Kitty walked ahead, oblivious to any danger the failed attempt at freedom might create.

Hanuš entered the house first, stopping immediately in the doorway, his mouth falling open in shock. "Papa, where is the furniture?" The flat had been picked over in their absence. Anything of value, including most of the furniture, was gone. The stove was cold, the woodpile gone.

Karel's tone was bitter. "We are Jews, Hanuš. No one thought we were coming back. Jews never come back. They took what they liked."

No longer under the protection of the Foreign Office Police, Karel prepared the family for a backlash. "There are those who will resent our attempt at freedom, even though it failed. Be careful who you speak to."

Kitty bit her lip. She hated to hear her father talk like that. He had been well-liked in the neighborhood before they left for Prague, always helping a neighbor in need with cash or food, sometimes to his own family's detriment. Within hours of their arrival, there was a knock on the door. Karel opened it warily, his shoulders slumped, wondering what new strife might be visited upon them. It was the wife of the neighbor across the street. She was an older woman with a kind face, grown thinner since Kitty had seen her last. Kitty stood behind Karel, and saw the woman's eyes scanning Kitty's sweater, noticing the absence of the yellow star.

"I don't want to intrude, but we saw you return. We saw what happened to the furniture while you were...away. My husband works at the sanitorium. He can bring two hospital beds tonight after dark for the children."

Karel was moved by the gesture. "Thank you, Fraulein. We appreciate that."

The woman winked at Kitty conspiratorially. "Make sure you get some fresh air, my dear." After the woman left, Kitty walked down the back stairway and into the yard. She scanned the small patch of grass; a squirrel sat, its tail twitching, on the dilapidated fence, slats curiously broken and missing since the family was here last. She watched the squirrel begin to claw at something hanging from the fence. Kitty gasped. "Shoo!" she waved her arms and ran to the fence, pulling two bags from the fence post.

Kitty opened the heavier of the two bags first, peering inside, then looked inside the other, lighter burlap sack. At the bottom she found a needle and thread and yellow fabric stars. She ran to show the contents to her father.

"It's like Christmas, Papa! A bag of potatoes and onions!" She held them up so he could see what the neighbor had left for them. "With the margarine and flour from the rations I can make something for dinner." Hanuš followed her into the kitchen.

"What will you use to light the stove?" He looked at the splinters of wood on the floor where a pile of firewood once sat.

"Break off a few slats from the fence out back. It looks as if someone else had the same idea." As Hanuš tended to the stove, Kitty sliced the potatoes and the onions and layered them in a dish. She placed small pats of margarine on the top and put the dish in the oven after it had warmed. She knew the gratin would taste better with a splash of milk but what they had would have to do. She sat down, feeling rather accomplished, and began the task of sewing a yellow star on her sweater.

Kitty's days in Dobřichovice were filled with activity, one blending into the other. She went to the market, cooked, cleaned. Bettina kept to herself, rarely lending a hand with household chores. She was silent, withdrawn. No matter. Kitty was the head of the household again, and she felt useful.

The day before Christmas, Karel received a telegram from his brother. "It's from Uncle Erich," said Karel. "He writes that Aunt Arna and baby Eva were sent from Prague to Terezin." Bettina sat stone-faced at the news. Kitty had planned a special dessert for dinner that night with items the neighbor had given her; now she wasn't sure she had the energy to assemble it.

After the fateful night of the pogrom when Uncle Erich had helped Hanuš and Kitty escape from Teplice, Uncle Erich became a hero in the family's eyes. He had gone back to Prague to check on his mother and sisters. While he was there, he met Arna and married her, and they lived with Arna's parents in a three-room apartment. Erich had been consigned to work for the Germans, constructing bomb shelters, forced to stay behind in Prague when his wife and infant daughter were deported.

It seemed a day rarely passed that Terezin, the Czech name for the Jewish resettlement community the Nazis now called Theresienstadt, was not on everyone's lips. This was the third time the shadow of this enigmatic Jewish ghetto had fallen on the family. It had been Otto and Frankie's last stop before being sent to the "East," and they had never been heard from again. Karel's sister, Bedriska, had been sent there in October. And now, Arna and baby Eva.

On Christmas morning it was cold. There were no presents to be distributed and very little wood for heat or cooking. The family sat solemnly in the main room. Everyone turned to look at Kitty as she walked into the room bearing a plate of apple strudel. The neighborhood Good Samaritan's most recent donation, apples and a spoonful of sugar, had brought tears to Kitty's eyes.

"But, Kitty, how? How did you do it?" Hanuš's mouth was open wide, and he licked his lips hungrily. When Kitty saw the precious ingredients, she had a flashback to making strudel with Oila in the kitchen in Teplice. Oila made Kitty memorize the proportions for the dough.

"And slice the apples thinly," Oila had instructed. They had stretched the dough together on the dining room table until it was paper thin, the parachute of dough floating up over the table and drifting back down. It had reminded Kitty of when the maids changed the sheets, the starched white cloth floating up over the bed and then landing silently on the mattress. That must have been why Oila had called it "making the bed." The dough was so thin, Kitty could see her hand through it. The neighbor had even included a pinch of cinnamon. That they were all together eating apple strudel was a Christmas miracle.

The memory of those days with Oila brought a smile to Kitty's face. She cut slices of strudel and put them on four chipped plates. Kitty looked around at her family and felt a glimmer of hope. The next morning, she found the plate she had given Bettina untouched, the slice of strudel intact.

Everyone was sleeping when the Czech police stormed the house. It was the coldest night in February. That very morning Hanuš had spoken hopefully about the family's safety, apparently just hours too soon.

"We have been back from Prague for months. Nothing is happening. Maybe the Nazis are losing the war."

Kitty woke to pounding on the door and shouting from the main room. "Get dressed! *Rychle!*" Hanuš and Kitty dressed quickly, an anxious look passing between them. If it was a search, Kitty and Hanuš had put the family's safety in jeopardy; there was contraband in the house.

The family had been living on rations meant for Jews: flour, potatoes margarine. They were not allowed sugar, dairy, milk, eggs. Those items were strictly *verboten*. Hanuš had recently traded pieces of the fence for eggs on the black market; a few remained, and they sat in a bowl in the kitchen in plain sight. If they were discovered, it posed a danger not only for the family, but for those who had bartered them.

Hanuš spoke to the guard nearest the kitchen as his parents dressed. "Excuse me. I need to use the latrine." On his way to the outhouse, Hanuš snatched the eggs. He put them down gently on the grass behind the latrine, hoping someone might find the precious items and use them.

Karel had seen the look pass between his children and tried to distract the guards. "What is this about? I demand an explanation." Karel spoke firmly to the Czech police, putting his shoes on, slowly tying them.

Kitty was left to deal with another problem. Jews were not permitted to borrow books from the public library, but the neighbor had been so kind as to loan Kitty a few. Now Kitty moved quickly, scooping up the books and putting them in her rucksack. She hung the bag on the back stairway for the neighbor with a note. "Thank you for your kindness."

"Hurry up! Now!" Kitty heard the police following her into the kitchen.

"Out! Now." The police pushed Hanuš and Karel out of the house and down the sidewalk to a waiting truck. They did not have time to grab their winter coats, and sat, shivering, as the truck lurched forward. Kitty could see her breath as they rumbled along in silence in the back of the truck. The benches were hard underneath them and when she tried to huddle near her father to stay warm, the guard shouted at her.

Kitty looked at Bettina sitting across from her in the back of the truck. Bettina had remained silent throughout the whole arrest. If their arrest had anything to do with the falsified citizenship papers given to them by the Foreign Office Police, Kitty assumed her mother must feel guilty and somehow responsible. Kitty did not blame her mother; she had done her best.

The truck stopped in front of the police station. It was three in the morning. Two Czech police led the family down a long hallway where the Gestapo officer in charge stood holding a clipboard. Kitty felt a chill wash over her when she saw his uniform; he was highly decorated, like the *Oberlandrat*.

The German officer barked orders at the younger officers. "Put them each in a separate room. *Schnell!*" Bettina, Karel, and Hanuš were led away down a dimly lit corridor. One of the Czech police shoved Kitty into a non-descript room lined with file cabinets. There was one lone chair and a desk, and a dim light bulb hung from the ceiling, casting the room in semi-darkness. Kitty was tired, and it was cold in the room. She was not properly dressed. She bit her nails, and sat down in the chair as her mind wandered, first to Oila and then to her father.

I will kill them if Papa has another heart attack, she thought, her teeth chattering. Anger boiled up in her as she waited for something to happen. She glanced at the desk, spotting a rubber stamp holder. Her mind went back to her father's office on Masaryk Street, and how she had "helped" her father with his office chores. It seemed like a lifetime ago.

The door opened and the *Kommandant* entered, throwing his hat on the desk. "Stand up." He was sullen. His eyes were dark, almost black and his face was pockmarked. His leather belt was cinched tight, his fat hanging over the edge of it. Kitty stood and took a few steps back.

"How old are you?"

"I will be fifteen soon," Kitty said proudly.

"What is the name of the man who signed your documents?" Kitty immediately regretted her honesty about her age. If she said she was younger, the German might not expect her to know anything. She looked for a way out of her previous statement, but it was too late.

"I have no idea who signed the papers." Kitty looked the man directly in the eye.

"Do you have any jewelry?" The Kommandant's eyes narrowed.

"No. Jews had to turn in their jewelry at a certain time. That is what we did."

"If you have any money, put it on the table. Now." He had a baton in his gloved hand. He tapped the table to indicate the spot.

Kitty drew in a breath. A string of excuses cascaded out. "I don't have any money. I don't need any money. I'm not going anywhere. I'm not buying anything. I don't have any money." She thought of her father, out there somewhere. She wanted to run out of the room and go to him. She was alone, and she could not think straight.

The Kommandant sensed he was making progress. "Every Jew," his voice filled with contempt, "every Jew must have some money. Don't tell me you don't have any money."

Kitty could accept bad treatment, but this man had crossed a line; he was insinuating that Kitty was a liar. What little self-control Kitty possessed left her along with the hunger, the cold, and the exhaustion. Her breathing quickened, and she clenched her fists.

"Don't be so cheeky. I will bring you down. You're going to be that small," he indicated with his pointer finger and thumb nearly touching, "when I get through with you."

Kitty turned her back to him, and reaching into the top of her stocking she drew out a coin, the smallest denomination of the Protectorate. It was the coin her father had given her for the good report card. She turned back around to face him. Kitty could see the man's face darkening in that moment. He barely moved as he watched her tremble and slowly place the single coin on the desk.

"This," Kitty said slowly, "is the only money I have."

The Kommandant acted quickly. Kitty lacked the energy to raise her arm to protect herself as the first blow fell. Kitty heard something crack. The second blow knocked her to the floor. Blood and saliva filled her mouth, spilling onto her chin. She spit two teeth into her hand, pushing her tongue against the spaces they left behind.

The interrogation had ended. Kitty remembered being shoved out the door of the small room and up against a wall. Hours passed and Kitty guessed by the light streaming in from under the doors that it was around noon.

Two guards brought Hanuš out, forcing him to stand next to Kitty. "Put your hands up and keep them there," barked the guard. When the guard walked away, Hanuš turned to look at Kitty. She smiled, revealing the two missing teeth, and her bruised and bloodied face. Hanuš's face crumbled, awash in anguish and pain.

"It's okay. Serves me right. I was being cheeky." Kitty played down the incident for her brother's sake. Despite the throbbing in her jaw and the growing welts on her face, she had stood up to her interrogator. She was proud of herself.

Twenty minutes later, two guards brought Karel out. They carried him under his arms, his legs dragging behind him and pushed him against the wall. Bettina followed. The family remained there, hands over their heads, Hanuš propping his father up to keep him from falling, until darkness fell. When no guards were present, Kitty cheated, relaxing her body against the wall. When she heard someone approach, she snapped back to attention.

"Hanuš," Kitty whispered. "I need to use the restroom." Since they arrived at three the previous morning, their most basic needs had been ignored. No food. No water. No toilet.

"Don't ask, Kitty. Please," Hanuš whispered back. She remembered the punch. The metallic taste of her blood lingered in her mouth, and her tongue found its way to the gaps where her teeth had been. Kitty knew this was not the worst. The worst was yet to come. How would Papa get through this, not just today but whatever lies ahead? She worried about the strain on his heart.

The Gestapo shouted for the Czech police. "Take them to the cage. Put them on the morning train." The Czech police led the family down another long corridor which ended in a large auditorium. In the room there were cages. One of the Czech police unlocked the door, motioning for them to get in.

As the police walked away, Bettina shouted after them. "I am an American citizen! Where are you taking us in the morning?" One of the men turned around and laughed.

In the morning the Czech police stood around them on the train platform, waiting for the next passenger train. Kitty heard her mother ask one of the guards for permission to go to the bathroom. He walked with her and stood outside the door. Bettina had somehow managed to keep her handbag and when she came out of the bathroom, Kitty could see she had used her lipstick.

The train pulled into the station, letting out a whoosh of steam. The Czech guards boarded the train along with the Löwis, and if it had not been for their presence, Kitty could imagine they were just going on holiday. They sat in a private car and the train jerked forward. As it picked up speed, Kitty looked out the frost-covered window at the passing countryside. Snow began to fall thick and fast, covering the ground in a blanket of white, muffling sound and shape alike.

"Hanuš," Kitty said, "remember how perfect the hill behind the house in Teplice was for sledding? Remember Otto, always the fastest to the bottom of the hill? And how Pavla loved it, always diving into the snow drifts?" Hanuš sat across from her, courting sleep, lulled by the rhythm of the train. He roused slightly. "And the look on Cook's face when Pavla came inside and shook the snow from her fur?" Hanuš smiled wistfully. Laughter was too much to muster under the circumstances.

Hours later, as the train pulled into its destination, Bohusovice, Bettina, her lipstick now faded, whispered in Kitty's ear. "I wrote a note with the lipstick I had in my purse. 'Whoever shall find this please notify the Swiss Embassy that an American citizen by the name of Bettina Löwi is being taken by the police to an unknown destination. February 16, 1943.' She had thrown the piece of paper out the window of the speeding train.

CHAPTER TEN

Vlada scratched at the frost that had etched a ragged, lacy pattern on the inside of the apartment window overlooking the street. Karel did not speak. Picking up his suitcase and Hermina's was enough to indicate it was time to go. The three descended the stairs, greeted by a stiff breeze and for the final time, Karel struggled to pull the apartment door closed. Hermina raised the collar of her coat around her face, shielding it from the wind.

Vlada did not feel the cold; he had been waiting months for this day. There was no love lost between Vlada and Pardubice in these last few months. He cringed remembering the fight with the man who stole his identity papers, and the subsequent humiliation with his father at the police station.

Vlada reached for the cart handle and began to pull it behind him, walking in the direction of the school. Vlada's pace quickened, the cart bumping along behind him over the cobblestone street as he picked up speed, eager to get to the destination. He was half a block's length in front of his parents when he turned onto Hlaváčova Street and ground to a halt, nearly crashing into the family in front of him.

The street was filled with people, dozens of families walking slowly in the same direction. The adults walked in silence; the only sound was an eerie clanging that filled the streets, echoing off the stone buildings and cobblestones.

How clever, thought Vlada, as his eyes adjusted to the scene surrounding him. Their suitcases stuffed to overflowing, some industrious souls had tied pots, cups, and utensils onto string and hung them from the rucksacks on their backs. Vlada passed two small children, pieces of crockery tied to strips of fabric, crisscrossed over their winter jackets. The tin and wooden supplies clanged together in a discordant melody not unlike a child banging out a tune on pots and pans with a wooden spoon.

The crowd grew, absorbing people from houses that emptied along the way. The motley assembly turned a collective left at Štefánikova, and approached the abandoned school. Hermina inhaled sharply at the sight that greeted them: hundreds of people, old, young, healthy, infirm, sat on suitcases or on the ground stretched out in front of the Obchodní Akademie. The three-story trade school on the south side of town had been pressed into service to house the city's Jews before their deportation to Terezin. Six hundred Jewish residents of the town – men, women, and children – had left for Terezin days earlier, herded from the school onto the train platform nearby and into the waiting rail cars. Vlada and his parents were among the next group of deportees. The last of the city's Jews were leaving. It was unclear if they would ever return.

Vlada smiled defiantly. He was glad to leave; Jews would be welcome at their next destination, he thought.

Karel removed the suitcases from the cart and set them on the ground, waving to a man standing on the fringes of the large crowd. The man was another friend of Karel's from the Czech Legion, the yellow star noticeably absent from the man's coat in the sea of Jewish families.

"I would have helped you, Karel," the man said under his breath. He was about Karel's age, and well-dressed. The man looked around, shaking his head in disbelief at the growing crowd.

"It wasn't worth the risk, Bhodan," Karel replied. Public displays of friendship with Jews were a risk best not taken. "My family and I thank you." Bhodan took the handle of the cart from Karel.

"Be safe, Karel." Bhodan looked at the sea of people milling around the building one last time, shook his head sadly, and walked away.

They passed an hour outside, the displaced families waiting for someone to allow them entry into the school, where they had been told they would be "processed" before deportation to Terezin. When the doors to the school opened, Hermina moved quickly, pushing her way inside the dim hallway of the school. Vlada and Karel followed her up a short flight of stairs as she ducked in the doorway of a half-empty classroom.

Hermina had changed under occupation, at times morose and helpless, at others, resourceful, efficient. Today Vlada watched his mother move with purpose, placing their belongings in a square around her, carving out a small section for her family against a wall in the corner of the room. The makeshift living space would be their home for the next few days until the Germans ordered it was time to leave.

Two days passed since they had arrived at the school. The school, which rarely had more than eighty students on the premises on any given day, groaned under the influx of hundreds of occupants and their worldly belongings, all crowded into its small rooms. The latrines could not handle the strain, and a few had ceased to work properly.

Hermina sat on her suitcase, a handkerchief to her nose. "Karel, the smell...." Within the close confines of the rooms, the odor of humanity was at its most pungent.

Karel nodded sympathetically. "I suppose we should be thankful they broke us up into two groups for deportation," Karel replied, smiling feebly, his attempt at levity falling flat.

Vlada sat cross-legged on a blanket on the floor. "How much longer are we staying here, Tati?" Vlada was growing tired of this stage of the adventure. They were unable to leave the building, so Vlada had sought out Jirka on another floor of the building. They spent their waking hours wandering from room to room, on the lookout for girls their age. The girls were usually with their parents making the game a questionable use of their time.

"It is out of our hands," Karel replied, shrugging his shoulders.

On the third day, SS guards flooded into the building, walking the halls of the school, banging their guns on doors, and shouting instructions. "Gather your belongings. Assemble in front of the building! Immediately!" Vlada watched his mother stuffing, still unfolded, the items they had used as bedding into her suitcase; his father threw cups and utensils in a rucksack without a thorough washing. Both his parents seemed to panic as the Czech gendarmes and the Germans barked orders into the crowd. Vlada looked away; these moments caught him off guard, gnawing at something inside him.

Wind whipped the red, white, and black Nazi flags flying above the train station as the remainder of the city's Jews crossed the street to board the passenger train cars waiting there. Women and children were crying; an elderly man fell as the crowd moved slowly across the street from the school and onto the train platform. A crowd had gathered, held back by the Czech police, to see their loved ones off on their journey. Women reached out their arms to their family members and friends, wailing and crying. This leave-taking was awkward, inglorious, muddied with conflicting emotions. Vlada stumbled. It was time to go.

Vlada boarded the train and found a seat next to a window, his parents taking the seats beside him. Babies cried inconsolably and people were still making their way through the aisle when the train lurched forward. There was a commotion on the train platform. Vlada recognized Černý, his boss from the radio factory, in his signature tweed suit, struggling to free himself as two SS guards dragged him off the platform.

Černý's face reddened as one of guards pinned his arms behind his back, while another guard shouted in his face. Černý spat out a response. Vlada had heard Černý swear on more than one occasion, and he was sure the SS were getting an earful. Others crowded the windows of the train car, hoping for a glimpse of the action.

Vlada stared in disbelief at what would be his last memory of Pardubice unfolding before his eyes, watching as the German guards forced Černý from the train platform and into a waiting car. Had the SS discovered that Černý allowed his young Jewish workers to listen to news of the war on the radios they were assembling? Vlada would never know the answer.

The Obchodní Akademie faded into the distance, the train chugging forward to its destination. Dark clouds hung low over the city as the train bearing the last of the Jews of Pardubice hurtled toward the unknown.

Vlada looked around the train car and spotted Nora sitting further up the car with her family. Vlada's optimism about the journey had faltered when he saw Černý manhandled on the train platform. But seeing Nora seemed like an auspicious sign, and a smile spread across Vlada's face.

At fourteen, Nora was tall for her age and looked much older. She had brown hair that fell around her shoulders. Vlada watched as her family took their seats and settled in, Nora firmly ensconced between her mother and father. Vlada wanted to talk to her. He stared at her, hoping to catch her eye until her older brother shot Vlada a threatening look. Vlada quickly looked away, resigning himself to watching her from across the train car. He and Nora had lost touch the last few months, but now it felt to Vlada like they were embarking on an adventure together. The two teens exchanged glances when their parents were not looking. Once they were settled, Vlada made a vow to seek her out.

Vlada longed to tell Jirka about Nora, and he wondered where on the train his friend was sitting. Jirka would have a field day with Vlada's flirtation with Nora. Vlada knew just what his friend would say. "Here we are being deported by the Germans and all you can think of is the pretty girl."

As they passed the days at the Obchodní Academie, Vlada had watched Jirka attempt to make the acquaintance of several girls. One evening Jirka approached two sisters in the hallway. If one did not respond to his flirtations, Jirka hoped the other one might; he gave himself a fifty/fifty chance. But within seconds of introducing himself, Jirka's attempts at romance evaporated.

From his train seat, Vlada watched Nora reach down to open the bag in front of her. She pulled out a book, and a strand of hair fell in front of her face. She looked up, locking eyes with Vlada. She held his gaze as she tucked the wisp of hair behind her ear. Vlada tried to imagine what it might be like to kiss Nora. Thoughts of her occupied Vlada for the remainder of the trip.

The train whistle roused its passengers from the spell of the rhythmic clacking over the course of the five-hour ride. It signaled their arrival at their destination and the anxious passengers gathered their belongings and disembarked the train, only to find that the rail line ended at Bohusovice station, a mile away from the camp that was Terezin.

Czech gendarmes in green uniforms and caps lined the platform, shouting instructions at the disoriented crowd. "Follow the carts to the camp! Your belongings will be returned to you after they are cleared of any contraband!" Families huddled together, uncertain, watching in unspoken protest as their carefully selected belongings were flung from the train cars onto waiting trucks below.

This was not the greeting Vlada had expected. They would have to walk the last mile toward their new life and Vlada felt nervous now, his anticipation of a grand adventure continually delayed. Among the crowd, groans rose up at the prospect of cajoling small children and the elderly over the worn, unpaved roads.

"Munks! Munks?" Vlada thought he must be imagining someone shouting his last name. He looked to his father and Karel returned a quizzical look, then began walking toward a young man who was calling out their name into the crowd.

"I am Karel Munk."

The young man in uniform turned to greet him. "I am Jan. Vera's fiancée," he said in a low voice. Vlada winced, caught off guard at the mention of his cousin, Vera. "Show me which is your luggage." Karel pointed to the bags that sat waiting to be loaded onto a large wooden cart. Jan was tall, fit, with an angular face. Vlada felt a pang of jealousy as he watched the man take charge of the family's belongings. "Those in charge of the luggage will steal from you. I will make sure your bags arrive safely. You may spend a few nights in the sluice but after that you will get housing, and these will be returned to you. It's not that bad, really, once you get used to it."

Get used to what? thought Vlada. Jan's eyes met Vlada's for an instant. Had Vera told him she had a younger cousin who had once had a terrible crush on her? His cheeks reddened at the thought that anyone besides Mirek might know his secret.

"Thank you, Jan," Vlada heard his father reply.

Hermina clung to her husband's arm. "Jan, can you tell us, how is Vera's mother, Anna?" But Jan had turned away. Hermina had not seen her sister since Anna's family had been deported to Terezin in February. "Karel," Hermina said, her voice sounded hollow.

"We will be there soon," Karel said to her, grasping her arm firmly. "We will find her when we get there." They fell in with the moving crowd, and Vlada found himself walking behind a young mother carrying a small child. The child looked over his mother's shoulder, his face stained with tears, nose running. Vlada pulled his face into a silly grin. The little boy turned his head onto his mother's shoulder and cried. The group walked forward in silence, the clanging of the crockery and people coughing up ahead the only sound they heard during the trek.

Vera. Engaged. It should have come as no surprise to Vlada; Vera always had a boyfriend. Vlada wondered if Jan knew his Jewish fiancée had converted to Catholicism. He thought, too, of his cousin, Mirek. Little if any word of his favorite cousin had reached them in Pardubice. Vlada would find Mirek as soon as they were settled.

Karel distracted Vlada from his uncertainty, sharing his knowledge of their destination with his son as they walked. "You know, Vlada, Terezin was the military fortress of Habsburg Emperor Joseph II, erected in honor of his mother, Empress Maria Theresa. It is a walled town, designed in the shape of a star. You can imagine the foresight and ingenuity that went into that process." Karel shook his head, impressed at the thought. "It was meant to be used for protection against invading troops, only the invaders never arrived," his father explained.

Vlada listened to his father's words, wondering how he could recite this bit of knowledge and remain calm. Vlada looked down at the yellow star sewn on his jacket. Were the Nazis being ironic? he wondered. They branded the Jews with a star and now a walled fortress in the shape of a star was to be the new home of the Jews of Czechoslovakia. More ironic still, Vlada remembered hearing mention of Maria Theresa's reputation as an ardent anti-Semite. He wondered what she would think of her namesake fortress now filled with Jews.

The path to the camp was worn, the ground rutted, dead and brown, with patches of snow scattered here and there. Hermina walked beside Vlada, her heeled shoes proving impractical over the rough terrain. Within minutes the new arrivals found themselves at the entrance to the elusive Terezin, the Jewish resettlement camp shrouded in mystery and thinly veiled in hope.

What medieval place is this? thought Vlada, taking in the camp's faded brick walls, its high ramparts topped with dirt and sod from some long-forgotten era. His thoughts traveled back to Kunětická Hora where he spent so many afternoons of his youth playing the knight clad in chain mail armor. Vlada felt a pang of sadness. Now here he was at another place that time had clearly forgotten.

The new arrivals fell into a long line outside the entrance to the camp. A table had been set up outside a gate with iron doors. A sign above the arched entry read *Arbeit Macht Frei*. Vlada knew enough German to translate: "Work will set you free." It was not a welcoming message.

Karel approached the Czech guards at the table when their turn arrived. "Karel, Hermina, and Vladimir Munk," he informed the uniformed guard. One of the men handed him three slips of paper.

"These are your special numbers," the man said in a gruff voice. "No one else has these numbers." Vlada fought back the urge to laugh. He hoped he and his father could have a chuckle about it all later. Karel held the "special numbers" in his hand. They included the letters of the transport they had just arrived on, Cg. Karel was Cg68, Hermina was Cg69 and Vlada was Cg70.

"And what do we do now?" Karel asked the man.

The man's head was close-shaven, and he wore wire-rim glasses. "Down there. The sluice," the man barked at them, already waving the next family up to the desk. Karel looked at Vlada and Hermina, then turned and began walking in the direction the guard had pointed to, down a long, sloping cement walkway into a dark, cavernous tunnel.

Vlada's eyes took a minute to adjust to the dim light of the tunnel. He could barely make out the shapes of people lying on the cold ground near the walls. Further along, a man waved to Karel. It was a former acquaintance from the synagogue in Pardubice.

"They are keeping us here for the night, Karel," the man said. He was a bit younger than Karel, tall and slim, and he wore a wool coat, the yellow star sewn on just above the breast pocket. His wife stood behind him, throwing straw on the ground to make a "bed" for their two small girls, one of whom was crying.

"I want Josef," the little girl cried, her mother attempting to quiet her.

"Our dog," the man explained. "We gave him to our neighbor, so the children were able to see him every day. Until now." The man shrugged disconsolately.

"Take care, Pavel," Vlada heard his father say. Along the bleak tunnel walls, a little further, they found an unclaimed spot on which to rest for the night. The dirt and brick walls wept, water dripping down in rivulets that joined together to make a thicker stream; the pile of straw in the spot they chose was wet and musty.

They could hear the voices of others in the darkness, sounds drifting pitifully through the echoing chambers, people moaning and children crying. Karel looked around the tunnel. "Things will look better in the morning," he said to Vlada and Hermina, attempting to sound upbeat, but his voice hoarse with emotion. Vlada lowered himself onto the damp ground. His mother remained silent, stunned by what she had seen and heard thus far.

In the morning, as the first rays of light shone into the tunnel from the far end, a Czech gendarme approached them. "Follow me," the man said, his comment directed at Karel. They got up and gathered their things, following the man, walking from the darkness of the sluice out into the blinding sunshine of a cold December day. Vlada shielded his eyes with his hand. "You and your son report to the Hanover Barrack," the guard pointed to a large building one block away. He looked at Hermina. "Are you pregnant?" She shook her head. Gesturing to Karel, the gendarme spoke again. "Your wife is in the house directly across the street. Now go!"

"Wait," Karel began to reply. The man waved his hand. The conversation was over. They stood in the middle of the street, dazed from lack of sleep, picking straw from their clothes, which were wet and musty from a night on the tunnel floor. Hunger from not having eaten in a day threatened to exacerbate the unwelcome news that they were being forced to separate as a family. Jan suddenly appeared, walking toward them, waving, pulling a cart with their belongings.

"Oh, thank you, Jan," Karel said, taking his suitcase from the cart. "Jan, we are being separated. Can you help us?"

"Men and women are separated. You are lucky your son isn't younger, or they would put him in the children's barrack. At least the two of you can be together in Hanover. It is one of the better buildings. I must go now. Good luck." Jan disappeared into the crowd. The din on the street as other newcomers digested similar news was deafening. Women were crying, hugging their husbands; babies clung to their mothers.

Vlada saw a look pass between his parents, his mother's eyes searching her husband's. The only time his parents had slept separately was when Vlada and his mother left early for the annual winter vacation. His parents stood in the middle of the street marked "Q2" and held each other, Hermina resting her head wearily on her husband's shoulder. Vlada was anxious to see their new home, but he waited patiently for his parents to part.

Tears filled Hermina's eyes as she reached her arms out to Vlada. Vlada hesitated; he was conflicted. Hugging his mother in the middle of the street in broad daylight, with people everywhere, passing by them? He reconsidered and quickly hugged his weeping mother before breaking away.

"Hermina," his father gently held her shoulders. "Go inside the house. Find your bed and we will meet you here later. It's going to be okay." Vlada did not think his father sounded convincing; he seemed distracted, preoccupied, glancing around in search of something. "Come, Vlada." The block they stood on was long, the buildings separate but joined one to the next. Karel motioned for Vlada to follow him into the huge barrack on the corner.

The first room they entered was cavernous and poorly lit. Vlada's heart sunk when he saw the sleeping arrangements; bunk beds were stacked, three levels high, fashioned from roughhewn wood, each bed covered with a straw mattress. The room looked like it housed fifty or more men. From what they could see through a doorway down a long corridor, the room was repeated many times over, making the building home to hundreds of men.

"Vlada...," his father began but did not finish the sentence. Karel's face was pained, his breathing ragged as he pointed to a lower-level bunk that looked unoccupied. Vlada looked up at the bunk two levels above it; he grabbed his suitcase and scrambled up the wooden ladder, lugging it behind him.

Vlada winced, pulling his hand off a rung of the ladder to see a sliver peeking out of the flesh of his palm. Welcome to Terezin.

"There must be over a thousand people living here," Karel observed. The surrounding rooms were crowded with men; the sounds of coughing echoed off the high ceilings in the bleak quarters, and unidentifiable smells hung in the stale air.

Vlada began unpacking his suitcase. It held multiple changes of clothes, kitchen implements, and a few of Vlada's favorite books. Vlada could see that when she was packing his mother had hedged her bets, hoping for the best yet preparing for the worst.

Vlada looked around the room at the other bunks and it was apparent others had made poor choices, guessing incorrectly what might be necessary for the conditions that greeted them at the camp. An odd mishmash of possessions, from the impractical to the sentimental, filled the shelves near each bunk and covered the small tables set in the middle of the room from musical instruments, clocks, and family photos to prayer shawls, dishes, and small tools. For some it would seem nostalgia had won out. For still others, confusion reigned. A few practical souls had packed small tools, thimbles, thread, and medical supplies.

An older man entered the room, settling himself on the bunk next to Karel. He was a small man, his face dotted with gray stubble. He opened a tattered suitcase. Immediately, he stood up and began shouting.

"My medicine! My money. They are gone!" he cried out, rifling through the items in the suitcase. He glared at Karel and Vlada as if they might be the thieves. From another bunk, another man was greeted with an unpleasant surprise: "My winter coat," the man lamented.

Karel looked around nervously, visibly shaken by the increasing tension in the room. "Let's go find your mother," Karel motioned to Vlada. They exited the barrack and crossed the street. Hermina stood waiting for them in front of her new home. She looked small and uncomfortable.

"How is it inside, Mami?" Vlada asked, hoping his mother's accommodation was better than what he and his father had just found.

Hermina spoke haltingly. "There are maybe thirty or forty women. One woman was kind and told me that my job is listed on the slip of paper they gave us," she took the paper from her coat pocket, handing it to Karel. "I will be working in the kitchen, taking food ration coupons." Hermina wrung her hands in front of her, trembling evident in her hands and voice.

"We will see each other every day, my darling," Karel put his arm around her. Vlada turned away, stiffening at his mother's distress.

"I have to find my mother," Hermina said, wiping her face. Babicka Emilie had arrived at the camp in September at the age of 78 and in poor health. Hermina's father had died at the camp in November and her face was lined with worry. Her eyes searched Karel's desperately. "I hope that Anna is with her. I will be back in time for dinner." Vlada watched his mother walk away, quickly swallowed up into the crowded street.

Everywhere Vlada looked, men, women, and children, all wore the yellow star. A cart barreled down the street among the hordes of newcomers, forcing Vlada to jump to the sidewalk. After the cart passed, Vlada returned to the street, absorbing the din surrounding him. Jews everywhere, every single one of them walking freely on the sidewalk, in the middle of the street, entering the park across from the barrack. There were no signs saying the sidewalk or the park were *Verboten*.

I am free, thought Vlada.

Vlada scanned the street, noticing the absence of elderly residents. Hadn't Terezin been formerly designated a retirement community, a 'spa' of sorts, for the elderly? Where are they? wondered Vlada. Maybe there is a special section for older people and that was where his mother would find his Babicka.

The sun passed behind a cloud, and Vlada shuddered from the chill. The movement on the street slowed under the cold, overcast sky, and the crowd was not so gay as Vlada had first imagined. He noticed that many of the people passing by looked thin, gaunt, desperate. With the sun gone away, everything was awash in a gray pall: the buildings, the streets, the faces of the people. Terezin was built to honor an empress, but if there was any beauty here, it had disappeared long ago.

Vlada looked out into the sea of humanity. His entire family was out here somewhere: all his Jewish aunts and uncles and cousins from cities across Czechoslovakia, all forcibly brought here by the Nazis. The thought simultaneously overwhelmed and gnawed at Vlada.

Jirka was out there somewhere, too. It had been Jirka and Vlada against the world at school. Now he needed his friend to make sense of the incongruities of this place, which were deepening by the minute. Vlada needed to find Jirka. And Nora, too. He had no idea where to begin.

Chapter Ten

Mary, Mary, quite contrary,
How does your garden grow?
With silver bells, and cockle shells,
And pretty maids all in a row ~

ENGLISH NURSERY RHYME

KITTY MAY 1943
TEREZIN, PROTECTORATE OF
BOHEMIA AND MORAVIA

Kitty closed her eyes and tried to sleep. It had been two months since the Löwis arrived at the camp via private transport. Kitty recalled the events as if it were yesterday: the Kommandant punching her, knocking out her teeth; her father's collapse. She opened her eyes to stop the visions from playing out in her head, pushing her tongue into the space the missing teeth once inhabited. It was dark in the women's barrack. Bettina was fast asleep beside her, breathing deeply.

The older girls whispered to each other in the dark from their neighboring bunks and Kitty strained to hear their conversations. On nights like these, when sleep eluded her, Kitty lay in her bunk and listened as they gave graphic descriptions after lights out of their recent carnal activities. Kitty, who could barely endure being naked in front of other women in the shower, listened on as the women talked of their naked encounters with men in the camp. While the level of detail shocked Kitty, it also made her self-conscious, highly aware of her own prudish behavior.

"Where did you go?" One voice asked in the dark.

"He has quarters above the Rathausgasse in the attic." The response was delivered cheekily.

"Weren't you afraid of getting caught?" a third voice asked.

"I brought cleaning supplies! No one asked what I was doing there."

And so the tales of sexual escapades continued, other voices chiming in, sharing more specific details, some perhaps exaggerated.

"His mother walked in!"

"It was his first time."

"My head was up against the door!"

"He put his hand..." Kitty blushed in the darkness. She hoped Bettina did not wake up.

She recognized one of the voices: it was Josefina, JoJo to her friends. "We are prisoners only if we allow ourselves to be. There are some things over which we have complete freedom. Our bodies, for one," Kitty heard JoJo say, one night when the conversation took on a more serious tone. JoJo's level of comfort with intimate details was high: she wore her encounters like a badge of honor, although whose army gave out such rewards Kitty had no clue. Kitty could tell that JoJo's opinions were not held by all, and there were times when Kitty could do nothing but plug her ears.

"I love him. He wants to marry me when this is all over." Kitty thought the voice belonged to Eliska. She was pretty, with long, dark hair and a nice figure. JoJo scoffed at her bunkmate's sentimentality.

"Good luck," Jojo replied. She had more sympathy for the girls who used their bodies as bartering tools, making deals during their dalliances that might benefit themselves or their families in the way of food or medicine.

The conversation continued for hours in the darkness after the lights went out. Not all the contributions were bawdy and light. The barely audible giggling was punctuated with occasional sobs. One night, someone wept openly, admitting to the other girls that she was pregnant.

"I want to keep it," Kitty heard the voice say. Kitty's mouth fell open, stifling a gasp. The declaration plunged the barracks into complete silence.

"Don't ruin your life, Klara," JoJo cautioned. JoJo knew everyone; if the girl needed help ending a pregnancy, she knew just who to go to.

Kitty held her breath, waiting for someone to speak. Klara began to weep, and something about her confession changed the tone of the discussion, leading it down a darker path. For a few of the women, their sexual encounters had not been of their choosing. Warnings were issued by those who had been coerced.

"Stay away from that one, you know, the one with the mole." Kitty's whole body tensed as the list of whom to avoid among the kapos, gendarmes, and even fellow prisoners grew. It was a long one. Kitty passed some of the offenders every day on her way to and from her job in the garden. She would never look at them the same way again.

"Bastards," JoJo spat the word out. She wanted revenge against the perpetrators. At some point, Kitty drifted off to sleep. She had fitful dreams, tossing and turning, and when she awoke the next morning, she was not at all rested. As she dressed, Kitty thought she recognized the girl who had spoken about being pregnant. She felt sorry for her. Her predicament was quite rare. From what Kitty had heard most of the women's menstrual cycles ceased after a few months of hard labor and limited food rations. The young woman had won an unlikely lottery.

Kitty had never had a boyfriend. The conversations she overheard in the barracks left her wondering why anyone would want one. Who has time for such drama? There were so many things to do every day. Back home in Teplice, Oila had been her favorite companion. They went for walks, to the store, to the movies, they made strudel. Kitty would never have traded Oila in for a boy, not even Otto. She felt a pang of sadness at the thought of her cousin; their childhood pact to marry each other if no one suitable turned up would remain unrequited after his death in Riga. Kitty dressed quickly for work, pushing thoughts of Otto and romance to the back of her mind.

The fortress that was Terezin had never suffered an attack by opposing forces, and neither had the soil surrounding it been broken by the sharp edge of a spade. Its grounds had remained largely barren and uncultivated for centuries until Terezin's internal Jewish administration, the Council of Elders, were instructed by their Nazi captors to cultivate the soil. It was backbreaking work — chopping up and separating grass from soil so that seeds could take hold and germinate. This work was to be carried out by the camp's child slave labor.

Kitty was part of the *Landwirtschaft*, the camp's agriculture work detail. She was part of the crew assigned to the *Jugendgarten*, the camp's youth garden, outside the main walls of the ghetto. Side by side, the teenage work force broke ground for vegetable gardens in acre upon acre of soil that had never been farmed before. For a girl who had not gardened or done a day of physical labor, each shovel filled with sod was a lesson in sweat and blisters. The work was demanding, but fortunately for Kitty, the work assignment came early in her incarceration, while her body was still young and well nourished. She was fourteen.

Kitty woke every morning at six, Bettina barely stirring in the bed next to her, and walked the long way to the spot where the youth garden crew gathered to make their way to the gardens by seven. Kitty took the long way so she could pass the barrack on the corner of Badhausgasse and Hauptstrasse where her father and Hanus lived. They had dinner together as a family at the end of every day, but it made Kitty feel closer to her father to know that he was in the big building somewhere, sleeping soundly. Karel was unable to work due to his heart condition, and Hanus's health was compromised as well, afflicted with staggering asthma since the family's arrival at the camp.

Bettina had been assigned work on a clothing detail and Kitty had to admit it suited her mother. Her job was to sort clothing confiscated from the new arrivals to the camp, the goal was to make sure nothing valuable — jewelry, money, food, even personal belongings with sentimental value — remained in the lining of the clothes as the new prisoners were absorbed into the camp. It was easy work but still, Bettina found something to complain about daily.

The Nazis regulated each inmate's food intake: those who worked received 800 calories of food rations per day; those who did not work received far less. According to the Nazis twisted logic, this ought to encourage even the laziest Jew to participate in the work force.

Kitty had heard stories: girls with parents younger than Karel and Bettina had died of starvation because their meager rations could not sustain them. That was all the motivation Kitty needed; the responsibility of feeding the family and keeping everyone alive fell squarely on Kitty's shoulders. She was glad to be busy. Oila, whom Kitty missed more than she could bear, had prepared her for a life that revolved around not being idle. Her phrase *Mach vas!* "Do something!" echoed in Kitty's ears.

Kitty no longer waited in line before work for the thin, brown liquid the ghetto cooks tried to pass off as coffee, preferring to start her day on an empty stomach rather than risk diarrhea. A long wait at the latrine might make her late for work, and Oila had also instilled a penchant for punctuality in her charge.

The vegetable gardens were situated outside the main wall of the fortress and each morning Kitty braced herself to leave the main camp. It was not the work itself she wished to avoid; rather, it was the gauntlet she and the other female workers were forced to pass through when exiting the main gate of the fortress.

Three checkpoints stood between the youth workers and the vegetable gardens: the Jewish police, appointed by the Council of Elders, the Czech gendarmes, and the German SS. The Jewish police wielded the least power, and for Kitty and her friends, passing through their checkpoint was a formality at best. Two men stood inside the fortress, checking the garden personnel's *Arbeitsklassifikation*, their work assignment. Kitty handed them her manila card, which she had received a month after arriving at the camp. They checked her occupation, gave her a quick glance to ensure she was in good overall health, and allowed her to pass through to the next checkpoint.

The Czech gendarmes were of two different dispositions, and in just a few short months, Kitty had come to differentiate the nuances between them. Kitty approached the checkpoint and was greeted by a few familiar faces. One older man always did his job without prejudice, keeping the line of workers moving, not of a mind to create trouble where there was none. He and others like him were compatriots who spoke in Czech and often met Kitty with a sympathetic gaze or a cheerful greeting. They shared a common sentiment: a deep hatred for the German occupiers of their native land.

Kitty approached the checkpoint that morning with trepidation. Two guards were processing the workers, and she had witnessed the work of one of them firsthand. The man had a cruel streak, doling out harsh words and discipline whenever the SS were in earshot, hoping to gain their favor. On one occasion he had withheld Kitty's work assignment card, claiming it to be a forgery. It was a lie, and it had backfired on him, making him even more eager to take revenge on Kitty.

At the last minute, the lines shifted, and Kitty ended up passing through the line of a friendly Czech guard she knew. The two kept their interaction formal, the guard looking at Kitty's card long enough to follow regulations lest anyone was looking for irregularities. The SS changed the personnel at the checkpoint frequently, to prevent relationships from developing between the prisoners and the Czech guards. Kitty grew to regret the appearance of a new face at the checkpoint. It often resulted in swapping out a sympathetic gatekeeper and replacing them with someone whose sympathies Kitty needed to establish from scratch.

Kitty felt sorry for some of the gendarmes. If they were kind they were at great risk; turning a blind eye to contraband the workers tried to smuggle from the garden could result in them being sent to the Little Fortress, the Gestapo prison on the outskirts of the camp, or worse yet, deported or shot for as little as a bootleg cucumber.

Today one of the guards was in a ruthless mood. "March! Hurry up, hurry up." The guard shouted to Kitty and the other workers as they passed by, swatting at them with a rag, laughing. "That will put a spring in your step." Kitty hurried to get clear of him.

Up ahead, Kitty could see the SS guards, the last checkpoint before the relative freedom on the other side of the fortress wall. Make no eye contact, keep walking, she told herself. Her family's survival depended upon her getting through each day unnoticed. Some days it was easy to slip by as if invisible. The Germans thought little of the Jews, especially the children, who received barely a glance, as if it might acknowledge in some small way that they were human. Kitty was fine with being ignored.

Growing up in Teplice, Kitty had never given a single thought to how fruits or vegetables arrived in Cook's kitchen. Now she loved gardening; it was fascinating to see the camp garden spring to life. The weeks of backbreaking planting and weeding, her fingernails ragged and chipped from digging without tools in the dirt, were worth it as she watched the crops she had planted – carrots, cauliflower, leeks, cabbage, and celery – push through the soil and thrive.

But the crops she watered and tended with care were not for her own consumption, or for anyone else in the camp. The harvest at Terezin was destined for the *Lazarette*, the field hospitals that nursed seriously injured German soldiers back to health, which existed outside the camp. She was feeding the enemy so that they could grow stronger, ensuring their continued oppression over her people.

There were no days off in the garden. Kitty weeded and picked all day on her hands and knees in cold, pouring rain, arriving back at the barrack soaked and shivering. Because of Bettina's job in the clothing depot, there was always dry clothing awaiting Kitty, brought to the house by her mother at considerable risk.

Bettina reminded Kitty daily how fortunate she was to be part of the essential labor force in the *Jugendgarten*. Although Kitty benefited from her mother's prominent status as an American citizen, the creation of the youth garden by the camp's Elders was one of their crowning achievements, shielding as many children as possible from potential deportation to the "East."

A vital job like the *Judengarten* could save your life, but it could also end it just as soon. The lure to steal extra food to supplement the camp's meager rations was an everyday temptation. There were various ethical codes in the camp, and pilfering from the garden of their captors was the antithesis of stealing in the mind of the camp's populace. Justification for theft was particularly acceptable if the bootlegged produce was destined for the garbage heap. Stealing to help one's family members survive was more than defensible. Some families in Terezin still had relatives on the outside who regularly sent them extra rations. For those who did not, like Kitty's, hunger pangs were constant, and malnutrition was common.

Kitty was aware of the risks of stealing from the garden. Guards had the right to shoot anyone caught trying to steal. The gardens sat in the shadow of the menacing black and white striped entrance to the Small Fortress, which served to discourage theft. The sounds emanating from the building on a still day were a chilling deterrent: one prisoner caught stealing pears was imprisoned there for months. Those not daring enough to smuggle contraband out of the garden took their chances nibbling at vegetables while working in the fields. But Kitty was not one of the timid.

Every day here is a risk, thought Kitty, so why not? She was smart and felt certain she could elude capture. And Kitty had friends inside. Her new friend Hanka, a Czech Jew who had come to the camp from Prague, was always eager to cue her in to the movements of the garden's supervisors. Kitty often shared the spoils with Hanka for her efforts.

"Today, I will steal a leek." Kitty confidently mouthed the words to Hanka. Once before, Kitty had tied a leek to her inner thigh with string. And tomatoes smuggled well, especially for girls whose breasts were not too large. If the tomatoes are firm, they can stand in for the real thing, as long as no one gropes where they are not supposed to, Kitty thought with disgust.

Supervisors patrolled the rows upon rows of teens as they weeded, harvested, and trimmed the acres of plants; they were older, usually women, Jewish prisoners like themselves. Kitty was a good judge of character, and she knew an opening when she saw one. "Supervisor Guttman. She is the same as us," Kitty had explained to Hanka. Not one to play up to the Germans, Guttman cooperated with the SS just enough to stay under the radar. It was under her watch that Kitty did some of her best thievery. She liked Guttman and did not want to get her in trouble, but if an opportunity arose, Kitty took it.

Kitty glanced around the garden and at the last moment opted for tomatoes over the leek. Success! Two green tomatoes now occupied each cup of her brassiere. Kitty felt a rush of adrenaline, her cheeks flushing slightly. Her excitement was short lived. Eluding detection out in the field was one thing; getting through the checkpoints at the end of the day was another. In the name of searching for contraband some Czech guards patted down the teens in places they did not want, or need, to be touched.

The day ended and Kitty fell into the queue leading to the gendarme checkpoint. She inhaled sharply. Just my luck, Kitty thought. Up ahead carrying out the exit inspection was the gendarme who fancied himself an SS officer. No one knew his name, but his reputation preceded him. Rumor had it if he found contraband, the offending party was forced to engage in sexual favors to elude exposure or worse yet, face deportation.

"He made me do things with him," Kitty heard one of the older girls crying one night in the barrack.

Kitty tried to remain calm, but her palms began to sweat, and her shoulders tightened. As she grew closer, she noticed a mole under his nose. "Turn around," he barked to Kitty, expecting each order to be quickly carried out. Her back to him, he reached around and squeezed Kitty's "breasts." After a not so gentle squeeze, she was instructed to turn around and face him. He was smiling.

The guard winked at Kitty. "Go on then," he ordered, sniggering as he turned toward his next victim. Kitty played the part of the innocent teen; she was an actor after all. Fool, thought Kitty.

On the walk back to the barracks Kitty took a different route. Rounding a corner, she caught her breath. There, in Stadt Park right before her were the most beautiful trees she had ever seen. Pear trees, in full bloom. The sight of them filled Kitty with a crushing sadness. "The trees don't know we are prisoners," she thought. "They don't know we are at war. They bloom regardless. How fortunate they are." Without trying, she had made a rhyme. She wiped a tear from her cheek.

Kitty recalled a poem, *Maj*, by the Czech poet, Karel Hynek Machá. The story was told that if a girl was not kissed under a tree while it was in bloom, she would wither and die within two months. Because she had not experienced romance firsthand, Kitty had always loved the story.

When Kitty arrived back at the barracks, she delivered the day's loot to her mother. Bettina accepted the bruised tomatoes, not bothering to inquire as to how they had gotten that way. Her mother's main concern was whether Kitty could clean the remaining dirt from under her fingernails before supper. With little running water and no soap, it was a nearly impossible task.

Each day spent in the camp's gardens, digging in the dirt, and tending to the acres of vegetables, deposited another layer of grime on Kitty's face, neck, ankles, and arms – no patch of exposed skin was safe. Had there been a mirror anywhere in the camp Kitty would not have recognized herself. Gone were the alabaster skin and thick, dark ringlets of the girl who had arrived months ago. Her hair was a tangled mess, and even her father had to refrain from telling her she no longer resembled Shirley Temple. In fact, she looked now more like a chimney sweep.

As if to add insult to injury, Bettina reminded her, "Tomorrow is shower day, Kitty." Kitty felt like she was making the best of everyday life in Terezin but showering in public was one thing that made her cringe. Every ten days, a pit formed in her stomach as the inevitable event arrived. The daily buildup of grit was such that no rag could wipe it away. But in Kitty's fourteen-year-old mind the alternative was even more disgusting.

Everyone has their limits, thought Kitty.

"I hope those cows keep their distance today," Kitty thought as she waited her turn in line at the showers the next morning. The women around her gossiped quietly as the line moved forward outside the barracks where the crime against Kitty's modesty would soon take place. She stripped, folding her clothes carefully and setting them on the floor of the makeshift dressing room. Kitty covered herself with her hands as best she could as the line inched forward. The women then formed into groups of five or six and were motioned by the female guards to stand underneath one of the dripping shower heads.

In stark contrast to how Kitty felt, many of the older women looked forward to this day, considering it one of the small luxuries of their grim daily existence. They were not going to let anyone come between them and the stream of lukewarm water that brought them some semblance of normalcy. For Kitty, this was the height of vulnerability. She had never been naked in front of anyone except her Oila. Oila had often joked that Kitty's mother had never even changed her diaper when she was an infant. This public washing pushed the barriers of personal comfort.

I'll try to stay on the outside, Kitty coached herself. I will turn my front outward, so I won't touch anyone. Kitty had heard the stories, whispers of advances that began in the shower and were requited in private. She was no wallflower, but anyone who tried would know with utmost certainty where she stood on the matter. She pitied the pampered girls new to the camp who might not know how to protect themselves.

Never mind that there was no soap to be had; Kitty loathed the proximity to the other adult women's naked bodies. Due to malnutrition and the stress of their new life in the camp, many of the women no longer menstruated. It was a small blessing, doing without the use of pads or rags, not having to worry about blood trickling down their legs in the fields or in the shower. But no matter how hard she tried, she could not rinse off without having another woman's body parts touch one of hers. She held her breath as the women, most of them twice her age, jostled and nudged her to gain a better position under the impotent shower spout.

"Watch it," one woman hissed at Kitty. "You are stepping on my foot."

"Ouch," another complained.

"Move your ass," another ordered.

Seen from afar, the women appeared to be engaged in a synchronized water ballet set to Johann Strauss' whimsical waltz *The Blue Danube*. Posteriors bumped anteriors, arms raised into the light stream of water and then fell as another reached in, elbows jabbed breasts of all sizes and shapes until Kitty found herself suddenly expelled from the group, dripping wet, mildly bruised and shivering, the other women's bodies undulating like one organism.

Her dignity barely intact, Kitty hurriedly pulled on the same dirty frock she had earlier folded with care. Her dress and undergarments had not been washed. In yet another German policy aimed at keeping the prison population off guard and confused, shower day did not coincide with laundry day.

CHAPTER
ELEVEN

Life in the ghetto was a combination of order and chaos, input and output. Vlada thought of the distillery, the oxen pulling the train car into the factory yard, unloading the chemicals, mixing the ingredients together in the laboratory using different equations to create new amalgamations, all the chemicals leaving the factory yard, albeit in a different form.

So, it was at Terezin: people thrown together to create order from chaos, so many moving parts needed to keep the camp functioning, and people coming and going, like bottles on the assembly line at Uncle Robert's soda factory, shuttling along the rollers and dumped out the other end.

In the first weeks at the camp, Vlada had struggled with the overcrowded streets, the unsanitary conditions at the barrack, the physical separation from his mother. It all seemed insurmountable. Every night Vlada crawled up to the private world he was creating on the top bunk and looked down at his father and the other men, who spoke in hushed voices, mindful of those who needed rest, sharing stories about their lives before the camp, helping each other with mending or writing a letter to someone in the outside world. Each night, Vlada turned his back to the men below, adjusting himself on the straw mattress, dreaming of places and things that disappeared like wisps of smoke upon waking each morning. Vlada was glad when he and his parents were given their work assignments. Each of them now had a role in the hive, worker bees responsible for the colony's activities.

Each morning Karel took his leave of the barrack, walking across the street to the enormous Magdeburg barrack, which took up almost an entire city block, where the Jewish self-government of the camp had taken up residence. Karel returned at the end of the day for supper, never shedding light on his daily activities. Hermina worked in one of the camp kitchens, at first glance a seemingly low-ranking job. But in Terezin, the pecking order of the outside world had been turned on its head.

Lawyers were of no use in the camp, the Nazis were the law now, so lawyers left behind their prestige and power upon entering. Those in charge of the food sat many rungs above them. Food meant power now.

It was a ten-minute walk across the camp from the Hanover Barrack to the *bauhof* where Vlada reported to his job at the locksmith shop each morning for the day's assignments. Every day except Sunday, the hub of workshops buzzed with activity; professional tradesman and their apprentices, blacksmiths, carpenters, electricians, locksmiths, and plumbers working in concert under the watchful eye of the camp's Jewish administration, working to maintain the ghetto's fragile infrastructure. The fortress, once home to five thousand residents, threatened to crumble under the weight of fifty thousand prisoners crammed inhumanely inside its walls.

Vlada crossed the camp under cold, grey skies. He entered the locksmith shop and inhaled deeply. He loved the smell of it, a combination of metal filings, wood shavings and grease. To an outside observer the shop looked disorganized, but Vlada looked down the length of the shop and saw everything in its place. He felt fortunate at having been assigned this line of work; he had learned a new skill, one which allowed him a certain amount of freedom. He was able to roam the camp at all hours after curfew while in the line of duty. The locksmith job also provided something with which to barter.

Vlada poked his head in the blacksmith shop next door. A wave of heat from the roaring fires warmed his cheeks, the loud clanging of the hammers as they hit the anvils assaulted his ears. Vlada waved to his friend, Ada. Adolf Lebenhart was from Prague, a year younger than Vlada, and the two young men had become friends. Ada stopped pounding on a molten rod, hammer poised in mid-air, and waved to his friend. "Hey, Vlada! Lunch later, eh?" Vlada nodded.

Felix was Vlada's assistant and he waited for Vlada that morning at a bench in the locksmith shop. Felix accompanied Vlada on the two-person jobs; he was as good a helper as he was a companion, holding doors in place while Vlada matched up a strike plate against a latch, or running back to the shop to fetch tools needed to complete a job. They worked well together, the days passing quickly.

The locksmith job sent Vlada to every corner of the camp, and one afternoon on his way to a repair, Vlada bumped into Nora on the street. She greeted Vlada warmly. A huge smile spread across her face, she threw her arms around his neck, then pulled away, embarrassed. Vlada stuttered out a response, looking around, wondering if anyone else had witnessed Nora's display of affection. They agreed to meet on the Haupstrasse after supper one night.

It was a bitter night for a walk, the wind whipping around the corners of the buildings, the streets nearly empty as darkness and curfew approached. Vlada and Nora walked together, their cheeks rosy from the cold.

"What do you miss the most about Pardubice, Vlada?" Nora's voice was soft and filled with melancholy. She had always been a bit dramatic. It was nearing curfew and Vlada looked at Nora in the fading light, realizing she was barely more than a child.

"My mother's cooking, my books, and the distillery," Vlada answered without hesitation. "You?" Vlada stopped walking, waiting for Nora's reply.

"I miss my dog, Jakub. We hid him right up until the last minute. And I miss *koblihy*." Nora laughed and then turned away, thoughts of Jakub bringing tears to her eyes.

Vlada changed the subject. "Oh, have I got a story for you about koblihy!"

Nora's older brother sought Vlada out the following day. Karel was six years older than his sister. "Stay away from Nora," Karel warned Vlada, his fists clenching, puffing out his chest.

Nice try, thought Vlada. It felt good to have a friend from home and Vlada was not about to give up Nora.

Nora teased Vlada on their evening walks, pumping her arms up and down and feigning importance. "Look, I am Vlada. I make keys." If his job at the camp gave him any feelings of self-importance, she immediately cut him down to size. Vlada tickled her until she cried out. "Stop, Vlada, stop!"

On some evenings, the duo became a trio, with Nora's friend, Eva, joining them after supper. The girls walked arm in arm, telling Vlada their childhood stories, the three odd companions talking and laughing for hours. Eva's grandfather had owned a large bakery in Pardubice before the occupation and every week Eva had visited Grandfather Schultz's bakery with her mother. "One day I asked my grandfather if I could help with a recipe for *medovnik*," Eva told Vlada and Nora. "I added salt instead of sugar and ruined the whole batch of honey cake!

"My favorite was his gingerbread," Nora smiled, smacking her lips together. A moment later they were all rubbing their stomachs, aching at the memory of eating one of Grandfather's sweets.

Any news of the war raging outside the camp's walls was taken with a grain of salt. Most information that filtered inside was patently false, rumors floating around the ghetto unsubstantiated or altered in their frequent retelling, often disproved within hours of the telling.

The family sat together eating supper one night at a makeshift table in Vlada and Karel's barrack. Karel rarely repeated camp gossip, but tonight he spoke in a conspiratorial tone, sharing news with Vlada and Hermina.

"Word is that the Poles are planning to revolt against the Nazis in Warsaw," Karel whispered the shocking, and dangerous, hearsay with conviction, shifting restlessly in his chair.

When neither Hermina nor Vlada responded, Karel added. "I have it on good account." Vlada wondered where the information had been revealed, so certain was Karel that it was true. Nevertheless, he was energized by news of this act of defiance coming from the oppressed of a ghetto in another Nazi-occupied nation.

"Do you think the same might happen here, Tati?" Vlada was not overjoyed with the conditions at the camp, but he was fearful of the ramifications of a rebellion against the Germans.

Vlada's question remained unanswered, but within days of the revelation, their world was sent into a tailspin. People did not show up for work at the *bauhof*, and Nora did not meet Vlada and Eva at their appointed spot. He went to the barracks where Nora lived with her mother.

"We are being sent to the "East," Vlada," Nora cried, packing her belongings in a small bag. Nora handed Vlada a slip with her name and a date: January 26. Vlada did not know what happened in the East. It seemed no one did. He hugged Nora.

"Let me talk to my father. There must be some mistake." Vlada ran all the way back to the Hanover Barrack and found his father alone in the makeshift sitting area. Karel's face was pale and drawn.

"Tati, what is happening? Nora said she is being sent to the East." Vlada was out of breath, and shocked to find his father in a state. He felt an uneasiness creep over him.

Karel paused for a moment, not looking at his son. "There is nothing we can do, Vlada." Vlada sat down on a bunk, staring at his father's back. He wanted an explanation, and his father gave him less than nothing. Vlada stared at the floor, the moment on the train when she had tucked the strand of hair behind her ear and their eyes met flashed in his mind.

The next morning, Vlada heard that Nora had been sent on a train to the "East" the previous day, along with her brother and her parents. He never saw her again.

Vlada did his best to console Eva after Nora's deportation. "Why, Vlada? Why?" Eva asked Vlada repeatedly. Eva's small features were no match for Nora's beauty, but she was sweet, nonetheless. Eva cried on Vlada's shoulder for hours over the loss of her friend. The trio of friends was irreparably broken.

Vlada and Eva became inseparable; each evening after their walk Vlada deposited Eva at her barracks, her arms around his neck, clinging to him. Vlada joked with her. "You are like the squid in *Twenty*

Thousand Leagues Under the Sea. I peel off your arms, but they reach right back out to grab me." The happy-go-lucky girl who had once laughed so easily was now a fearful child. Vlada kissed the top of her head each time they parted, gently removing her arms from around his neck. "I am not going anywhere, Eva," he told her gently.

Sometimes Vlada and Eva walked to the Central Bakery at one end of the camp. Grandfather Schultz's reputation as a baker had preceded him, and he was immediately put to work turning out bread for the camp's inhabitants. Once the owner of the city's renowned gingerbread bakery, he was now tasked by the Nazis to make bread from flour that resembled sawdust. The generous baker offered Vlada loaves of bread, which he smuggled home in his toolbox and shared with his parents.

Less than a week passed, and one night Eva did not show up for their regular date. Vlada ran to the bakery, knocking frantically at the back door. Grandfather Schultz appeared outside, shaking his head. "This morning," the baker started to speak, barely lifting his head to look at Vlada, then turned and walked back inside.

Vlada had cared for both girls and now they were gone, sent to some godforsaken place where no one was ever heard from again. But that was not the worst of it. The worst blow came when he returned to the barrack that evening. His parents sat on a bench; his mother's face twisted in pain. Vlada looked questioningly at his father. Karel shook his head, gradually revealing the ugly news to his son.

The sun rose over the camp and the world outside it the next morning, the mere act of its appearance allowing the prisoners to do what humans have done since the beginning of time — hope. Each day that dawned meant another night survived. But the fiery dawn that February morning was different. Muffled cries could be heard around the camp. The events of January and February had been like a series of waves crashing over Terezin, leaving only destruction in their wake, the weight of each swell threatening to crush the spirit of even the strongest prisoner. Vlada, stoic and even keeled, was among those suffering the camp's collective tragedy.

The metamorphosis was excruciating. Vlada was bitter at his naivete, at the excitement and promise he felt just a few months earlier when he and his parents boarded the train in Pardubice bound for Terezin. In a few weeks, Vlada would turn eighteen, but he could not summon even the smallest reason to celebrate this milestone to manhood. His coming of age had arrived early.

The Nazi promise of a Jewish community and retirement settlement for the elderly Jews of the Protectorate was revealed to be a lie, with the illusion that life in the camp was one over which the prisoners had a modicum of control stripped away. The events of the past few months had ripped the blinders off. Out of lies and deception, Vlada saw the truth emerge, and it was worse than he could have imagined.

Vlada and the other inhabitants of the camp were faced with two options. Wear blinders, and slip into the illusion or, keep them off, and admit that you live in a world without hope, where every moment you are a pawn in a game, subject to the arbitrary whims of your captors. Was even that choice itself an illusion?

Vlada had a crush on Vera for as long as he could remember; her dark hair and eyes cast a spell over him. She laughed often, a laugh that was deep and husky. Vera was two years older than Vlada, making her by default more mysterious than girls his own age. There always seemed to be a boy lingering around Vera's house, hoping for a moment with her, or, she was on her way out to meet one. Vera paid little if any attention to Vlada; in fact, his presence barely registered with her. She was unattainable, which made Vlada even more smitten. In the end, one obstacle guaranteed Vlada's crush would go unrequited: Vera was Vlada's first cousin.

As a young boy, Vlada loved visiting the Eisners. Hermina's sister Anna, her husband Robert, and Vlada's cousins Vera and Mirek, lived in a spacious home in Beroun, to the south and west of Prague. Their comfortable home was made possible by his uncle's lucrative business venture, a soda factory that occupied the entire first floor of the building. The high points of Vlada's visits to Beroun were twofold: he succeeded in drinking all the ice-cold soda pop he wanted, and he got to see Vera.

Often Vlada left a visit to Aunt Anna's house disappointed. Vera was usually out with her latest beau, and when she was at home, she walked right past her younger brother, Mirek, and her infatuated cousin, the one with the puppy dog eyes, as if they were invisible.

"Come on, Vlada," Mirek teased his cousin. "She's too old for you." Vlada was forced to drown the sorrows of Vera's unreturned affections in liter upon liter of sweet soda pop and daily trips to the swimming hole on the banks of the Berounka River. One sunny day, Vlada held his breath underwater for what he was sure was the longest time ever. Seeing no sign of Vlada returning to the surface, Mirek ran, terrified, to fetch his mother.

"Vlada," Aunt Anna screamed, standing on the edge of the riverbank, her apron still tied around her waist. Moments later, Vlada popped up for air, grinning madly. Neither Aunt Anna nor Mirek found Vlada's antics amusing.

Mirek plotted his revenge. One day Mirek filled a soda pop bottle with coffee. "Here you go, cousin. Your favorite flavor — chocolate!" Mirek watched as Vlada took his first sip.

"Ptthew!" Vlada spit out the coffee, both boys laughing and rolling on the floor until their stomachs hurt. Their mothers' annual summer visits, catching up on family gossip and taking afternoon walks, were far from a hardship for the two boys, as they had each other. They were great companions.

Mirek loved to play the factory tour guide, pointing out his favorite features inside the walls of the sweet-smelling plant.

"This," Mirek said officiously, "is where Father keeps the ice." Mirek opened the thick door just a crack to reveal a sealed cooler, having been warned never to leave it open or the massive blocks of ice were at risk of melting. A fine mist escaped through the crack in the door, the cold within meeting the heat of the summer day. Vlada had an icebox at the flat back in Pardubice, but it was nothing like this; here the blocks of ice had to weigh more than he and Mirek combined.

"Wow." Vlada's eyes grew wide. The colossal chunks of frozen water never ceased to impress him. "Close it! Quickly, Mirek!" Vlada did not want to risk disaster or the wrath of his uncle.

The soda production was automated and partitioned off by task: one area was dedicated to mixing the soda ingredients, one for washing the bottles, and one for filling them. It was a banner day when Uncle Robert allowed Vlada to see the factory in full operation. Watching the assembly line was like stepping into a futuristic world, the bottles clanking noisily along on a conveyor belt, topped off to a fill line with the sticky sweet liquid. At the end of the line, the bottles were capped and crimped.

"What do you think, Vlada?" Uncle Robert shouted above the din, the machines hissing and bottles jangling. He was proud of the business and of his small fleet of trucks that delivered soda throughout the region. Vlada loved the distillery, but this was something altogether different.

Each evening after supper, Mirek and Vlada engaged in a tradition and grabbed a couple of bottles of soda, sneaking them up to Mirek's bedroom. Mirek whipped off the caps. Vlada closed his eyes, listening to the hissing sound the bubbles made as they escaped from the bottle. The boys drank in deep gulps of soda, thirsty from the day's activities, and proceeded to burp. Their mothers would not have approved.

The two boys sat on the floor of Mirek's room in their pajamas and told stories of the day's events and the things they planned to do in between sips.

"Tomorrow I am going to hold my breath underwater longer than you," Mirek threatened.

"Good luck!" Vlada laughed, and considered letting Mirek win the next one. Life was sweet.

In return for Vlada's visits to the Eisners, Hermina invited her nephew to stay with the family in Pardubice. The cousins played in the factory yard until it was time to catch the bus to the family's annual summer vacation spot in the Krkonoše mountains.

Mirek's parents had a car, so he rarely had the opportunity to ride a bus or train. He was the first to run up the steps and hand his ticket to the driver, making his way to the very back of the bus, motioning for Vlada to follow. Mirek gazed out the window of the bus from the moment it pulled out of the station, barely taking his attention away from the passing scenery during the entire hour-long ride. The family arrived at the mountain midmorning, and dropped their bags at the small cabin they would call home for the next two weeks.

"Mami, Tati, can we please take Mirek on the gondola?" Vlada begged his parents to take the cable car to the top of Sněžka Mountain, the highest peak in the mountain range. "You can see Poland from the top, Mirek!"

They walked to the base of the mountain and boarded the enclosed cable car. Mirek tightly gripped the handrails as the car swayed slightly, dangling off the cables and inching its way up the mountain's broad side. The only sound was the rhythmic squeaking of the cable. Everyone aboard, including the boys, gazed out the large windows, mesmerized by the sweeping view of the countryside. When they arrived at the summit, the boys spun in circles, arms outstretched, taking in the three hundred sixty-degree panorama under cobalt skies.

"Don't try to cross the border, boys. The Polish guards will be waiting to lock you up!" Karel teased. Mirek's eyes grew wide with fear.

"Leave him alone, Karel," Hermina scolded her husband, as they lingered at the top, looking out onto the green mountains stretching off as far as the eye could see. The sun changed its angle in the sky, beckoning them to begin the hike back down the mountain on a well-worn, slightly steep path.

As they made their way down the trail, Vlada began to sing his favorite hiking song. His parents joined in and sang along, Karel pumping his arms up and down in a silly, exaggerated march. Hermina broke out in a huge smile, laughing at her husband's antics. Vlada loved the sound of his mother's laugh.

The sing-song melody of the tune kept a perfect rhythm as they marched down to the town at the mountain's base. "La da da da da da." It was a simple ditty, and after a couple of rounds, Mirek learned the words and joined in.

"*Chytila patrola prostitutku mladou.*" Vlada began to sing one of the songs he knew made Mirek blush, a salty pub song with a polka melody about a prostitute who is caught by the police crossing the Charles Bridge. The woman falls into the river and all that can be seen of her as she floats away is her bottom bobbing up and down in the water. Vlada shouted the punch line.

"Stop, Vlada!" Mirek protested, almost losing his footing, and laughing until his belly hurt.

Tired and happy, they reached the base of the mountain, the four of them marching into the tourist village of Špindlerův Mlyn as if they were part of a parade. The resort town's main street was wide and lined with stores, coffeehouses, and buildings with Scandinavian architecture.

They settled in a booth in their favorite restaurant, and Vlada's parents ordered beer. Vlada watched as his mother sipped the golden liquid, her eyes sparkling, her spirits high. She and Karel clinked their glasses and joined in the drinking songs played by a band of musicians wearing lederhosen.

"Mami, it's *Pes Jitrničku sežnal.*" Vlada heard the familiar strains of the song which told the tale of a dog who ate sausage in the kitchen of a restaurant and was caught by the cook, who quickly did away with him. All the other dogs cried and built their friend a grave. The band repeated the chorus, and the singing in the small restaurant grew loud and spirited, beer mugs crashing into each other with gusto.

The waitress arrived and placed steaming bowls of *Krkonošské kyselo* in front of Vlada and Mirek. Vlada and Mirek looked at each other and then dug in greedily. They ate until their bellies were stuffed. Mirek groaned and said he had never eaten so much in one sitting.

One year younger than Vlada, Mirek felt more like a sibling than a cousin, his presence transforming their small family of three into a robust family of four. Those were blissful summer days for Vlada, singing and hiking and eating to contentment, surrounded by his favorite people and the mountain's breathtaking scenery.

Now they were gone. Mirek. Vera. Aunt Anna and Robert. On February 1, the entire family was forced onto one of the camp's many winter transports to the "East." Hermina was devastated. She feared the worst for her sister and her family and Karel could do little to dissuade her.

Vlada tried to make sense of it. He thought back to a time not long after the German occupation, the day his mother told him that Vera had been sent to a Catholic school.

"They are trying to keep Vera safe, Vlada." Hermina spoke as if under a great weight, cupping Vlada's face between her hands and looking in his eyes in a way that confused him.

"Will she be okay, Mami?" Vlada did not comprehend the gravity of the situation. "Should she not have made bat mitzvah?"

Like Vlada's family, the Eisners followed a relaxed observance of Jewish religious traditions. Vlada was his father's son, the son of a Czech Legionnaire and, therefore, no stranger to the concept of Czech first, Jew second. He wondered if Czech first made it easier for the Eisners to allow Vera's conversion to Catholicism. If Vlada understood correctly, her parents had counseled Vera to renounce her religion to keep her from under the German's radar. In that case, why hadn't Vlada's parents asked him to do the same?

To her family's surprise, Vera converted not only in name but in spirit, making it known that she had deeply embraced the dogma of the Catholic Church. Vlada remembered the last time he saw Vera; it was the summer of 1941. It was a bright summer day and the sun glinted off the gold cross that hung from her neck. Mesmerized by her, Vlada watched as she absentmindedly played with the cross as they exchanged pleasantries. Later, Mirek told Vlada how strange it was to hear his sister reciting the Lord's Prayer in her bedroom each night. Vlada could only imagine her despair when a few months later, Deputy Reich Protector Heydrich decreed that all Jews must wear the yellow star with the word *Jude* on it while in public.

Vera had no choice but to comply. The Nazis were unimpressed with Vera's conversion; they did not recognize her as anything other than a Jew. The final insult was to send her to Terezin along with her family, a Catholic convert among Jews.

Vlada wondered where Vera's Catholic God was when the Eisners were loaded onto a train bound for the "East" after a year of living in relative peace in Terezin. Maybe He was in the same place as Yahweh. Nowhere.

Aunt Anna had been Babicka Emilie's faithful caretaker from the day her mother arrived at the camp the previous fall. Blind and infirm at age seventy-eight, Vlada's maternal grandmother had been ripped away from her daughter Berta's home in Prague and deported to Terezin. Babicka Emilie was assigned to live in the Jager Barrack, a low, moss-covered building on the edge of the camp. The barrack was jammed to capacity with the camp's elderly and infirm, who lived in squalid conditions, barely surviving on the meager rations allotted to those who could not work. It was a death sentence.

After Anna and her family were sent east, Emilie's care fell to Hermina. She tried to supplement her mother's diet with her own rations, and with items pilfered from her job in the kitchen. But her efforts were in vain. Poor nutrition and the camp's harsh conditions had already taken a toll on her mother.

"My mother is heartbroken over Anna and the children," Hermina reported, still reeling from the loss herself. Babicka Emilie died two weeks later. The final blow had fallen.

Vlada arrived early at the locksmith shop on his birthday, before the other workers. No one would have questioned his presence there; he was a trusted employee. He worked quietly, efficiently, meticulously, and when he was done, he walked to the courtyard where his mother was doling out portions of stew from a large pot.

"For Babicka Emilie," Vlada said, handing his mother a small metal box with a tight-fitting lid, his grandmother's name etched on the top. Hermina held back tears, taking the box from her son, understanding its purpose immediately. She would transfer her mother's ashes from the cardboard box the ghetto guards had given her to the beautiful metal box Vlada had made.

"Her ashes will be stored in the Columbarium, Vlada. Along with grandfather." His mother was repeating what she had been told by the Czech crematorium staff. She avoided making eye contact, instead her eyes fixed on the box.

"Their ashes will be returned to us when we are freed from this place. Then we can take them home and give them both a proper burial in Pardubice." She held the box in her hands, her whole body thick with grief. She had forgotten Vlada's birthday. It's for the best, thought Vlada. He could find no reason to celebrate turning eighteen.

Nora and Eva were gone. The Eisners were gone. And his grandmother, too. Vlada had no faith that what his mother had been promised would ever come to pass.

CHAPTER ELEVEN

Bettina stood in front of Kitty in the middle of the women's barrack on the corner of Haupstrasse and Badhausgasse, excitedly holding something behind her back. Kitty sat on her bunk, eyes closed, complying with her mother's request. When Kitty opened her eyes, her mother presented her with a small package, bending at the waist, as if she were bestowing crown jewels. The package was tied with old newsprint with a scrap of fabric for a bow, and Kitty tore it open eagerly.

Inside was a cotton pillowcase, light blue with tiny white squares: gingham. Kitty held it at the corners allowing it to unfurl, admiring it. Her immediate fondness for it forced Kitty to admit Bettina knew her preferences well when it came to fabric: tiny flower prints, pastels, small patterns, and anything on which Kitty could embroider if there was thread to be had. The pillowcase was Kitty's birthday present, pilfered from Bettina's job in the clothing detail.

"Herzlichen Gluckwunsch zum Geburtstag, Kitty." Kitty frowned when her mother wished her happy birthday in German. Why can't she just speak to me in Czech? Kitty groused. There were rumors

spreading among the garden staff of an impending visit by the Danish Red Cross. Did Bettina want her daughter to look her best when they came for the inspection? Her mother wore a plain, short sleeve blouse, the yellow star sewn over the left breast, and a dotted skirt. Kitty bit her lip. Bettina had been more than tolerable, kind even, since their arrival at the camp, and Kitty felt a wave of guilt wash over her for her unkind thoughts.

Kitty stared down at the pillowcase, with its sweet pattern and fabric unblemished by dirt and wear. It was ripe with possibilities. She sat down on her bunk and began loosening the stitching on the seams to create openings for her head and arms. Bettina watched as Kitty threaded a needle with red thread she had been saving for a special occasion, keeping it tucked away under her bunk. Kitty pierced the fabric the way Oila had taught her, each stitch combining with the previous one to slowly reveal a petal, a few more still becoming a flower right before Bettina's eyes.

Kitty threaded the needle again, this time with green thread, embroidering a few leaves near the flowers around the neck of the shirt. After a half hour's work, Kitty set the needle down, admiring her handiwork. Oila would be proud. Kitty whipped off her old blouse, sliding the former pillowcase over her head and letting it fall in place.

Bettina sat down on her bunk, releasing a melancholy sigh. Her eyes drifted to some faraway place, and she became so lost in thought that she failed to notice Kitty had left off the yellow star from her new creation. Kitty prepared to leave the barrack, looking down at the shirt proudly, hoping to show it off. She waved to Bettina, who absentmindedly lifted her hand, waving back. Kitty's cheeks flushed, and smiled at her coup. If Bettina had noticed the absence of the star, it would have spoiled everything. The blouse was perfect without it.

It was a beautiful evening in June, and Kitty walked briskly, energized by her own daring. She passed the barracks next to hers on Badhausgasse, and saw a woman sitting on the steps, a young girl on the step in front of her. The girl had long brown hair and was noticeably younger than Kitty. The girl's mother sang a lilting song quietly under her breath, all the while brushing her daughter's hair. Mother and daughter smiled and laughed.

Kitty could not remember a time Bettina had ever brushed her hair. Her smile faded, the joy at the beautiful blouse she had created from her mother's gift turned briefly to sadness at the absence of Oila, her hairdresser, her teacher, her companion.

It had rained earlier in the afternoon and fat drops had fallen on the dry, cracked streets of the ghetto. A lingering cloud passed in front of the sun, casting Kitty's face in shadow. A breeze picked up, and she was transported back to Masaryk Street in Teplice, and the image of linens hanging on the clothesline lifting gently in the wind. The sun reappeared, warming Kitty's face, and her envy of the closeness between mother and daughter and sadness over missing Oila evaporated as quickly as the clouds in the skies.

Kitty stopped for a moment and closed her eyes before turning to the right onto Hauptstrasse; it was her birthday, and she had forgotten to make a wish. In her mind's eye she imagined she was not in a prison, that the walk around the block she was embarking on was as a free person. Kitty opened her eyes, turned the corner, and found to her delight that her mental trick had worked: although the faces that greeted her were gaunt, the inhabitants dressed in shabby clothing, she convinced herself it was just another evening in any Czech town. Kitty joined the throngs in the streets escaping into the cool summer evening. Happy birthday to me, she thought.

Kitty walked confidently, head held high, shoulders thrown back, daring someone to take note of her missing star. When no one noticed, she returned to people-watching, hoping for an interesting distraction. She caught a glimpse of her reflection in the window of a building and smiled to herself. But the excitement she had expected when she set out without the star was not materializing. She was not cross, just disappointed as she turned back in the direction of her barrack. She would sit outside and read from a biochemistry book she had borrowed from a friend on the garden crew.

Oh, thought Kitty. That one again. Kitty had noticed the young man on the other side of the street before. He was handsome, with an aquiline nose and brown hair. She had seen him in the early morning on her walk to the *Judengarten*, when the streets of the camp were still quiet, and few people were about. The young man walked purposefully, carrying a heavy box of tools. Kitty thought he must be very important, always coming and going in the camp at all hours. She watched him for a moment and smiled inwardly; she was just about to look away when his eyes caught hers.

The young man shouted to her from across the cobblestone street. "Hey, you, Miss! You forgot your star!" Kitty looked quickly down the street, afraid the young man's shouts might have aroused the attention of a Czech gendarme or worse, a German guard.

When it was clear no one had heard his comment, Kitty shouted back. "Well, that doesn't concern you!" Her stomach performed an unfamiliar flutter. She looked away, cheeks reddening, just in time to see her friend Hanka from the *Judengarten* approach.

"Kitty. Have you not met Vlada?" Hanka waved to the young man, motioning him to their side of the street. Kitty felt frozen in place on the sidewalk, her breathing shallow as she watched Vlada approach.

"Vlada, meet Kitty. Kitty, Vlada. Well, I must be going." And just as quickly as Hanka had appeared, she disappeared, turning, and walking away, leaving Vlada and Kitty standing awkwardly next to each other on the sidewalk.

"So, about your star," Vlada said cheekily. He lowered his head, his hand on his chin and looked directly into her eyes. Kitty felt strange. Her body trembled slightly. "You really should get back to your barrack before anyone else notices it. But tomorrow after work I think you should meet me right here, and you can tell me more about it." He raised his eyebrows, waiting for her response.

Kitty nodded, afraid to speak, afraid of what her voice might sound like, unsure of herself in these most unusual circumstances. Vlada smiled and walked briskly down the street to whatever important business kept him coming and going about the camp.

What just happened? thought Kitty, her stomach doing somersaults, her mouth open in astonishment. Her small act of defiance, walking in public without the star, on her fifteenth birthday no less, had given her a brief illusion of freedom. Yet in that moment of freedom, this person, this handsome young man, this Vlada, had turned Kitty's orderly world on its side.

Kitty walked slowly back to the women's barracks, her eyes wandering, alighting on every crack in the sidewalk, every tree as if she were seeing it for the first time. Something had changed. Everything in the camp had been seen through a sepia lens before that moment, as if a fine, brown dust had settled over everything she set her eyes on, muting its beauty. She had not been unhappy in the camp but suddenly, everything she passed – every crack, every sidewalk, every tree – was lovely and vibrant and colorful. She did not understand why.

Once she had been in church with Oila and heard of holy things. Kitty turned the brief encounter with Vlada over in her mind, thinking that it might qualify as divine. She entered the women's barrack, her breath coming quickly, worried that her smile might arouse suspicion. One of the young women in the barracks noticed Kitty's flushed cheeks and elbowed one of the other girls; they knew a co-conspirator when they saw one, but they dared not tease Kitty with Bettina nearby.

Bettina noticed neither Kitty's dazzling smile nor the missing star.

The following day Kitty mooned about the barracks after dinner. She rarely spoke to the older girls, but tonight she needed to find JoJo, the clever girl who knew the inner workings of the camp's black market. JoJo had something Kitty wanted. Someone had discovered that when they mixed a red medicine dispensed for urinary tract infections with Vaseline it gave the appearance of lipstick. The "lipstick" had been making the rounds of the camp. Kitty was going to meet Vlada, and she wanted to look older, more sophisticated, and she was willing to pay.

"How much?" Kitty pointed at JoJo's tinted lips.

"Oh, who is it, Kitty? Do tell." JoJo wanted all the details. Kitty was not ready to tell anyone about Vlada. She possessed so few things in the camp, in the world for that matter. This was her secret, and hers alone, she was holding the thought of him close, and she wanted to keep it for herself for just a little while. And besides that, JoJo was a gossip who held no secret as sacred.

"I can pay." Kitty directed JoJo's attention back to the matter at hand. She revealed her bargaining chip, a green tomato smuggled that day from the garden.

"Okay, so it's just business then." Jojo brought out a small tin of the mixture. "Hold still," she told Kitty, applying the tint to Kitty's lips with her fingertips. "Now smack them together, like this." JoJo pressed her lips together to make a popping sound. "Beautiful, dahling."

Kitty dropped the small green tomato into JoJo's open palm. "Thank you!" Kitty said over her shoulder, running from JoJo, afraid she might be late for her meeting with Vlada.

Kitty walked briskly to the spot where she had met Vlada the day before, trying not to arouse attention. She had hoped to get to the spot first; she had played out scenarios in her mind all day as she weeded the garden, and the one she liked the least was where Vlada got there first and she had to walk toward him. Kitty knew nothing of dating etiquette. She did not care about appearing over-eager. She had another reason for wanting to get there quickly: she needed to get to the meeting spot before the lipstick wore off.

Where was it? Kitty looked down at the sidewalk as if there might be an "X" marking the spot where she had been introduced to Vlada the night before. She was wearing her favorite blue sweater, the one she had embroidered with tiny, swirling stitches; it was soft from numerous washings but not yet threadbare. It was a warmer night than last and Kitty reconsidered her sweater choice.

Kitty had tried to fix her hair for the occasion. She no longer had the long, dark locks that Oila used to coax into tight, shiny curls; Bettina had cut Kitty's hair when the threat of lice had gone through the barrack. Kitty had done her best, but without a mirror she had no idea how she looked. It was the first time since arriving at the camp that she had cared about her appearance.

Kitty dared not touch her lips; the sticky mixture threatened to run down her chin after her exertions to get to the meeting spot. If Bettina could see her, she would have been mortified.

She waited. Minutes passed. Whatever is taking this Vlada so long? Kitty was naïve where matters of the heart were concerned. She never even considered the possibility that Vlada might not show up. Every night she had heard the older girls sobbing over broken engagements and unreturned affections but she had never once put herself in their shoes. She looked down at her sweater, with its loosely stitched yellow star. Underneath she wore the blouse made from the pillowcase, the one that had prompted the introduction. Her heart felt like a hammer beating madly in her chest.

A few more minutes passed without a sign of Vlada. Kitty waited dutifully at the appointed spot; she had no intention of abandoning her post. She smoothed over the wrinkles on her skirt, glancing around to see if anyone had noticed. Her mind wandered to her mother, who had not been informed of Kitty's plans that evening.

What does Bettina know about love? She almost made a mistake and married the wrong man. It took her mother years to realize that Karel was indeed "the one." It was only by virtue of Kitty's father's steadfast patience that the two had united. But the delay in their nuptials had one significant advantage: the year they were wed, the law changed, allowing Bettina, an American married to a Czech, to retain her American citizenship. Without that, who knew where the family would be?

Kitty, her chin set in a determined manner, vowed to do things differently than Bettina. If someone loves me, I won't make them wait, thought Kitty. At that precise moment, Kitty felt a light tap on her shoulder. She turned around and found herself staring up into Vlada's brown eyes. She drew in a quick breath.

"Now tell me about your missing star, young lady."

Chapter Twelve

Vlada strode confidently into the locksmith shop, smiling to himself. The familiar smells of the shop intensified in the summer heat and he breathed them in deeply. While others complained about the warm weather, Vlada had barely noticed, spending every available moment in Kitty's company since the moment they met in June. Each night, they pushed the limits of curfew, staying out until the last possible hour, Vlada depositing Kitty on the doorstep of her barrack just minutes before the clock struck eight. Kitty's mother was not amused, but Vlada had never felt surer of himself. There had been no deportations to the East since spring, and his job was going well. Vlada was walking on air.

Vlada turned to his assistant, Felix, who was gathering tools for the day's assignments. "How do things look this morning, my friend? Broken locks? Replacement keys? The usual?" Felix's brown hair stuck to his forehead, perspiration glistening from his furrowed brow, the look of dread on the young man's face indicating things were not business as usual.

In July, the camp had come under the leadership of a new Nazi SS *Lagerkommandant*. Anton Burger earned the post after his predecessor, *Hauptsturmführer* Siedfried Siedl, botched a visit by the Danish Red Cross, revealing too much about the true state of the ghetto's living conditions. During their tour of the camp, the humanitarian organization had seen unmistakable evidence of the camp's overcrowding, disease, lack of food and sanitation. They left intent on reporting their findings to the outside world.

Burger was an unwelcome replacement, and his reputation preceded him. Within hours at his new post as head of Terezin, he made his preferences known around the camp: he had a soft spot for the camp's German and Austrian prisoners. As for the Czechs, dislike was too kind a word. He loathed them.

Vlada sought out Ada to discuss the new leadership of the camp one day before work. They met in the back of the smithy, the sounds of the hammers hitting the anvils and the roar of the fires drowning out their covert conversation. "What does Burger have against us?" Vlada's father had been his main source of information about goings on in the ghetto, but his father had become strangely tight-lipped as of late. Now Ada was Vlada's confidante, and his sources were good. Too good, perhaps.

"I have it on good authority that Burger was born in Austria," Ada explained. "He became a German citizen and a member of the Nazi party." Ada theorized that Terezin's new commander felt more affinity for his German and Austrian charges, even if they were Jews, because they had the Fatherland in common. He held no sympathy for the Czechs imprisoned in their own country.

"He may make it tough for us, Vlada. I heard he was stationed briefly at another camp before being transferred here; rumor has it he picked up some troubling ideas about how a camp should be run. Let's hope we don't find out what they are."

Vlada had caught sight of Burger briefly, shuddering at his remarkable likeness to the Führer, right down to the mustache. Vlada knew it was foolish to hope their similarities ended there.

Vlada and Kitty walked arm in arm down the Rauthausgasse toward the park. The air was still and humid, and Kitty dabbed at her forehead with a square of fabric, not wanting Vlada to see her sweat. Vlada stopped walking and turned to look at her. *What is it about this girl that I forget all about the time when I am with her?* wondered Vlada.

"I have something for you." Vlada reached slowly into his pocket and pulled out a small, metal charm. Kitty brought her hands to her cheeks and gasped with delight.

"Oh, let me see," Kitty said, taking the small item from his hand and turning it over. A custom had arisen in the camp of melting down items that no longer held value in the outside world-- spoons, cutlery, picture frames-- and commissioning charms to be created out of them. Kitty had heard a few of the girls in the barrack talk of receiving charms with the Terezin coat of arms engraved on them. The one Vlada gave her was different; it was shiny and smooth, and it was in the shape of a small spoon.

"I love it," said Kitty, standing on her tiptoes and throwing her arms around Vlada's neck. Vlada leaned into her, feeling the warmth of her skin against his. In the first few weeks of their relationship, Kitty had been self-conscious about displaying affection with Vlada in public. But time had weakened her defenses and he indulged himself in it.

Kitty smiled at him, and Vlada cupped her chin in his hand and kissed her on the lips. He inhaled deeply. He loved her scent, a mix of fresh air and the rich, loamy soil from the garden filling his lungs. Kitty rested her head on Vlada's chest, and they lingered like that for a moment, the last light of day fading, casting a golden glow over the lovers.

Within weeks of Burger's arrival, the camp, which had settled back into a familiar, if often unpleasant, routine after the deportations earlier in the year, was turned on its head. On his way to the locksmith shop, Vlada felt a chilling sense of foreboding when he observed senior SS officers walking through the camp, stopping at different locations to inspect various buildings and houses, and taking measurements.

Shortly thereafter, residents of the *Sudeten Kaserne*, one of the largest housing units on the western side of the camp, and prisoners living in surrounding houses, received instructions that they had twenty-four hours to evacuate the premises. The command came from the Gestapo and was to be executed by the camp's Jewish self-administration, who would oversee the eviction and relocation of the buildings' 6,000 residents.

Vlada took a different route to the *bauhof* one morning, curious to catch a glimpse of the activity on the west side of the camp. He quickly regretted his choice. The scene that unfolded before his eyes was tragic.

The Sudeten barracks was enormous, housing fifty men per room, all of them crammed together in bunks stacked three high. Thousands of men who called the barracks home filed in and out of the building carrying their meager possessions. Some stood near the windows on the upper floors and threw their belongings onto carts that waited below. Women helped their husbands and sons, many of them crying as they struggled to complete the task before the evening's curfew.

Wood planks from the disassembled bunks were heaved out of windows, narrowly missing the forlorn tenants walking below. Vlada felt a lump in his throat. But at the end of the workday, he could not help but take the same route home. The building stood empty and silent, tattered sweaters and soiled blankets, a hairbrush atop men's ripped trousers, these and more were left behind on the ground.

Vlada arrived back at his own barrack to a scene of utter chaos; scores of the evicted men stood in a line that stretched out the door and around the building, carrying their belongings in blankets and boxes. Karel and Vlada were no strangers to overcrowding. Men in the latrines slipped on urine-soaked floors, and typhus sent roomfuls to the infirmary. Now more were about to join them and things would only get worse.

"Say hello to our new neighbors, Vlada." Karel joked, sweat dripping from his forehead. The temperature in the room felt like it was rising by the minute, and his father absentmindedly dabbed at his bald pate with a rag.

"But why here, Tati?" Vlada said petulantly, pushing his way toward his own bunk. A naked bulb hung above his bed; he had wired it himself so when lights out was enforced at ten o'clock each evening, he could continue to read from his books by its dim glow. His father sat in his own bunk below. Vlada wasted no time scrambling up the ladder to his bunk to stake his claim. He was not going to lose his proximity to his father to one of the displaced men.

Karel grimaced at his son's lack of generosity as dozens milled about the second floor hoping some kind soul might offer them half a bunk and a place to set their belongings. All night, men streamed into the barrack, until Vlada, exasperated and resentful, thought the building might burst at the seams. The heat of the extra bodies made the summer night even more oppressive.

From his perch on the third bunk, Vlada looked down to see men his father's age and older, sitting upright against the walls of the room, attempting to sleep. The older men would most likely be moved to the Jager Barrack, out of sight of the main population, to wither and die. Vlada hung his head at the sight, regretting his uncharitable behavior. Every man deserved his own bunk and decent rations.

We are all victims, thought Vlada. We are not at fault. Hours later, sweating, and miserable, Vlada fell into a fitful sleep.

In the coming days and weeks, Vlada watched as prisoners showed up for work at the recently emptied barracks, constructing new rooms, cleaning, and painting them for some yet undisclosed purpose. Then suddenly all activity at the barrack ceased. Amidst horrific overcrowding and in the middle of the oppressive summer heat, the Sudeten building and surrounding houses, painted and ready, stood vacant.

Vlada reported for work at the *bauhof* every day as usual, meeting Ada for lunch whenever possible. Before Vlada met Kitty, he and Ada had spent many evenings together, walking and talking and attending the camp's lectures, and he did not want his friend to feel neglected.

Today they climbed up on the roof of the locksmith shop, eating a lunch of thin soup. While they talked, Ada poked absently at the ancient, weathered bricks in the building's chimney. One of the bricks dislodged with little effort, revealing a small, tightly wrapped package tucked inside. Ada reached for the package and gingerly pulled away the brown paper.

"Cigarettes!" he exclaimed. He rolled one between his fingers, the paper and the tobacco beginning to crumble in his lap. "These are dry. What do you think Vlada? Oh, the things we could barter for with these." Ada conjured up images of margarine, sugar, bread, even, perhaps, a small piece of meat.

Vlada thought of his father who had, without complaint, sacrificed the pleasure he took from smoking since the family's arrival at Terezin six months earlier. Everyone in the camp knew that cigarettes were strictly *verboten*, the SS linking one's possession of cigarettes as reliable evidence of contact with the outside world. The penalty for having contraband was severe: a stint in the Little Fortress, or deportation to the "East."

The two shared a serious look. "Put them back, Ada," Vlada cautioned. Ada returned the cigarettes to their hiding spot, reluctantly tapping the brick back into place.

The locksmith shop employed fifteen workers under the supervision of Kurt Lowenstein. He was a big man, a German Jew who Vlada considered to be an old man, only to find out he was barely thirty. Vlada liked him. "You can run Terezin without lawyers, but not without locksmiths," Kurt told Vlada, laughing.

On the first day Vlada reported for work at the *bauhof*, Kurt assigned him to apprentice with a wizened old man who did not speak a word of Czech. For his first lesson, the man gave Vlada a hammer. He held Vlada's hand in his, guiding both at an angle into the head of a large nail protruding from a thick wooden beam. Vlada had protested. "I know how to hold a hammer, old man." Vlada knew he was being disrespectful, but the old man would never know. Vlada raised the hammer on his own, striking at the nail and missing, the hammer landing sharply on the wood. He tried again and missed again.

On the third try, he rolled his eyes and let the old man guide his hand, and Vlada hit the nail perfectly on the head. Vlada looked at the man, smiling and nodding his head, and they both began to laugh. The old man shared his repertoire of locksmithing skills with Vlada. They spent one day installing hinges into door frames, carving out the perfect indentation in the wood; another day they wandered the camp, repairing broken window locks. One entire day was spent making and duplicating keys, the old man working slowly, and with the precision that the job required. Within weeks, Vlada had mastered the entire repertoire of locksmith's duties, and had worked in locations of the camp he had not known existed.

Vlada loved to make keys. He loved the feel of pressing the key into the soft lead, making an impression, and then patiently filing the key until it was perfect. His attention to detail allowed him to enter the inner circle of the older locksmiths. "Come here." One of the men beckoned to Vlada as the shop was closing one evening. "Hold this." The man handed him a stethoscope, motioning for Vlada to hold it up to a safe that sat on a bench in the workshop. The man turned the dial on the safe. "Listen. Do you hear it?" Vlada could not believe his ears; he could hear the 'click, click' of the tumblers as they fell into place. One final click and the door of the safe popped open with a creak.

Fixing a broken lock on a prisoner's suitcase, Vlada soon learned, was a valuable skill and could be exchanged for a slice of bread and margarine or some sugar. As Vlada's locksmithing reputation grew, he was stopped often on the street and asked to fix various items in exchange for something else of value.

"A trunk? Why yes, I can open that."

"You say you have a briefcase and you've lost the key? Bring it to me."

Kitty looked forward to the fruits of Vlada's labor. "What have you for me tonight, Mr. Locksmith?" Kitty greeted him coyly. Vlada responded first by deeply kissing her on the lips. "You must have done something very challenging in exchange for that," Kitty teased, then searched his pocket for food and other trinkets.

The summer heat, the lack of space, lice, and fleas – all competed daily for the preeminent source of discomfort. The influx of bodies into the Hanover Barrack had brought with it a proliferation of vermin. Not an evening passed that Vlada did not watch his father brush the fleas off his ankles as he walked to his bunk. The odor of unwashed bodies had graduated to a stench now that the barrack was stretched to capacity, its latrines crippled by a lack of soap or steadily running water.

It pained Vlada to walk by the buildings that sat empty while Hanover and other barracks exploded at the seams, overrun with all manner of infestations. Three weeks later a Gestapo contingent arrived from Berlin; the black limousines sped into the camp, flags waving. The cars were followed by dozens of military trucks kicking up dust as they traveled over the parched ground. The Czech guards began to unload the trucks, revealing their unusual cargo: hundreds of file cabinets from the Gestapo's central archives at the Reich Security Office.

Vlada wanted details on the mysterious file cabinets and sought out Ada for the particulars. "So, it seems that the Gestapo headquarters in Berlin and a satellite warehouse in Hamburg were the targets of Allied bombs. If only the Allies had been successful," Ada whispered under his breath, glancing warily around the *bauhof* yard. "They transferred all the files, millions of them, to the Sudeten Kaserne for protection," Ada continued. "If the Allies do a fly over Terezin, the Nazis are counting on them to just keep going." Additional trucks brought in furnishings for the newly constructed offices and for the keepers of the files and the camp's new residents: the German secretarial staff, the SS, and their families.

Vlada was summoned into Lowenstein's office at the workshop the following morning. "Vlada," Lowenstein cleared his throat. "Those file cabinets that arrived from Berlin have been damaged." Vlada's body tensed. He wished he could flee the shop before hearing what came next. "I have been asked to find someone reliable to repair them. There are broken locks, keys that need replacing, standard tasks."

Vlada blocked out the rest of Lowenstein's speech. All he could hear was a ringing in his ears. Vlada had seen the file cabinets; there had to be thousands of them. He was being ordered to spend days, if not weeks, in the presence of Gestapo officials and Reich Main Security Office personnel. When Lowenstein finished speaking, Vlada paused for a moment, breathing unsteadily. "Will Felix accompany me?" Vlada knew the answer before the question escaped his lips.

After the meeting, Vlada frantically searched the blacksmith shop for Ada. He took his friend by the arm and pulled him outside. "What do you think it means, Ada? Are the Nazis running scared? Does the transfer mean the Germans are losing and the end of the war is near?" Vlada peppered his friend with questions. Ada shrugged, eyeing his friend nervously.

Vlada had been forced to look on as the relocation of the Nazi files to Terezin had impacted the camp's inhabitants in untold ways. The Gestapo had erected a fence around the barracks and the houses on the west side. It cut deeply into the ghetto, further shrinking the living space of the camp's forty thousand inhabitants.

In just over six months Vlada had risen in the ranks at his job. He was always on time, and he was known for being discreet, respectful, and unobtrusive. Kitty was proud of him and she had told him so.

Now, because of his hard work and locksmithing skills, Vlada was being forced to go in alone, past the fence, into the lion's den. His every move there would have to be perfect, or there would be hell to pay.

Vlada was too nervous to eat the morning of his first day of work at the Sudeten Barrack. Kitty had done her best to encourage Vlada the night before, whispering sweet things in his ear, and tickling him, trying to make him laugh.

"Don't worry, Vlada," his father had told him that morning before walking off in the direction of the Magdeburg Barrack. "This is just another job, one that you will do well, like always." Vlada searched his father's face, wanting to take comfort in his words.

No one in the locksmith shop envied Vlada his new work assignment. When he entered the workshop that morning to pick up his tools, the men stopped what they were doing. A few turned away, avoiding eye contact, which did nothing to allay Vlada's concerns. Felix's face bore a taut expression, and Vlada smiled weakly at his friend. He picked up his toolbox and walked back the way he had come. "Good luck, Vlada," someone called after him, more out of obligation than purpose.

The sky was overcast, thick, dark clouds tinged with pink hung over the camp. Looking to the west, Vlada saw patches of blue. He walked slowly in the direction of the Sudeten Barrack. *Zutritt verboten!* The forbidding signs the Nazis had posted every hundred yards around the file compound were unnecessary; they needn't worry about anyone wandering into the area without authorization, but the effect of the fence was the same as if it had been surrounded by a concrete wall and barbed wire. No one walked into a den of SS unless it was on purpose, Vlada could attest to that.

The Sudeten Barrack had gained notoriety even before the Germans made it their file storehouse. Vlada had heard the stories from his father, how the first arrivals at the camp had lived there, in early November of 1941. They slept on the cold cement floor in the dirty, deserted building, rationing what little food they had brought with them until it ran out. Such were the auspicious first days of Terezin. Now the building that held the camp's first Jewish prisoners hid a vast portion of the secrets of the Third Reich.

Vlada presented his credentials to the SS guard at the barrier and after a thorough inspection, he was allowed entry. He entered the first floor of the building and saw that it had been transformed. There were walls where bunks had been, offices where the male prisoners had once slept. Vlada tried to remain expressionless, but it was jarring to him how normal it all looked now.

A quick scan of the room revealed the absence of SS uniforms. Vlada quickly inferred that the day-to-day keepers of the files were German civilian staff, and he breathed a deep sigh of relief. It was a small blessing, one Vlada was happy to accept.

Before Vlada could speak, a woman at the desk spoke first. "You are here for the file cabinets, correct?" She addressed him in German and Vlada nodded his reply. "Follow me." The woman wore a tan suit and a collared shirt made of silky fabric, a gold pin in the shape of an "A" attached to her lapel. The pin reminded Vlada of one his mother had worn almost every day, before Terezin; a gold "H" for Hermina. Vlada could not remember the last time he had seen her wear it. What could have happened to it? How his mother loved that pin. The thought of it going missing irritated him so much he forgot to be nervous.

The heat made Vlada conscious of the rough fabric of his long-sleeved shirt rubbing against his wrists. The German secretary opened the door to a vast room filled from corner to corner with filing cabinets, many looking battered and worse for wear after bouncing around on trucks on the trip from Berlin. Vlada took stock of the room, and his shoulders fell as he realized the breadth of the work before him. He set the toolbox down and wiped the sweat from his brow. A window was open partway, the warm breeze stirring the air in the room, ruffling stacks of papers yet to be filed. He opened his toolbox and extracted the necessary tools for his first repair.

As the day progressed, Vlada fell into a comfortable routine. This is not so bad, he thought. No one was directly supervising him, thus allowing him to work at his own pace. It was comfortable in the large room. He had at least a month of work ahead of him, and while everyone felt sorry for him back at the shop, he was beginning to see the upside.

The contrast between the conditions at the Sudeten Barrack and that of the Hanover Barrack were in sharp relief. Vlada went to work every morning, and spent the day in the clean, dry, relative peace of the file cabinets, only to return home to a barrack, at first overrun with men, and now with bugs. Fleas attacked his ankles upon entering the building and bedbugs spotted the lower bunks, his father's included.

"I wish I could get you out of here, Vlada," Karel said with concern. Bedbugs were a mild inconvenience, but the real concern lay with the fleas and lice. Both carried typhus and in such close quarters, an outbreak could be deadly.

Signs posted everywhere in the camp read, *Lice =Typhoid!* Other signs urged prisoners to wash their hands after meals and after using the latrine. In a world where soap was hard to come by and hot water was nonexistent, the warning signs had become something of a joke in the camp.

Before the arrival of the new inhabitants, the latrines at the barrack had been barely adequate. Now, water trickled from only a few spigots, and those designated to keep the latrines clean appeared to have given up. Because Vlada was not allowed to use the latrine at work, he was forced to wait all day to use the latrine at the barrack. The stench, compounded by the heat, did nothing to quell his desperation.

During the winter months, Vlada was the envy of many as the heat rose and he stayed warm and dry above the fray. Now his bunk below the ceiling captured each day's oppressive heat. The smell of sweat and excrement invaded Vlada's nighttime sanctuary, forcing him to spend every possible moment out of the barrack in the evening, walking with Kitty until curfew gave him no choice but to go back inside. Each night, Vlada waited for sleep to come as he stared up at the ceiling in his bunk. He knew that in the morning he could leave the bug-ridden barracks for the relative comfort of his job.

Weeks passed and the unsanitary conditions grew worse. Karel did not seem surprised when the dreaded rash indicating typhus appeared on a handful of men on the third floor. "Be prepared to move," his father told him. Karel had caught wind of a possible evacuation to keep the highly infectious disease from spreading. Vlada trusted his father's information but wondered as to its source. Within days the Czech gendarmes were at the barracks.

"Anyone on the second floor, follow us immediately," they shouted into each room. "Leave your bedding behind." The gendarmes swept through the bunks with urgency, leaving Vlada no time to grab one of his books. The ragtag residents of the second floor were led to a small barrack used solely for quarantine and they were assigned beds. A makeshift fence cordoned off the building, indicating it was off-limits to visitors. The inhabitants would be released after two weeks if they showed no signs of infection. It turned out there was one insect even the Nazis feared: lice.

If Vlada's solitary days working among the file cabinets were a small blessing, quarantine was divine intervention. Vlada and the other prisoners made themselves at home in their new living quarters. The straw mattress he slept on was clean and dry, and their meals were brought to them. Until they were cleared, they did not have to report to work. "God forbid we get the SS infected," Vlada heard one of the quarantine bunkmates joke.

Vlada and Karel played chess each day, and Kitty visited Vlada each evening after dinner. The lovers talked across the fence, Kitty maintaining a safe distance, right up until minutes before curfew. Vlada looked longingly across the fence at Kitty, yearning to break the rules and give her a good night kiss.

Those who had become infected with typhus were taken to the Hohenelbe Barracks, the Central Hospital for the camp. The infection had spread quickly under the camp's unsanitary conditions and close quarters, and the hospital wards swelled to overflowing with prisoners suffering from fever, chills, and delirium, some barely able to walk. New beds opened when the sick perished.

Both father and son remained free of the dreaded signs of infection. "All good things must come to an end, Vlada," his father said. The doctor informed them both that they were free to return to their original lodging. They walked to the Hanover Barrack together. Vlada stepped reluctantly into the dimly lit room breathing through his mouth to lessen the stench of unwashed bodies and the latrines. Karel immediately set off in the direction of Magdeburg.

It was lunch time and Vlada escaped the oppression of the barrack, his stomach growling, and entered the courtyard at Hanover in search of food. He joined the lunchtime queue clutching his food ration coupon. Up ahead he saw his mother, gathering the ration coupons from the prisoners. Hermina had traded her work assignment that day hoping to catch a glimpse of her son. They had been separated for two weeks, the longest separation mother and son had ever faced.

Hermina's face lit up as Vlada approached her in the queue, her head bobbing around the people in front of him, hoping for a glimpse.

"Vlada!" A huge smile crossed her face but she was forced to keep the line moving. "This is my son," she said, nudging the woman next to her serving the soup. The woman acknowledged the information by dipping the ladle deep into the bottom of the vat. When she lifted the ladle out, a chunk of potato and a piece of gristle poked out of the thin, brown liquid. Hermina handed her son the cup, thick wisps of steam rising from the vat, billowing around her face already damp with sweat. Vlada thought his mother looked beautiful. He had not realized how much he had missed her.

A rush of memories from another life, long ago and far away, brought Vlada back to laundry day at the flat in Pardubice, his mother supervising the maid, grabbing the stick from her to show her how to evenly distribute the sheets in their steamy bath. He recalled the corn meal mush slathered in blueberry jam that he had barely been able to stomach back then.

He lost sight of his mother's face for a moment in the steam rising over the soup. What I would not give now for that meal I once loathed, thought Vlada. He grinned back at his mother, overwhelmed with love for her, smiling so hard his face hurt. Vlada took too long in the queue, and the man behind him pushed him, forcing Vlada out of the line of sight of his mother. He took the cup of soup and slowly walked away.

CHAPTER TWELVE

By midsummer, the *Judengarten* was lush and overgrown: Kitty, Hanka and the other young women on the work detail spent entire days staking row upon row of tomato plants, their stems heavy, laden with large, green tomatoes, the braided stalks of the leeks thick and ready to harvest, cabbages blossoming like flowers, planted early and awaiting a sharp cut at the base, severing them from the rich earth that had given them life.

"Vlada, Vlada, Vlada," Hanka teased Kitty one morning, pushing a wheelbarrow over the bumpy ground through the narrow rows of vegetables. "That's all you think about." Kitty blushed, glancing furtively around the garden where they walked in the bright sunlight. Each evening in the darkness after the lights went out, the older girls in the barrack continued to share risqué details of their affairs. Kitty did not join in; she had decided she would not share a single detail with anyone – not even Hanka. What happened between her and Vlada -- the sweet kisses, the smell of his neck, his hand on the small of her back -- was theirs, and theirs alone.

Before Vlada, Kitty had listened fervently to the camp gossip about the war and the world outside, each day little tributaries of information siphoning off from an ongoing stream of speculation about who was winning the war, where the heaviest fighting was taking place and what might or might not be occurring in other camps and ghettos. For months, no one had speculated about the future. No one dared.

Since the beginning of the summer, the inhabitants of the camp had endured food shortages, overcrowding and outbreaks of disease and infection. But one thing was noticeably absent: deportations. The void left by the lack of grim roundups, separating families and instilling fear and uncertainty, had allowed the rarest of crops to ripen and mature in its place: hope.

Kitty cut the heads of cabbage off their stalks. She shook her head and smiled dreamily to herself, picturing Vlada's face, the feel of his arms around her waist. She wanted to run through the garden and shout his name but that was unacceptable. I must look daft, she thought.

The days after the two lovers met had drifted one into the other; something had changed in just that short time. She could still picture her beloved hometown of Teplice, and she smiled tenderly at the memories of the girl she once was: what presents might I receive for Christmas? What was Cook making for dinner? When would we leave for Jesenice? Such childish things, Kitty thought. Her childhood self was a far-off memory now. I am in love, thought Kitty with abandon, throwing a cabbage into the wheelbarrow.

It was not that she did not care about what happened now, it was just that Vlada occupied all the space in her heart and in her mind. Hanka was right: Vlada. Vlada. Vlada. Each day was a means to an end; Kitty worked, she shared a quick meal with her parents and Hanuš, and then she went out with Vlada. They walked hand in hand, sometimes arm in arm, and the whole world fell away, if only for a few hours.

Tonight, Kitty was waiting for Vlada outside her barrack. She wore a navy dress with polka dots and a white collar, and she carried a yellow sweater. Her dark hair was short now, and she had adopted the habit of nervously tucking it behind her ears.

Kitty's face lit up when she saw Vlada walking toward her. Vlada looked Kitty up and down, shaking his head. "I don't know how you do it in this place. You look beautiful."

Kitty blushed, inhaling sharply. Vlada reached for her hand, it felt warm and rough in hers and Kitty fell in step next to him. The streets were crowded with people – parents with children, women walking arm in arm. Vlada and Kitty walked what was now their usual route, up the Lange Strasse. Most nights they turned onto Rathausgasse but tonight it appeared to have a lot of foot traffic, so they proceeded one more block up to Berggasse, in pursuit of a little privacy.

"What did you have for dinner tonight, Vlada?" Kitty asked, slipping her arm in his.

"Lentil 'soup.'" Vlada rolled his eyes.

"At least your mother cooks!" Kitty said. "Bettina is hopeless. I made cabbage and potatoes with some scraps from the garden. Otherwise, we would have starved. Did you see her looking out the window when you picked me up?"

"Bettina, as you refer to her, does not care for me. I did see her, but I think I will keep my distance." Arm in arm, they continued down the main street. They walked until the light began to fade. Kitty wanted to know everything about Vlada, and each evening she posed question after question, with Vlada insisting she give her answer first.

"I want to know your favorite dessert," said Kitty. Vlada nodded, prompting Kitty to answer.

"Apple strudel, of course," Kitty answered. "Fresh from the oven with a dusting of powdered sugar and the edges still crispy and warm." Kitty licked her lips as if she were biting into the strudel and savoring it.

Vlada shook his head, chuckling. "You. Always with the apple strudel. You would think they never served you real food growing up, only strudel the way you talk about it." Kitty smiled, but she was flustered. Was her yearning for strudel too much? As she contemplated this, Vlada began to tickle her waist.

"Stop! Vlada, stop." Kitty pretended to run away. Vlada pulled her around the building at the corner of Berggasse, where few prisoners found themselves after hours. Kitty leaned against the brick wall, breathing hard. Vlada pressed against her, looking into her dark eyes.

Vlada did not consider himself a romantic, but he found himself doing and saying things around this girl he had never done before. "Your eyes remind me of a poem." He looked down at the ground, stepping away from her to gather his resolve.

"Oh, Vlada," Kitty said sweetly. No one had ever spoken to her in such a fanciful way, and she suddenly felt aware of her every movement.

"The widest of all seas are human eyes ... such also were you, my love, your white sail trimmed for the shore." Kitty watched as Vlada nervously recited the lines from memory. Before Kitty could comment, he kissed her on the lips.

Kitty had never kissed another boy before, and she hoped she was doing it right. The way their lips lingered near each other, slightly apart, his warm breath on hers, made her feel like she was. When their lips met, Kitty's were soft and responsive. When Vlada pulled away from her, Kitty put her hand to her chest.

"Vlada, you took my breath away." She was breathing heavily, her cheeks flushed.

"Good." He winked, trying to make light of the moment. Something between them had shifted with the kiss. Kitty felt butterflies in her stomach; nervousness and excitement collided all at once. She tucked her hair behind her ear and quickly launched into a conversation about family pets.

"I still miss my dear Pavla, you know. I will never forgive Bettina." Kitty was still leaning against the building, and Vlada saw her eyes begin to tear up.

"When we get out of this place, I am going to get you another dog," said Vlada. "And if you like you can call it Pavla. Unless it is a boy and then we will have to think about that!" Kitty's shoulders relaxed, and she burrowed against him. Vlada kissed her forehead, his arms surrounding her, and Kitty felt safe and out of harm's way.

The sweet moment was interrupted as a flatbed carriage hobbled past the lovers and down the cobblestone street. During the day, the repurposed hearses transported the camp's dry and dusty bread from the bakery where Eva's grandfather worked at the far end of the camp, distributing it to the various kitchens. Tonight, the cart had been returned to its original function: it bore the bodies of the camp's dead. The cadavers were destined for the crematorium, built the year before out of necessity, when simply burying the thousands who died of disease, starvation and lack of sanitation was no longer a viable option.

Kitty turned to look at the cart, immediately regretting it. "Oh, Vlada." A thin, gray arm and other shriveled limbs hung off the side of the flatbed, visible because a tarp had been thrown carelessly over them. Vlada pulled Kitty close, caressing her hair. A petulant frown crossed Kitty's face. This place. It always ruins everything, thought Kitty.

She pulled away from Vlada, pushing away her selfish thoughts. A new awareness washed over her face. "I know seeing that must bring back sad memories for you, Vlada. I am so sorry." Kitty touched his cheek lightly with the back of her hand, caressing him.

Kitty had read his thoughts. "My babicka had her sense of humor right up until the end. She called her living quarters 'The Lower Depths,'" Vlada said with a grim chuckle. "I think she would have liked you." Vlada took Kitty's hand from his cheek and brought it to his lips.

I do believe Vlada is the most handsome man in the entire camp, thought Kitty. She looked up at him adoringly, her heart full and aching. The young lovers passed their nights in this manner; one moment filled with laughter and light, the next a tumble into the shadow of death and darkness, and then back again. They walked home on the Haptstrasse, the street quiet in the moments before curfew except for the sound of crickets chirping. Vlada deposited Kitty on the steps of her barrack in the nick of time. Such was an evening in Terezin.

The next morning, Kitty looked over at her mother sleeping in the bunk next to her, a light sheet she had pilfered from her job covering the length of her. She looked small, vulnerable. Bettina's face wore a pleasant smile during slumber that was rarely visible during her waking hours. Kitty let her sleep for another moment. Her mother had a busy night, and the two women had nearly crashed into each other to reach the barrack before curfew.

Bettina flew in the door of their residence, out of breath, her golden hair pasted to her forehead with sweat, her clothes disheveled. She flung herself down on her bunk, exhausted, and picked up a handkerchief with her initials on it: how she had managed to hold on to it all these months Kitty could not begin to guess. Her mother pushed her hair back from her forehead, patting the sweat on her brow, breathing in and exhaling a sigh of accomplishment.

"You have a new cousin," Bettina announced proudly.

Kitty had begun dressing for bed, and she whirled around to face her. "Boy or girl?" Kitty asked eagerly. Uncle Erich's wife Arna had carried the ultimate contraband into the camp in her belly eight months prior, and Bettina had promised she would be there for the delivery.

"Well, it was a difficult birth, but baby Eva has a little brother, Petr." Bettina smiled for a moment, then turned away from Kitty.

"What is it? What's wrong?" Kitty had been waiting for this baby for months. Kitty remembered her parents talking about Uncle Erich back in Dobricoviche; he and Arna had endured severe food rationing under the German occupation in Prague, but Erich's work building barracks for the Germans had earned him favors that kept the family going. Arna was deported to Terezin on Transport Cc in November of 1942 with little Eva, a healthy 9-month-old beauty and one small twist: Petr had sneaked into the camp, unknowingly even to Arna, in utero. Erich had been forced to stay on in Prague, continuing his work for the Germans.

When the Löwis arrived at Terezin, Arna was three months pregnant, and her growing belly was a source of wonder to Kitty. As her pregnancy with Petr advanced, Arna tried to hide it under loose fitting clothing so she could continue to work and get full rations. By early summer, she could no longer keep the pregnancy secret. Unable to work in the final months, the loss of rations endangered both Arna's pregnancy and that of her child. Kitty noticed Arna's stomach stopped growing; she was giving what meager rations she received to little Eva.

Still Kitty was excited for the arrival of the baby. I only hope they get along better than Hanuš and I, Kitty thought. She did not think that Arna would play favorites with her children like Bettina had.

On the nights when Vlada was called away for locksmith duty in another part of the camp, Kitty walked to the barrack where Arna lived with her little girl. After supper, Arna sat outside on the steps and let Eva play with a ball in the small courtyard nearby.

Kitty liked to sneak up behind her little cousin, grabbing her by the waist and whispering "boo" in Eva's ear. Each time, Eva turned around, giggling, her eyes lighting up when she saw Kitty, her tiny face surrounded by dark curls. Eva held out her arms and Kitty picked her up, holding her close, breathing in her baby scent. Karel thought she was the spitting image of Kitty when she was little.

When Arna first arrived at the camp, the child had tiny rolls of baby fat, knees and elbows dimpled healthily. Now, at one and a half, her legs and arms were thin and straight as pins, her cheeks wan, and underneath her eyes were dark circles.

Kitty did not need anyone to tell her that the child needed more food; she was already pilfering items from the summer garden for her parents and Hanuš, and she added Arna and Eva to the list of recipients. She worried how much good a green tomato, or a few radishes would do for a growing child.

Now Kitty could not bear to hear bad news, but she pressed Bettina now about Petr. "Arna is so thin. It was difficult for her to carry the baby to term," Bettina explained. She smiled, looking Kitty in the eye. "Petr is strong, but so tiny." Kitty wanted to comfort her mother and help the baby; instead, she stood helpless as her mother continued.

"I don't know how much milk she will be able to produce," Bettina's voice broke, trailing off. "How does one nurse a baby when you don't have any food to eat?" Five days after Petr was born, the Nazis issued a general ban on births in the camp. The punishment for violating the ban was deportation to the "East."

Kitty's days were filled with schemes of how to maneuver more food out of the garden and into the bellies of the people she loved. Her thoughts became focused on two pursuits: getting food for Arna and the babies and seeing Vlada.

One afternoon at the end of the workday, Hanka and Kitty hurried their way through a particularly aggressive pat down at the hands of one of the Czech gendarmes. "You are scaring me, Kitty," Hanka whispered to her friend when they were out of earshot. Each day Kitty had grown more aggressive in her pursuit of smuggling vegetables. As Kitty's lookout, Hanka had grown uneasy at her friend's lack of discretion. "You are going to get us both caught." The risk of deportation to the "East" was low, but the chances of ending up in the Little Fortress might be a worse fate. The screams of the prisoners behind the forbidding black and white striped prison entrance, subjected to unspeakable torture at the hands of the Gestapo were a warning to all who heard them.

Kitty looked at her friend, hearing her for the first time in weeks. Hanka's russet hair was covered in a headscarf, the skin on her freckled nose peeling from the hot sun beating down each day, her brown eyes cautioning her friend. Kitty's shoulders fell. The last thing she wanted to do was harm anyone; the tomatoes in her bra had gone unnoticed this time, but if there was a changing of the guard, it could be a different story. Kitty was torn: who would feed Arna and the babies if she did not? She nodded to Hanka that she heard her friend's concerns. She would try to be more careful.

As Hitler cleansed Czechoslovakia of Jews, Terezin's walls had slowly filled with the country's finest writers, historians, philosophers, composers, and psychologists, the prisoners clinging to the identities that had distinguished them prior to being imprisoned in the ghetto. The irony was not lost on Kitty; what the prisoners lacked in sustenance, they gained with nightly lectures, music, and performances, food for their spirits and minds. The SS turned a blind eye to what they considered harmless pursuits.

One night, Vlada arrived at the barrack and presented Kitty with tickets to a performance taking place that evening. At first Kitty smiled, thinking of Vlada's thoughtfulness, but then she thought of Eva and tiny Petr. How could she go out and have fun when the little ones were suffering? But the look on Vlada's face won Kitty over; he took her by the hand, and she felt her body soften, the urgency of her worries fading in his company. The lovers had barely begun to explore the cultural life of the ghetto together.

"You know, I spent most evenings before I met you with Ada on the lookout for avant-garde pursuits," Vlada told Kitty as they walked down the dusty cobblestone street. "I think he is a little jealous now." He winked at Kitty, and she blushed slightly. "Ada always said, 'It only takes one German officer in the audience to ruin the best performance, eh, Vlada?'"

It was common knowledge that although the SS spent little time restricting the content of the prisoners' cultural activities, the threat loomed large that they might attend an event on any given evening. Kitty shushed Vlada, worried his comment might be overheard by the wrong people.

"What are we going to see tonight?" Kitty could see they were headed in the direction of one of the warehouses where the attic was often used for performances.

"*The Water Sprite*," Vlada replied. "We needed tickets for this one. Ada thinks some of the Krauts might show up. This is right up their alley." Kitty clapped her hands together with delight. It was a recitation of the poem by Karel Jarom Erben, and if Kitty remembered correctly, it was extremely dark. Yes, the Germans would like something like that.

"You should join the recitation group, Vlada." Kitty was quite impressed with Vlada's ability to recount epic poems. He had shared his favorite, *The Ballad of Charles IV* by Neruda, with her.

Vlada turned to face her. "Maybe I will at that, young lady." Vlada put his arm comfortably around her shoulders as they walked; it was late August but there was a hint of autumn in the air. Some of the leaves on the linden trees had already turned golden and fallen. They scuttled along the rough cobblestone street in the cool evening breeze.

They arrived at the warehouse and walked three flights to the attic to find the low-ceilinged space packed with spectators. Four people stood on a makeshift stage in the front of the room, three men and one woman. Kitty and Vlada found seats as a hush fell over the attic and the first performer began to speak.

Vlada held Kitty's hand and she closed her eyes and listened, trying to recall if she had ever heard the poem in its entirety. If so, she had forgotten its gruesome nature. A shiver ran down her spine as the players on the stage recited the stanzas, each filled with foreboding. After completing their portion, the actors each turned their back to the audience. Kitty sat in rapt attention, her eyes shone in the dimly lit space, inspired by the gravity of the performances.

The Water Sprite begins with a mother warning her young daughter not to go to the water that day to wash her scarves out of a haunting fear for the young woman's safety. The daughter, despite her mother's fearful premonition, goes to the water and falls in. She is taken prisoner by a water sprite, an underwater bogeyman who holds the girl against her will beneath the lake in his dark, lonely home. The young woman bears a child with her captor, and although she loves her child dearly, she longs for her own mother's embrace and to see the sun once more. One day the water sprite, tired of the young woman's pitiable pleas, agrees to let her visit land for one day, under certain conditions. She must leave their child behind, and she must promise not to touch her mother or any other human.

At this point in the performance, the three male actors had recited their stanzas and turned away from the audience. The lone woman on the small stage was left to recite the final verse. The attic audience was deathly silent as she began to speak, her voice full of pathos, as if she were experiencing the daughter's fear and longing firsthand.

"What would a reunion be like without a warm embrace?" The audience members sat unmoving as the woman delivered the final line and turned her back to them. Absorbing the story's brutal ending, the sound of weeping could be overheard in the crowd, Kitty among them.

A grim silence descended over the room, followed by an explosion of applause. The sound was deafening in the small space, reverberating off the ceiling. The story had struck some hidden chord in Kitty, taking her by surprise. How could the young mother not embrace her mother while on land? Unfortunately, the evil water sprite made her pay dearly for her betrayal. Kitty opened her eyes, trying to shake the imagery the voice had conjured so clearly in her mind, that of the young mother arriving back at her watery home after reveling in the sunshine and her mother's embrace, only to find the lifeless body of her only child.

On Kitty's recommendation, Vlada joined the recitation group as its youngest member. Kitty sat in the audience, grinning proudly, and watched as he performed works by Czech poets, Nezval's *Edison* and Wolker's *Ballad of a Sailor*. The revolutionary nature of the subject matter ignited a passion she had never seen Vlada exhibit before, and she held her breath when it was his turn to speak.

Vlada's performances inspired Kitty and she signed up for a part in the children's performance of the musical *Brundibár*. "Now, tell me again about this play," Vlada asked Kitty during one of their evening walks.

"Oh, Vlada! I do think it is going to be wonderful!" Kitty gushed. "I know I am only in the chorus, but it is still so exciting. You know I was lucky to get a part. I so wanted to play the role of the cat." The original production of *Brundibár* had been performed in Prague until the cast of children and their parents were deported to Terezin, where many of them were preparing to reprise their roles.

Kitty went on, her cheeks rosy with excitement. "It is the story of the evil organ grinder *Brundibár* who the children hope to defeat, with the help of some brave animals. Oh, Vlada! I can't wait." Kitty grabbed his arm breathlessly, then practiced taking a bow. She blushed, embarrassed by her enthusiasm.

Vlada broke into a grin. "Well, I hope they can defeat this evil man." Kitty gave him a sideways glance. "And if you can't wait then neither can I. I will try to get a front-row seat."

CHAPTER
THIRTEEN

At the end of the workday Vlada found himself stopping back at the locksmith shop at the *bauhof* to restock his tool kit with nails, screws, and small metal picks. Kitty was often busy with after-supper rehearsals for the premiere performance of *Brundibár*, so Vlada took his time replenishing each compartment.

The shop was empty save for an older locksmith who had the same idea. "Good night, Vlada," the man said as he snapped shut his now-heavy toolbox. He tipped his cap and stepped out into the quiet street. Within moments he was back. "There is someone outside who says they need to speak with you, Vlada," the man said with a wink.

Vlada lifted the toolbox off the workbench and headed toward the door. At first glance, the courtyard appeared empty. Then Vlada saw a young woman beckoning him toward her.

"Vlada!" The woman called, waving frantically. As he came closer, he was surprised to find Hanka, Kitty's friend from the vegetable garden. She was out of breath, as if she had been running.

"Hanka, what is it? Is Kitty okay?"

Hanka was in visible distress, and tears welled in her eyes. "Vlada, haven't you heard the train whistle blowing all day?" The question sounded accusatory, and Hanka's eyes searched his for an explanation.

When Vlada and his family first arrived at Terezin, they were forced to walk the last mile from the train station at Bohušovice to the camp. The Nazis, with their penchant for efficiency, had since laid down train tracks that connected the train station to the camp, delivering Jewish prisoners straight to the ghetto.

The sound of the train whistle brought with it a sense of foreboding. It pierced the air at unpredictable times, signaling the arrival of more prisoners from the far reaches of Czechoslovakia and departures to the "East." Vlada would never forget the shrill sound of the whistle in January, when Nora was deported, or in March when Eva disappeared, never to return. The whistle's menacing cry made Vlada tense and he had grown accustomed to its absence over the past months when deportations out of the camp had ground to a halt. Now Vlada realized that he had heard the whistle today. It had been faint, almost a whisper, easy to ignore as he worked all day on the furthest side of the camp.

"Oh, yes. I did hear it. What does it mean, Hanka?" He took Kitty's friend by the shoulders and looked into her eyes, preparing himself for the worst. "Did something happen to Kitty?"

"No, Vlada. Not Kitty. It's her brother. It's Hanuš." Hanka paused for a moment. "He's gone."

It took days to sort out what had happened to Hanuš. Kitty had gently pressed Bettina for information, but to no avail. Her mother took to her bunk and lay in it, unmoving, refusing to respond even to the simplest questions, her eyes staring straight ahead but not seeing.

Karel took Kitty aside and shared the few details he was able to uncover, out of earshot of Bettina. Kitty gasped at her father's appearance. His hands trembled and what little color he had was drained from his face.

"They were gathering families, parents with their children, for a labor transport. It sounds like it was an awful scene, children crying and parents struggling to keep them calm." He noticed that his hands were shaking uncontrollably. "Hanuš should not have been on that list because of your mother's status as a *prominent*.

Bettina had been designated as part of the camp's contingent of *prominent* Jewish prisoners because of her American citizenship, which she had been fortunate to retain. The Löwis were married after the law that disallowed women who married foreign born men from retaining their citizenship was rescinded. The group of *prominent* prisoners also included those who were of some renown either by profession or status in the outside world. Some were low-level aristocracy. *Prominent* status did not allow for privileges regarding work details or food rations. But the one privilege it did confer outweighed all others: *prominent* individuals and their families were deemed to be exempt from deportation to the "East."

Karel struggled to continue, and Kitty felt like she was watching her father's body crumble in on itself. "Someone bribed a guard and they put Hanuš' name on the list to be sent away. They said he did not have access to Bettina's privileges any longer because he was eighteen and he was an adult." Kitty bit her lip, her breath coming in shallow gulps. Bettina's *prominent* status was the one thing Kitty gave her mother credit for and it had failed them. As cruel as the transports were, the Nazis did attempt to keep families intact. "This should never have happened." Her father stuttered, his face set in a grimace of pain. "Your mother." Karel could no longer continue.

"Yes, Father." No further words passed between them.

The crippling events found Kitty running between her own barracks and that of her father's for the remainder of the week, checking on the condition of both her parents. Worn out, she and Vlada finally met at their usual spot after supper. Vlada held out his arms when he saw her, and Kitty ran to him, her eyes puffy and red, and collapsed in his arms. She relayed the events of Hanuš's deportation with the addition of a tragic detail. "My father heard some men talking that they took someone else's child off the transport and put Hanuš on, all for an extra teaspoon of margarine." She looked up at Vlada, her voice cracking, her eyes searching his to somehow make sense of it all.

Vlada gently led Kitty to a bench at the edge of the Stadt Park. Groups of prisoners walked by and Vlada shielded Kitty from their prying eyes. His mind buzzed furiously, searching for the right words to say. He would not tell Kitty that his family had also been impacted by the transport. Hermina had been distraught upon discovering that her oldest sister, Kamila, and her husband, Max, were on the same train, along with Karel's nephew, Joseph. Vlada's friend, Vera, from the radio factory in Pardubice, had been forced on the train as well. They were all unfortunate victims, but what happened to Hanuš was wrong; he was the victim of a wrongful act of greed.

They sat in silence for a moment, as Vlada searched for the right words to say. He felt anxious as he was caught off guard by how Kitty's heartbreak affected him. He wanted to avenge the wrong done to her brother and see her happy once again. But he was powerless, except for his words. "He is going to be safe, Kitty. Hanuš is going to be just fine." He looked into her dark eyes, to see if his words hit their mark. Fat tears spilled onto her cheeks.

"Tell that to Bettina," Kitty said as she wiped roughly at her eyes.

Kitty released a deep breath and sank deeper into his arms, allowing Vlada to stroke her hair and gently kiss the top of her head. Vlada could have stayed with her that way all night. Vlada lifted his head as a golden sunset began to spread across the cloudless evening sky. Its beauty ignited a fresh wave of anger in him. How can such beauty and such ugliness exist in the same moment, he wondered.

He looked at his watch, a barter he had received from another prisoner for fixing the lock on a suitcase. "It is almost curfew, Kitty. Let me walk you home."

He lifted her gently by her elbows, and they walked in step back down the main street in the fading light. Later, Kitty told Vlada that when she arrived back at her quarters, she found Bettina in the same position she had been in earlier. Kitty had walked toward her mother and Bettina, sensing her proximity, had rolled over on the bunk, turning her back to her daughter without ever saying a word.

The forced departure of five thousand of the camp's inhabitants to an unknown destination set off a chain reaction of events, illuminating the interconnectedness of each of the prisoners to the other. The next time Vlada and Kitty met, she relayed the events that transpired to Vlada.

She had arrived for a play rehearsal at the cellar of the boys' barracks as the director was assembling the cast for an important speech. "Frantisek Zelenka stood in front of everyone. Vlada, he was so sad,"

Kitty recounted. "After all the children had quieted down, he told us that due to recent 'events,' he needed to make some changes to the cast." Kitty's voice was choked with emotion. She looked down at her hands. "He told us there was a new cast list posted on the wall."

Kitty had stood behind the other children, waiting for a glimpse of the cast roles. When it was her turn in line, she found her name had been removed from the chorus. She scanned the sheet again and discovered she had been cast in the role of the Cat. Kitty bit her lip, conflicted, her body torn between wanting to jump for joy over the coveted role and crushing sadness that it was the result of someone else's misfortune. She knew each stage direction and all the Cat's lines, having watched the previous actor's every move, memorizing the role as if she were the official understudy. Kitty hung her head, despondent with the knowledge that she was given the role because the previous girl had been deported along with Hanuš.

"Vlada, I feel awful."

"It's not your fault, Kitty." Vlada hugged her tightly. "You are going to be the best cat *Brundibár* has ever seen."

Kitty smiled weakly. "Now the other cast members must quickly learn their new roles. Zelenska is determined to prepare for the opening."

The premiere performance of *Brundibár* took place in the attic of the Magdeburg barrack, the building where Vlada's father spent most of his waking hours. Vlada entered the makeshift theater and saw Kitty looking out at the audience from the edge of the painted backdrop that served as the stage. He waved and she waved back, excitedly pointing to her costume, which was little more than the blue checked dress she sometimes wore for work in the *Judengarten*. But acting in the play was the only time the children were allowed to remove the yellow star from their clothing while in the camp. It seemed fitting somehow, the missing star on her play costume. The absence of the star on her blouse was how she and Vlada had met, a day that now seemed like a lifetime ago.

Vlada watched as the audience began to file in, an unnerving mix of SS guards in their uniforms and shiny boots, and children from the camp in worn clothing, laughing, and talking gaily as they filled the rows of seats closest to the stage. The house lights went dark, and the play began. Vlada was unaware of the exact plot except for the few general details Kitty had told him. He watched as the story unfolded on the makeshift stage, a sheet painted with a large fence, a city scene rising behind it. His body grew tense, and he glanced nervously at the SS in the audience, wondering if they grasped the play's thinly veiled allegory: a battle between good and evil, the evil organ grinder, complete with dark mustache, eerily reminiscent of the Führer. Would there be retribution for the slight against their leader? wondered Vlada.

Kitty took the stage as the Cat, and Vlada found himself grinning in the darkened attic. He watched Kitty joyfully sing the tunes he had heard her humming under her breath. The children and those playing the animals filled the stage, singing a triumphant finale after their victory over the villain. The standing room only crowd rose to its feet, shouting affirmations. Vlada stood up, too, applauding enthusiastically. The SS clapped, having missed the story's central theme. Vlada had forgotten. Most of them did not speak Czech.

Vlada waited for Kitty outside the barrack afterward. "Brava," he shouted, waving her over. Kitty ran to him, her stage makeup still on, her tears ruining her greasepaint whiskers.

"Oh, Vlada! My parents didn't come to the performance," she cried. "Bettina just lays on the bed saying, 'My son, my son.'" Kitty hung her head, her shoulders slumping. "I am such a foolish girl, trying to pretend we are not in a horrible camp by acting in a silly play."

Vlada recalled a conversation he and Kitty had when they first met. Vlada had commented on the lack of original cultural material in the ghetto. "Not a lot is created here," he had said. "Literature and the classics are used to escape the present by concentrating on something else. Much is performed here, but little is created." He reminded Kitty of that early conversation. "Remember what you said to me, Kitty? About why we don't write plays or poems about life here?" asked Vlada. "You said, 'You don't put up a play about the life that you are living.' You helped everyone in the audience tonight forget where they were for a little while. That is all that really matters."

Chapter Thirteen

A month had passed since Hanuš was forcibly deported to parts unknown. Each evening after work, Kitty watched as Bettina tried to track down anyone with a family member who might have been on the same train as Hanuš. When someone told her there was a woman whose son had been on the fateful transport, Bettina tracked her down, peppering her with questions. "Have you heard from your son? What did he say? Does he have enough food?" The poor woman, her face drawn, a worn shawl drawn tightly around her shoulders, shook her head sadly and walked away. Kitty felt pity for the woman, wondering if her son had been sold out for a bit of margarine, too.

Kitty entered her father's barrack for their evening meal together to find Bettina wringing her hands and pacing back and forth. Kitty's father sat in a straight back chair, grimacing in pain. His eyes met Kitty's and he shook his head. He nodded to Bettina, who was gripping a postcard tightly in her hand.

"Darling, give it to Kitty," his father said soberly. Bettina held out the postcard and Kitty took it from her mother cautiously. There was no one within earshot, so Kitty read it aloud.

"October 26, 1943

Dear Parents and Sister!

I arrived here and am all right. I wrote to Kurt and he sent me a package.

How is my little sister Kitty? Regards to Uncle Gustl and Aunt Lisl. I would like to hear from them soon. I didn't speak to Erich.

How is my dear Mama? I think of you often. Elsa is here with me and sends her regards to all of you.

Many kisses, your son,

Hans

Kitty turned the postcard over and looked at the return address. The letter came from Birkenau -Labor Camp.

Karel addressed Kitty. "It is the best we could hope for. I don't know where this Birkenau Labor Camp is, but I pray they do not work him too hard." Bettina took the postcard back from Kitty, pressing it to her chest.

The following evening, while Bettina was still with her father at his barrack, Kitty reached beneath Bettina's pillow and took the postcard from its hiding spot. Kitty met Vlada and when they had settled on a bench in the park, she handed him the postcard. Vlada read it in silence, and looked up, his mind poring over Hanuš's cryptic message.

"He is alive, Kitty. At least that much is certain," Vlada said.

Kitty looked at Vlada guiltily, her eyes downcast, a lump in her throat. Vlada had been so kind and loving, comforting Kitty after the shock of her brother's disappearance. He had waited days, only then reluctantly sharing that he had lost family members to the transfer as well: his aunt and uncle, his cousin, and Vera.

"I am sorry, Vlada. I shouldn't have shown that to you knowing that you have not heard from your family yet."

Vlada shook his head. He handed the letter back to Kitty, their fingers brushing against each other. The brief physical contact sent a thrilling shock through Kitty. That hollow, fluttery sensation in the pit of her stomach happened more often lately: when they touched, when Vlada's lips brushed against hers, when he placed his hand on the small of her back. Those fleeting moments made Kitty's heart race, and she wondered if Vlada felt the same. She demurely cast her eyes down, forgetting about her brother and the other lost ones for a moment. Twilight descended over the camp.

"Your eyes look beautiful tonight," Vlada said breathlessly. People began to hurry down the street past the lovers, prompting Vlada to look at his watch. "Oh, no, Kitty...the time!" Vlada was dismayed. It was yet another in a series of tender moments cut short as they hastened down the street to beat the curfew. Kitty looked at Vlada longingly as they ran, hand in hand, in the fading light.

Terezin did not recover from the labor camp deportations; more accurately, it reached an uneasy compromise. Those who remained felt a slight reprieve from the overcrowded conditions, and some believed rations became more plentiful. But Kitty knew better. The only people she did not hear repeating the misconceptions of plenty were her parents. They could find no comfort in extra rations, perceived or otherwise. They would rather die than credit an extra ration of sugar each week with the loss of their son.

After work, Kitty walked to her father's barrack to share the evening meal with her parents. She stopped outside the door, gathering her wits about her. Lately, she felt guilty about everything. She found herself trying to atone for the loss of Hanuš, even though she knew she was not responsible. She felt remorse each time she emptied the dwindling produce from her pockets as the *Judengarten* crops began to wither and die in the autumn frost, and she felt shame that she would rather be with Vlada than here with her parents. The only place she had found comfort these past few months was in his arms.

She forced a weak smile, squared her shoulders and entered the barrack. Her father was where she always found him, lying prostrate in his bunk. Kitty cheerlessly deposited her meager draw from the garden on the table. She helped Bettina chop up the few small potatoes she had pilfered; the sooner the meal was done the sooner she could be with Vlada.

In mid-October, a notice arrived instructing Kitty that she was being transferred to work in the central laundry. From the first day, Kitty loathed working in the laundry, her hands in and out of hot and cold water all day, the small amount of lye soap cracking and reddening her skin. Her back ached as she picked up heavy baskets filled to overflowing with piles of wet clothing and bedding. By the end of each day, she was tired and irritable. She donned a cheerful demeanor around Vlada but it was hardly necessary. Vlada had his own concerns, his thoughts dark and distracted during their evening walks.

"Something is going on at the Magdeburg Barrack," Vlada informed Kitty one evening. He handed her a piece of bread he had bartered for a lock repair, and she tucked it in her pocket, fretting over who would be the recipient: her father or Arna, who would use it to feed the little ones.

Vlada reached for Kitty's hand, and she quickly pulled it away, embarrassed by the rough texture of her skin, sore to the touch where it was cracked and dry. Vlada took her hand gently, looked at it, and put it to his lips. Kitty closed her eyes, a warm flush enveloping her body. She opened her eyes to see Vlada intently staring at her.

"We need privacy," he said in a low voice that made Kitty shiver. There was a chill in the air, and they stood and began walking briskly to shake it off. Kitty left Vlada's suggestion unanswered, but it lingered in her mind. Later that night when they parted ways, Kitty undressed, changing into her nightclothes, playing what Vlada had said, his voice husky, his gaze piercing, over again in her mind. She slipped under the covers and lay in bed in the dark, trembling in anticipation at the thought of it.

The next morning, just after sunrise, the entire camp awoke to shock and confusion. Czech gendarmes and Gestapo marched menacingly down the middle of the main avenues of the camp, banging on doors and shouting.

"Everyone out, now!" Guards crashed through the doors of Kitty's barrack, entering each room, and pulling prisoners from their beds. Boots stomped noisily as the men moved from room to room, ensuring every bunk was emptied. Kitty had been dreaming of Teplice, but all tender thoughts disintegrated amid the clamor of the guards and the cries of her bunkmates. Bettina and Kitty shared a wordless look and walked hurriedly out the door and into the street, where throngs of frightened prisoners flowed out of every barrack.

The guards herded the prisoners toward the main entrance, most dressed in their nightclothes, with only the quickest among them grabbing a coat or sweater to ward off the chill of the cold November morning. The throngs of prisoners were corralled into a large field adjacent to the wall of the fortress. Wild-eyed, many of the prisoners had not seen the outside world in well over a year and were terrified to know the reason behind this sudden evacuation.

Kitty lost Bettina in the crowd as they were jostled and pushed out onto the grassy lot, still wet with dew. The guards fanned out and formed a perimeter, training their machine guns on their captives. Kitty turned around, aghast at the enormous crowd of people surrounding her. She had never seen the entire population of the camp in one place at one time. The guards were emptying the whole of the camp, for what reason she could not imagine.

"Form into groups of one hundred!" the Czech gendarmes instructed. "Remain standing! Ten by ten in a square, now!"

At the instructions, utter confusion erupted; family members did not want to be separated while the goal of the grim exercise remained unclear. If they were to be shot, they wanted to have their loved ones near them. Kitty could hear children crying, and anxiety rose in her. She wondered where Arna and little Petr and Eva were in the sea of thousands.

An SS officer with a brutish, pockmarked face walked slowly down the rows of prisoners, his shiny black leather boots becoming plastered with wet grass. He counted off groups of one hundred to a guard walking beside him holding a clipboard. Oh, no, thought Kitty. They are counting us. They are going to count every living soul. Her thoughts turned to Vlada, wondering where he was in the crowd, but she quickly moved to find a place.

The shouting continued. "This is a *volkszahlung*. You will cooperate and immediately stand in groups of one hundred and be counted."

A census, thought Kitty. But why? Kitty looked out over the sea of bodies. She saw a group of the ghetto's administrators from the Magdeburg barrack far off in the crowd. She wondered if Vlada's father was among them. Every single camp inhabitant was out in the field. Kitty could hear women calling out their children's names – 'Rudolf? Where are you, Rudolf?' – and men screaming in prayer toward the skies. Women huddled together in small groups, holding hands, and Kitty saw a group of elderly prisoners struggling to help each other stand. The moans and cries were drowned out as a group of SS guards made their way threateningly down the perimeter of the crowd, barking instructions. Kitty urgently wanted to find Vlada. Where was her love in this horrible scene?

Kitty shivered, her teeth chattering. The sun had risen higher in the sky, but the temperature had not. She was sure it was close to freezing and even after being counted, the guards were not allowing anyone to return indoors. The prisoners huddled in groups, cold and hungry, trying to maintain their rows while seeking each other out for warmth. When a prisoner needed to relieve themselves, they were instructed to go to the perimeter. Women walked hesitantly to the edge of the formation, the guards' guns trained on them, as they lowered their underwear, and squatted. Kitty and a few other women moved to surround them; they linked arms to form a human fence, shielding them from the prying eyes of the guards. Is there worse to come? Kitty wondered.

An SS officer began shouting angrily at the Czech guards and other officers. He screamed at them that they would have to begin the counting all over again, the count having been corrupted in some way. A prisoner made the mistake of asking the officer a question and the officer approached, his face contorted in anger, pulling a baton from his belt. He raised the baton and began beating the man, continuing the beating even after the man fell to the ground, the man's wife crying out each time he landed a blow. The officer replaced the baton in his belt and walked away.

Late in the afternoon, Kitty watched as an elderly man, who had been propped up by someone in his group, collapsed on the ground. One of the Czech guards ran over, pushing the man with the butt of the gun, shouting at him to stand up. It was clear to those around him that he would not be standing, not now or ever again. The guard shouted to two of the men in the group to take the man and move him to outside the perimeter and then return immediately to their places. The two men, with anguished faces, carried the old man, his arms around their shoulders, his legs dragging behind him. They laid him gently in the grass. Wailing, an elderly woman wrapped in a blue shawl tried to free herself from the throngs, and stumble over the uneven ground in the direction of the body. Two women took her by the arms, holding her tightly. Kitty hung her head, helpless.

Darkness descended over the masses, and more bodies were brought outside the perimeter. Kitty heard cries of "My baby! My baby!" and thought of Arna and the little ones. She hugged her shoulders and stomped her feet. At around 11 p.m., just when Kitty thought she might not be able to stand another minute, the guards began to shout. "Go back to your barracks." With hundreds of dead bodies left lying on the freezing ground, the crowds listlessly dispersed in the direction of the fortress.

Chapter Fourteen

It was only late February and it had been a terrible winter. Christmas and Hannukkah had seen two mass deportations headed to the "East": one on December 15 and one on December 18, each transport bearing 2,500 prisoners, and once again shattering the stability of the camp's inhabitants. After the census in November, Vlada had noticed his father was extremely on edge. He responded sharply to simple questions. When the family gathered for their evening meal, Karel was reserved and distracted, lost in his own faraway thoughts. His abrupt change in demeanor aroused worry in Hermina as well.

One evening at supper, Hermina ladled soup with one chunk of gristle each into each of their bowls. She set them down and they began to eat; the only sound was that of the spoon hitting the edge of the bowls. The comfortable hum of conversation and her husband's kindhearted compliments about the meal were noticeably absent as Karel stared distractedly into his bowl. Hermina gathered up the bowls and utensils in silence, and Vlada stepped outside the barrack with his father. Karel inhaled deeply, breathing in the cold, fresh air, a welcome change from the stifling, airless atmosphere of the barrack. Now that they were alone, Vlada pressed his father. "Tati, what is it? What's wrong?"

As Karel began to speak, Vlada could see the weight fall from his father's shoulders. "The Kommandant ordered the census in November based on a rumor that some prisoners had escaped. He suspected some of the ghetto administrators, Jakob Edelstein for one, were attempting a cover-up. The count revealed the first part was true: the prisoner count was off by over fifty people." Karel paused for a moment, exhaling like a man who had kept a secret burden for too long. "The SS arrested Edelstein. The Kommandant let some time pass, allowing us all to think there would be no repercussions now that Edelstein was in custody." Karel spat the words out. "Then the Kommandant ordered those two transports in December, as punishment. Edelstein was on the first train."

Vlada listened as his father told the gruesome tale, wondering how he was privy to such high-level information. What did he mean by "us all?" Vlada shuddered to himself. If the camp's top administrator was not safe from deportation, who was?

As he strode confidently toward the newly built latrines on the other side of the camp, Vlada could see his breath in the cold air. It was barely past dawn, and the camp was still asleep. His thoughts turned toward his father's rules for safety. He trusted his father, despite the recent secrecy, and he put his suggestions into practice at every opportunity. They were not meant as casual advice, but as protection, ammunition even.

Rule number one: Walk with purpose. Karel counted on this rule to protect Vlada from the vagaries and whims of their captors. Vlada employed it often, even when he was going to relieve himself. He had seen firsthand the unwanted attention that meandering or loitering attracted from the wrong people: the Germans, and the Czech gendarmes.

There was a predictable script that played out. First came the stern address, "You, there! Stop! Where are you going?" That was invariably followed up by, "Who gave you permission?" If the questions were not answered precisely, it might result in beatings, or even imprisonment. If anyone stopped him this morning, Vlada had a valid answer at the ready.

Rule number two: Never volunteer. Karel likened the Czech gendarmes and SS guards at Terezin to the lazy, cruel, and corrupt characters in the dark satire *The Good Soldier Svejk*. Any good graces one hoped to gain by lending a helping hand were sure to come back to haunt you. Better to keep a low profile. In a world filled with corruption and hypocrisy, no good ever came from being good.

The newly constructed pit latrine came into view. Some of Czechoslovakia's best engineers were imprisoned at the camp and although the latrine's purpose was simple, it was a feat of technology. It had been built in early 1943, after sanitary conditions and disease had liquidated almost half of the camp's population. Vlada marveled as he approached that it still looked brand new, underutilized as it was. He could not understand how the men in the camp preferred the horrific conditions of the barrack latrines to the relative cleanliness and seclusion of the one before him.

Set apart as it was, it was rarely supervised and still more infrequently occupied, and Vlada had taken to regularly venturing there in the early morning hours. Despite living communally in the ghetto for well over a year, Vlada was still shy when it came to privacy of bodily functions.

He climbed the short flight of wooden stairs and glanced at the trio of old men, early morning regulars who gathered at the far end of the long wooden bench. If it were not wartime, they could easily have been mistaken for elderly gents taking a sauna at a bathhouse. They ignored his arrival, too busy relishing the few stolen moments shared amongst men their own age. One of them joked and the others laughed, a low laugh no one except Vlada could hear.

The old Czech gents reminded Vlada of home, and his mind traveled back to the coffee shop in Pardubice where his father would meet friends for a drink and conversation while Vlada flipped the pages of *Time Magazine*, his favorite. He rarely allowed himself to look back at the past. This memory, especially, was a painful one. He imagined his father in a suit, the picture of sartorial perfection, sporting his beautiful striped ties, and highly polished shoes. He recalled the high esteem with which his father was held among his peers, for his role as a Czech Legionnaire and as a knowledgeable chemist. The memories jarred with the reality of his father's present life at the camp.

Vlada shook himself out of his reverie. As the old men joked and laughed, Vlada unzipped his jacket and pulled out the book Kitty had presented to him for his birthday just days earlier. He rubbed the leather binding with his thumb. It felt smooth, precious, unyielding.

She is full of surprises, thought Vlada. He could not imagine how she had gotten her hands on something so valuable. In the *Judengarten* Kitty had bartered for special items with vegetables. In early winter, she had been transferred to work in the central laundry, and he wondered what bartering tools she had at her disposal there. By whatever means Kitty had obtained the volume Vlada now held in his hands, he was aware of what this gift meant. In the outside world, books were verboten, inside Terezin, they were prized and treasured. In a word, Kitty's gift of this book meant nothing short of one thing: Kitty loved him, and she wanted him to know, even at great risk to herself.

In their long walks before curfew, Vlada had told Kitty of his love of books, a love he shared with his father. He treasured his walks with her, their hushed tones as they shared their passions and worries. Those moments left them both feeling like the world was theirs alone, and they were transported out of the miseries of the camp, if only for that moment. Vlada was surprised daily at the feelings he had for Kitty. He felt at once possessive, worrying about her welfare, and wanting to make her proud of him.

Vlada told Kitty of the precious birthday gift, the book *Babička*, that he had received from his parents as a young boy, and how his class had visited the château in Ratibořice where the story was set. Kitty knew the book well, and she wanted to know every detail of his visit there, having never been herself. "What did you see? What was your favorite part?" Kitty begged for details.

"Being there was like a fairy tale unfolding before my eyes," Vlada said dramatically, winking at Kitty.

"Don't tease, Vlada. Did you go to the well?" Her eyes searched his face, hanging on every word.

"Of course!" Vlada replied, puffing his chest out proudly. "We even have a photo of my class in front of the statue of Babicka and her grandchildren."

Kitty's eyes lit up. "Go on," she encouraged.

"Oh, and I almost fell into the dam; the water was rushing, and it was so loud. My mother saved me," Vlada told her. Kitty held Vlada's arm tightly, transporting herself away from the mundane daily life at Terezin and imagining Vlada teetering on the edge of the dam below.

Vlada stopped in the street, aware of the growing darkness enveloping them. "It's getting dark now, Kitty." He looked at her flushed face, so open and eager to hear more. He was caught off guard by the depth of emotion that washed over him, and he wanted to sweep her up in his arms and keep her safe and happy.

"But we still have a few minutes. Please, Vlada!" She tugged at his sleeve, her gaze softening.

"Okay, okay." He threw his hands up, feigning surrender. "The château was grand. It's pink. Did you know that? And the old bleaching ground had a thatched roof and a small attic window. My mother told me it reminded her of her childhood home." They walked, and Vlada continued his tale of the visit to *Babiččino údolí*, the Grandmother's Valley, embellishing the story, with Kitty gripping his arm tighter at each new detail.

Finally, they had come to stand in front of Kitty's barrack. A threadbare curtain moved in one of the lower windows. It was Bettina, keeping an eye on the young lovers. She did not hide her dissatisfaction about where, and with whom, Kitty spent her time each evening.

Vlada glanced toward the window and laughed. "She is going to have to try harder than that to discourage me."

Kitty blushed. "Wait here," she whispered in his ear. Vlada felt her warm breath, and he turned to face her, but she was gone, having dashed inside the barracks. Vlada stood awkwardly outside. He felt the gaze of the young girls who were now gathering at the window to see the young man who lingered alone in the street.

Kitty reappeared, taking the steps two at a time, holding something wrapped in what resembled a pillowcase. She proudly handed him the fabric-covered parcel.

"For you," Kitty announced. "Happy birthday, Vlada Munk." Before he could reply, she gave Vlada a fleeting peck on the cheek and hurried inside.

Vlada returned to his own barrack and climbed up to his bunk on the third level, wanted to inspect Kitty's gift in private. He could tell by its heft that it was a book. He slowly removed the pillowcase, the leather cover revealing its title in the dim light: *The Jewish War*. It was a biography of Josephus Flavius, a rebel commander and military prisoner, who later became a brilliant Roman historian. He told the story of the destruction of the Second Temple in Jerusalem and the depopulation of Palestine.

Vlada could not believe his eyes; he opened the book with a reverence he reserved for few things in the camp, carefully turning the pages printed on tissue-thin paper.

He was instantly captivated. The walls built around the ancient cities reminded Vlada of Terezin's fortress walls, as did the calamities that unfolded as Jerusalem was taken. As the barracks darkened and the lights went out, Vlada vowed to get up early the next morning and continue reading. He would take the book with him to the latrine and escape, if just for a few moments, into its pages once again. It would be the perfect start to his day.

The elderly trio at the end of the long bench kept up their dialogue as Vlada sat down on the rough wood of the latrine, Kitty's gift in hand, to accomplish two tasks before work. He opened the book and began where he had left off, enthralled by the tale of the Roman legions' discipline. He turned the tissue-thin pages with reverence, forgetting the cold, the lean-to behind him provided little in the way of protection from the elements when the wind was blowing from the east. Vlada turned the pages, allowing the story to transport him up and out of Terezin. He wished he could hide up there forever and read to his heart's content.

At the top of the latrine, Vlada read, lingering much longer than he anticipated. The men at the other end of the row of toilet seats were standing to take their leave, and the sky was brightening. He reluctantly closed the book and set it on the wooden bench beside him. He proceeded to pull up his pants. There was no toilet paper, no running water, and no soap to be had. Rushing to buckle his belt, Vlada's knee nudged the book from its place on the ledge and *–plop—*down it went into the dark abyss. Vlada cursed under his breath. He looked down into the cavernous hole below and saw the book, sitting atop a murky ooze, forever lost to a place where things were only deposited, never retrieved.

How will I tell Kitty? he worried. He could not believe his clumsiness. Will she ever forgive me?

Vlada allowed himself one last glance downward. The book's title stared up at him, mocking him. He looked to the end of bench to see if the men had noticed. One of them looked at Vlada, then at the other two men, and all three burst into laughter, slapping their knees, and guffawing loudly at his predicament. Vlada shook his head and ran down the stairs.

CHAPTER FOURTEEN

Kitty's cheeks burned red with shame. Shame and humiliation. The feelings were so unfamiliar, they were causing her physical pain. She felt sick to her stomach, and her head ached.

There was some other emotion mixed in, something completely different and far more terrible. It was fear.

Kitty felt her body trembling uncontrollably.

How did I get here?

The weather had turned warmer, and prisoners spilled from their barracks out into the street after dinner to linger in the balmy evening air right up until the 8 o'clock curfew. It was a welcome reprieve from the cool, wet spring when everything felt covered in dampness. The streets were crowded but Kitty barely noticed. Each time she saw Vlada waiting on the main street for her, she felt her heart soar, and the tiny flutter in her stomach was ever-present. The smile on his face, and the urgency with which he took her hand, encouraged her to think he felt the same excitement.

They immediately fell into step with each other, and their conversation flowed easily. The feel of her hand in Vlada's strong and calloused one never ceased to thrill her. Parting at the end of each evening was difficult, but Kitty eagerly anticipated the compensation: Vlada's breathtaking kisses.

"Time with you goes by so fast." Kitty lamented the witching hour as she stood outside her barrack and prepared to bid Vlada good night. Vlada kissed Kitty on the forehead, then stepped back. They stood, their faces inches apart, so close that Kitty could feel Vlada's warm breath on her cheeks. Her breath began to quicken, and they stayed that way, not moving, for over a minute. Vlada tilted her head so that she was looking directly into his eyes. He kissed her. His lips were warm, and rough, and Kitty responded. She pursed her lips the way the actors did in the movies she'd seen a lifetime ago. Vlada parted his lips slightly, and Kitty surrendered hers in return.

Vlada pulled away and Kitty felt her cheeks flush. "Goodnight, Vlada," her voice wavered, sounding unfamiliar to her.

"Goodnight, Kitty," Vlada responded. He lowered his head, looking her in the eye, and she blushed again. She felt self-conscious and giddy, like he was seeing her without her clothes on. Kitty caught her breath and entered the barrack, a light film of sweat on her forehead. She lowered her eyes, trying to avoid eye contact with Bettina, but her body language revealed her secret without the two women even having to speak. Bettina scowled at her, shaking her head.

She knows nothing of romance, thought Kitty. Kitty could not remember the last time she had seen her parents share a kiss. Kitty laid down on her bunk. She closed her eyes and replayed the moment with Vlada over and over again in her mind.

Bettina slept soundly the following morning as Kitty dressed for work. Kitty chose a blue sweater, throwing it over a thin cotton print dress. Her mother secured the clothing at great risk, pulling the items out from under her full skirt at the end of the workday, breathless at the thrill of it. It was a side of her mother Kitty had never seen before, and she liked it.

The blue sweater was Kitty's favorite. It had embroidery stitched on the front and fabric-covered buttons. The weather was cool in the early morning hours, comfortable. If the sun came out later in the day, Kitty would peel off the sweater and tie it around her waist for safekeeping.

Kitty liked walking to work as the camp was beginning to wake up. Birds chirped and the rumble of a cart bumping over the cobblestone streets carrying bread to the camp's kitchens was soothing and familiar. Her thoughts turned to Vlada and the night before when the warm feel of his lips met hers; a demure smile crossed her face. She tried to control her daydreaming about Vlada, but it was nearly impossible. It often resulted in an elbow from Hanka, shaking Kitty out of her lovelorn reverie and back to earth. Hanka had long gotten over the excitement of hearing about Kitty's evenings with "my Vlada."

"What witticisms did your dear Vlada utter last night, Kitty?" Hanka teased, rolling her eyes, as she walked alongside Kitty to the *Judengarten*. The girls' friendship enjoyed an easy banter, and teasing each other took their minds away from the necessity of foraging for food. They had been happy to discover they were both assigned to the garden again as part of the summer work detail.

Hanka and Kitty had built solid reputations as good workers, and they had earned the privilege of loose oversight. When they arrived at the garden, the Czech overseer motioned them over to a patch of green beans that were ready for picking. They walked through the now-familiar garden, past the sweet peas, its bright green tendrils winding around tall wooden trellises, the onions sticking out of the dark earth. They stopped in front of the green beans.

Both girls needed extra rations: Kitty's father was ill and unable to work, and Hanuš was gone. She could not count on Bettina for help; her mother rarely completed her "norm," that is, the work necessary to obtain her daily allotment of full food rations. Kitty was the primary breadwinner for the family, and she also felt pressure to help Arna feed the little ones. Poor Hanka has even more people depending on her for their survival, thought Kitty.

She observed the plants, thick with beans, and Kitty and Hanka shared a look of pleasant surprise. Kitty could feel this was going to be a good day: the beans were plentiful, and they began grabbing thick fistfuls, cutting them from the vines and dropping them in a large woven basket. For every handful of beans Kitty picked for the *lazarotte*, the

German wounded who were the recipients of each day's harvest, Kitty picked a handful for herself.

Kitty worked fast, while Hanka acted as lookout. The stockpile of beans for her own use grew, and Kitty felt her shoulders relax at the knowledge that she would have more than enough to supplement her parents' daily allotment. She and Hanka would split the day's take once safely outside the gauntlet. On any given day, Kitty and Hanka switched roles, one working as lookout, the other securing the contraband.

The other women in the garden whispered to each other as they worked, sharing the camp gossip of the day. The rumor mill in the camp had been relentless of late, churning out so much flotsam and jetsam it was nearly impossible to discern fact from fiction. The camp's inhabitants were eager for a bright light amidst the daily diet of hunger, disease, death, and degradation, and they devoured anything with a happy ending, no matter how much it jarred reality. Many had pinned their hopes on a recent fiction of a prisoner exchange. It was a pleasant alternative to a loved one being sent to a labor camp, or worse. Kitty wished she could be one of the hopeful ones, placing faith in such rumors.

Sadly, on the rare occasion when there was a hint of truth, the information was bandied about in a capricious version of the childhood game "Telephone," rendering it completely unrecognizable by its final iteration. Many rumors petered out over the course of a few days from lack of authentication.

Today's gossip had a different feel; there was a buzz in the garden and the camp, the momentum building for days. The few trustworthy Czech gendarmes who had access to news from the outside world had seemed to confirm it.

A friendly Czech overseer whispered the news discreetly to Kitty as she passed by. "The Allies have prevailed over the Germans in France." The implications of this piece of news were too much to hope for: if France were liberated, surely Czechoslovakia could not be far behind.

Hanka had bought into the rumor completely; she was already planning what she would do now that freedom seemed imminent. "I am going back to Prague," Hanka said confidently, using a hoe to weed between rows of onions. "I am going to be a secretary."

Kitty shook her head and frowned, pulling up weeds with her bare hands. She worried this type of thinking was premature. "We have heard this all before," Kitty whispered to her friend. The last time a rumor of this magnitude had spread, it disintegrated into little more than crushed dreams, sinking some of the prisoners further into darkness and despair.

The veracity of this latest news mattered little to Kitty and the empty bellies she needed to fill right now, but she would gladly use the ripples of distraction it caused to her advantage. She greedily stuffed handfuls of beans into her makeshift bra, only stopping when Hanka slid her finger across her throat in warning.

At the end of the day, Kitty and Hanka walked through the post-garden gauntlet. Kitty breathed a sigh of relief at the sight of a couple of the more friendly gendarmes who ignored the women's noticeably bulky bosoms. Kitty returned to the barrack to wash up and change her clothes. She scrubbed the dirt from under her fingernails beneath a trickle of water that dripped from the sink in the latrine.

Oila would be proud of me, of my work ethic and my resourcefulness, thought Kitty, pulling a clean dress over her head. Bettina had done well in choosing this dress which had a tiny floral print and a small bow at the neck. It fit Kitty perfectly. She pinched her cheeks to add a little color and ran her fingers through her short hair; hairbrushes were a liability due to an outbreak of lice.

Kitty promised herself to be as cheerful as possible at supper that evening. The family meals had become increasingly somber of late. Bettina was in mourning, her thoughts often far away, worrying constantly over the fate of her only son. Kitty's father's health had declined further in recent months, and he could do little to give his wife solace. That left Kitty to provide comfort to Bettina. Kitty eyed her mother coolly, resentful of the change in roles. She never wiped a tear after a skinned knee back in Teplice, thought Kitty. No matter. The sooner dinner is over, the sooner I can meet Vlada.

"What have you brought us today, Kitty?" Bettina inspected Kitty, looking her up and down for garden contraband.

Kitty looked at her mother angrily, scanning the surroundings to see who might have heard her question. This woman does not know to lower her voice, thought Kitty. There were spies everywhere who would turn Kitty in for a few stolen green beans if it meant an extra slice of bread or salami for the informant. Did her mother want to lose the family's primary breadwinner? Infuriated, Kitty reached into her pockets and pulled out the spoils, handing them to Bettina.

They ate in silence at the small table in her father's barrack, the conversation of others around them amplified the family's lack of interaction. It became so uncomfortable Kitty felt obligated to bring up a topic for conversation. "Have you heard the rumors about the Allies in France?" Kitty saw a flicker of interest in her father's eyes, then he immediately went back to eating his soup. Her mother did not take the bait; Bettina's mind was elsewhere, probably on Hanuš and her guilt over not having been able to prevent his deportation. Kitty felt a wave of sadness wash over her at the thought of her brother out there somewhere, but she refused to spend her time before curfew comforting Bettina. Those were Kitty's precious hours of freedom. Hours for Vlada.

It had been a year since they first met and barely a day went by that the two did not meet at their appointed spot, a midway point on Hauptstrasse. One night they talked of music, another night literature. She knew all Vlada's favorite books by now. She could listen to him talk for hours, each evening spent in their own private bubble of laughter and affection. No matter what the chosen topic, their conversations always worked their way back to food.

"Bread," Vlada said dreamily. "Good, fresh bread."

"Oila and I used to stretch the strudel dough out on the kitchen table until it was so thin, we thought it might tear, and then we brushed it with melted butter. Then we added another layer of dough and still yet another layer." Kitty could almost taste the buttery sweetness, her description prompting her stomach to growl from hunger, the thin soup and handful of green beans she had for supper no match for her memory of freshly baked apple strudel.

This night Kitty met Vlada at their usual spot. "Come with me," Vlada requested, looking serious. Vlada grabbed her hand and led her down a side street Kitty did not recognize. Vlada drew Kitty inside the doorway of one of the barracks, pulling her with an unfamiliar urgency up the stairway in front of them.

Kitty followed, excited, and slightly confused. "Vlada, where are you taking me?" Before Vlada replied, Kitty already knew the answer. Vlada had mentioned that his friend Jirka knew of a kumbal, a cubbyhole used for privacy. But he neglected to tell Kitty the whole story of how Jirka knew of the kumbal as it would have put her off.

Vlada made his way to the far end of the attic and pulled back the curtain of a makeshift closet. A blanket had been laid out on some cushions; a single light bulb hung over head. "Vlada!" Kitty protested. He put a finger to her lips to silence her, then pulled her inside the cubbyhole and let the curtain fall over the opening, obscuring them from view.

Vlada sat down on the makeshift bed and beckoned Kitty to join him. Kitty took his hand and sat down. They stared into each other's eyes and then Vlada cupped Kitty's face and began to kiss her. Kitty closed her eyes, and at the same moment, the light bulb went out, and everything in the tiny cubbyhole was a hazy gray, hovering somewhere between day and night.

Kitty could hear Vlada whispering her name, his hot breath in her ear. She felt the warmth of him, wrapping her up in his arms. His hands, rough from his work in the locksmith shop, caressed her softly and the stubble from his beard scratched her mouth as he kissed her strongly, persuasively.

They fumbled in the darkness of the room. Kitty barely felt the wool blanket scratch her bare legs. A warm flush rose in her cheeks and she was glad to be in the velvety twilight of the room, barely able to see Vlada's eyes glittering in the darkness. Every sorrowful thought was wiped away by Vlada's touch. She felt beautiful and passionate, loved and adored.

Kitty dozed, awaking with a start to total darkness. "Vlada, what time is it?" Kitty asked nervously.

"I don't know," Vlada said drowsily, pulling her close.

Kitty pulled the curtain of the kumbal to the side to find the attic room outside enveloped in darkness. "Vlada, it's late. I must hurry," she leaned down and kissed him on the lips, lingering for a moment.

Kitty thought her heart might burst; the passion of their earlier moment was reignited, and Kitty felt her breath coming in short gasps as Vlada returned her kiss. Her body relaxed as she put her arms around his neck. She wanted to stay. She did not care what time it was. She would risk anything for this intimacy, this affection.

It was late. She gently pushed Vlada away and dressed hurriedly. Vlada did the same and soon they were at the bottom of the stairs and out in the street, headed for Kitty's barrack. All was quiet. She dragged her feet as they approached the building.

Oh, how I want to be grown up, thought Kitty. Inside was Bettina, who Kitty was certain would give her daughter an accusatory once-over. Outside was Vlada. Warm, sweet, strong Vlada.

"It isn't fair," Kitty said petulantly. She wished the whole world would instantly right itself so their time together would never be cut short again. Vlada opened the screen door to Kitty's barrack. They stood there in the semi-darkness, hovering between the illusion of being the only two people on the planet and the reality of life in an overcrowded camp.

Vlada hushed her, covering her face with kisses, her anger at the world subsiding under his tender caresses. He gave her one last kiss on her forehead. Kitty clung tightly to him and looked up into his eyes. At that moment Kitty saw a flicker of movement under the streetlamp nearby. Her body froze. She moved to bolt inside the barrack, but it was too late.

A man stepped into the light and shouted. "Stop! You two! Give me your names, immediately!"

Vlada stepped forward into the light of the streetlamp, pushing Kitty behind him. "There is nothing here for you to be concerned about." Vlada spoke confidently. His job as a locksmith allowed him to be out after curfew, giving him the run of the camp. He was not breaking any rules.

"Oh, but I think there is," the man responded ominously. He wore the cap of *die ghettowache*, a civilian ghetto guard. Their reputation was notorious. Kitty recognized the man as one of those connected to the census the previous year. Three hundred people had died that day waiting to be counted by the likes of him.

"It is ten minutes past curfew, and I need both of your names at once. This is a serious offense." The man spoke officiously. Vlada assessed the man and took a chance that he might be open to negotiation.

"Let her go, please. This all is my fault," Vlada appealed. The man strode toward them with his hand on the club hanging from his side. Kitty trembled behind Vlada, the sweetness of their earlier moment together had all but vanished, replaced by fear.

"Identification papers, now. And you, there, show yourself." The guard's tone was unnecessarily harsh. It was clear he hoped something more untoward was afoot. Kitty stepped into the light next to Vlada, her head bowed. Vlada reached in his pocket for his identification. The man gave Vlada's papers a quick glance before handing them back to him.

Kitty reached into the pocket of her dress and produced her papers. The guard snatched it out of her hand, and yanked her chin, the chin that Vlada had held so gently just minutes ago, turning it this way and that with disdain so he could see her in the dim light. Can he tell what I've just done? Kitty wondered.

"Well, now this is a problem, is it not?" The guard began to toy with Kitty, delighting in her discomfort as she struggled to hold back tears. "Out after curfew and under the age of sixteen. This looks like a case for the Juvenile Court. Your father will be notified of your offense. Failure to appear could result in unpleasant consequences, for you and your family. Now get inside. *Schnell!*" He turned on his heel and walked back into the black night.

Kitty broke down in tears. "He is a traitor," she cried to Vlada. Whether Czech or German, weren't they all Jews imprisoned in this camp because of the Nazis? Did they not owe each other some sort of solidarity? Kitty's shoulders heaved. "He could have let me go with a warning. Why are people so cruel?"

Vlada held her, whispering angrily in her ear. "One prisoner arresting another. This is how he saves his own skin from being sent to the "East." He should feel foolish and small." Vlada felt the sting, remembering his encounter with the man in the park back in Pardubice.

"He is despicable." Kitty hated the man for his arrogance. He had ruined the most beautiful night of her life. And now he was going to make it dirty, public.

Vlada held her shoulders and looked directly into her eyes. "Listen to me, Kitty. No harm will come to you." Vlada's words sounded convincing, but Kitty's mind raced with all the potential ramifications.

"How could I be so stupid? My parents just lost Hanuš, they can't lose me as well. What will become of them if I am not here to bring them extra food? What will they do to me? What if they send me to the "East?" I can't leave you!" She broke down in shuddering sobs, throwing her arms around Vlada's neck. Women had begun gathering in the windows of the barrack, peering out.

Vlada hugged Kitty one last time on the landing. "We will find a way out of this," Vlada said. Bettina opened the door. Kitty immediately felt her mother's disapproval, emblazoning her with a scarlet letter.

The air was fraught with Bettina's icy presence. Vlada told Kitty later that he felt something different. The words were unspoken. When Bettina looked at Vlada, she was judging his worthiness. "Why is this boy still here? Why is my son gone?"

Kitty went inside, her head hung in shame. It would only get worse: tomorrow her father would hear the news of her broken curfew and her secret tryst with Vlada. She had disappointed her parents; worse yet, she was embarrassed in front of Vlada. The incident emphasized the difference in their ages at a moment when she wanted nothing more than for him to see her as an adult. A grown up. A woman. She threw herself on her bunk and began to sob quietly, her shoulders rising and falling with each wave of emotion.

"*Mach vas!*" Oila's refrain echoed in her ears. "Do something!" Kitty sat up and wiped her tears with the back of her hand and probed with her tongue the empty space where her tooth had once been. She was not one to be pushed around or trifled with. She had proven that to herself when she stood up to the SS officer the day her family was deported to Terezin. She would not give up now because a puny guard who was a traitor to his Jewish compatriots had turned her in for the smallest of infractions.

They want me to give up, but I won't, thought Kitty. There must be a way out of this mess. She would make Oila, and Vlada, proud. She looked out the window before drifting off to sleep, and she could see stars glittering in the heavens over the camp.

Mach vas! In the morning, Kitty vowed, she would just that.

CHAPTER FIFTEEN

Kitty repeatedly read the summons calling her to the Juvenile Court, each review prompting a fresh wave of humiliation. The summons was issued by the Jewish Self Government in Theresienstadt, the German name for Terezin, and it had requested both Kitty and her father's presence in front of the court in the matter of Kitty violating curfew as a minor.

Kitty had stood next to her father in the somber courtroom, the camp's elders peppering him with questions, as Karel struggled to remain standing. Kitty stood immobile, her legs feeling like great blocks of stone. She wanted to run from the room, but she accepted that escape was not an option. Instead, as the charges were read against her, Kitty hung her head, Bettina's judgmental eyes burning a hole in her back from where she sat.

The judge had dismissed the family and Karel, Bettina and Kitty had walked back to her father's barrack in an uneasy silence. Karel collapsed on his bunk. Perspiration dampened his shirt, and his breath came in short, heaving gasps.

With her arms crossed, Bettina stood next to the bed, a dam of anger and humiliation within her poised to burst at any moment. Kitty sat stiffly in a chair next to the bed, fretting a small handkerchief in her lap, avoiding eye contact. Her emotions alternated between embarrassment, outrage, and frustration: embarrassment that Vlada had to be reminded of her age in such a public way; outrage at the horrible ghetto guard who had caused all this injury. In five days, thought Kitty, I will turn sixteen, and none of this will have mattered.

Her father cleared his throat. "Kitty, the court has informed us that they are unable to consider your case for at least four weeks. That means you must sit with the offense hanging over your head for that time. If there are deportations, people with offenses are often the most at risk." He looked at her, his eyes betraying his powerlessness.

Bettina gasped, collapsing onto the bed. She looked at Kitty, sympathetically this time. "Karel," she said, her voice cracking. "I can't lose another child."

"I have a friend in the infirmary," Karel continued. "He has suggested a plan that might keep Kitty safe."

Bettina went to where her husband lay uncomfortably in the bunk and urgently took his hand. "Tell us, Karel. What is it? What do we need to do?"

Kitty's heart swelled with love for her father, and her cheeks grew red with shame, knowing that he must be involved in the subterfuge. Whatever the plan was, she was willing to do anything he asked.

He sat up a little straighter on the bunk, looking at them both. "It will require a little acting on your part, Kitty, but I am sure you can play it well," her father said. "You're going to pretend to have encephalitis. My friend said there are no tests to confirm it, and they will want to quarantine you in the infirmary until you are 'better,' that is, until the next court date. You will be safe there, I have it on good authority." The short speech and the evening's events had exhausted him, and he fell back in the bunk.

Bettina sat on the bed, adjusted the pillow, and handed her husband a glass of water. "Thank you, darling," she said, the relief in her voice palpable. Bettina turned her gaze to Kitty; their eyes met, her mother's emotions transparent as she regarded her daughter with a mixture of love and resentment. "My hopelessly frustrating girl." Bettina shook her head, biting her lip, and held out her arms to Kitty. Her eyes welling with tears, Kitty went to her mother, allowing Bettina's arms to envelope her.

"I'm sorry," Kitty choked, her shoulders heaving with emotion. "I will do my best." They stayed like that, the family of three, comforting each other for a few more moments as the room began to darken.

The infirmary was located at the far end of the camp. Kitty walked there the next day with Bettina, feigning fatigue and dizziness. Karel had coached Kitty on the symptoms associated with the ailment, and Bettina cautioned her that when it came to feigning her illness, less was more. They were directed to an examination room, where a kind doctor, his face haggard under the weight of the camp's ill and dying, conducted a thorough examination of Kitty. The doctor and Karel were friends, and he was taking a great risk in admitting her to the clinic.

Kitty nodded during the exam and said all the right things. "Yes, terrible headaches. A stiff neck. I have no appetite, and I want to throw up." Bettina chimed in. "Oh, yes. A very high fever." The doctor immediately admitted Kitty. Mother and daughter said goodbye, and Kitty was ushered by a nurse to a private room in the children's wing. Unexpected memories of Oila came to the surface as Kitty remembered her bout with appendicitis and Oila's devotions to her day and night.

In bed, she lay on her side on clean white sheets, reading a book from the children's bookshelf. Occasionally, she set the book down and moaned dolefully to keep from arousing the nurse's suspicions as they performed their rounds. Kitty understood why Vlada had loved being under quarantine: she was excused from work, and the nurses brought her three meals a day.

In the evening, Vlada appeared outside her hospital room window bearing a beautiful crimson rose. Kitty squealed with delight and then scolded Vlada for the risk he took picking it. The rose had been part of an elaborate hoax of beautifying the camp for a Red Cross inspection. She took the flower, regarding its delicate petals like the rare and exotic thing it was. The only beauty Kitty had ever experienced at the camp were the verdant *Judengarten* overflowing just before harvest, and the pear tree covered with tiny white petals when it bloomed in the spring.

"You gave me a scare, Kitty." Vlada spoke in a low voice, his look one of tender concern. "I'm sorry, Kitty." He glanced at the ground, his face bearing his contrition. It was the first time they had seen each other since that fateful night and Kitty felt fluttery and nervous around him, searching his eyes for a clue to his feelings.

Kitty mustered a reply. "It wasn't your fault." She looked down at him adoringly. "And I would do it all over again." She blushed, disbelieving she had the nerve to speak so frankly.

Vlada looked up and shook his head, grinning. "Then get better soon," he said.

Weeks passed and Kitty continued to rest in the infirmary feigning encephalitis and waiting for the Juvenile Court to hear her case. At the end of the third week, her parents received another, more intimidating, request. They were ordered to appear at the office of the camp Kommandant, Karl Rahm, a cruel and uncompromising Nazi. It was rare for prisoners at the camp to come in close contact with the Kommandant at Terezin, let alone receive an order for a private hearing. Bettina hurried to the infirmary with a handwritten request asking that Kitty be released for a few hours to attend the meeting.

Bettina was visibly shaken when she arrived at the infirmary. Her hand trembled as she handed the doctor the note. He took it from her, eying it nervously, and then signed his initials approving the excursion. Bettina grabbed Kitty's hand, crushing it in hers, searching her daughter's eyes for some small comfort, and they stepped out of the dim light of the infirmary and into the harsh sunlight.

The blue sky shimmered above and the warmth from the cobblestones radiated upward. The day lost its golden glow as Kitty shifted her attention to Bettina. Her mother was dressed as her former self, wearing a shabby checked suit that she must have pilfered from the clothing detail. A fabric flower was pinned to the lapel. It might have looked gay ten years ago, but it was crumpled and faded with time. Kitty was overwhelmed with sadness at the sight of her.

Since the day of Hanuš's sudden departure, Kitty had walked on eggshells around her mother. Bettina was equal parts angry and fearful; angry that the privilege she held as a prominent had been cast aside, worth nothing in a moment of such great consequence, and fearful of the outcome of that betrayal. Bettina did her best to avoid the camp gossip but what bits of information filtered back to her about the fate of those sent to the "East" made her fear the worst for her son.

Kitty had never seen her mother in such a state. She stopped a block from the Kommandant's office and tried to smooth her mother's hair and clothing, tucking a wisp of parched blonde hair behind her ear and pinching her cheeks. Bettina stared off into the distance, her mind somewhere else entirely.

Kitty's thoughts turned to her father. I hope they don't see his weakness, Kitty worried. Whatever transpired, they must comport themselves in a manner that left the camp's top commander with the impression that they were useful and healthy. It could mean life or death.

Karel was waiting outside of his barracks and Kitty breathed in sharply when she saw her father. He was grey. Ashen. The pity she had come to reserve for him was replaced by a wave of love, the love she had felt for him as a little girl. It welled up inside her as she slipped her arm into his. She patted his arm lovingly. His reply came in the form of a weak smile.

Her parents had perfected a dance around the disappearance of their son. They both knew the steps and they were simple to execute. No one was to mention him; the pain it churned up was just too great. If her father said her brother's name, the dance would be over. It would be like scratching the needle across the record they were dancing to, grinding the illusion of Hanuš's safe return to a halt.

With some difficulty, they crossed the camp, arriving in front of SS-Sturmbannführer Rahm's office. Kitty had heard other prisoners speak about Karl Rahm since his arrival in February, about his working-class upbringing and his disdain for the intelligentsia and privileged classes. Good thing he did not see us at our best when we first arrived, thought Kitty.

They entered the office, and Kitty immediately felt how their worn clothes stood in sharp contrast to the officers in their clean, starched uniforms and shiny boots. We are powerless, thought Kitty, as they waited in the anteroom, one door between them and a man who held their fate in his hands. They waited as if invisible, with no acknowledgment on the part of the guards, who crisscrossed the room with a purpose unknown to the prisoners.

Kitty felt awkward and angry. She looked down at the floor. The wood was pale and golden; it shone in the light that came in through one of the room's windows. In an instant Kitty was transported back to the house in Teplice. She had rarely paid attention to such things, but in this most unusual of places she remembered the burnished floors in her old home, how she had loved skipping from one room to another in the flat, the click of her shoes on the shiny hardwood. She remembered laughing back then, always laughing.

Kitty snapped out of her reverie when one of the young officers shouted their names. "Löwi!" In an instant, they were ushered into the office and made to stand before the Kommandant's desk. Kitty took the measure of the room. This is not meant to be a conversation, Kitty thought, her understanding of what was about to transpire becoming clearer with each moment that passed.

This is an interrogation. Its purpose, however, eluded her. She looked at the man responsible for the deportations, the rations, the lack of sanitary conditions, the single individual who held power over tens of thousands of Jews. He was not a tall man. His face was long, and he had a dark, neatly trimmed mustache and a receding hairline. But it was his uniform that held Kitty transfixed. The sharp, pointed collar was decorated on one side with the lightning bolt insignia of the SS. The four silver pips on the other side defined his rank as assault unit leader. It struck her at that moment how fitting the symbol of the lightning bolt was – like the strongest electrical force in nature, they left destruction in their wake.

Kitty flashbacked to the night her family was captured and interrogated, and out of habit, she plumbed the space where her tooth should have been with her tongue. She felt her body tremble at the memory of the blow that had knocked it out. The man who dealt that blow had been wearing a uniform much like the man she now stood before. Even if not of equal rank, the two men were clearly equal in their ability to inflict cruelty.

Kitty had learned much during the past year in the camp. She understood there was great risk in speaking and acting out, risk much greater than a silly tooth. Kitty's eyes wandered to a large map on the wall behind the Kommandant's desk. It looked nothing like what she had learned in school. In this version, it looked like Germany was swallowing Czechoslovakia whole. She felt dizzy.

After what seemed like an eternity, the Kommandant lifted his head, stared at them, motionless, and spoke. "Tell me, why are there only three of you when this letter from the Swiss Consulate says there should be four?" He spoke in German with tempered disdain. He understood that Bettina was protected due to her American citizenship, but she was still Czech, and a Jew.

Kitty's body tensed when she heard her mother's uneasy reply. "My son was sent away."

"And why was that?" The Kommandant sounded bored with the conversation already. Kitty had promised her mother she would not speak unless spoken to. Angry questions swirled around in her brain. You are a Nazi! Kitty wanted to scream. You oversee this camp! Do you not know everything?

"His transport number was very high, and it was changed at the last minute to very low." Bettina looked anywhere and everywhere, her eyes flitting to the corners of the ceiling, to the Kommandant's desk, to Kitty and Karel's faces, her hand absently tugging at the wilted flower on her lapel. Kitty worried that the Kommandant would find Bettina's behavior disrespectful.

"Hmmph," he replied, shuffling the papers in front of him. He looked down at one paper and scanned it closely, adjusting himself in his hard wooden chair. Then, his mood changed, and he looked up at Bettina, seeming to notice her for the first time. What was that look? Kitty had an awful feeling in the pit of her stomach. Was it...pity?

"I... am an American citizen," she heard her mother say haltingly. "Please tell me what happened to my son."

Kommandant Rahm took a red pencil and without any hesitation scribbled the letters "RU" on the paper in front of him. Kitty did not know what "RU" meant, but her concerns turned toward her father. This was the longest her father had stood in months, and she could see his legs beginning to buckle.

"Very well, then. You may return to your barrack." The interview was over. They were dismissed.

With Kitty on one side and Bettina on the other, the two women supported her father, each taking a forearm and moving as quickly as possible under the circumstances. Bettina let go of her husband the minute they were outside the building, and stumbled to the side, leaving

Kitty to support her father's full weight. She walked jerkily, covering her face with her hands, her shoulders heaving. Kitty could hear her mother sucking in large gulps of air. She had never seen her mother cry. Bettina staggered ahead, bereft of reason.

Kitty reflected on her mother's favoritism of Hanuš, and she understood, for the first time, how her perception gave her strength. She had filled the void created by the absence of her mother with Oila and her father, and both had been a source of joy and knowledge for her. As Kitty and Hanuš grew older and more independent, they no longer sought approval from their parents, but from their friends at school, their teachers and their cousins, Otto, and Frantisek. Their childhood squabbling and rivalry faded when they learned to see each other as individuals.

One of Kitty's fondest memories with Hanuš was of the early days of the German occupation. The two had eaten glorious lunches and watched movies all day in the darkness of the Dobřichovice theatre. The natural order was unraveling around them, but they had found pockets of joy in a world with no parental supervision, watching Charlie Chan solve crimes and Tom Mix ride off into the sunset.

Hanuš was one of the brightest people I have ever known, Kitty thought. She wished she could have seen what great things he might have done with his life. Kitty thought back to the bicycle incident. Rather than have his favorite bicycle end up in the hands of the Germans, Hanuš had given it to a friend. Had Hanuš retained that rebellious spirit of his youth in the last days of his life? I hope so, thought Kitty, tears welling up in her eyes.

Bettina shuffled on ahead of Kitty and her father, like a ship at sea, adrift. She clutched the fabric flower, tore it from her jacket and tossed it on the ground.

Kitty grasped the gravity of the red letters, 'RU', which the Kommandant had hastily scribbled across Hanuš's papers. That night Vlada reluctantly informed her of their true meaning. 'RU', or *Rückkehr unerwünscht* was German for 'return undesirable.' It was an informal death sentence by the Gestapo, Hanuš's fate sealed from the moment he stepped aboard the train. Hanuš was never meant to return.

The following morning Karel received a notice that Kitty had been pardoned, the severe reprimand was declared null and void.

Chapter Fifteen

Vlada 10/01/1944
Terezin, Protectorate of Bohemia
and Moravia and Auschwitz-Birkenau
Concentration Camp, Poland

A strong wind blew through the ghetto in late autumn, carrying with it a rumor of a rebellion brewing in the camp's underground movement. News had filtered into the camp that the Nazis were in a weakened state from heavy losses due to the liberation of Rome and Paris, and from successful offenses mounted by the Russians. Each loss was like a blow to the Führer himself, which had coinciding effects; if he felt pain, then someone else must suffer.

Hermina returned to the Hanover Barrack one evening, sat down on a bench and began to cry quietly. Karel sat down beside her, and she slumped into his arms. Vlada stood by, helpless, as his father whispered gently in Hermina's ear.

"What is it, Hermina? What has happened?" Karel held her hands in his, his voice calm and steady.

"My brother," she said, barely above a whisper. "Who will take care of Marta and Jan?" Hermina looked imploringly into her husband's eyes, her shoulders sagging. Karel understood, and he turned away from his wife, the guilt-ridden look he gave Vlada betraying some prior knowledge of the distressing event.

Hermina slowly relayed what she had discovered on her recent visit with her sister-in-law and her two-year-old nephew. Hermina's brother, Karel, and the majority of the camp's doctors, were being forcibly transported to the "East" in a matter of days, leaving Marta and young Jan behind. She trembled as she told the story, pulling her tattered shawl tightly around her shoulders.

Vlada had heard the rumors. The Nazis were losing their iron grip on the war and their paranoia of an insurrection had magnified. The SS were panicking and the blows were going to fall hard on the inhabitants of Terezin.

Karel poured Hermina a cup of water from a pot simmering on a hot plate. He handed her the chipped porcelain cup, and she cradled it in her hands, letting it warm her. He did not seem shocked by the news; on the contrary, he tried to make it seem like a normal turn of events.

"I had heard from the camp elders that doctors were needed to accompany outgoing transports in case anyone fell ill." His father's tone was unconvincing, his voice trailing off, and Hermina did not take notice. Vlada watched his mother sip from the cup, her gaze absent, her mind working out how she would take care of Marta and Jan with her brother gone.

In the morning, Karel found Vlada at the *bauhof* organizing his tools before work. He took Vlada by the arm and led him outside the locksmith shop, looking furtively around the courtyard. He reached into the pocket of his jacket and pulled out two transport requests, both for the same departure date as Hermina's brother.

Vlada took the slip with his name on it from his father, barely concealing his shock. It contained instructions to report to the back door of the Hanover Barrack with his luggage at the appropriate date and time. Vlada was so angry he wanted to rip the slip into a thousand pieces.

"Vlada, don't worry. I will do my best to make sure we are not on that train," his father said. He put his hand on Vlada's arm to reassure him. Vlada gently pulled away, regarding his father.

"How will you do that, Tati?" Vlada's thoughts turned immediately to Kitty. He did not wait for a reply. "I have to go." He left his father standing alone in the courtyard of the *bauhof*, his own deportation slip in his hand.

The ghetto population was reeling at the prospect of the upcoming deportations. Vlada could see the tension in the faces of the people he passed on the street that evening, many rushing to say their last goodbyes to those unfortunate enough to have received a slip. Kitty was waiting for Vlada at their appointed spot, and she ran to him, throwing her arms around her neck. "They can't do this," she sobbed into his jacket, staining it with tears. "You can't leave!" Vlada led her to their favorite bench at the Stadt Park and held her, stroking her hair and whispering in her ear.

When she had calmed, Kitty relayed gossip she had overheard in the central laundry. "I heard that the camp leadership are the ones that used to make the lists for deportation." Kitty scowled, wondering who had been responsible for putting Hanuš's name on a list. "Now the SS have taken control of the deportation lists."

Vlada had heard a similar story. Now it made sense why the whole of the camp administration was on the first transport as well. The SS was doing some serious housecleaning, eliminating those who used to do their dirty work and anyone else who might possibly organize a resistance. Vlada remembered how in his younger days he had been in awe of the Nazis' strategic prowess. He no longer felt that way, he saw clearly now how their every move was rooted in evil.

Vlada recounted to Kitty his father's unusual reaction to their slips. "Vlada, your father works in the Magdeburg Barrack," Kitty said, matter-of-factly. "The entire Jewish administration of the camp is on that transport." The implications of Kitty's statement were not lost on Vlada. He had often wondered what role his father played in the administration. Had he chosen names for transport? Had he kept their names off all this time due to his position? Did he still have any influence? Having his suspicions confirmed did not give him comfort. It was rather the opposite.

The moon was almost full, hanging low and red in the sky over the camp, and the night sky was vast and full of silvery stars. Kitty clung to Vlada, gazing up. "Where shall we meet when the war is over, Vlada?"

Vlada responded by kissing her on the forehead and wiping a tear from the corner of her eye.

"In Prague, of course," Vlada spoke with certainty. "Find my Aunt Berta."

The night before, the lovers had vowed to reunite on the other side of the war. Now they stood, wrapped in each other's arms, along with hundreds of other passengers waiting next to the train that would take the camp's husbands, brothers, and sons to the "East." Vlada released Kitty with one final peck on the forehead. Kitty did not cry; she was all out of tears. She had made a pact with herself that the last thing he would see was her smile.

Hermina clung to her son, and when Karel pulled her away from him, she seemed small, vulnerable. A Czech guard spoke roughly to Hermina and Kitty, forcing them to move away as Karel and Vlada picked up their small leather bags and took their place in line under the cloudless September sky.

Suddenly, another Czech gendarme approached Karel and Vlada, motioning to them and pulling them out of the queue. A conversation ensued, and they held out their deportation slips for inspection. The guard motioned, and they began to follow him back in the direction of the holding building. Vlada glanced over his shoulder and waved to Kitty. The women watched in disbelief as Vlada and Karel were led away from the outbound train.

Marta began to wail, waving frantically to her husband who still stood in the queue that inched toward the open train cars. Jan began to bawl in response to his mother's upset, tears streaming down his cheeks. Hermina took the child from Marta, bouncing him up and down on her hip. The train whistle released its plaintive cry and pulled away from the camp, without Vlada and Karel on board.

There was a lightness in his step as Vlada followed along behind the gendarme. Was it possible that his father had been right? Would they be released back into the camp population? He had never been so happy to be within the walls at Terezin. Vlada and Karel were taken back to the collection point where they sat down on the floor, bags by their sides, and waited, along with fifty or so other men, all night and into the next day without any further explanation.

In the morning they woke to the sound of the train whistle signaling the departure of another full transport. A restless day ensued and there was much speculation among the remaining men. Why had they been pulled from the transport? Were they to be the next camp administration? Karel paced decisively, as if the strength of his footfalls somehow dictated their destiny. Vlada kept to himself, not trusting the vagaries being bandied about. He was raised by a man of science. He would wait for proof.

On the third day, all was quiet. It was Vlada's turn to pace. He recalled the limbo of awaiting deportation to Terezin. It had not turned out exactly how he had hoped but he had met Kitty. He wavered between optimism and fear, wishing he could see Kitty one last time. Karel kept to himself; he was stoic, his face set in a grim line. Vlada did not question him, lest it break the spell of his father's prediction.

On the morning of the fourth day, a gendarme entered the building and approached them, his face drawn and guilt-ridden. "It's time," the man said. Karel told the man there must be some mistake, and Vlada had to look away. The sky was dark and pitiless as they followed the guard out of the holding building, a steely rain greeting them. The guard put his hand up and stopped them, waving to someone in the train yard. Hermina and Kitty appeared. Vlada laughed at his good fortune; he had gotten at least one of his wishes.

He held Kitty for as long as possible, the familiar feel of her back causing the corners of his mouth to relax into a contented grin. He reluctantly let her go and Hermina and her son shared a look, their eyes locking, his mother's love and unselfish manner throughout every moment of his young life encompassed in that brief glance. Karel briefly took his wife's hand in his, and then let go. Then the two men were moving forward, Vlada and Karel, toward the "East," and the unknown.

Vlada and Karel sat pressed together in the passenger train car as a crush of prisoners poured in, pushing and jostling each other to find seats. Two women held hands, one pulling the other forward through the crowded aisle. One of the women stopped, looking overly disheveled for the start of the journey, and stared at Karel. Her whole body began to tremble as she reached in front of Vlada, and began clawing at him, scratching at the lapels of his jacket with her hands.

"Where did they take my husband? Where are we going? I know that you know! Tell me! Tell me!" Her eyes darted back and forth, looking at Karel and then at Vlada, pleading for an answer. Vlada pressed himself to the back of his seat hoping to avoid contact with the woman. Prisoners were piling up behind the woman in the aisle, and an SS officer got on the car and shouted into the crowd.

"Keep moving! Now! Move! Raus!" He pushed his way to where the woman was standing and shoved her forward, forcing her to release her grip on Karel's jacket. The woman's friend put her arm around her, gently guiding her forward.

"Where is Paul? Where is he?" The woman continued, shouting the question over her shoulder, her voice fading as she and her companion crossed haltingly into another train car.

Vlada looked at his father, who was smoothing his jacket. "What was that about? Why did she think you would know where her husband was, Tati?"

"I don't know, Vlada. Maybe her husband was on the first transport, the one we were removed from." Karel did not elaborate further. He looked away, his body visibly stiffening, signaling an end to the conversation. Vlada turned the interaction over in his mind, and discovered he had more questions than answers.

The train lurched forward. People standing in the aisles grasped at nearby seats to steady themselves. As the train began to pick up speed, leaving Terezin behind in the distance, the car was filled with the soulful sounds of women wailing and men praying.

Karel looked out the window, the sky a dark shell, the wind driving the rain in thick rivulets across the window. Anguished cries rose, and Vlada could hear weeping. The laments of the women on the train pained Vlada, prompting thoughts of his mother. He looked out the window, but there was nothing to see except endless flat, grey terrain, strewn with the occasional piece of deserted agriculture machinery, rusted from lack of use. The train chugged rhythmically forward and within an hour many of the prisoners had quieted.

Karel looked at his son intently. "I never told you about my time in the Czech Legion, did I, Vlada?" Karel sat up straight in his seat, a wistful smile crossing his face.

Really, Tati? thought Vlada. They were prisoners of the Nazis on a train during wartime, not on a pleasure trip. Vlada looked at his father, the lines in his face and around his eyes had deepened, making him look perpetually sad. Vlada's anger faded. He had always wanted to hear his father's war stories, the accounts behind the medals. Perhaps a story might help him take his mind off Kitty. He pictured her clearly, her dark hair, the sweetness of her lips, the feeling of her small hand in his.

A hush had fallen over the train car as the skies darkened to black, and some of the prisoners dozed off even though it was barely mid-afternoon.

"Tell me, Tati," Vlada said. "Please tell me everything."

Karel looked out the window and began to talk. "I was in my third year of studies at the university in Prague. I loved my life as a student." Karel smiled. "Then I was drafted into the Austro-Hungarian army. They gave me the rank of *Fahnrich* and sent me to the Eastern Front. I had no idea what I was doing, Vlada." Karel laughed softly, shaking his head. "And that, Vlada, was the end of my education."

Vlada's studies had been halted by war as well. Instead of becoming an officer, I became a prisoner, thought Vlada.

"They gave me a subordinate; can you believe it? A rank-and-file soldier who shined my boots and kept my uniform ironed. It was awkward to say the least," Karel paused, reflecting on his younger self. Vlada thought back to the flat in Pardubice, his father was never comfortable giving orders to the maids.

"And there was such hypocrisy. For years the emperor ignored the pleas of the Czech people and now he was demanding that we fight for him. And against our Slavic brethren, no less." Karel spoke with the passion he had as a young man. "We would sooner defect if it meant taking up arms against the Russians. But desertion was not an option."

"You mean you actually considered it, Tati?" Vlada leaned in closer, listening intently, enthralled by the tale his father had begun to weave.

"The penalty for desertion was death, Vlada. You never knew your grandmother, my mother, but she could not have borne that. But we could surrender, so a group of us made our way to the front and did just that. That is how I became a Russian prisoner of war."

Vlada pictured his father, crossing enemy lines and voluntarily laying down his arms to the Russians. The story was like the stuff of Vlada's favorite epic books. It was impressive. He remembered a photo he had seen of his father at the POW camp, a roughhewn cabin in the background. And no matter how rustic the conditions, Karel was the picture of sartorial splendor, cigarette in hand. What a life he led in those early years, thought Vlada.

"Now, we wanted to fight alongside the Russians against the Central Powers, but it was not that simple, so we lived in limbo for months in that dreary POW camp." Vlada listened thoughtfully, his eyes narrowing, as he began to make connections between his father's story and his own life. I know a little about being in limbo, thought Vlada. He had felt that way since the occupation over four years ago.

"Finally, we were organized into special units as an independent Czech army, the Czech Legion. We vowed to fight side by side with the Russians. And we won a decisive battle," his father said proudly, "but then the political landscape of Russia was turned on its head."

"The Bolsheviks, Tati?" It was growing dark inside the train car, and it added to the suspense of his father's tale.

"Millions of Russian soldiers lay dead on the battlefields, there were massive food shortages, and the Tsar abdicated the throne. The Bolsheviks stepped in amidst the madness and declared an end to Russian involvement in the war. We found ourselves in Russia in the middle of a civil war."

Prisoners in seats nearby had begun listening intently to Karel's story. Vlada's eyes shone with pride. The train began to slow as it approached a station, and then picked up speed again.

Karel seemed momentarily distracted. Vlada searched his father's face, but Karel was lost in the past. "Go on, Tati," Vlada encouraged him.

"The Bolsheviks were not pleased to have the Czech Legion in their midst. At first, they promised us safe passage to the sea...." Karel's voice turned bitter. "We had a heedless altercation with some Austrian POWs, but then the Bolsheviks imprisoned some of my compatriots and demanded we lay down our arms. We refused. We commandeered an armored train, the "Orlik", or Little Eagle. It was wrapped in steel with machine guns and cannons and we began traveling East on the Trans-Siberian railway. That train became our home away from home."

The clicking of the train along the tracks provided the perfect backdrop for Karel's story. Vlada pictured the Czech fighters, in fur hats and coats, traveling on the speeding train across war-torn Russia. His thoughts traveled back to the factory yard and the childhood games he had played with Lada on the train car – make-believe scenarios where they were brave Legionnaires aboard one of the legendary armored trains, clacking across the frozen tundra.

"It was a most interesting group on that train, Vlada; there were writers, laborers, tailors, doctors, artisans, and academics."

"Sounds a lot like Terezin, Tati." His father nodded at the comparison.

"Yes, only we had power, Vlada." Karel raised his hand in a clenched fist, his voice was strong, and filled with pride. "We fought and won battle after battle at each station. We repaired blown up train tracks and bridges and we kept inching forward, east to Vladivostok. News of our plight and our victories were broadcast as far as America. It felt like the whole world was watching us." He paused for a moment, his face lighting up joyfully. "Vlada, I was thousands of miles from home in a tattered uniform with barely enough food to survive, protecting a railway from the enemy. Then the news reached us: Masaryk had declared Czech independence on October 28, 1918." Masaryk, the founder of Czechoslovakia, was his father's hero. "We made it past the Urals, and Lake Baikal, and arrived at the sea. We expected a hero's welcome but there was no one waiting there to take us to freedom."

Vlada felt a chill and the hair on the back of his neck stood up, imagining his father and his brave compatriots experiencing such great dishonor. Night had fallen and they had been traveling for hours. People had begun sobbing and moaning again, crying out at odd intervals. Vlada could not see the features of his father's face in the dark train car, but they sat, shoulder to shoulder, and Vlada felt a closeness to his father, as men, that he had never felt before. Why had it taken this set of circumstances to feel and share this moment with him? Vlada wondered.

The sounds of grief and illness ebbed and flowed in the background, voices in pain and emotional distress rising and falling rhythmically, in grating contrast to his father's journey of strength and honor. "What happened next, Tati?" Vlada knew there was more to the story, and he needed a distraction from the suffering around them on the train.

"The Supreme Allied Command decided they had a use for us: keep the railway out of the hands of the Bolsheviks. We were stuck on that

God-forsaken track for another year. Rations and morale were low, and we felt we had done enough; we made our own deal with the Russians for a safe exit. Only half of us made it home. I had been gone for over two years."

Karel had talked through the night and into the gray early hours of the next morning. The sound of his father's voice and the rhythmic chugging of the train won out over the cries and lamentations of the other passengers and lulled Vlada to sleep. He drifted off just as his father's story came to its triumphant conclusion. "I still remember it, Vlada, as if it was yesterday: walking through the Powder Gate in Prague with my compatriots, to a hero's welcome in free, independent Czechoslovakia." Karel's voice was strong, jubilant, almost. It was the homecoming the weary and honorable survivors of the Czech Legion deserved.

When Vlada woke again it was late afternoon and dark once more. They had been traveling for thirty hours. Vlada's dreams and his father's story had blurred together in his consciousness as he struggled to awaken fully. Karel slept, his head pressed against the window of the train, and Vlada regarded his father with pride. He had missed his father's lecture at Terezin about his time in the Czech Legion because he had been too busy with Kitty. His heart felt full having finally heard his father's tale, his role in the fight for Czech independence. His father was a hero.

The prisoners in the train car began to stir, an anxious energy enveloping the group. Vlada peered outside where he could see blinding spotlights shining up ahead piercing the black night, illuminating a large watchtower with a gate below through which the train was about to pass.

The train whistle made a shrill cry and began to slow down. Vlada imagined the gate they were approaching was a gaping maw, with two windows for eyes below the watchtower. In an instant, the gate swallowed the train and spit it back out the other side.

The monotonous sound of coughs, moans, and whispers came to an abrupt halt, replaced by silence as if the hundreds of prisoners had collectively sucked in all the air on the train. They held their breath as the train came to a full stop. A shiver went through Vlada at the sound of scraping metal on metal as the door of the train car was opened. Karel looked at his son one last time. Their eyes met and his father nodded. "Vlada," his father's voice was hoarse; he had talked for hours without a single drop of water.

"*Raus, raus.* Out, out! Get out immediately! Leave any belongings on the train!" SS guards shouted orders as the prisoners descended the ramp outside the train, their voices barely audible over the vicious dogs that barked and lunged, leashes taut, teeth bared, at the prisoners. The guards landed blows wherever they could on the heads and backs of those disembarking the train, and Vlada took it as his cue to hunch his back and keep his head down. The spotlights gave the illusion of daylight and Vlada had to shield his eyes with his hand to help them adjust from the gloom of the train. He dropped the small bag he had brought with him on the ground. Under the circumstances, it already felt gratuitous.

The prisoners formed a ragged line, and Vlada fell into place behind Karel. The shouting continued, harsh and ear-piercing, an assault on the senses after the quiet, soulful ululations of the train ride. Terezin was a spa compared to this place, thought Vlada. He thought of Kitty and Hermina, taking a brief, fleeting comfort that they did not know the truth about this destination.

Vlada looked at his father's back, a wave of tenderness washing over him as he examined his father's bald pate, his bare neck, his shoulders sloping down on either side. Vlada noticed for the first time that the jacket he wore no longer fit him properly; it hung loosely on his thin frame. His pants were loose, too, the fabric ballooning out from his legs, and his shoes were scuffed beyond repair.

Vlada watched as Karel waited his turn in a line that slowly made its way toward two SS officers seated at a table. An old man in front of Karel stood before the men at the table, and then slowly shuffled to the left. It was Karel's turn to step forward. Vlada willed his father to pull up his shoulders and stride confidently toward the table. The man asking the questions flicked a small whip in his gloved hand to the left and Karel walked in that direction, the same direction the old man before him had gone.

Vlada walked forward and stood in front of the man, the man's eyes narrowing slightly. For a moment, their eyes met, and everything stopped: the dogs, the shouting. The man seated next to him addressed him. "Dr. Mengele?"

Mengele cleared his throat. He flicked the switch in his hand to the right, dismissing Vlada. Not a word had passed between them. Vlada walked toward a small group on the right and waited. The noise level was deafening.

Hours passed. The strange sorting process, once complete, left around three hundred prisoners in Vlada's group out of the 1,500 prisoners that had departed a day earlier from Terezin. An SS guard directed them to a sidewalk, his baton raining a beating down on anyone who held their head up as they passed by him. Vlada did not dare betray his shock, but his eyes darted in every direction as he attempted to make sense of the strange hell they had descended into.

Out of the corner of his eye, Vlada saw a group of women in grey striped dresses, their heads close-cropped, on the other side of a high barbed wire fence. Some of them started running parallel to the new prisoners, their arms stretched out in front of them. "Give us bread! Bread!"

Shots rang out overhead and Vlada cowered, flinching. He looked up in the direction of the sound and saw a guard firing a gun from the nearest wooden watchtower. One of the women running toward the fence came to an abrupt halt, her head whipping back. She fell backward into what looked to be a tide of thick mud. The others turned to run back the way they had come, but it was too late. Vlada heard another series of shots, and a second woman fell in the mud. A third shot missed its intended target.

The last woman from the group ran and screamed, trying to zigzag to evade the next bullet. Then she stopped. She turned and stood still, looking up at the soldier in the tower. There was a pause. Vlada did not move, and in that moment time froze. The guard shot five more times. Vlada watched as the woman's left shoulder whipsawed from the force of the first bullet. The gunman's methodical cruelty filled Vlada with horror; his body trembled, and he had to command his legs to move him forward.

I am in hell, thought Vlada.

The kapos who walked alongside the prisoners repeated their orders.

"You must turn everything in now."

"You must turn in any jewelry or other belongings, or you will be beaten."

Vlada flinched. He had only one thing of value left, a watch that he had bartered his locksmith services for back in Terezin.

He did not have to think about it. I will not give them the watch, thought Vlada. If I do, I will have nothing left to bargain with. Vlada stepped and knelt, pretending to tie his shoe. The ground was muddy and soft, and he made a hole in the mud, pushing the watch down until the mud made a sucking sound and the watch was completely submerged. He looked at the number of the nearby barrack, planning to recover the watch later.

He stood up just as a kapo landed a blow on his shoulders. "Get up! Move!" Vlada stood up, the pain from the blow radiating through his upper back. He did as he was told, falling in line with the rest of the prisoners and following the kapos into the cold, dark bowels of the barrack. There were no beds, only a damp concrete floor. The kapos glared at the new arrivals, hands gripping their clubs, daring any of the new prisoners to make a comment about the accommodations.

Vlada slumped down against a wall onto the floor, dazed, fearful and exhausted. He had to see his father in the morning; this was going to be hard on him.

Vlada struggled to keep his eyelids open, searching for a familiar face from the camp in the dim light of the room, but he finally succumbed to an all-encompassing torpor.

"What has this inhumanity to do with war?" was Vlada's last thought before falling asleep.

CHAPTER SIXTEEN

KITTY, OCTOBER 1944
TEREZIN, PROTECTORATE OF
BOHEMIA AND MORAVIA

How do you kill all hope? Ask the Nazis, thought Kitty. They had perfected it.

When Karel and Vlada were spared from the first transport, Kitty felt a wave of relief wash over her. She knew deep down that that moment, chaotic and rushed, was not meant to be their final goodbye. She had been slightly jealous, having to share Vlada with his mother when she had envisioned a more romantic, more intimate farewell. Kitty felt a pang of guilt afterward. She understood the mother-son connection better than most, she had seen how Bettina had been robbed of a similar circumstance with Hanuš. The realization of that missed opportunity haunted her.

Rising early every morning, Kitty walked to the train platform, buttoning her favorite blue sweater to chase away the autumn chill. When the platform was in sight, Kitty hid at the edge of a barrack and waited. She was not sure what she expected to see: Vlada being released back into the camp population, running to her, and sweeping her up in his arms? Vlada and his father being forced aboard another train?

Kitty did not pray, but if she did, she would certainly have prayed for the former.

Hermina had the same idea as Kitty. Each morning she lingered on the outskirts of the loading area, too, hoping for a glimpse of Karel and Vlada, or a clue as to their condition. Some mornings she was joined by her sister-in-law, the one named Marta, and Marta's son, Jan. Kitty had mistaken Marta for Hermina's younger sister; the two women looked so much alike. Dark eyes, dark hair – drawn up in a bun – and both similarly attired in simple cotton dresses. Kitty and Hermina did not approach one another, or speak. But Hermina nodded to Kitty, a tiny acknowledgment that made her feel very grown up.

Three days passed in a similar fashion. On the third morning, Kitty detected activity among the Czech guards, the warning signs that they were preparing to load another transport with prisoners: the train whistle blew a few short blasts, and all the doors to the third-class train cars opened, gaping maws waiting to lock up and swallow another meal of innocent victims.

A queue of men and women began to shuffle out of the holding building and cross the yard in the direction of the train. Kitty struggled to find Vlada in the crowd; she thought her heart might explode when she recognized him. He walked slowly, searching the surrounding yard for Kitty. When their eyes met across the dirt yard, Kitty raised her hand to wave to him. A sympathetic Czech gendarme noticed the interaction and motioned to both Hermina and Kitty to come quickly.

Vlada and Karel stepped aside as the other prisoners continued to trudge past them toward the open train cars. Kitty could not believe their good fortune. They were being allowed, through this stranger's generosity, the simple gift of saying a proper goodbye.

Kitty ran to Vlada, and he swept her up in his arms, just as she had envisioned. Kitty breathed in his scent, hoping to preserve it for the days and weeks ahead. In the nights leading up to their deportation, Vlada and Kitty had spoken all the words they needed to say. There were no promises left to utter, just the feeling of Vlada's warm body against hers.

Vlada gave Kitty one last tight squeeze. He whispered in her ear, his warm breath intoxicating to Kitty. "Prague, Kitty. My Aunt Berta's apartment. Don't be late." He released her, the rough stubble of his beard scratching her cheek as they separated. Kitty felt like she was losing a limb; their fingers brushed against each other's and then they were separated.

Karel took his wife's hand and lifted it to his lips and Kitty stood by her hand on her heart, as Vlada and his mother locked eyes, Hermina hugging her son to her with a gentleness Kitty had never seen before. The gesture filled Kitty with sense of grace and understanding for the love shared by a mother and her son.

And then it was over. Vlada and Karel picked up their small bags from the ground and joined the queue. The train was surrounded by German police, and Kitty recognized a man from Teplice, the father of a girl she knew from school. The man stood at the door to the train car, pushing people up and into the train. Kitty was ashamed of the man and wanted to shout at him, imploring him to remember these people were his friends and neighbors. He won't recognize me, Kitty thought. I am a woman now. The last time he saw me I was a girl.

The moment Kitty and Vlada shared had filled her with optimism; the feeling of his strong body against hers and the words he left her with kept her tears at bay for the moment. Kitty stood, resolute, as a light rain began to fall.

The parting had not had the same effect on Hermina. She walked toward Marta, her body wavering, her legs buckling under the weight of her emotions, utterly impotent as her son and husband disappeared aboard the transport. Marta walked toward Hermina but before she could catch her, she crumpled to the ground like a broken doll. Marta reached under Hermina's arms, lifting her up from where she knelt in the dirt, her head hung low on her chest. She supported her, took her arm gently, and walked with her away from the trains.

Soon after, the train blew its final whistle of departure and rolled away. The skies opened, and rain began to fall heavily, the heavens releasing a deluge on the dusty ground of Terezin.

The three transports were just the beginning of a methodical purging of the camp by the German SS. Morale reached an all-time low as families were torn apart, and women, children, the sick, and the elderly were loaded onto an endless string of trains leaving the camp for the "East." The Germans were emptying the camp and the remaining prisoners were hopeless to predict how or when the purging would continue.

Soon after Vlada's departure, Kitty went to check on Hermina. She walked to her barrack and entered the dimly lit building. A woman was sorting large piles of clothing on a few of the lower bunks. The clothing belonged to those who had been recently deported. The woman was wiry and pale.

"You want anything?" She held up a dress that looked like it was Kitty's size. "Take it. No charge."

Kitty shook her head. "I'm looking for Hermina Munk. Do you know her?"

"Oh, yes. So sad," the woman turned away from Kitty. "Yesterday's transport. With that other woman and the little boy."

It was Kitty's turn to crumble; she felt like she had been punched in the stomach. She steadied herself, holding onto the wooden beam of the bunk as she pictured Hermina boarding a train with Marta and Jan.

Bunks had emptied around Kitty and Bettina daily, and yet Kitty had held out hope that the Nazis would tire of the deportations and cease the cruelty. Kitty thought she might go mad each time a deportation slip appeared on the bunk of someone she knew. Its discovery was invariably followed by cries of anguish at being torn away from family and friends and a desperate, growing fear of what really awaited them in the "East." The train whistle blew every few days, its appetite for the camp's prisoners insatiable.

Why had she not seen this coming? she wondered. Hermina loved Karel and Vlada so much, thought Kitty. Maybe she was glad to go, hoping for a happy family reunion on the other end of the line. Kitty could not convince herself there was an upside to the devastating information. Instead, the news caused a crisis of confidence.

Are Bettina, Father and I next? she wondered.

Each day, Kitty concocted a different story about the benefits of Vlada's absence. Kitty would soon be forced to return to the central laundry and within days her hands would be cracked and dry again. Thank goodness he won't be here to see them, Kitty consoled herself. Each story was a lie. If Vlada were here he would kiss her hands, erasing the shame she felt at their rough appearance.

Evenings after supper stretched on forever – without Vlada to laugh and walk with. Kitty began to visit Arna and the little ones nearly every night to fill the hours. Arna was a strong woman, but months in the camp without Uncle Erich, and caring for their two children alone on her meager rations, eroded her will. Kitty remembered how Arna had struggled in the early months after Petr's birth to produce enough milk to keep him alive. When Petr's first birthday arrived in July, it felt like a miracle. He was tiny but strong.

Kitty walked across the camp on the Haupstrasse after another moribund supper with her parents, Bettina had tried to muster sympathy for Kitty's despondency, but her own thoughts always returned to Hanuš. It quickly became evident it was best when no one spoke.

The streets of the camp were the quietest Kitty had ever seen them; The young and able were the ones she and Vlada saw on their walks every evening, and now they were gone. Vlada would have loved these quiet streets, thought Kitty, as she passed the bench on the edge of Stadt Park where they sat so many nights. Two weeks had passed since Vlada had left.

Kitty turned the corner onto Berggasse and braced herself for the two tiny figures barreling toward her. She stood, legs apart, in the cobblestone courtyard as the children raced toward her. She barely felt the impact as Eva and then Petr crashed into her. Eva threw her arms around Kitty's legs and started tugging her. "Kitty! Kitty!" Eva said in the sweetest voice. "What did you bring for us today?"

Eva searched Kitty's pockets, rifling through first one, then the other, for treats and she frowned at Kitty upon finding them both empty. Kitty brought the carrot she had been hiding from behind her back, producing it with a flourish. Eva's eyes grew wide, she smiled up at Kitty, her mouth formed in a tiny "o," as if Kitty were a magician who had just pulled a rabbit out of a hat. Eva took the carrot from Kitty, the greens bouncing as she ran to present it to her mother.

Eva and Petr were copies of each other; they both had thick, dark hair and deep brown eyes surrounded by long eyelashes. They took after their mother.

Kitty tousled Eva's hair and crouched down, hands formed into imaginary claws, and growled like a bear. The children giggled, pretending to be scared, running to their mother for safety and then running right back to Kitty for another round of tickling. Kitty pulled Eva up onto her lap as she joined Arna where she sat, looking tired and drawn.

"Sweet, precious thing," Kitty whispered as she nuzzled the back of the little girl's neck. Eva's brown curls were pasted to the back of her neck, sweaty from the joy of running that even starvation could not curb.

Each week Kitty had reveled in the milestones the babies passed. She was so happy to have been present to see the smile on Eva's face as she took her first, wobbling steps toward her mother, the day Petr held his head up on his own, and the day he crawled toward his sister, Eva clapping all the while and saying his name in her tiny voice.

Kitty looked at the children where they sat on the rough cobblestones, filling a tin cup with stones and pouring them into another container. Gone was the dimpled baby fat Eva had when she arrived at the camp a year ago. Petr, born inside the camp, had not been given that luxury. Kitty's pride in the children's progress was later replaced with concern. She was shocked when she noticed her precious Eva losing weight due to the family's meager rations, her dresses hanging on her thin frame, her bony knees peeking out from underneath them. Petr's head looked large and out of proportion for his body, and he resembled a tiny bobblehead figurine. The scarcities brought on by the war had robbed the innocent babes of normal growth. Born barely a year and a half apart, they were often mistaken for twins.

Kitty walked over to where the children were, picking up the tin cup filled with tiny stones. "May I? she asked Eva. Eva nodded, her eyes lighting up with excitement that Kitty had come to play with them.

Kitty poured the stones out on the ground and spelled out Eva's name with them on the rough surface. She pointed to the letters.

"E. V. A. Eva!" Eva clapped her hands together with excitement, giggling. At that moment, Kitty made a vow to herself to do better. I can't do anything for Vlada now, thought Kitty. But you two are worth any risk.

Kitty and Hanka stabbed at the depleted earth of the *Judengarten* with large garden forks, each forkful getting caught up in a tangle of roots and rocks. There had already been a hard frost and they were days away from putting the acres of spent garden soil to bed for the winter, and time was running out for Kitty to overturn some last bits of sustenance for the children. They worked their way methodically down one row, inspecting each clump of earth for one last unharvested vegetable. A rumor had circulated among the work detail that the current Kommandant liked to watch the activities in the garden from a vantage point in his office, hoping to catch someone in the act of stealing. Kitty felt there were eyes watching her every movement.

Hanka raised her garden fork, shaking off the roots, the dark soil below revealing a couple of small, purple beets. She looked casually around the garden, taking note of the location of the supervisor and the guards, and nodded to Kitty that the coast was clear. They were seasoned pilferers and Kitty's next move was well practiced. She bent down over the soil, her hand reaching for the beets, when a disturbance in the far corner of the garden stopped her hand in midair.

An SS officer from the Small Fortress was in the garden proper, which was enough to send a chill down Kitty's spine. An older man from the work detail cowered on the ground in front of him. The Nazi guard shouted in German, hissing at the man. "Jew Pig!" The guard spat the words out. "What makes you think you can steal from the Führer and get away with it? Hand it over. Now!"

The kneeling man slowly unzipped his jacket, revealing a large, fully formed cauliflower, which he placed on the ground in front of the guard. The man bowed his head and put his hands in the air in a prayerful position, prostrating himself in front of the officer. All work ground to a halt, the workers, including Hanka and Kitty, stopping to gape, watching the scene in both admiration for the man's brave move and disgust at the guard's response.

The supervisor shouted to the garden detail. "Back to work!" Kitty put her head down, and she and Hanka went back to working the soil, Kitty's eyes still focused intently on the beets.

A moment later, they heard a horrible sound; Kitty turned to see the German officer kicking the kneeling man in the stomach. The man doubled over, crying out, earning another kick from the officer. The guard continued in a forceful rage, kicking, and stomping while the old man's guttural cries echoed off the brick walls of the ramparts that surrounded the garden. The officer stopped kicking when the old man fell silent.

Kitty blinked back tears, for the man who had been so mercilessly beaten, and for the children who were starving. Retrieving the beets would have to wait for another day. It would do no one any good if Kitty were caught stealing and received a similar beating, or worse yet, was deported. She resumed piercing the soil with the garden instrument, her body trembling uncontrollably, making a mental note of the row where Hanka had overturned the delinquent beets. She would try again tomorrow.

After the brutal beating in the garden, Kitty grappled with guilt over her failure to secure food for the hungry little ones. Thankfully, that morning the prisoners had received their weekly ration of ten dekagrams of margarine and a spoonful of sugar. Rather than using the sugar to sweeten the camp's "coffee," and the margarine to moisten the bread that was dry as sawdust, Kitty and Hanka mixed the sugar and margarine together and formed it into little balls. It was a special treat, and they pretended it was candy. Kitty mixed the "candy," tucked the balls in a bit of paper and set out for Arna's.

Kitty passed the pear tree at the edge of the park. A month ago, it had been heavily laden with fruit but no one harvested the ripe pears, and many had fallen on the ground where they had rotted in the warm autumn weather. No one in the camp had dared pick the perfect fruit from the tree, nor scoop the rotting fruit from the ground for fear of a week in the Little Fortress or deportation. This is the Nazis' legacy, she thought. That the babies and the elderly of the camp would starve to death while the perfectly edible fruit rotted on the ground.

Eva's eyes grew wide as Kitty revealed the "candy" she had brought. Arna and Kitty shared a wordless look, and Kitty placed three pieces of candy in each of their hands. Arna set the candy on her tongue, her cheeks hollow from malnutrition, letting it melt slowly, savoring it. The children greedily popped their candy in their mouths, grinning and chewing the soft treats.

Kitty sat Eva on her lap, her smocked dress dirty from playing in the street, and began to tell her the story of Snow White. "And the old woman came to the door with a shiny red apple, tempting Snow White to take a bite."

Eva interrupted her. "Kitty?" Eva asked in her sweet, tiny voice. "What is an apple?" A child of the ghetto, Eva had never seen an apple.

Kitty smiled sadly. Eva jumped from her lap and chased after her brother, who toddled gleefully toward his sister in a game for which only they knew the rules. Petr's smile was infectious; he ran squealing back to Kitty and reached his arms up in the air, indicating his desire to be picked up. She obliged. The little boy was light as a feather. He grinned at her, completely unaware that he was starving.

One evening, toward the end of October, Kitty made a deal with one of the Danish girls: her favorite blue sweater in exchange for some powdered milk. The barter successfully concluded, Kitty tucked the glassine package packet containing the powdered milk in the pocket of her dress and walked briskly to the courtyard outside of Arna's barrack, worrying the package with her fingers. She arrived breathless to find the courtyard was empty. Kitty looked around nervously, her chest heaving from the brisk walk.

A woman stepped outside of the barrack, brushing at the stoop with a broom. She saw Kitty and recognized her from her frequent visits. She stopped sweeping. "They left today. All three of them."

Kitty's face fell. She wanted to run after them. She wanted to hold the children again. She wanted another chance. She would do better this time. She would find more food, she promised. No, not them, Kitty cried to herself. Not the little ones.

She reached in her pocket for the packet of powdered milk. Her fingers had worn a hole in the glassine envelope, and a dusty white film covered her fingertips. Kitty's shoulders fell in utter despair and she handed what was left to the woman. "Here," said Kitty, suddenly weary. "Give this to someone who needs it."

Kitty felt like the last actor left on stage after a play, only her fear of abandonment was real. She now stayed in the barrack with her father after supper each evening, reading to him as he lay on his bunk, his breath coming in shallow gasps. He smiled weakly, and Kitty knew he was happy to have her near again. She hated the reason why.

Kitty lay in bed each night before lights-out and thought of Vlada. She had created a ritual to keep the memory of him close. Each night she took out the collection of charms Vlada had commissioned for her. They included her transport number, a small mess tin, a thermos and the one that always made her laugh: a lice comb with small tines. She tried to picture the moment he had given each one to her and played the interaction over in her mind. The last part of the ritual involved replaying their goodbye kiss and her eyes closed in solemn remembrance. Only after that ritual was complete was she ready to drift off to sleep.

With winter approaching, the garden closed and Kitty went to back to work at the central laundry. One day after work she found a transport slip on her bunk; the SS knew where she lived, and the notice said she was to report at four a.m. the day after next for transport to a "labor camp."

Kitty sat on her bunk clasping the slip to her chest. She thought of Hanna Krauskopf, an older girl from the barrack, who had voluntarily boarded an earlier train going to the "East" to join her boyfriend. Kitty turned the idea over in her mind. Would Vlada want me to accept the deportation and follow him? What would her Oila say? Kitty could hear her voice in her head. "Kitty, you can't expect anything to get better if you leave. It can only get worse."

Kitty shrugged, turning her options over in her mind. If she managed somehow to avoid deportation, she would have to work very hard to evade the busybody Czech gendarmes who would love to turn her in to the Gestapo for disobeying the deportation order. I can handle the Czech gendarmes, thought Kitty. She crumpled the slip and hid it in an empty bunk.

When the last transport left the camp on October 28, 1944, Kitty was not on it. She slept in Hanna Krauskopf's bunk from that day forward. Bettina was assigned to a new job as a maid for a prominent man whose family was quite wealthy. Igor had a Swiss bank account, and he regularly signed over to Bettina housekeeping money. Although Bettina's new employer was very generous, Kitty found the arrangement strange.

Kitty missed Arna and the babies. She missed Vlada. She looked at her parents as they ate supper one evening, their bellies filled with extra rations, the bittersweet result of the cruel string of deportations.

A deep gash had rent the camp; the bleeding had stopped but the pain it left behind was deep.

CHAPTER SIXTEEN

VLADA OCTOBER -DECEMBER 1944
AUSCHWITZ-BIRKENAU
CONCENTRATION CAMP, POLAND

The kapos woke the new arrivals for the day ahead by slamming their batons on the ground within inches of the prisoners' feet. Many, including Vlada, had slept sitting up against a wall of the barrack on the cold cement floor. Vlada struggled to regain consciousness. But when his mind began to replay the events of the previous day – the dogs, the women shot in front of his eyes, the queue where he was separated from his father – he longed to withdraw again into sleep. The alternative was a waking nightmare.

His father had been such a comfort, packed as they were on the train among the other prisoners. After hearing his father's story in such vivid detail, Vlada wished he would have told him how proud he was of his time in the Czech Legion. He would tell him first thing when he saw him again.

The kapos barked instructions. "Sit down! You are to write back to Terezin. You are permitted to write twenty to thirty words. You are not to mention Auschwitz. Write to people you know are alive. Don't try anything tricky. Do not try to write in a secret code. You will be found out and punished accordingly."

Vlada quickly stood up and found a seat at one of the rough wooden tables that filled the large room, shocked he had not noticed them the night before. Those who took too long to stand were beaten. Vlada watched as a young man from the same transport stood up, pressed his back against the wall, and did not move. Vlada could not tell if he was doing so in protest, or if he was paralyzed by fear. It made no difference as one of the kapos, a wiry man in oversized clothing, set upon the man with his club and began to beat the young man mercilessly.

The kapos did not make eye contact with the prisoners. No butcher would make eye contact with an animal before the slaughter, thought Vlada. There was no pity here, no empathy. He was sure men were beaten for lesser offenses.

Vlada stared at the postcard in front of him. *Do I write to my mother, or to my girlfriend?* He tried to think but each minute that passed was an assault on his senses. The shouting never ceased, and the din in the barrack threatened his sanity. He tried again to focus. *Kitty is the one most likely to remain in Terezin due to Bettina's prominent status and her age.* He did not want to consider it, but he knew his mother was at risk of deportation. There had been many women on the train to this horrid place with Vlada and his father.

He thought back to the postcard Hanuš had sent his family from this place. Hanuš had been forced to write to his family and tell them he was alive. It was the Nazis way of covering the tracks. It had since been discovered that family in Terezin received postcards from Auschwitz from people who were long dead. Hanuš tried to conceal a message in the words he wrote, about the date when his postcard was truly written, who he was with and what the conditions were but it had been too difficult to decipher. Vlada needed to do better. His life depended on him being strategic.

The kapos were stopping at every table now, and smashing their batons on the table if they did not like the prisoner's progress on their postcard to Terezin. The kapo who had beaten the young man was working his way down the row of tables Vlada was seated in. Vlada began to sweat even though it was the dead of winter. He dipped the pen in the ink and wrote the salutation. His pen hovered above the postcards. Think, Vlada. Think!

A moment later, the cruel kapo began raining blow after blow on the man at the table next to Vlada. The man cried out, stripping his eyeglasses from his face to wipe his eyes. The kapo knocked them out of his hand. The wire rim spectacles fell to the cement floor and the kapo crushed them under his boot.

Vlada froze in his chair. He had to start writing or he too could be beaten. He needed to convey as much information as possible in a few words, but he had attracted the attention of other guards and now they shouted at him.

"Write something! Who do you think you are? Shakespeare? Hurry up!"

Vlada brought the pen to the paper and began to write in German. "Dear Kitty, I arrived in good health to the destination and hope the same about my father. I will work somewhere in my profession. I met your brother Hanuš. Many kisses to my mom. Greetings and kisses, Your Vlada."

As soon as Vlada had finished writing, and the ink was barely dry, the card was ripped away from his hand. Vlada and the others were forced out into the light of day and marched to another nearby barrack. Vlada did his best to take note of his surroundings without attracting attention, surreptitiously scanning the moving crowds.

A kapo stood at the front of a large room, a long row of chairs in front of him. "Take off your clothes!" Two other kapos spread out into the crowd of men, prodding them with the end of their clubs to move faster. The men stood naked, shivering in the cool autumn air, some holding their hands in front of their genitals, others standing with their arms at their sides. "Sit down!" the kapos shouted, forcing the naked prisoners to take part in a hideous version of the childhood game of musical chairs, standing and sitting at the kapos' bidding for the next ritual of induction into the camp.

Vlada sat down in one of the chairs and flinched when he felt the cold razor against the back of his neck. He thought of his father, bald since before Vlada was born. At least this is one indignity you will not need to go through, Tati. Clumps of hair fell on his bare shoulders.

Once or twice the kapo broke the skin of his scalp, but Vlada did not dare wince.

"Stand up." Vlada did as he was told and stood while the barber moved around to the front of him and shaved the hair surrounding his genitals. Vlada stared straight ahead, unable to think of anything to distract himself from the abasement. His shoulders itched from the remnants of hair that clung to the perspiration on his skin, but Vlada did not dare scratch them.

"Move! Move!" The kapos ushered the shorn and naked men into another room, where they were ordered to form a line. Vlada's breath came in shallow gulps. He had no prior experience of wretchedness to compare the events to as he shuffled forward in silence toward the next torment. He saw the men in the front of the line bowing their bleeding, denuded heads. Shivering, Vlada moved closer to the front of the line of naked men. Men were falling out of the queue, vomiting noiselessly, beaten back into line by the kapos.

Vlada came face to face with the source of disgust. A kapo with a large brush in his hand stood behind a tin bucket containing a murky liquid. He dipped the brush in the bucket and shouted, "Head down!" Vlada bowed his head, and the man scraped the rough brush across his wounded scalp. Vlada bit his lip to keep from crying out as the disinfectant permeated his open cuts.

Vlada brought his head up, gritting his teeth, and the man motioned for him to turn around. The man dipped the brush in the bucket of disinfectant again, ordering Vlada to spread his cheeks. The disinfectant trickled off Vlada's scalp, stinging his eyes and making them water. He did not want to appear to be crying. He did as he was told and bent over as the kapo swiped the disinfectant on his backside.

Bile rose in the back of Vlada's mouth. He gagged inwardly at the realization that all the men before him had gone through the same disinfecting process. He looked for an escape route from the madness that surrounded him – hundreds of shorn and naked men, kapos barking orders, the cold and grim surroundings – but there was none. At least, this must be the last of it, he thought.

Then the men were forced into the showers and Vlada struggled for a spot under a spigot with lukewarm trickling water. He ran his hands over his scalp, reaching for hair that was no longer there. Barely seconds under the water, a kapo with a scar above his eye shouted at him to move on. Vlada stood in front of the man, dripping water and shivering, as the man looked him over and threw clothes at him from large piles on the ground: pants, shirt and a jacket. Vlada spotted the huge pile of shoes.

Whose shoes are these? Vlada began to tremble, slowly wrapping his feet with rags that the kapos clearly intended for the prisoners to use as socks. He did not want to put the shoes on. Everything was wrong here. He wanted to stand up and scream: Whose shoes are these? But he was not ready to die for asking questions, and in this hellish place that was a real possibility.

A kapo seated at a table nearby shouted. "Over here! Shivering and mortified by the repeated assaults on his person, Vlada hurried and stood in front of the table.

"Name."

"Munk, Vladimir." His voice came out hoarse, unrecognizable. The kapo wrote his name next to a number in a large ledger.

"Put your arm on the table." The one who had written his name held his left arm down with more strength than Vlada thought necessary. The other man held a small piece of wood with a needle sticking out. Vlada flinched instinctively. The man glared up at Vlada and then roughly tapped and pricked a letter and series of numbers from the ledger onto Vlada's forearm: B11673. Tiny bubbles of dark red blood filled the holes left by the needle. The kapo dipped a cloth in thick, black ink and smeared it over the tattoo.

Vlada stepped away and looked down at his arm. Red welts slowly rose around the barely legible tattoo. Vlada recognized that, to the Nazis, he was a number. He had grown to adulthood in captivity. He was nineteen, he had nothing, and the Nazis were taking away the last thing he had: his name. He could not foresee that when he identified himself to the kapo, it would be the very last time he spoke his name at Auschwitz.

Days passed interminably. The hundreds of new prisoners fell into a predictable daily routine. Every morning the barrack emptied out into a clearing between two buildings for roll call. For hours, Vlada stood with the other prisoners at attention in the muddy yard, sometimes in the freezing rain, while the guards counted and recounted them. Every day, Vlada searched the faces in the crowd for his father.

The sky over the camp was rarely clear. At first glance, Vlada thought the sky was filled with birds, circling overhead in search of carrion. But what he thought were birds was ash, thick black flecks of ash, and black smoke churning out of the huge brick chimneys at the far end of the camp. The ash floated down onto the ground around them. Every breath Vlada took filled his nostrils with a sickly-sweet smell that permeated everything. There were no birds in the sky. Even they had deserted the prisoners.

At the end of the first week, Vlada got up his nerve and spoke under his breath to a Polish prisoner who stood next to him in the muddy yard.

"Do you know what happened to the people who were separated and went to the other side? The ones who went to the right? My father went that way." Vlada earnestly searched the man's face, trying not to appear desperate. It had taken all his strength to ask the question and Vlada held his breath for the man's response.

"You see the smoke there?" The man indicated the flecks of ash and smoke that filled the air. "That is where your father is. He went up the chimney." The man tilted his head, sizing Vlada up and watching for his reaction. Then he shrugged his shoulders and turned away.

Vlada struggled with the information. Was this the truth? Was this the Nazis' plan all along? All the missing pieces over all the years began to fall into place: the decrees, the yellow star, the deportations to Terezin, the outgoing trains to the "East."

Vlada's face contorted in pain. The grief came in waves, almost knocking Vlada to the ground. How could I have been so stupid? He looked up at the dark sky above. Ash crackled out of the chimneys and up into the sky.

He watched the flakes catch in the wind and float up. Vlada reeled, momentarily losing his grip on reality. Each piece of ash, still red with embers, was a soul, needing to be gathered up and revered, paid homage to on its way heavenward. He willed the thick flecks of ash not to fall back down to earth. If they did, he would get down on his knees and scoop up the mud and ash and put his father back together again.

When the prisoners were released to their barracks for the night, Vlada went directly to his bunk and fell asleep. His sleep was fitful. He dreamed he and his father were on a small island, with water surrounding them. Inch by inch, the water level creeped up, thick, black, viscous liquid overtaking the island, and leaving them standing knee-deep as it threatened to envelop them. After that first night, it became a recurring dream, but Vlada did not mind. It was the only place he saw his father.

The daily routine at the camp droned on. Nothing stopped. Every day he stood, surrounded by hundreds of other men, in a field between two barracks to be counted, recounted, and counted again. In the morning, the ground was frozen and rutted, and as the day wore on, it softened, turning into a thick mud. One day, Vlada watched as the man next to him tried to shift his feet, but his shoes had sunk so deeply in the mud he could not extract them. It would have been comical if it had not been so tragic. Finally, the man freed one leg up and out of the muck, and it made a loud sucking sound.

On a warmish day in December, during the counting, a man cried out and fell over. Two kapos ran up, and dragged the body of the unmoving, emaciated prisoner from the yard. There was no sucking sound as they pulled him out, leaving Vlada to surmise the man's boots had been left behind in the muck.

Vlada watched as two men behind him performed what he thought must be a well-choreographed dance. They fell into the line, but only after one stood guard, while his counterpart retrieved the boots left behind by the dead man and tucked them in his baggy striped jacket. The man who had stolen the dead man's boots had a scar on his cheek.

Later, in the line for soup, Vlada looked down at the boot thief's feet. He had done well to steal the dead man's boots. They were free of holes. Vlada observed that the two thieves looked like twins – shaved heads, striped jackets, cheekbones jutting out below hollow eye sockets. Vlada's depression was so deep, so all encompassing, he did not realize until that moment he looked just like them.

Ever since he had discovered the dark secret of Auschwitz, and the truth about his father, Vlada barely ate, he was visited daily with waves of nausea. He did not dare wretch in front of anyone for fear of attracting unwanted attention. Instead, he clamped his teeth shut, swallowing the bile that rose in the back of his throat.

Today he looked around at the squalor and depravity of the camp and drank the entire portion of thin, brown liquid, searching the bottom for something solid. Something had changed in him. He needed to regain his strength. He was going to get revenge for the death of his father. He was going to kill the Nazis.

Chapter Seventeen

FOLK SONG

KITTY NOVEMBER 1944
TEREZIN, PROTECTORATE OF
BOHEMIA AND MORAVIA

The Czech gendarmes marched the women of the camp down the middle of the Haupstrasse under cool, blue skies. If Kitty had not known better, they might have been taking part in a lovely fall outing. The group was made up mostly of young women, many of the faces, including Hanka's, familiar to Kitty from the *Judengarten*. The guards had begun by assembling the prisoners first in the Hanover courtyard while several SS guards hovered nervously on the perimeter of the group. Kitty stood among them, arms crossed, awaiting further instructions. She caught Hanka's eye and mouthed wordlessly, "What's going on?" Hanka shrugged, discreetly rolling her eyes.

The SS had forced the prisoners of Terezin to do so many senseless things since Kitty and her family had arrived at the camp. Each day, they introduced new rules, restrictions, and procedures, eliminating any sense of stability from one day to the next. But something was different this time. The SS were on edge today. With their eyes narrowed, they shifted nervously, looking to each other for reinforcement of their next move. Kitty watched them from the edge of the crowd wondering what strange whim, what dirty work, the women of the camp would be forced to perform for them.

The women began to march toward the undisclosed destination, and two SS guards fell into the rear of the formation. The group shuffled past the Stadt Park, startling a flock of grey wood pigeons in the large stand of trees. They flew upwards in a wild flurry, ascending higher with each flap of their wings, heading south.

They are going to Prague, thought Kitty wistfully. Thoughts of Vlada filled Kitty with a mix of melancholy and optimism. A month had passed since they said goodbye, and everywhere she looked since then had been a reminder of him: the locksmith shop, the Hanover Barrack, the attic apartment. Kitty bit her lip. A familiar flutter passed through her and she clutched at her chest, overwhelmed with a hopeful feeling.

The women had walked the length of the camp before turning right and crossing the dry moat that surrounded the fortress in the direction of the river. As they drew closer, Kitty recognized the river as the Ohre; she had been forced to swim in it back in September when the men had come to the camp to make the film. The film was a big lie, meant to convince the outside world that the Jews of the camp were happy and healthy and living under wonderful conditions. The ghetto Kommandant Rahm ordered the creation of outdoor cafes where flowers bloomed from planters and concerts were performed, including *Brundibar*.

A fellow prisoner had heard that Kitty was a good swimmer, and the filmmaker, a prisoner named Gerron, rounded up Kitty and a handful of boys, taking them down to the river and instructing them to splash around while he filmed them from the shore. Kitty remembered stepping down from the grassy bank of the river and into the cool, rushing stream. She had waded out into the middle where the water was deepest, the rushing water flowing against her legs, her fingertips grazing the water's surface, and submerged herself. When she popped back up she began to tread water, her legs dangling below her in the cool depths. She floated, the rush of the water filling her ears, feeling free for the first time since arriving at the camp. One of the SS guards had watched her closely. He needn't worry, thought Kitty at the time, this is the closest to freedom I will venture today.

The boys in the group were not as adventurous. They nervously waded in the shallows by the shore, unable to enjoy the water because they were paying more attention to the SS guards who were overseeing the outing.

The group had arrived at the river to begin filming in the late afternoon. Kitty had immediately drifted into the water, even though the camera equipment had not yet been set up. By the time they finished filming, the sun was setting, the light dappling through the trees that hugged the river's banks, and Kitty never wanted to leave. The guards had neglected to bring towels for the swimmers and Kitty shivered in the cool September evening, a trail of water dripping from her swim clothes all the way back to her barrack.

Today the sun sparkled on the rippling water, catching the sunlight, and refracting it into a million tiny diamonds on the surface. The women formed a line that went from the mortuary, up and over the dry moat, and concluded on the edge of the riverbank. Two SS guards came down the line and stationed themselves at the river's shore, sharing nervous glances that set Kitty on edge.

There was a commotion down the line of women, and Kitty turned toward the Dutch girl next to her, searching her face for some clue as to why they had been assembled here. It was abundantly clear they were not there for a swim. And then she saw the first few dozen cardboard boxes and glassine bags come into view, being passed bucket brigade style, from one set of young hands to the other.

"Ready!" the SS guards shouted, although Kitty was confused as to whom their announcement was directed. The boxes moved fast, and soon one was in the hands of the Dutch girl, who turned toward Kitty, placing it in her hands. Kitty stared down at the cardboard box; a name was written upon it in white greasepaint or chalk, but Kitty could not make it out.

"Shnell!" One of the SS shouted at Kitty, and she turned to her left and handed the box to the young woman next to her. There were only a few more prisoners between Kitty and the riverbank. The last woman in the line, her dark hair pulled back in a bun, held the box with two hands and stared at the guards, a quizzical look on her face. One of the guards motioned to her to heave the box into the river.

The dark-haired woman followed the order, sending the box airborne over the water. The cardboard top separated from the bottom, and the contents of the box, a dark grey dust mixed with stark, white slivers, scattered in the breeze, half of it falling into the river and the other half blowing back on the woman. She cried out in anguish as the dust hit her skirt and shins.

For a moment Kitty was in denial, and her mind struggled to come to terms with what she had just seen. Her eyes disbelieved what her heart knew to be true. Soon Kitty had another box in her hands and was passing it on, realizing that each box passing through her hands contained the human remains of one of the camp's dead.

Kitty's mind raced as packages slipped through her hands and on to the person next to her. The line of women had become a ghastly human chain to rid the camp of the ashes of those cremated there. Kitty's anguish overwhelmed her. But why? she asked. They are getting rid of the evidence of the camp's conditions —disease, unsanitary conditions, and malnutrition. Have they forgotten that we are still here to tell the story? That these people once existed and that they were innocent, and we will never allow them to be forgotten? Kitty felt like running and screaming to each person surrounding her. "Remember them, remember them!"

There were occasional cries from further up the line when a box was dropped or a glassine bag tore open, scattering ashes and bits of bone on the shoes of the prisoners and into the dirt.

Kitty remembered overhearing one of the girls in her barrack talking one night. The girl was "dating" a Czech gendarme, their dates consisting of having intercourse in an attic room over one of the barracks while everyone else was at work. Kitty listened as the girl, whose name she did not know, talked about her 'boyfriend' and his duties at the camp.

"Frantisek told me why all of the gendarmes were so miserable when we first arrived," the girl paused before continuing. "For the first few years it was their job to bury the camp's dead. He remembers burying up to one hundred prisoners a day. Poor baby. It was backbreaking work, you know? Then they made the gendarmes build the crematoriums, so instead of hauling corpses they were hauling bricks. So, his back was still aching. That's why he must lay on his back while I ...," the girl laughed, and the other girls giggled along with her. Kitty had not seen the humor at the time.

Since the crematoriums were built, the camp had cremated thousands of bodies. For the women standing in line, the boxes kept coming with no end in sight. Sweating, Kitty pushed her hair back from her brow. The woman to her left motioned to Kitty to wipe her forehead where a trace of ash had mixed with her perspiration. As the hours passed, the frantic pace of the early assembly line began to slow. The women's bodies were fatigued, but their trauma, as they acknowledged their participation in their gruesome task, probed depths they had not known.

The line of boxes finally slowed. Kitty was able to look down at the one in her hands and realize that it was different from the others. It was well constructed from tin with a tight-fitting lid. Kitty knew in an instant that it had been made by Vlada in the locksmith shop. He had told her about this box; he had made it with great care. It held the remains of Vlada's maternal grandmother, Emilie Gesmai.

After enduring the deportation of her children and their families to the camp, Emilie, at the age seventy-eight, had been forced onto a train and sent from Prague to Terezin, alone and blind. Once at the camp, she was briefly reunited with some of her children, only to mourn as one after another of them were deported yet again, this time to the "East." In less than six months, she succumbed to malnourishment, the camp's unsanitary conditions, and despair. Her earthly body was returned to dust in the camp's newly built crematorium.

By the time Kitty and her family had arrived at the camp in February of 1943, Emilie was already dead. Vlada had spoken of her and of the box he had made. It was the only thing they could do for Emilie to honor her in some small way in this wretched place. Holding the box made Kitty feel closer to Vlada somehow. She could just make out 'Emilie Gesmai' marked in chalk on the top.

The Dutch girl hissed at Kitty under her breath. "You are holding up the line! What are you doing?" Despite the pressure to keep the line moving, Kitty stood frozen. She needed to think fast. Only once during her time in the camp had Kitty come dangerously close to disciplinary action by the SS and that was enough. If their grisly assembly line ground to a halt, someone would have to pay. It was not going to be her.

Kitty fell back on her *Judengarten* skills; she took a moment to locate the SS guards and Czech gendarmes overseeing the operation. The gendarmes were distracted, handing out dustpans and brooms to a few of the prisoners.

The SS were nervously laughing and smoking, paying no attention to their ash-covered charges. They were clearly on edge and their agitation was a possible indication, Kitty believed, that the Germans were edging closer to losing the war. But the more tightly wound they were, the more likely they were to descend on her with their clubs or boots.

Kitty had mere seconds to act. "Mach vas! Do something!" She heard her fraulein's phrase echoing in her head. Kitty was used to hiding tomatoes and other vegetables in the folds of her dress when working in the agricultural detail. But the box with Emilie's remains was too big for that. She locked eyes with the Dutch girl, pleading for solidarity. The girl hesitated. Kitty was on the verge of panicking when the girl rolled her eyes and nodded. Kitty stepped back, out of the line, and the Dutch girl quickly moved in to fill the gap left behind by Kitty.

A stand of willow trees rose directly behind Kitty, towering on the edge of the riverbank, their delicate branches drooping over the river. I'll be able to easily find this spot again, thought Kitty. She bent at the knees and gently placed the tin box on the grass at the base of one of the willows. She could barely hear the rush of the river over the pounding of her heart in her ears.

Kitty inched forward and resumed her place in line. The Dutch girl glowered at her. I know...I'm sorry, thought Kitty, smiling weakly. She had put the woman in harm's way for the sake of her own private mission. After this horror was over, she would find a way to show her gratitude.

Now that she had acknowledged the contents of the containers, all Kitty could see were the names of the dead, their Ghetto numbers, birth and death dates written in chalk. She began passing the boxes gingerly to the girl on her left with reverence for who they once were.

Even taking the greatest care, the names written in chalk were unintentionally wiped away. The people who once lived their lives and raised their families in cities, towns and villages across Czechoslovakia were tossed, nameless, into the river. Anyone who believed their loved one would have a proper burial after the war was stripped of that idea in the harshest fashion. Kitty remembered reading the Hebrew inscription at the base of the columbarium once before. Translated, it read: "And the Lord God will wipe away tears from all faces...." (Book of Isaiah, 25:8). Kitty looked around at the faces of the women, many of whom were weeping and covered in ash, and she wondered where God was right now.

In the shadow of the Little Fortress, the women toiled for hours, some collapsing from the strain and exposure. The guards ordered the crew to take breaks in shifts, and Kitty was pulled from the assembly line to rest. When she resumed her place in line again, she positioned herself nearer to the willow tree.

The day had been humid, and it was becoming more difficult to wipe or sweep up any spilled remains. Muffled laughter punctuated the grim silence of the late afternoon as a dark joke began to circulate among the women. They hoped the river flowed downstream and became drinking water for the Nazis.

It was growing dark, the fading light the perfect cover for Kitty to grab the box containing Emilie's remains and take it for safekeeping. The gendarmes lit oil lamps by which to work, but that only made things worse as the flamelight cast eerie shadows on the women's grimy faces, making their task more ghoulish. In this new light, Kitty noticed she, too, was covered in a thin layer of greyish-brown dust. She felt sick.

Women began falling to their knees from exhaustion while the last of the boxes passed down the line. Kitty had no idea where Vlada was, but she knew that she had to make this last small effort to secure Emilie's remains. For a second time she slipped out of line and into the darkness. The base of the willow tree was barely visible, but she knew she had the right one. In the darkness, Kitty's hands brushed along the base of the tree. She crouched low and crawled, trying to remain unseen.

I know it's here, she thought. She continued her search, panicking as she patted carefully at the dirt and grass so as not to upend the box. She was running out of time; the line began to break apart as the women prepared to make the walk back inside the fortress. This is not possible, Kitty cried. She could not find the box. What have I done?

The box containing Emilie's remains was gone. Someone must have seen it during her brief time away from the line and thrown it in the river with the rest of the dead. Kitty was horrified and ashamed. She began the walk back to the barrack, dirty and dejected, the harrowing weight of the day bearing down upon her stooped shoulders. Turning to see a faint breeze blowing upon the branches of the willow trees, Kitty watched the lingering leaves release into the flow of the river in the twilight.

Up ahead, the line of women filed slowly past the Czech gendarmes. The guards were placing something in the outstretched palm of each prisoner as they passed. When it was Kitty's turn, she held out her hand, wondering what they considered a suitable reward for the gruesome task they had just performed. She looked down at the small object in the palm of her hand. It was a lump of sugar. She wanted to cry out in frustration, from the loss of Emilie, the loss of Vlada, the loss of everyone, but she withheld her cries.

Kitty threw the lump of sugar in the dirt, and continued walking. The woman behind her picked up the lump of sugar, dusted it off, and put it in her mouth.

CHAPTER SEVENTEEN

"This must be what it is like to be a dying man looking back over a long, lost life," Vlada thought. In a little over a month, he would turn twenty. He had grown from childhood into adulthood under Nazi rule. During that time, he had lost everything.

Vlada likened the effects of the Nazi occupation of his homeland to the frog in the pot of water. The concessions, degradations, and deprivations his family had borne under the Third Reich had been gradual at first. Memories flashed in his mind, bursts of light like a projector in a movie theater warming up to show a film. There had been the stamp collection, then the radio, Tati forcing him to develop the photos, and martial law after the attentat of Heydrich. There was the giving away of all their worldly possessions, his mother at the piano, Cigy, Terezin, Nora and Eva and Mirek and Vera. Then Auschwitz.

The heat had been turned up on the Jews in such small increments as to seem almost imperceptible. Now the water was boiling, and the frog had lost any chance of climbing out of the pot.

"I am the frog," thought Vlada. His arms hung weakly at his sides. He had been forced aboard a train at Auschwitz and now found himself part of a slave labor detail at Gleiwitz I, a sub-camp of Auschwitz, selected to repair Nazi rail cars damaged by Allied bombs. Whispers of the camp's reputation for backbreaking labor and a low rate of survival had circulated on the train.

If memory served him at all, Vlada had eaten less since arriving at Gleiwitz than he had at Auschwitz. The Nazis had calculated how many calories were needed to keep the laborers alive for three months. The dueling menace of inadequate rations and freezing temperatures were taking a toll on the men around him. The prisoners shuffled in silence from one side of the railyard to the other, their feet wrapped in rags, mistaking their movements for well-being. Some were nearing expiration.

A large fire burned in the center of the yard, but it was not for the prisoners' comfort. Iron rivets glowed white in the flames. An older prisoner lifted a rivet out of the flames with tongs. He ran, if one could call it that, at a metal plate that covered the splintered wood of a damaged rail car and found a point of entry, the rivet piercing through to the other side. Another man inside the train car hammered the molten iron down, securing the metal plate in place. The older man fell to the ground, weak from the exertion.

He won't last the week, thought Vlada. He had become skilled at predicting survival based on a few key factors – their physical state and what was going on in their head. No one improved under these conditions, they only got worse. He took in the scene around him. Many had lost hope. He could see it in their eyes. If they gave up now, death was a certainty.

Vlada willed himself to move. Time to look busy, he told himself. He grabbed a brush and picked up a bucket of grease, his hands trembling from the cold. Vlada allowed his mind to wander to thoughts of his father. I am like *The Good Soldier Sjevk*, thought Vlada. See, Tati. I was paying attention. But Vlada's mind closed the door on that memory before a yearning pain marched through. Vlada had taken to greasing the wheels of the train cars to appear useful if an SS guard happened upon him. An idle Jew was a dead Jew.

The first time Vlada walked the length of the tracks, dipping the brush in the bucket and swiping the metal wheels with the thick grease, he had a disturbing flashback. He was back in Auschwitz, in the disinfection line. The man ahead of him spread his buttocks and the guard swiped him with disinfectant. Then it was Vlada's turn. He stepped forward and watched as the guard dipped the same brush in the bucket, and then wiped it over Vlada's freshly shorn and bloodied scalp. Vlada winced remembering the pain as the disinfectant seeped into the cuts made by the dull razor. He reached his hand up and rubbed the scratchy stubble that had grown in since then.

Because of the cold, Vlada walked haltingly, and greased a few more wheels. The guards paid him no attention. A bit further down the line, he poked his head inside an open rail car. Wincing with the effort, Vlada pulled himself up and into the rail car, summoning what little strength he had remaining. He looked down at his hands, barely recognizing them. His skin was white from the cold, with red spots where the molten tie rods had burned his skin. These hands which had once performed the most delicate operations as a locksmith now failed him for anything more precise than holding a cup of weak tea.

A small, shadowy object in a darkened corner of the railway car aroused his curiosity. He reached toward it and his frozen fingers struggled to close around it. A turnip. He pawed at it, managing to lift it and drop it in the pocket of his threadbare jacket. In the other corner lurked a small potato. He scooped it up with numb fingers and stared at it. It sat like a precious jewel in his hand.

He closed his eyes and imagined it was an apple, remembering the way an apple's flesh snapped as it was bitten into. He bit into the potato. The skin snapped under his teeth, and the force made his gums bleed. It was frozen solid.

Food sat right here in his hand. He was starving. and he could not eat it. Like a man possessed, Vlada could think of nothing except how to get the potato and the turnip into an edible state. He slid the potato into his pocket. All fear left him. He understood stealing from the Germans was an act punishable by death. He did not care that he would be beaten within an inch of his life if the SS caught him with a few scraps of vegetables. At that moment it was worth any risk.

Vlada shuffled back to his work area, looking officious with the bucket and the brush. The metal tongs the elderly man had used to grab the hot rivet sat in a bucket of water. Vlada flinched as he thought back to the day he had plunged his frostbitten hands into the bucket to warm them. His hands had met with an instant, searing pain. The water was lukewarm at best, but it had burned his frozen skin. Now, the bucket of warm water would be his friend. He looked around to make sure no one was watching.

He had nothing to worry about. No one paid any attention to his movements. Each man on the work detail was in his own private hell of hunger and despair. The SS gave him a wide berth when they saw the white-hot rods in the tongs he carried. Who knew what a crazy Jew might do with nothing to lose?

No one saw the precious root vegetables slip silently from his frozen hands into the hot water. Vlada busied himself nearby, keeping a watchful eye over his precious treasures. Within an hour of stewing in the warm water, the vegetables were soft.

Up until that moment, Vlada had pushed aside his physical hunger, subsisting instead on a daily diet of hate. His need for revenge was a loud monster that quelled the racket emanating from his empty belly. Hatred, he had discovered, is its own form of sustenance. There was no room for hope in Vladimir's mind right now. He could no longer imagine a world where he would be reunited with his beloved Kitty or see his mother, Hermina, again.

I will live to see the Nazis lose the war, Vlada pledged. Until then, I will kill as many of them as I possibly can. He turned his back to the other men and chewed greedily on the now tender vegetables. This time they yielded to his sore gums as he swallowed them in large, dry gulps. After the first few swallows, he began to chew more slowly, savoring the small mouthfuls. It dawned on him that revenge would be even sweeter with a full belly.

Everywhere his eyes rested in the camp, Vlada saw death. He woke in the morning to the groans of the older men in the bunks surrounding him, wondering who would make it through the day. In the latrines it was worse. Some of the men's bodies were so broken as to have given up all normal function. The men lost most of their remaining hope in the food lines, faced with the knowledge that the thin broth ladled into a tin cup held little in the way of solids. It would not sustain them for the hours of physical labor ahead. The food was a mirage of sorts, momentarily tricking the eye but not the belly of the recipient.

Vlada was no longer able to bring himself to look at his physical surroundings, which were bleaker than anything he could have imagined. He looked up and considered the ominous, grey clouds pressing down over the camp. The rumbling in the distance threatened a cold rain, or more likely snow. Why do they call the sky 'the heavens?' he wondered.

Vlada remembered childhood trips with his parents to catch a glimpse of the stork of Bohdaneč, a spa town not far from Pardubice. He wished the stork that had made its nest in the chimney of the grand building would come and get him now. He wanted to be lifted: up, out, away from the camp. Away from the dead and dying. Toward life. He wanted to be reborn, as a newborn baby. He wanted the chance to start all over again in a world far away from the Nazis, one where his family never had to suffer again. What had started out as an adventure on the train from Pardubice to Terezin over two years ago had veered off the path into a cold, dark nightmare.

His head was filled with dark thoughts, as dark as the threatening sky. No one is coming to save you, stupid. Still, he allowed himself to indulge in the daydream. If I were to be carried away, where would I go?

Vlada had always loved the mountains of Krkonose. Now when he pictured that icy, otherworldly landscape, the one he had once imagined was another planet as a young boy, he realized it was no longer an option. If I survive, I will never be cold again. I will never ski, or ice skate or climb a snow-covered mountain ever again. Never.

He struggled, discouraged. What was wrong with him? Why could he not picture paradise? Why could he not see anything of beauty? He screwed his face in concentration, but nothing revealed itself. This is my darkest hour, thought Vlada. I cannot believe the Nazis have taken this one last thing from me – the ability to wish for something – anything – good.

A kapo, a Pole with a pockmarked face, had been studying Vlada from across the yard. He saw the shadow fall over Vlada's face the moment he descended into despair. He had seen that look before, right before someone killed themselves. Not on his watch. They needed every able body.

He sidled up to Vlada. "Are you okay, my friend? Not thinking about doing anything stupid, now, are we?" Vlada's eyes regained their focus.

Something had changed. He looked up at the sky again and a smile began to spread across his face.

"Ah, feeling better, I see." The kapo began to put his arm around Vlada's shoulders, but Vlada shrugged him away. "What are you smiling about, you fool? You are starving and on the verge of freezing to death. What have you got to smile about? What's on your mind? Tell me! I must know!"

Vlada did not look at the kapo. He just kept smiling. He looked up at the sky again, an ever-widening patch of blue insinuating itself through the clouds, confirming his suspicions. The rumbling he had heard was not thunder after all. It was the sound of Russian tanks, and they were getting closer. That could only mean one thing.

Revenge, first. Then freedom.

Chapter Eighteen

The sound of a gunshot further up the line of prisoners shocked Vlada back to his surroundings. The last thing he remembered was being roused from a deep sleep, the German guards shouting for the prisoners to get up and out of the barrack. "Raus! Raus!" Vlada was one of the lucky ones. Those who did not move to an upright position in their bunks quickly enough to satisfy the SS were shot where they lay. That was how the death march began.

Now, it was difficult to know how long they had been marching. The sun refused to rise further than three-quarters above the horizon and from that angle cast long shadows over everything the ragged group of prisoners passed. The trees that lined the deeply rutted road over which they struggled had thick trunks, their branches nearly cracking under the weight of recent heavy snow. Beneath the branches, only darkness was visible. The wind was dry and soulless, as the Germans forced the prisoners onward. Both the prisoners and their captors were like tiny characters in a snow globe Vlada had seen in a store in Krkonose. Trapped. There was no way out.

Years of living under Nazi rule had made Vlada no stranger to irony. The only reason he was alive to take part in this forced march with the other men from the camp was because of Leon. Leon Müller was a wiry, fast talking kapo, a German prisoner who had been in the camp longer than he cared to divulge.

On his first day at Gleiwitz, Leon had sidled up to Vlada. "Do you come here often?" The impish kapo chuckled at his own joke. A black inverted triangle was sewn onto Leon's clothing, signifying non-conformity or vagrancy. Vlada was shell-shocked. The weeks standing under the ash-filled skies of Auschwitz, and the bitterness and grief over the loss of his father, had changed something inside of him, turned him inside out.

From the moment he arrived at the labor camp, Vlada felt lonely and isolated. The older men working in the train car yard, the Hungarians, shook their arms wildly to warn him away from the smooth-talking lackey to the SS. But Vlada watched them as if in a fog, a fog that grew thicker each day with cold and hunger.

Once Vlada had figured out how to procure a few root vegetables from his forays in the train cars, he had shared them with some of the other men. But his generosity was self-serving. On a frigid day, one of the Hungarians saw him slip a turnip into his pocket. The man looked pleadingly into Vlada's eyes. Later, Vlada took the man by the arm, and offered him the bit of contraband. Hunger, it turned out, was a universal language. From that moment the man was indebted to him. Vlada had no idea how or when he might call in the debt, but it lay there, a part of every future interaction, like an open wound.

A few weeks into his time at Gleiwitz, Vlada woke in his bunk to the stench of sour breath and an incessant tapping on his shoulder. "Pssst." It was past midnight and Leon's face hovered in the semi-darkness, inches away from Vlada's. "Come with me." Vlada cleared the sleep from his eyes, careful not to make a sound, as he gritted his teeth and lowered himself from the second bunk. He followed behind the lean little man, struggling to keep up with the fast pace he set.

The camp was quiet, most of the prisoners motionless in their bunks, half dead from exhaustion. Leon moved from one building to the next with ease, acknowledging every sound, pausing until he knew its source, and then moving again when he had determined the coast was clear. They finally came to a stop at the end of a narrow hallway in front of the door to Leon's living quarters.

With a flourish, Leon threw open the door. "Home, sweet, home." Vlada peered into the simply furnished room. There was a bed with a blanket, a chair, and a lamp on a small table. It was warm, dry, and free of vermin but beyond that Vlada wondered how he might benefit from this late-night excursion with the odd little kapo. He looked at the man and began to regret his decision to leave his bunk.

"Why did you bring me here?" Vlada hissed under his breath. He did not care at that moment if he sounded rude. This man was nothing but another prisoner. A sellout to the Nazis.

Leon held up his hands, palms out, hoping to calm Vlada. "Whoa. Take it easy. I plan on making it worth your while." He smiled, revealing teeth, sparse and brown. He looked slightly less trustworthy and a good deal more deranged in the flickering lamplight than he had during the light of day when they made the plan to meet. Leon removed his cap, revealing short, red hair. In the dim light, he looked elfin.

Leon held his hand up like a magician about to perform a trick. He tugged on each cuff of his jacket with the opposite hand. "Nothing up my sleeve." Vlada gritted his teeth and turned away. He would find his own way back to the barrack, even if it was at great risk.

"Wait." Leon pointed to a wall near his bed and brought his finger to his lips. He grasped a section of the wall that until then had blended perfectly with the rest, revealing a stash that made Vlada's mouth water. Shelves inside the wall were stocked with cans of food, potatoes, and something that resembled ham and bread. Leon took a small loaf of bread from one of the shelves and ripped off a chunk. He wiped the bread in a battered tin cup filled with margarine and handed the "buttered" bread to Vlada.

"What do you want for it?" Vlada asked warily, taking a step back. He gazed longingly at the buttered bread, his stomach growling, but he refused to raise his hand to accept the food until he received a satisfactory reply. Vlada had heard rumors about Leon. Even though he did not understand Hungarian, the hand gestures the men used made it clear they suspected he was a homosexual. Vlada looked at the wild little man in front of him and the bread in his outstretched hand. I am starving but not that starving, Vlada thought.

"I like you Vlada. I want to look after you." Leon sat down on the bed, patting the space next to him.

How could I have been so stupid? thought Vlada. I should have known better.

Leon's face crumbled; his brown eyes shone with tears. "I'm sorry, Vlada. I'm not a bad person. I'm just so lonely here. I had to try." He extended the bread to Vlada again. "Don't leave. Here. Take it. No strings attached. I promise."

Vlada grabbed the bread from Leon's hand and proceeded to bite off large pieces, chewing greedily. After swallowing the first few mouthfuls, he sat in the chair next to the bed. Leon offered him a cup of water.

"So, what books did you like to read, you know, before?" Leon asked. Vlada took a sip of the water. He relaxed a bit. "*Three Musketeers, Twenty Thousand Leagues Under the Sea.* Karel Capek. You?" They talked about books for a half hour and then Leon stood up. Vlada looked at Leon closely. It was warm in the room, and Vlada's shoulders relaxed. He felt guilty for having judged the little man so harshly.

"Let's get you back." Leon stepped in front of Vlada, and set off at a fast pace. He paused for a moment outside Vlada's barrack, putting his finger to his lips. They could hear the voices of two German guards. It was a tense conversation that seemed to go on forever. Vlada began to shake, partly from fear and partly from the cold.

For a few bites of bread, I will be discovered and shot, thought Vlada. Then one of the guards laughed, launching into a story about an indelicate situation with a woman. Leon edged forward, leading Vlada to his bunk. He winked, his eyes shining in the darkness, and was gone.

Each night Vlada traveled with Leon to his room for some tinned beef or a stale piece of bread, and conversation. A few days passed, and a group of prisoners stood outside the barracks in the cold morning air stomping their feet to keep warm. Injured train cars lined the track, their wood and steel doors blown to bits by Allied bombs. One of the Hungarians caught Vlada's eye, conveying a lewd message with his hands. Vlada caught its meaning. It was about Leon.

"Ha," the man's breath came out in great, icy bursts, as the other men around him chuckled at the coarse joke. The Hungarians had a beautiful way of swearing. It rolled off their tongues, lilting phrases that, when translated, were quite vulgar.

They are just jealous, thought Vlada. What they were insinuating was a lie. He and Leon had come to an agreement: a few extra rations for companionship and conversation. Nothing more.

"They would never believe me if I told them I trust him," thought Vlada. The small, tightly wound man was growing on him. Moments shared with even the most eccentric friend were days spent less isolated.

The next morning, Vlada woke to sharp abdominal pain. He scurried to the latrine, holding his stomach, barely making it in time to deposit a painful, watery stool. Leon appeared in the doorway of the latrine. "Pssst," he warned his new friend. "It's time for roll call. Why aren't you outside?"

Vlada hunched over on the seat, wretching in response.

Leon tried to lift Vlada. "Come on. I can't cover for you. You must come out and work."

Vlada doubled over in pain, moaning, his insides twisting painfully. "I can't. Something is wrong." He wretched onto the floor in front of him and then sat down in time for a deluge from the other end.

"Stand up. Let me look," Leon ordered. Vlada stood, forgetting all modesty, and Leon looked down the latrine hole behind him and gagged. "Shit" said Leon. "You're shitting blood. It's dysentery. Come with me. Now. I am taking you to the infirmary." Vlada pulled up his pants and obeyed, following Leon, and falling behind the kapo's brisk pace.

It was a short walk to the makeshift infirmary. Leon spoke to the young kapo at the desk with a tone of authority. "This is one of my best workers," he nodded to Vlada, who stood next to him, gripping his stomach. "He has the runs. Fix him up. I need him back at work in a day or two." The young man nodded vacantly. The orderly was plump from the extra food rations he took as bribes. Leon pressed a sausage wrapped in brown paper into his outstretched hand, eliminating the need for questions. Before he departed, Leon turned to Vlada. "I'm not going to let anything happen to you."

The orderly led Vlada to a room filled with bunks. It did not look sterile, or even tidy. Every bunk was full, and the orderly motioned Vlada to a bunk where one of the Hungarians lay on his side, moaning softly. Vlada lowered himself onto the bunk, hugging the edge, giving the sick man a wide berth. For hours Vlada lay on the edge of the bunk. It had begun to grow dark when another orderly arrived, holding a small cup. "This is not a cure, but a little bismuth should help with the cramps." Vlada swallowed the pink liquid, nearly gagging with every sip. He collapsed back on the bunk and looked at the window above him. Ice had formed in lacy patterns on the panes of glass. Vlada could see his breath and he was not sure whether the chattering teeth he heard were his own, or those of the man on the bunk next to him.

That evening Vlada dozed fitfully. He awoke to find Leon's impish face looking down on him. "How is the patient? I will miss our visit tonight," he said in a low voice. Leon winked jokingly. Vlada was too weak to raise his head to make sure no one had heard him.

Leon looked over at Vlada's bunkmate and pushed the man onto his back. Vlada realized he had not heard the man moaning in a few hours. The Hungarian's eyes were open, staring vacantly at nothing. No beautiful swearing would pass from his lips ever again.

"Orderly!" Leon called out.

The man who had given Vlada the bismuth came in and stood by the bed. He glanced at the dead man unflinchingly. "I'll take care of it," the orderly told Leon in a voice devoid of emotion.

The night was filled with a blur of crazy dreams of Vlada fishing with his father at Polabiny. He woke frequently, the heartbreaking dreams punctuated by trips to the latrine. The next morning, the dead man was gone, and light streamed through the windows of the infirmary. Vlada sat upright in the bunk and waited, watching the door for Leon. His trips to the latrine became less frequent and night fell with no visit from his friend.

The next morning, Vlada walked slowly to the desk and found the young kapo who had admitted him humming to himself. "Do you know what happened to the kapo who brought me here? Müller? It has been two days. I thought he would be back to drag me out of here and back to work."

The young man looked at Vlada, eyes narrowing. "Oh, yeah. They rounded him up with a few other German kapos, and converted their prison sentences. The poor idiots were celebrating until they realized that meant they were being drafted and sent to the Front."

Vlada stood frozen as the kapo continued. "That's the Russian offensive you hear," the kapo lifted his finger in the air. He had barely finished speaking when Vlada's ears tuned in to a rhythmic booming of cannon fire in the distance. "The Germans have nothing to lose now. They're throwing anyone they can find at the advancing troops. Better them than me." The kapo shrugged his shoulders at Vlada's lack of camaraderie and turned and walked away.

Vlada walked slowly out of the infirmary, unsure of what to do. He was angry. And sad. And a little scared. After years in the camp, getting blood from a stone, forcing work out of dying men, they sent Leon to the front, another expendable, thought Vlada. He had not thought about eating in days, but he placed his hand on his stomach, anticipating the hunger pangs would begin again in earnest, wondering how he would replace the extra rations Leon had given him.

Vlada went back to work on the train car repair line. While he waited for the bolts to heat up, he traveled from one train car to the next with his bucket of grease and a large brush, stepping up his search for vegetables. One of the older Hungarians was emboldened now that Leon was gone. Vlada returned from a successful foraging with a potato in his pocket. Aggressively, the man held out his hand. His eyes narrowed, boring into Vlada's, daring him to deny him. The man's wrinkles were deep and dry like a cracked riverbed, his beard thick with wiry grey hair.

This man has never shed a tear, thought Vlada. He grudgingly placed the potato in the man's hand, and watched as he crossed the train yard. The bearded man handed the potato to the newly promoted Polish kapo as a bribe. The Polish kapos were the worst. Always beating prisoners in front of the SS to ingratiate themselves with their captors.

The shelling from the Soviet offensive grew louder each day. Vlada saw the German officers flinch when a shot landed close to the edge of the camp. He smiled inwardly when he saw the disgust in their eyes turn to something else - fear. The guards had received orders from the high command to evacuate the labor camp. Not a single prisoner was to be liberated by the approaching Russian troops. The Nazis would kill all of them before they would let that happen.

On the verge of collapse, Vlada now found himself on the third day of the westward death march. He was weak from his bout with dysentery, the lack of food and water, and the freezing temperatures. The cold made his blood thunder in his ears. He stumbled forward, lurching in the thick snow. Keep walking, he told himself. Those who fell to the ground and did not get up were immediately shot.

Vlada had seen it happen. Men stumbled and fell to their knees on the frozen ground. If they did not get up, they were shot where they took their last steps. The day before, Vlada had managed to work his way to the front line of prisoners, laboring to lift one foot in front of the other. He stepped to the side to relieve himself and the grisly parade of half-dead prisoners edged forward, a mass of grey disturbing the pristine snow.

A man fell and another man ran to him, reaching under his arms and slowly dragging him to the edge of the moving column. "Stoppen!" one of the guards shouted at the good Samaritan. The man hesitated, his face contorting in anguish, and then he let the body fall gently to the ground. The guard grew fat during the war, his throat pinched by the collar of his uniform, his cheeks plump and red from the cold. The fat German drew his gun and fired two shots into the body on the ground. The dead man's friend staggered forward. His eyes met the guard's for a moment, blinking and questioning his actions. The guard sneered and spat on the ground, then turned and began to march. The dead man's friend and another man pulled the body off the path, leaving blood-smeared streaks in the snow.

A wagon bumped along at the front of the column carrying the belongings of the SS officers. I must get to the wagon and allow it to pull me forward, Vlada thought. It is my only chance.

He summoned his last reserves and moved forward. He felt like he was crawling through mountains of snow and still, he passed hundreds of struggling prisoners. His toe caught on the body of a corpse in the middle of the road, yet he managed to lift himself up and over the dead man. Another shot rang out. Vlada flinched. Keep going, he told himself.

He could see the wagon up ahead. It was almost within reach. His feet scraped across the snow. *Thwap!* Finally, Vlada's frozen hand connected with the sideboard. He immediately felt the tug of the wagon's forward momentum.

The gate at the entrance to Blechhammer, another sub-camp of Auschwitz, was made of crudely assembled wood. The SS shouted orders as the ragged group of starving prisoners filed into the camp. "Report to a barracks and remain there until morning!"

Vlada collapsed in a bunk in the back of one of the barracks. He struggled to remember the last time he had eaten. Every part of him cried out: from pain, from hunger, from exposure to the elements. The only way to quiet the pain was to sleep. But the peace he sought in sleep eluded him.

Remnants of the recurring dream of his father at Polabiny filled his head. In the dream an inky, black liquid covered his father's face, obliterating his features. Suddenly his father opened his eyes, the whites stark against the black ooze that covered him. In the dream Vlada heard a sucking sound, like the sound of the dead man's boots in the thick mud of the yard at Auschwitz.

Now Vlada understood what the black ooze represented. It was the Nazis, pulling his father down under their terrible grip, swallowing him whole. Vlada felt the comforting urge for revenge wash over him again.

In the morning Vlada awoke to the smell of death and rot filling his nostrils. He struggled to stand. He peered cautiously out the door of the barrack, and seeing the courtyard empty, he walked slowly toward it. The sky was dark and ominous, and threatening snow.

Vlada saw another young prisoner and called out. "Hey, where is everybody?" The young man put his finger to his lips and motioned to Vlada to follow him. He ran to another barrack nearby, Vlada following as quickly as his broken body would take him, the sound of gunfire spurring him on. At the barrack, Vlada arrived in time to see the young man run to the back and dive underneath a bunk. Vlada instinctively followed. A moment later, the front of the building was sprayed with a burst of machine gun fire.

The *rat-tat-tat* continued in short bursts, followed by shouting in German. "Give yourselves up, now. You are surrounded," the Nazi guards shouted in the direction of the building.

Vlada looked at the stranger for answers. "They think we are trying to escape. Their orders are to leave no prisoners behind." The young man's voice was drowned out by an explosion that tore a hole in the front of the barrack, sending shards of wood and glass flying. The explosion was followed by a few less enthusiastic rounds of gunfire before the camp went silent.

Dusk fell and a cold wind howled through the holes in the barrack made by the detonation of the grenade. Vlada and the young prisoner huddled under the bunk and whispered awkward introductions.

"I am Emil." The Romanian stuck out his hand for Vlada to shake.

Vlada introduced himself, eyeing the Romanian with suspicion. What little war news had trickled in over the past years had the Romanians siding with the Axis and Hitler.

Emil sensed Vlada's concern. "If you are wondering, I am a Jew."

Vlada and his new companion lay on the frozen ground under the bunk, starving and frostbitten, for two days, not trusting that the camp was truly deserted. Overcome by hunger, Vlada was the first to crawl, stiff and broken, out of the hiding place under the bunk. He peered out through the bullet holes in the walls of the barrack and into the camp. "Empty," he whispered, his voice relaying his distrust that what he saw was real.

The two men walked toward the front of the barrack. A cold wind blew through the gaping hole. Emil pointed to a cluster of houses in the distance. "Down there." The two men set off down the hill and entered a small, deserted village. Vlada did not know what to do next. His mind had passed the threshold of pain and hunger. Emil desperately kicked open the door of a small, abandoned house, shattering glass.

The Romanian stepped into the house while Vlada stood guard outside. "Oh my God!" Emil exclaimed. Vlada's heart sunk and he fell against the fence outside the house, unable to face another horror or hardship. "Come quick, Vlada!"

Vlada pushed himself off the fence and stumbled into the house. He found Emil in the small kitchen. The table looked as if the occupants had been there only moments earlier. There was bread on the table, and an open pot of jam, the red mash of berries punctured by a silver spoon. Two teacups sat on the table, half full. Emil reached for the bread and broke the loaf roughly in half. He handed half to Vlada, smiling.

Vlada held the bread stiffly in his hand. He could not reconcile it with the last three weeks of his life. How could a string of lifeless men on a death march have passed this close to fresh bread and jam and tea? He took the first bite. If I am shot at this moment, it will have been worth it, he thought. He chewed nervously, greedily, watching the door. He washed a mouthful of bread down with the tepid tea, then tore into the loaf again.

They pulled out chairs from the kitchen table and sat down. Vlada poured cold tea from the pot into the cups and the two men made a toast. "Let Death kiss our ass!" Emil shouted enthusiastically. Shells exploded in the distance, and both men flinched.

"We can't stay here," Vlada warned. "We must get back to the camp before nightfall." Vlada stood up with difficulty. He caught a glimpse of movement in the mirror above the sideboard. A man looked back at him, a man with deep-set, dark eyes and hollow cheeks, the man's head and face bearing an equal amount of rough stubble. Whoever you are, you are free, he said to the reflection. You are free! Do you hear that?

Emil followed Vlada out and they began the walk back to the deserted camp. The snow crunched noisily with each footfall, dusted the night before with a fresh layer of glittery snow. Across the vast, white field, two soldiers with rifles approached. Their military uniforms were obscured by white capes they used as camouflage. One of the soldiers motioned to the prisoners to advance.

Vlada's heart sank. There was nowhere to hide.

"Maybe it's the Russkis," Emil added hopefully. The two soldiers approached quickly, the Nazi uniforms coming into focus.

"Halt!" One of the shoulders shouted. "Stop right where you are. Don't move!" The German staccato cut through Vlada like a knife. "Have you seen any Russian soldiers come this way? Tell the truth!" Vlada could see the face of the man who spoke. They looked to be the same age, twenty or so.

They are just as afraid of us as we are of them, only they have guns, thought Vlada. They were the hunter and now they had become the prey of the Russian army. Vlada wondered how it felt to have the tables turned.

Emil replied forcefully. "No. We have not seen any Russians."

The two Germans looked at each other. They did not bother with a response but broke into a run in the opposite direction of the shelling, scrambling off over the hill. Vlada and Emil walked as fast as their worn-out bodies would propel them, turning around frequently to make sure the Germans were receding. Every time he turned his back on the soldiers, Vlada's buttocks tightened in fear. It would be just my luck, thought Vlada. On the day I am to be liberated, I am shot by German soldiers.

He waited for a shot between the shoulder blades or if they were good marksmen, a bullet to the brain. But it never came. The next time Vlada saw German soldiers, they were prisoners of war.

Darkness fell. The two men shivered in the barrack, cold air pouring in through its side, splintered from grenades and mortar. A slice of the black night sky was visible through the gaping hole.

Vlada did not know it, but he would soon embark on a hero's journey. Would he journey home? Where was home?

Chapter Eighteen

Kitty walked slowly through the streets of the camp, always so serenely quiet right before dawn. She found herself wishing the morning light would hold off for a few more hours as she made her way toward the house on Haupstraffe.

The streets were damp from the previous night's rain, and it sparked a memory from Teplice, of the day Kitty returned home from the hospital after her appendicitis attack. Teplice. She could picture the villa. Oila, Pavla, Otto, Hanuš, her father, so robust and industrious, the Bettina of old, perfectly coiffed. *How can that feel like a lifetime ago when I am only turning seventeen?* Kitty wondered.

The great emptying of the camp the previous fall had set in motion a game of musical bunks for the thousands of prisoners who were not deported. Entire barracks sat empty now, their residents moving into smaller houses, some with kitchens and private rooms. Bettina and Kitty had moved to a small, two-story house. There was no one left to take issue.

Bettina had insisted that Kitty be in attendance as her mother assisted one of the few remaining nurses in the camp at a birth in one of the houses on the main street. "Assisted" was a generous term. Bettina usually boiled water in whatever makeshift way necessary – on a hotplate or in the kitchen of a house – supplying the nurse with a steady supply of relatively clean, hot towels during the delivery.

Kitty hesitated on the front steps of the house. The peaceful silence of the camp was shattered the moment Kitty turned the door handle and pushed open the door. A young woman lay on a bed in the front room, crying out in anguish and clenching her fists, her body frozen in a wave of pain. Then she fell back exhausted on the pillow. Kitty winced.

"Just in time, Kitty." Bettina motioned for Kitty to move quickly. "Here. Hold this on her forehead," she said, shaking a wet rag in Kitty's direction.

Kitty sat on a chair next to the bed and gently pressed the cool cloth against the woman's furrowed brow. Kitty realized she had seen the young woman before, in late winter the year prior, when a truckload of potatoes was delivered to the commissary. Word spread quickly about their unusual nature. They were perfect. Unblemished. No eyes, no rot.

One evening after dark, there was a knock on the door. Kitty opened it to find a young woman standing outside, holding her apron by the corners. It was filled with potatoes, their earthy scent beckoning, promising, reminiscent of the loamy bouquet of the *Judengarten* Kitty had grown to love.

"I hear you have a hot plate. If you let me borrow it, I will cook some of these for you," the young woman offered. Her face was serious, frank. Her name was Kamila.

Kitty scurried through the sparsely furnished house to fetch the hotplate; she was not going to hold her breath for the promised goods. Kamila looked like she needed the cooked potatoes more than Kitty did. But the following morning, Kitty stepped out of the house and almost tripped over a tin cup filled with still-warm potato wedges, the edges crispy from a well-seasoned skillet. Kitty looked up and down the street, hoping for a glimpse of the girl who had kept her promise. Reflecting, Kitty realized Kamila had been pregnant at the time.

The gut-wrenching cries in the small room began afresh. Kitty dipped the rag in cool water, wringing out the excess, and returned it to

Kamila's forehead, hoping that it might comfort her. The pain and cries came in ever-tightening waves, until bright sunlight streamed through the curtains, signaling midday. Suddenly, in a rush of bodily fluids, the baby appeared, tiny but active, her arms and legs moving in tiny, jerking movements. Kitty gagged, turning her head away, swallowing hard at the bile that rose in her throat from the smells she was unprepared for.

The nurse gently wiped the infant clean, swaddled her in a clean cloth, and placed the squirming baby in her mother's arms for the first time. "It's a girl," the nurse said.

Kamila lay back on the pillow, pale and weak, and looked down at the child in her arms. "I am going to call her Nadia because it is the closest name to *naděje*. Hope." The baby squirmed, appearing to make eye contact with her mother, acknowledging the name bestowed on her. The nurse let out a satisfied sigh and began to gather up the bed sheets and rags.

"Nadia." Kitty spoke the name out loud. "That's beautiful." Kitty helped her mother and the nurse gather the dirty laundry, stopping to watch Kamila coo over the baby, and plant tiny kisses on the infant's forehead. Nadia responded with tiny mewling cries. This was the first birth Kitty had witnessed; she had not been present when Bettina had assisted at the birth of Arna's little Petr. She stood awkwardly, soiled bed sheets bundled in her arms, feeling like an outsider witnessing this intimate moment between mother and child.

Kitty also felt a shocking bitterness well up inside her for the mothers and babies who had not been so fortunate as Kamila. This baby has a better chance for survival than Petr, thought Kitty. Arna had nursed Petr to life almost at the expense of her own. And poor JoJo, thought Kitty.

Kitty recalled her former bunkmate JoJo, the camp's black-market expert who had applied Kitty's lipstick for her first meeting with Vlada. JoJo had fallen in love and found herself pregnant, a mistake which she had cautioned others against. The Nazis had issued a ban on births in the camp, but some women had managed to hide their pregnancies and to secretly give birth. All the women who knew of JoJo's pregnancy thought she could manage the necessary ruse, including Kitty.

By six months JoJo was underweight with little if any belly to hide. Her bunkmates watched as JoJo pursued desperate measures to keep her baby viable, smuggling more bread, margarine, and sugar, to supplement her work rations. One day, she was careless, and a Czech gendarme turned her in for stealing. Kitty had watched, helpless, as the Czech gendarmes dragged the pregnant girl away, screaming "My baby, please. My baby." JoJo was forced to serve two weeks for her crime in The Little Fortress, the Gestapo's infamous prison, known for its horrific treatment of prisoners.

When JoJo was released two weeks later, she was emaciated and withdrawn. She never spoke of the baby again. Just weeks later, after the camp was emptied of its strongest, the most able-bodied inhabitants sent to the "East", food became plentiful and JoJo never had had to steal again. Such was the fickle nature of life in the camps, Kitty thought. Matters of life and death came down to weeks, sometimes even days or hours.

The nurse assisted Kamila in unbuttoning her nightgown, exposing one breast, the new mother awkwardly offering it to the child. Nadia rooted around hungrily until she discovered the source of sustenance and latched on, sucking greedily. Kitty watched the infant feeding, her eyes welling up with tears, her cheeks burning with shame at her previous selfish thoughts. Why doesn't Kamila's baby deserve to survive? Why should this child suffer? The Nazis are responsible for all the death, Kitty remembered. All we can do is try to protect the life that is still here.

Kitty turned at the door and looked back at Kamila. She felt her shoulders relax, and a sense of compassion for mother and child enveloped her. There had been no word for months from the men who left in the fall transports, Vlada included. Kitty wondered if baby Nadia would ever know her father?

Bettina mistook Kitty's silence and her parting glance at Kamila for longing. She offered Kitty the laundry basket, watching Kitty closely as Kitty put the soiled linens on top. "Having the baby is the easy part, Kitty. Raising it alone, now that will be the challenge." Kitty reprimanded her mother with a discouraging look; they were barely out of earshot of the new mother.

Kitty remembered her mother watching her body like a hawk, looking for signs of a thickening waistline, or a growing belly underneath Kitty's dress, unwanted developments in the months after she had stayed out past curfew with Vlada. Bettina had worried herself sick for no reason: there had been no tiny consolation prize, no pregnancy.

Kitty had her hopes pinned on Vlada's safe return. She wanted him. Only him. Nothing else would do. Maybe someday she would experience the sheer love between mother and child, the love and dependency she had witnessed between Kamila and Nadia. But for now, only Vlada would do.

In the first days after the camp was emptied, and Vlada was sent to the "East," Kitty remained optimistic. No one left behind in the camp had been untouched by the deportations, and the spirits of many who remained had been crushed. But Kitty willed herself to stay positive, writing unsent letters to Vlada, making small crafts for him, performing her nighttime ritual of tenderly examining the gifts he had given her in their short time together, and conjuring memories of the moments they had shared on the bench in Stadt Park, a snowy walk down the Haupstrasse, their tender, halting moments in the attic kumbal.

But the holidays came and went with no word, and then the new year arrived. The final blow had been Vlada's birthday in February. Her love was out there, somewhere, a man of twenty, and she had no idea when she would see him again. Doubt began to creep in. Kitty fell into a depression. She was raw, reeling, a delayed reaction to the loss of the man she adored. One day blended into another – wake-work-eat-sleep – and Kitty cried herself to sleep each night, hugging the trinkets Vlada had given her, tossing and turning, her dreams filled with nightmare scenarios of finding him injured or dead. Bettina's attempts to comfort Kitty were bound up with her own suffering and bitterness over the loss of Hanuš. Kitty felt worse after Bettina's ministrations, guilty almost, wondering if her mother wished it was Hanuš who might still have a shot of survival rather than Vlada.

That winter, Kitty was sent to a new work detail as part of the German war effort. The mica factory occupied two large wooden barracks just outside the camp. Over a thousand women were assigned to leave the camp daily, although closer to eight hundred showed up due to malnutrition or disease. Kitty stood among the crew of Dutch, Czech,

Russian, and Hungarian women as the Czech gendarmes counted them inside the ghetto wall. She then trudged to the barrack where she was assigned a stool at one of the long wooden tables.

She stared at the block of mica in front of her, unmoving, and watched as a supervisor demonstrated how to use the special knife to strip the worthless surface layer of mica off the block, revealing the valuable inner sheets, which the Nazis used as insulation in their war planes. She was instructed to drop the inner sheets in a metal box at her station to be weighed at the end of the day. Bettina sat next to Kitty on the mica detail, and her mother struggled daily to meet her quota, prompting Kitty to work doubly hard to fill both boxes. The work, while not physically tiring, was repetitive and boring, leaving Kitty's thoughts to wander.

She thought of Vlada and of Oila. Neither of them would want to see her this way: listless, lifeless, depressed. She was healthy due to the extra rations, and she vowed to stay that way. She had to be ready when the war ended to find Vlada wherever he was. She worked harder. Helping her mother and the other women made her feel needed. And Vlada needed her, too. She had a mission, and it imbued her daily life with purpose.

When she crossed the threshold of the camp, escaping the fortress walls, her mood lightened. One day, I will find Vlada and leave this place behind forever, thought Kitty. She felt her spirits lift with each passing day.

Now Kitty prepared to leave the house, casting one last glance at Kamila and Nadia. "I need some air. I am going to walk a bit," Kitty told her mother.

Bettina followed Kitty out of the house. Her mother looked exhausted. Her arms hung by her sides, her eyelids were heavy, and Kitty immediately regretted dismissing her. She stood in the street outside the house and watched as her mother walked away. The empty camp meant fewer guards. Freedom to walk the streets without fear of repercussion had become its own small form of liberation.

Kitty thought back to those late nights listening to the older girls in their bunks as they talked about men – and boys pretending to be men.

Their infatuations, obsessions, rejections, betrayals. She was not one of them, thank you very much. Her hand reached for the charm that hung on a simple chain around her neck. She remembered the day Vlada had given it to her.

"Close your eyes, girl," he commanded.

"We only have a few moments, Vlada. Stop playing games." Kitty had looked around the street, impatiently.

Looking back, she felt a pang of guilt for rushing him. He had wanted to bestow upon her with fanfare what would be the last of a string of gifts. One final sigh of exasperation escaped her before she consented. Her eyes closed, and she felt his hand on her arm, caressing the length of it until he arrived at her fingertips. She shivered at his touch. He slowly, gently unfurled her fingers, still lightly clenched from her earlier irritation, and placed a rough object in her palm.

"Ah, ah, ah! Not yet," Vlada warned her. He closed her fingers lightly around the object. He kissed her hand. "Now you can open them."

Kitty opened her eyes and looked down at the small piece of burlap tied with string. She tugged at the knot and unfolded the scrap of fabric. There, in the palm of her hand, was the most perfect thing she had ever seen: a replica of the Terezin coat of arms engraved into a golden charm. It was all there: the camp's stone fortress, two towers rising on either side and a lion brandishing a sword. The details were magnificent.

"But how, Vlada?" Kitty started to ask.

"Shhh. Turn it over." On the back, the charm was engraved with her transport number, Ez199 and the date she arrived at the camp: 16-II-1943. She had told Vlada that day in February was her lucky day because she had met him there. She stared at the charm in her palm, her eyes welling up with tears, almost to the point of overflowing her thick, dark lashes.

Now, she stood in the street of the camp, trying to picture his face again. It had been six months since he boarded the train. She could see him clearly in her mind's eye. His eyes. His smile. Oh, his smile! This was not a broken heart. Their story would be different.

"We will see each other again, Vlada. In Prague. Just like we promised," Kitty vowed. She opened her eyes and realized she had been standing in the middle of the street, a cup of weak tea from the morning still in her hand.

Kitty stopped in her tracks and a chill washed over her. The tin cup fell from her hands and bounced off the cobblestones, splashing tepid liquid over her ankles. She barely noticed.

Hundreds of skeletons the color of ash and mud shuffled slowly toward her, some of them with their arms outstretched. A scream rose in Kitty's throat and stopped there. Kitty's mind could not make sense of the horrific sight before her. Her lips remained parted, but no sound escaped them.

The only monster Kitty had ever heard of was in the tale of the Golem of Prague. When her brother, Hanuš, wanted to scare her, he would tell the story of the Golem, an ancient being made from mud, not fully human, who was called forth to help in times of crisis. She remembered something about how it would come to life when sacred words written on a piece of paper were placed in its mouth. She stared ahead as the courtyard of the camp filled with what looked to be a thousand Golems.

Who put the sacred words in their mouths and brought them back to life? Why are they here?

As they approached, the only sounds Kitty could hear were the rustling of the rags they wore, their feet sliding in the dirt as they walked. Then, like the barely audible mew of a newborn kitten, the tiniest cries poured forth from their dry, cracked lips and scorched tongues.

"Help...water...please." She heard someone cough. The haunting refrain frightened Kitty, and then the coughing exploded into a cacophony, coming first from one section of the crowd and then another. A woman shuffled toward Kitty and Kitty stood frozen, hands clenched at her sides, as the woman fell to the ground in front of her. The uneven cobblestones under her feet threw her off balance, but Kitty continued to stand, immobile, as the sea of figures parted around her and continued walking past.

A wave of fear washed over Kitty as the throng stirred the air around her, a pungent scent of death and disease assaulting her nostrils. How do I make them stop? she asked herself. She remembered then how the Golem was relieved of his power: the paper with the sacred words was removed from its mouth.

Plagued by horror, Kitty began to think irrationally. There is no way I am putting my hand in the mouths of any of these things. Kitty shuddered, the hair on her arms standing up, a cool film of sweat forming on her brow. Still the figures shuffled forward, and Kitty was certain they numbered in the hundreds, if not thousands, their skeletal bodies moving in a shocking morass.

Kitty continued to back away, tripping, and catching herself. A cry that had begun to form in her throat turned to a sigh of relief as she saw the prisoners of the camp sweeping out of their houses and into the street. Whatever was happening, Kitty was not alone in facing it. A woman she recognized from the mica detail strode past her, throwing her shawl into the street behind her, and began to search the faces in the approaching horde.

She cupped her hands around her mouth, shouting into the crowd, shifting from one side to the other, eyes desperately searching. "Edvard? Edvard? Hanka? Is that you?" The woman stood in the path of the grey, skeletal figures, shouting the names at every one that passed. Soon she began screaming the names together in a singsong way, the names blending into one long name.

"Edvardhankaedvardhankaedvardhanka!"

As the throng walking toward her came into clearer focus, Kitty realized what, or who, they were. Kitty could make out features now, their hair and clothing, striped uniforms, the star.

"Wait. Is it possible?" Kitty wondered.

It's them, she realized with certainty. Those sent to the "East," months and years ago. She was certain her Vlada survived. Was this what had become of him?

"If this is how he has returned to me, I will accept him. I will bring him back to life," thought Kitty.

Her shoulders fell and she began to search the faces for that of her beloved. They were ashen, their eyes sunken as deep as the sockets on a skull, but she was no longer afraid. She felt her legs come back to life, the dampness of the tea present on her ankles. Then she screamed.

"Vlada! Vlada?"

EPILOGUE

VLADA AND **KITTY** FEBRUARY 1950
PRAGUE, CZECHOSLOVAKIA

Kitty sat at the small table in the sparsely furnished dormitory room and watched Vlada as he slept. It was warm in the room, and he stirred, tossing fitfully in the small bed they shared on weekends, covered only in a sheet. She cast a loving gaze over her husband. Husband, thought Kitty, turning the word over in her mind with a reverence she reserved for few things. What a long road it has been to this moment, she thought.

After searching for Vlada's face among the disease-ridden prisoners who lurched eerily into the ghetto, Kitty was stoic. The SS fled the camp not long after the masses arrived, skirmishing with the Red Army on their way out, a final burst of explosions rocking the camp. Russian tanks rolled into Terezin to liberate the camp on a clear evening in May.

Days passed and the Soviet medical units struggled to restore order in the camp and contain those infected with typhus. Hundreds of newly liberated prisoners dropped in the streets from hunger and malnutrition, and hundreds more were dying from a myriad of maladies, including tuberculosis and dysentery. Kitty approached a Russian soldier who was barely a few years older than her. He wore the traditional Ushanka bearing the hammer and sickle, despite the day's warmth. "I speak a little Russian. I can help," Kitty offered.

She stood behind a table set up in the Hanover courtyard and translated instructions from the Russian officers into Czech for the prisoners, old and new. "The Sudeten Barrack is now a quarantine station for typhus patients," Kitty instructed. She wished Vlada were there to laugh with her at the irony. The building the SS had commandeered to protect their precious files was now being used to contain an epidemic.

Another affliction swept through the camp along with those who survived the death marches: thievery. Kitty stood in line in the Hanover courtyard for her extra rations after spending the morning translating for the Russians. She looked around at the sea of unfamiliar faces. Her eyes came to rest on the woman in front of her in line, the woman's shoulder blades protruding from the back of her thin cotton dress. Kitty felt pity for the poor soul. While we received increased rations after the camp was emptied, Kitty realized, prisoners in other neighboring camps were being beaten and starved. Her sympathy was tested when a malnourished arrival bumped into her, knocked her ration cup from her hand, and ran away with it. Theft had been a rare occurrence in the camp, except when it came to stealing from the Germans. The prisoners had rarely stolen from each other, and now thievery – be it food, medicine, clothing – was a daily occurrence.

The entire population of the camp, including the healthy, were not permitted to leave, and Kitty became resigned to it. A week later, she was surprised when Bettina told her to pack her things. Kitty did as her mother instructed. She was preoccupied as she placed several dresses and sweaters in a small valise, carefully tucking the charms Vlada had given her in among her clothing for safekeeping. She was torn. Her fingers grazed his letter where it sat hidden in the pocket of her dress. It was a touchstone, an oracle she hoped might give her an answer as to what to do next.

Should she wait for Vlada at the camp, with the sick and dying, or leave with her parents for Prague? "Meet me at Berta's," Vlada had told her. Kitty sat on her bunk, conflicted, her eyes darting around the room, imagining every scenario that might upend the plan she and Vlada had made so many months before.

Like a baby bird kicked out of the nest, Kitty prepared to leave the relative safety of the fortress walls for the unknown world outside. She was afraid to bid farewell to Terezin, but she had no choice. From the back of a military vehicle bound for Prague, and freedom, she watched *Arbeit Macht Frei,* the words over the gate, appear to grow smaller and smaller.

Kitty remembered little of the family's departure from the ghetto. She felt untethered, like she was floating, watching the scenery pass as if through someone else's eyes. "Kitty!" Bettina took hold of her daughter by the shoulders in the back of the truck, shaking her gently, her voice filled with concern. They crossed the city limits and Kitty became aware of the blue sky and the sound of thunder, which seemed incongruous.

"Is it going to rain?" Kitty asked her parents in a dreamy, far-off voice.

Her father turned toward her, his eyes scanning her for the source of her affectation. "The city is still under siege, Kitty," her father gently explained. Although Prague had been liberated, German tanks still fired rounds in the old town square. Terezin had been removed from the violence and destruction of war, and the bursts of gunfire made Kitty flinch. She nervously twisted the chain around her neck that held the charm Vlada had made for her. "We will be safe at my cousin's flat," her father assured her.

No longer imprisoned, liberated Jews faced a world that had not yet caught up with their reentry into society. As a Jew, Karel's cousin had been assigned a room, not a flat, and now five people inhabited the small space.

The transition from the insulated and proscribed world of the ghetto to the vast openness and visibility of life in the city left Kitty feeling dazed and vulnerable. On the street, she walked hesitantly, feeling exposed and unsafe. In the confines of the tiny, overcrowded apartment, she felt claustrophobic. She longed to shrink against the wall or into a corner of the room. She closed her eyes and pictured herself back in the small house she and Bettina had shared with her mother's employer in Terezin. She longed to feel safe again, and she wanted Vlada. She felt herself suffocating in the small flat.

One day Bettina went off to search for the family's Persian carpets that had been left in the care of some Christian acquaintances. Kitty took the opportunity to escape the confines of the flat, running outside the building, breathing in deep gulps. She stopped, suddenly recognizing a familiar face.

"Hanka!" Kitty ran to her friend, grasping her by the shoulders and staring into her face. "Is it really you?" Her friend turned to Kitty, confused at first and then registering recognition. Hanka threw her arms around Kitty, her body suddenly wracked with sobs of joy and relief. Hanka's mother had died from a botched operation at Terezin even before the mass deportations. Her father was deported on the same train as Vlada and Karel. The two friends sat on a bench and held each other's hands.

"I am an orphan, Kitty," Hanka said. There had been no word of her father's whereabouts, and she assumed he was dead. He had been missing the same amount of time as Vlada, and the young women shared a wordless moment as the implication settled over them. Hanka searched Kitty's eyes for the common pain of loss. But she was surprised to find it lacking in her friend.

"You think he's still alive, don't you?" said Hanka. Kitty felt a flash of anger at the accusatory tone in her friend's words. Her cheeks reddened, but she just as quickly calmed herself. Yes, Kitty thought. But she said nothing, holding her hope for Vlada's safe return in strong reserve. She would not share with Hanka how every day, from its hiding spot in her bureau, she took the letter Vlada had written to her at Auschwitz. How she slowly and gently unfolded it, taking great care to keep it intact, examining the ebb and flow of his handwriting and attaching her own secret meaning to each phrase. She can't understand, thought Kitty. Like the letter, Kitty kept her hope for Vlada's safe return locked away where no one could see it and destroy it.

Late in May, Kitty returned to the flat after running an errand. She found her parents and Hanka sitting at the small kitchen table, acting strangely on edge. Kitty felt the hair on her arms stand up. She feared the worst. But a moment later, the kitchen door swung open and Vlada was standing there in front of her. Their eyes met and she felt a flash of anger. Why had he not let her know he was alive? His shoulders fell at the sight of her. The corners of his mouth turned up in a smile Kitty barely recognized; Vlada's face was familiar, yet deeply changed, filled with a vulnerability and depth of feeling he had not possessed at Terezin.

Kitty's anger dissolved immediately and ignoring her parents' prying eyes, she walked toward Vlada and stood in front of him. They stood, inches apart, and Kitty felt the spark, the familiar flutter in her stomach. She exhaled sharply. She lowered her eyes as they both broke into wide grins, their bodies speaking their own private language. "Welcome home, Vlada," Kitty said in a gravelly voice she barely recognized. They fell into each other, their bodies melding into the other, so they had no idea where one left off and the other began. An awkward silence descended over the group of bystanders – Bettina, Karel, Hanka, and Karel's cousin. They averted their eyes, looking at each other, but it was impossible to offer the young lovers privacy in the tiny room. Bettina stepped forward slightly, arms crossed, and engaged in an exaggerated clearing of her throat, causing the room to erupt in laughter. Kitty and Vlada parted, and Karel walked forward and shook Vlada's hand. Hanka giddily hugged Kitty. Bettina removed herself from the felicitations of the crowd, her face frozen in a taut smile.

At the first opportunity, the reunited lovers left the flat and for hours walked the streets of Prague. They fell in step with each other, arm in arm, Kitty leaning into Vlada, walking like they had in Terezin. Vlada told her everything.

Vlada had been returned to Gleiwitz. Russian troops poured into the camp, but there were few men left alive to liberate. The Russians set up a mess hall and Vlada ate potatoes, cabbage, and beets, and aside from the stolen bread, it was the first solid food he had eaten in months. He chewed slowly, nervously, disbelieving more food would follow. He felt like an animal, feral, wild, undomesticated in his rags. His father had spoken with pride of fighting beside his Slavic brethren. Vlada would have loved to have told his father that it was his Slavic brethren who had liberated him from his bondage. He forced the memory of his father away and stared out through hollow eyes at the activity around him. Trucks pulled in and carried prisoners away, and those in dire need of medical care were taken on stretchers to the infirmary. The camp activities seemed normal, civilized. Vlada felt anger rise in him as the chaos and violence he had experienced under the SS metamorphosed into a calm and ordered existence under the liberators.

What was it all for then? The years lost, the imprisonment, the killings? Vlada wondered. Are we to just go back to normal? A Russian foot soldier walked over to where Vlada sat on the frozen ground and handed him an official-looking ticket. Through a brief exchange, Vlada gathered he had been given a ticket to anywhere in Poland. His mind was clouded and he picked his way through a murky haze. Vlada struggled to stand; the soldier reached for his arm to help him up. "Kraków?" Vlada blurted. At the moment, it was the only city he could think of. The soldier nodded at one of the covered trucks in the yard where the driver leaned against the door, waiting for passengers. Vlada walked over and handed the man the ticket.

The truck rumbled over deeply rutted roads, passing Russian tanks headed in the opposite direction. The only Germans they passed lay in ditches on the roadside, shot dead from bullet wounds to the head. When the truck arrived in Kraków, Vlada slowly rose, his bony backside bruised from the rough wooden seat. He lowered himself from the truck bed, and began to walk, wandering aimlessly down a city block. An older couple stopped him, and the man handed Vlada a few slips of unfamiliar currency. Vlada blankly stared down at the money, his mind slow to respond to the man's courtesy.

Kraków appeared unblemished, unscathed by the vicious war. But Vlada soon found himself in a public square where a half a dozen women were seated in a row of chairs; some had split lips and torn clothing, their heads bowed in shame. A man stood behind them with a razor, shouting. "These women slept with the Nazis. Shame on the collaborators!" The man noticed Vlada. "You, there. These whores slept with your jailers. Want to give one of these young ladies a haircut?" He waved the razor at Vlada.

The day had begun to take on the surreal quality of a carnival freakshow. Vlada staggered on and saw another young man in ragged attire, watching the spectacle. Their eyes met and they walked toward each other in a strange kinship reserved for damned souls. They stood in silence for a moment. "I've had pretty good luck begging if you'd like to join me," the man said in German.

Vlada squinted his eyes at the man. "What country are we in?"

The man looked at Vlada, his eyes narrowing. "Are you joking? We are in Poland." Vlada stood in the unfamiliar square, in the unfamiliar city, and struggled to get his bearings. His chest was heavy, and his breathing was labored. He leaned against a nearby building to steady himself. Vlada sagged and the man put his arm around Vlada's waist. "You're ill. Let me take you to the hospital. It's a block away." The stranger guided Vlada to the hospital, depositing him on the front steps where Vlada collapsed. Within minutes a nurse, dressed in white, a rosary hanging from her neck, found him, and called for assistance to move him inside.

Vlada awoke days later in a hospital bed as a doctor sympathetically looked over him. "You are in the Catholic hospital in Kraków. You have pneumonia," the doctor explained. "You are lucky to be alive." The doctor turned and walked a few feet to the next patient. Vlada felt a tickle on his chest and looked down to see a host of lice swarming in his chest hair. A rush of panic washed over him as visions of the last days of those infected with typhus washed over him. The lice needed to go.

Vlada was systematically crushing each louse between his thumbnails when an older priest wearing long vestments approached him. "Are you saying the rosary, young man?" Vlada stopped cracking the lice between his thumbnails and dropped his hands to his sides exposing the vermin crawling on his chest. The priest gasped in horror, and quickly turned to minister to another patient.

In and out of consciousness, Vlada had the recurring dream about his father covered in the thick, black ooze. At other times his mother came to him in his dreams, but in those versions, he was a young boy. Each day, prayed over and fed by the hospital staff and clergy, Vlada grew stronger. He began to sit up straighter in his hospital bed and he walked farther each day around the halls of the hospital floor. Several wings were filled with gravely wounded men, their life expectancy seemingly linked to the putrid scent emanating from their amputated limbs. Vlada's mind gained clarity, but he lacked direction. He knew there was something he needed to do, but it eluded him.

A volunteer from the Red Cross brought Vlada a clean shirt and pants prior to his discharge from the hospital: the military green shirt had been handed down from a member of the Afrika Korps. Vlada hoped he did not get shot wearing it. After twenty-one days, he was released from the hospital. The sky that April morning in Kraków was overcast. Vlada knew where he needed to go. He needed to find his mother.

The military transport headed west out of Kraków and Vlada shuddered an hour later as it passed Gleiwitz. His shoulders relaxed when the truck kept going, heading in a southward direction toward the border of Czechoslovakia. A while later, the sign for Ostrava loomed up ahead, and Vlada gritted his teeth. The memory of his first separation from his father bubbled up to the present moment. He felt his jaw clench, as he pictured his petulant childhood self, a boy of thirteen, inconvenienced by his father's brief military deployment. He shook his head and looked out the side of the truck.

The streets of Pardubice looked the same, but Vlada knew better. He had expected to walk unnoticed, like a ghost, an apparition. But his return attracted attention, much of it unwanted. He walked slowly, an entourage growing around him as if he were some freakish wartime Pied Piper, picking up all manner of townspeople, each with their own agenda. People spoke to him, some pleading, others apologetic, so he knew he was at least visible.

"You are alive," one woman cried. "Why you? Why not my son?"

"Have you seen my brother, Vlada? He left on the same transport as you."

"My daughter, Ilsa. Did you see her?"

"My grandfather stopped writing back in October of last year. Do you know anything?"

The questions were all just noise. Vlada discovered no one had seen his mother, and he did not know whether he should give up hope. He walked to the distillery and found the gate wide open; a smattering of coal dust occupied the spot where the mountain of coal he had played on once stood, the doors to all the flats locked, the laboratory shuttered.

He wandered out, past the town's familiar landmarks, the tennis club, and the riding school, and he wondered if Mr. Lochman was still in business. He passed the school, and stopped, surprised to see signs of life on the grounds. He had been kicked out of school in 1940. He would never forget his mother's expression when she heard the news. His non-Jewish classmates had been allowed to continue their studies and they had all since moved on. They will be starting university in the fall, he thought.

Gazing up at the building, the seeds of a plan began to form in Vlada's mind. He would return to school. He would pass all the equivalency tests. He would join his former classmates in university in the fall. It was what his parents would have wanted.

Vlada walked as if through mud to the home of Jirka's parents. He hesitated before knocking on the door, memories of Jirka flashing through his mind: their solidarity in Latin class each day under the abusive Pan Jicha, his friend's admitted lack of romantic prowess, Jirka's support at the Junak for Vlada's bid for the Eagle Feather badge, fishing with rum soaked bait at Polabiny. Sighing, Vlada rapped on the door. A moment later, Jirka's mother opened it, wiping her hands on her apron. She looked up to see Vlada, her face brightening noticeably.

"Oh, Vlada!" Mrs. Friedman exclaimed, taking him by the shoulders. "You're alive!"

Vlada held his breath and waited for news of his friend. "Jirka survived as well!" she continued. "But he is not here. He has been ill from his time in Auschwitz. He was sent to a sanitorium to recuperate." Vlada exhaled, heaving a sigh of relief. Mrs. Friedman apologetically put her arm on Vlada's shoulder. "You can stay here if you like." He saw sympathy in her eyes. But he was not ready to give up the search for his mother. It was time to go to Prague and find Aunt Berta. Berta would know about his mother. And then he would find Kitty.

Kitty watched as Vlada struggled toward wakefulness, her heart bursting with tenderness. She recalled the Vlada of long ago who had taken so long to find his way back to her after the war ended. He was lost, orphaned at the age of twenty, his inner compass smashed to bits, unable to discern which road would point him in the direction of home. She did not take his slow return as a sign that his love for her had faltered. He had been broken, and whether he knew it or not, he spent those months finding pieces of himself, and finding his way back to her.

Vlada woke to find Kitty watching him. He sat up, wiping the sleep from his eyes. "Good morning," he said, looking at Kitty, who was clutching her pocketbook and buttoning her coat. "And where are you off to this morning?"

Kitty stood and walked to the door of the dormitory room. "Good morning, sleepyhead. My father's cousin phoned. The wedding photos are finally ready and I'm off to fetch them." She smiled as she glanced around the little love nest they had created. Vlada had been studying to complete his degree at the university. Large tomes with titles like *Industrial Chemistry* and *The Engineering of Chemical Reactions*, and papers with scribbles Kitty could not decipher, were piled high on the small kitchen table. More occupied the floor on Vlada's side of the bed. Her side of the bed was still warm from where they had earlier lain in each other's arms.

Vlada jumped from the bed. "Not so fast, Mrs. Munk." He grabbed Kitty by the waist and pulled her close to him, looking her up and down. "A kiss before you go for your poor husband – who is up to his ears in schoolwork. You look just as beautiful now as you did on our wedding day." The ocelot print coat was the same one she had worn on their wedding day just a few months earlier.

"Darling, you never need to ask." Their lips met and lingered. Kitty pushed him away. "I will be back soon!"

Since their wedding on November 12, the newlyweds had fallen into an unconventional routine. Vlada was in university and lived on the campus, while Kitty lived with her cousins in a villa in Prague. But the weekends were theirs to share. On Friday evenings, Kitty signed in with the dormitory staff and spent two nights in her husband's arms. They lingered in bed each morning, looking outside the window at whatever weather the day had in store. Today it was sunny, with a deep February chill that would not release its grip.

After Kitty left, Vlada put water on the hot plate for tea, reflecting on his previous night's dreams. The recurring dream with his father was thankfully a distant memory, but occasionally, other odd images rose to the surface as he slept. He frequently shared the brief fragments he could recall with Kitty, and she gave her best interpretation of them. He woke one morning to lingering images of Čigy at his father's camp in Polabiny, barking at something in the tall grasses that lined the shore. Kitty lay next to him, nodding and listening intently. Vlada had propped himself up on one elbow, gazing down where she lay next to him, overcome with affection for her. She talked animatedly, intuiting that the dream meant they needed to get a dog. He chuckled at how she always cast some positive symbolism over his dreams, no matter how dark a shadow they left behind.

Kitty walked briskly in the cool morning air. She breathed in deeply as she crossed the Charles Bridge, the chunky heels of her shoes clicking on the cobblestones. The underside of the clouds were tinged with pink and gold, hovering high over the narrow spires and copper roofs. She paused for a moment to watch the river's swiftly flowing current. The city was waking up. She could hear the sound of cars and trucks rumbling through the streets, echoing across the city. The swans that usually hugged the shore were absent this morning, perhaps frightened away by the cacophony of vehicles.

Kitty missed her father. She was thankful, and frankly surprised, that he had survived the war and the family's imprisonment in Terezin. He had been disappointed to find his former company in the process of being nationalized after the war. Looking back, Kitty understood how difficult it would have been for him to find employment, but her parents' decision to move to America — and take her with them – had devastated her.

Kitty stood looking out over the river, recalling the day Bettina informed her she must emigrate to the United States with her parents. She made no attempt to sugar coat the news. "Kitty, you are not yet an adult. You are coming to America with us." It did not matter that she had spent barely a year reunited with Vlada. At nineteen, she was a minor and considered unable to make her own decisions.

"I will write to you, and we will plot our reunion," Kitty remembered confidently telling Vlada. There were no schoolgirl tears then, only determination. How she had hated that journey on the Queen Elizabeth, the elegant ship taking her further and further from her love. Once in America, Kitty had tolerated the family's frequent moves from one relative to another. She stopped explaining to each new relative she met that she was only in America temporarily; that at the first opportunity, she would return to Czechoslovakia. To Vlada. No one understood, but her heart was certain. Still, she was forever grateful for those final years with her father. Kitty smiled, knowing her father would share her happiness.

Kitty looked across the river in the direction of Prague Castle, high on a hill on the other side of the bridge. Oh, Prague! Kitty thought it must be the most beautiful city in the world. I could love any city, she mused. As long as I am with Vlada.

Just over the bridge, Kitty stood in front of the photographer's studio. She pushed open the door and a bell tinkled. The small front room smelled of photographic chemicals, and the walls were lined with black and white framed portraits of men, women, and families. A man's friendly voice shouted from behind a curtain. "Just a minute, please!" A moment later the curtains parted, and her father's cousin, Arnost, appeared, smiling at the sight of Kitty. He was older, bald, with twinkling eyes, and he wore a leather apron. "I was developing some photos. My apologies for the delay, Mrs. Munk." Arnost winked at the mention of her new title.

Kitty smiled gracefully. Mrs. Munk. She did not think she would ever tire of hearing it. She knew she was one of the lucky ones. After liberation, vile gossip spread about how young women like herself had managed to survive the camps. The gossip left many young women feeling as damned as the women accused of sleeping with the SS: scorned, and bearing a wartime scarlet letter. It had been four years since the war ended, but for some, the fallout endured.

"I have your photos here, young lady. That coat of yours photographed beautifully." Arnost gathered up a brown cardboard envelope and handed it to Kitty, the corners of his eyes crinkling when he smiled. "Take these proofs and let me know how many copies you would like by month's end."

Kitty excitedly took the package and began the walk back to the dormitory. She held the photos eagerly, but kept the package sealed, having promised Vlada they would look at them for the first time together.

A light snow began to fall as she crossed the bridge. She pulled the collar of her coat up around her neck, clutching the envelope against her, taking care not to crush the photos inside, and bent her head down as she walked forward into the swirling snow. She loved the feel of the cold air on her cheeks. The smell of roasting chestnuts filled her nostrils, conjuring the image of Hermina as a young woman crossing the same bridge and finding love. Kitty slowed, and she sat down on a bench, her fingers straying to the clasp of the envelope.

Her mind was awash in memories. Kitty bit her lip remembering her reunion with Vlada after liberation. He had been so lost after the Russians freed the prisoners in the camps, offering them transportation to wherever they wanted to go. He could not remember which direction home was, or if he even had one. Kitty did not begrudge Vlada those lost months, months spent wandering the countryside and cities of Poland, ill, heartbroken, relying on the kindness of strangers and begging for food and money, not even owning the shirt on his back. He was afraid to go back to Pardubice because that would confirm the horrible truth: that his parents had both perished, and that he was alone. And so, he had wandered like Job, questioning the existence of God, and punishing himself for surviving.

Kitty remembered the dying and disease-ridden prisoners filling the camp, she remembered feeding them, and the camp being put under quarantine. The planes flying overhead and the sound of bombing in the distance. And then, after Terezin was liberated, she remembered a celebration in the streets of the ghetto that she and her parents did not attend. Her last memory of the camp was sitting next to her father, who was very ill, Bettina across from them, in the back of a truck that rode out the front gate of the ghetto in the direction of Prague. They had been lost then, too, only they had each other, save for Hanuš. Bettina wanted to leave the country. She wanted to put the place of so many bad memories behind her.

With no word from Vlada, Kitty's heart had broken a little every day. Did she think him dead? Fallen out of love? No. She sensed him out there, somewhere, alive, but not quite.

She relived their reunion in Prague that May, in all its detail. One day she returned to the kitchen of the family's flat to find Bettina acting strangely. "What took you so long, Kitty?" her mother asked, her eyes wide, darting frequently to the door that led into the living room. Kitty froze as the door slowly opened to reveal Vlada, not the version of him that had left Terezin in October of the previous year, but a different Vlada, a man, slim and serious, and every bit as handsome as she remembered him.

He walked toward Kitty, and a smile spread over her face. He took her face in his hands and then hugged her around her waist until Kitty thought she would lose her breath. His arms. His lips. His breath as he whispered cheekily in Kitty's ear. "I thought I told you to meet me at Berta's."

Had it all been a dream? Was Terezin a dream? One part of her wanted it to be a dream so she could wake up and find that Hermina and Karel and Hanuš were all still alive. But if it had been a dream she would not be here, now, with Vlada. Kitty stood up and began to walk briskly toward Vlada. Her cheeks were wet with tears by the time she reached the flat.

Vlada had made tea and toasted bread. The small table was set with cups and plates, marmalade, and butter. He noticed Kitty's distress, gently took the envelope from her hands, and led her to the table.

"Eat first, darling." Kitty sat reluctantly at the table and obediently took a sip of tea.

"No," she said. "No more waiting." She quickly cleared the table and placed the envelope in the center. She unhooked the clasp and a pile of black and white photos tumbled out. Kitty's face fell.

"What is it, darling?" Vlada put his hand on her shoulder and looked down at the photos. He held one up. "You look beautiful." Kitty's shoulders heaved up and down, her breathing became shallow, and thick, fat tears clung to her black eyelashes, threatening to roll down her cheeks, still flushed from the cold. She took one of the photos, searching it. "Ha – Ha – Hanuš." She stuttered, the name of her brother pouring out in a series of short breaths.

"I'm sorry, Kitty. He should have been there." When Vlada had returned home from his wanderings, it had occurred to Kitty that Bettina could have 'adopted' Vlada: he was an orphan and Bettina had lost her son. Of course, Vlada could never take the place of Hanuš, but she could have welcomed him to the family. There would have been a certain symmetry to it.

Kitty had often wondered what drove Bettina's detachment when it came to Vlada. Did Kitty's relationship with her mother play a role? She and Bettina had never been close. Kitty had often thought Bettina disliked her optimism, her zest for life. She had no patience for Kitty's romantic sentimentality, a fact that made Kitty pity her father. She doubted her mother had a passionate bone in her body. Or was it as simple as the loss of Hanuš that had forced her mother to close off her heart, denying entry to any object that might try to replace him?

After the early delight in his safe return, there had been no love lost between Bettina and Kitty's future husband. Instead, they had made an uneasy peace between them when they could have had so much more. Bettina had not made the trip from America for their wedding.

"Your – parents," Kitty continued, looking at a photo, the wedding couple surrounded by Aunt Berta and a handful of acquaintances. Vlada was silent as Kitty continued. "Eva. Petr. Uncle Erich. Arna."

Vlada took up where she left off. "Vera. Mirek. Uncle Max. Uncle Karel, Marta, and Jan."

He held Kitty by the shoulders as she fell into his arms and wept. He took her chin in his hand and looked into her dark eyes. "They were there darling. They were with us. We will never forget them, nor they us. They will always be with us, my love. Forever."

Later that day, Vlada took two small crystal glasses from a shelf, saved from his parent's belongings, and filled them with brandy. He handed one glass to Kitty. "L'chaim," Vlada said, looking into Kitty's eyes.

Kitty was surprised by Vlada's toast. It was their custom to toast in Czech. A curious tickle radiated from her stomach and she gently placed a hand over the spot where it had occurred. She still felt the flutter of butterflies when Vlada looked at her a certain way, but this was somehow different. One hand lingered on her belly, and she raised her glass with the other. "To life," Kitty replied, smiling.

Vlada woke in the morning to a hint of a dream. He was alone in the yard at Terezin and a flock of birds, dozens of them, rose over a high fence, flapping their wings gracefully and rising, up, into the direction of the sun. Vlada watched Kitty as she slept soundly next to him, her dark hair spread across the pillow, her cheeks slightly flushed with a hint of pink. When she woke, he would ask her what she thought it meant.

AFTERWORD

Vladimir Munk was born to Karel and Hermina Munk in Pardubice, Czechoslovakia, on February 27, 1925. Kitty Löwi was born to Karel and Bertha Löwi on June 15, 1928, in Teplice, Czechoslovakia.

After the German occupation in March 1939, Czechoslovakia became part of the Third Reich, and its name changed to Protectorate of Bohemia and Moravia. Germany's laws and anti-Jewish orders became valid in the conquered territory. There, on December 6, 1942, all the Jews of Pardubice were deported to Terezin Concentration Camp and Ghetto. Kitty and her family were deported to Terezin on February 16, 1943, by special transport due to her mother's American citizenship. In the spring of 1943, Vladimir and Kitty met in Terezin, where they fell in love.

Vladimir and his father were sent to Auschwitz-Birkenau on October 1, 1944, while Kitty remained behind in Terezin. Vladimir's mother, Hermina, was sent to Auschwitz on October 12. He never saw his parents again. Vladimir was sent from Auschwitz to a subcamp, Gleiwitz I, where the prisoners repaired railroad cars. The camp was evacuated on January 18, 1945, and Vladimir was forced to march for three days to Blechhammer concentration camp. The following day the camp was emptied. Some prisoners, Vladimir among them, succeeded in escaping and were liberated by Soviet soldiers.

Vladimir remained in Poland during the winter and spring of 1945. When he returned to Pardubice at the beginning of May, he found that Čigy, the family dog, survived the war. Vladimir and Kitty reunited in Prague. Vladimir finished his high school education and passed the final exams. He moved to Prague and, in September of 1945, enrolled in the Technical University to study chemistry. In 1948, following a coup d'état, Czechoslovakia became a Communist country.

Kitty enrolled at Charles University in Prague and studied English, Russian, and German. Her family emigrated to the United States, where her parents both had relatives, in 1947. Kitty moved from Asbury Park, New Jersey, to Kansas City, Missouri, and after her father died, to Chicago with her mother and Aunt Rose. When Kitty turned 21 in June of 1949, she returned to Prague. She and Vladimir were married in November of 1949.

Vladimir graduated in January 1950 with an MS in Chemical Engineering and after another three years of graduate studies received a Ph.D. in Biochemistry and Microbiology. He worked as a research scientist from 1953 until 1969 in several research institutes in Prague and published numerous scientific papers and patents. He was awarded the State Prize of Czechoslovak Republic in May 1968. Kitty worked in the Technical Universities Library until the birth of their son Peter in 1950.

In August 1968, when the Soviet Union and Warsaw Pact countries invaded Czechoslovakia, Vladimir decided that for his family's safety they must leave the country. Vladimir accepted an invitation from the Dean of Science at SUNY Plattsburgh in northern New York and joined the faculty as a visiting professor. The new Czech government cancelled previously issued visas that would have allowed the Munk family – Vladimir, Kitty, and their two sons, Peter and Paul – to remain in the United States for one full year, ordering them to return two months early. Vladimir refused, and the college supported his decision, changing his status from "visiting" to "tenured." He retired in 1990 after twenty-one years of teaching.

In addition to raising their two sons in Plattsburgh, Vladimir and Kitty enjoyed raising three dachshunds. For the rest of her life, Kitty kept the letter Vladimir wrote to her from Auschwitz. Kitty and Oila maintained a correspondence until Oila passed away in Austria. Kitty died of complications from Alzheimer's disease in January 2015. Vladimir continues to live in Plattsburgh, New York. In January of 2020, on the 75th anniversary of Auschwitz's liberation, Vladimir returned to Auschwitz to pay his respects to his loved ones who perished there, among them his parents, Karel and Hermina Munk, and Kitty's brother, Hanuš. Vladimir was accompanied by the author.

- Over 155, 000 Jews were transferred to Terezin ghetto during the Holocaust. 35,000 died there while another 88,000 were deported to points East and almost certainly to their deaths.
- In September and October of 1944, 18,402 prisoners were deported from Terezin to Auschwitz, including Karel, Hermina, and Vladimir Munk.
- In November of 1944, Heimlich Himmler ordered the gas chambers and crematoriums at Auschwitz to be partially dismantled, disabling their functions.
- 1,574 survived the autumn transfers to Auschwitz. Vladimir was one of the survivors.

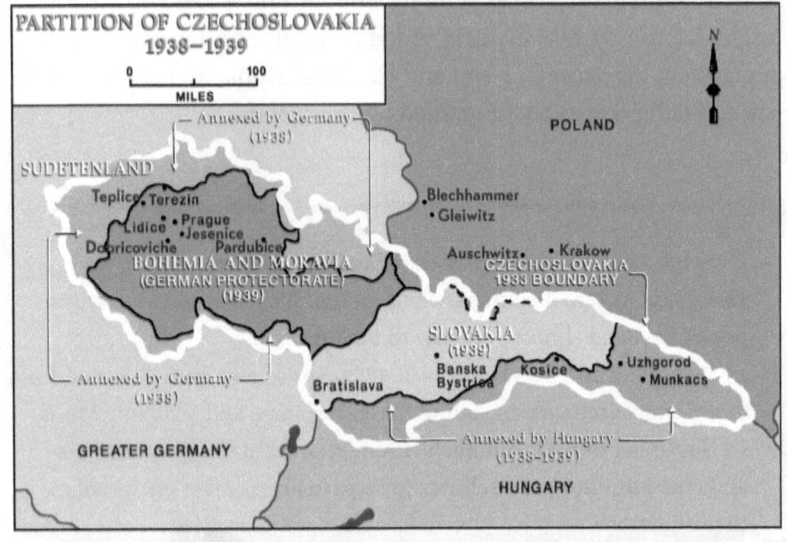

Partition of Czechoslovakia, 1938-1939

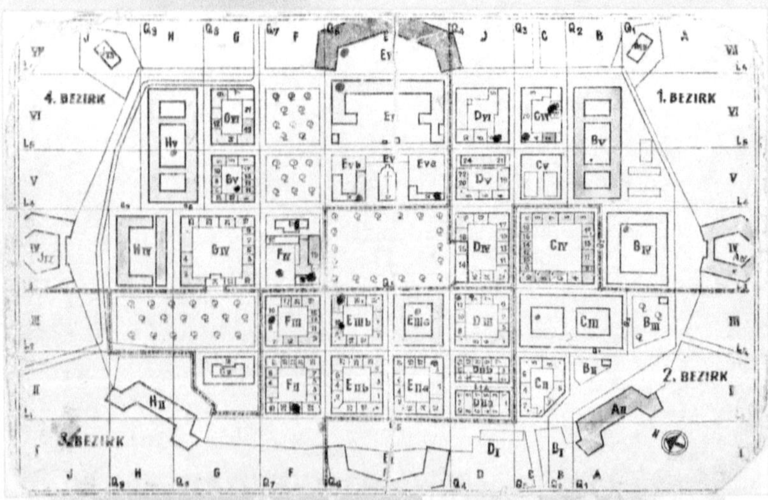

Terezin, circa 1940

Vlada, Hermina and Karel Munk, 1929

Vlada and Čigy, circa 1940

Kitty Löwi, 1936

Kitty, Oila and Hanuš, 1934

Kitty and Vlada, November 12, 1949

Acknowledgments

There are your steadfast supporters, in it for the long haul, and there are those who play key roles along the journey, dropping in and then moving on. I have the deepest gratitude for wherever the following people fall on that spectrum. This book could not have been written without your love, support, and expertise. Thank you.

Alice Munk – Kitty's daughter-in-law – one conversation with you changed the trajectory of this book. Thank you for reminding me that Kitty had a story too.

To my Writing in Community cohorts: Terri Tomoff - look up steadfast support and encouragement in the dictionary and you will find Terri's picture. David Reynolds – your encouragement, time, and genuine interest in Vladimir's story was a quiet port in a storm.

To Richard Schaefer - the breadth of your historical knowledge made me feel like I had the Library of Congress at my fingertips.

To my readers and friends: Erena Fulton – your frequent check ins picked me up and I apologize for asking you to read those early drafts. Brianne Bonner – your unwavering love and support transcends coasts and time zones. No words. Anne Racette - your red pen on those early drafts was invaluable, the glass of wine eased the pain, and the other fun distractions kept me sane. Kate Foldy - you jumped in, guns blazing, for the late assist.

Kim Cummins – whim supporter and website crafter, thank you for always making things look like magic.

Paul Frederick and Bruce Carlin – thank you for helping me bring Vladimir's story to the screen. It made me realize there were so many more stories that needed to be told.

Renáta Růžičková – thank you for sharing your love and intimate knowledge of Pardubice with me. Your friendship is the icing on the cake.

Petr Mücke - the once in a lifetime tour of Kunětická Hora with you brought the stuff of Vladimir's childhood to life for me.

For those unfortunate souls like me who struggle to get the words right, I had the amazing good fortune to have not one, but two amazing editors enter my orbit:

Paul Steinmetz - for your unwavering support of "Team Julie" without whose encouragement from the very beginning I might very well have given up. So grateful to have you there every step of the way, although some day we will have to discuss your semicolon vendetta.

Lisa Lewis – my apologies for making your work so difficult. You are a horticulturist of words. I am not sure what flower we ended up with, but I am forever grateful for the tending.

To my daughter, Ava Jeanine - your love, support, and repeated advice to "Just finish the book" is the stuff mothers dreams of. Love my girl.

To my husband, Tony - you enabled, supported, and fed the monster – with endless love and gratitude.

Select Bibliography

Holocaust.cz. www.Holocaust.cz. Accessed Day Date, Year. Accessed on May 1, 2020

"Return of Legions." http://sechtl-vosecek.ucw.cz/cml/dir/legions.html

"The Czechoslovak legions: myth, reality, gold and glory." https://archiv.radio.cz/en/static/world-war-i

Waleik, Gary, "The Czech Countess Who Took On The Nazi SS In Steeplechase." *WBUR Boston's NPR News Station*, 20 Dec. 2019. https://www.wbur.org/onlyagame/2019/12/20/lata-brandisova-grand-pardubice-czechoslovakia-nazi-germany.

Karel Hynek Machá. *Maj.* https://www.lupomesky.cz/maj/may.html

Němcová, Božena. *Babicka.* Published 1855, public domain.

Krása, Hans, and Adolf Hoffmeister. *Brundibár.* Published 1938

https://www.holocaust.cz/en/history/events/brundibar/

Busch, Wilhelm. *Max and Moritz: A Story of Seven Boyish Pranks.* Published in 1865, public domain.

Háj, Felix, and Andrej Kováčik. *Skolak Kaja Marik*. Published in 1926.

Erben, Karel. *The Water Sprite*. Published 1853, public domain.

Langová, Alžběta, and Renata Růžičková. *Traces of the Jews in the Pardubice Region*. Pardubice, Štěpán Bartoš, 2018

Humphreys, Rob, and Susie Lunt. *The Rough Guide to The Czech and Slovak Republics*. London, Penguin, 2002.

Levy, Esther V. *Legacies, Lies and Lullabies: World of a Second Generation Holocaust Survivor*. Sarasota FL, First Edition Design, 2013.

The Jews of Czechoslovakia. U.S., The Jewish Publication Society of America, 1968.

"Pilsen," *Jewish Virtual Library*. 2008. https://www.jewishvirtuallibrary.org/pilsen.

Makarova, Elena et al. *University Over the Abyss: The Story behind 489 lecturers and 2309 lecturers in KZ Theresienstadt 1942-1944*. Jerusalem, Verba, 2000.

Neruda, Jan. "The ballad of Charles IV (Romance o Karlu IV. in English)" Visegrad Magic Cube, n.d. https://www.visegradliterature.net/works/cz/Neruda%2C_Jan-1834/ Romance_o_Karlu_IV./en/63861-The_ballad_of_Charles_ IV?tr_id=10008.

Weiner, Pavel. *A Boy in Terezín: The Private Diary of Pavel Weiner*. Evanston, Illinois, Northwestern University Press, 2012.

Hájková, Anna. "Women as Citizens in the Theresienstadt Prisoner Community." SciencesPo Mas Miolence and Resistance — Research Network, 27 June , 2016. https://www.sciencespo.fr/ mass-violence-war-massacre-resistance/en/document/women-citizens-theresienstadt-prisoner-community.html.

"Josef — Pardubice Nightingale." *Pardubicky Slavin*, http://www.pardubickyslavin.cz/index.php/property/pirka-josef/.

"Feathers Josef." *Pavel Scheufler*, http://www.scheufler.cz/cs-CZ/ fotohistorie/fotografove,p,pirka-josef,262.html.

Agnew, Hugh. *The Czechs and the Lands of the Bohemian Crown*. Menlo Park, Hoover Press, 2004.

"Adolph Hitler Becomes Leader of the Reestablished Nazi Party." *United States Holocaust Memorial Museum*. https://www.ushmm.org/learn/timeline-of-events/before-1933/adolf-hitler-becomes-leader-of-the-reestablished-nazi-party.

Seton-Watson, R. W. *History of the Czechs and Slovaks*. Hamden CT, Archon Books, 1965.

"Rudolf Popler." *Armed Conflicts*. https://www.armedconflicts.com/Popler-Rudolf-t104141.

Jenkins, Tom. "Grand Pardubice Steeplechase: The World's Toughest Horse Race — A Photo Essay." The Guardian. https://www.theguardian.com/sport/2018/oct/18/grand-pardubice-steeplechase-the-worlds-toughest-horse-race-a-photo-essay.

"Heroes or Cowards? Czechs in World War II." *Radio Prague International*. https://english.radio.cz/heroes-or-cowards-czechs-world-war-ii-8098640.

Mcguire Mohr, Joan. *The Czech and Slovak Legion in Siberia 1917-1922*. Jefferson NC, McFarland, 2012.

He was the only one to stand up for the Jews during their deportation from Pardubice. He paid for it with his life | Memory of Nations (pametnaroda.cz)

"Legionnaire Databases." *My Czech Roots*. https://www.myczechroots.com/records/military/legionnaire-databases.

"Soldier's Record (Karel Munk)." *Military Central Archive*. http://www.vuapraha.cz/soldier/19174448.

"Prisoners of War (Russian Empire)." *1914-1918 International Encyclopedia of The First World War*. https://encyclopedia.1914-1918-online.net/article/prisoners_of_war_russian_empire.

"Charlotte, A Holocaust Memoir: Remembering Theresienstadt. As Shared With Robert A. Warren." https://www.jewishgen.org/yizkor/charlotte/CharlotteforWeb.pdf

"From Ghetto in Theresienstadt to Auschwitz II-Birkenau." *Auschwitz-Birkenau State Museum — Google Arts & Culture.* https://artsandculture.google.com/exhibit/gQiyloEi.

Chalmers, Beverly. "Jewish Women's Sexual Behaviour and Sexualized Abuse During the Nazi Era." *The Canadian Journal of Human Sexuality.* https://www.utpjournals.press/doi/full/10.3138/cjhs.242-A10.

Cameron, Rob. "Former Terezin Guard Sentenced to Life in Prison For Killing Jewish Inmate." *Radio Prague International.* Former Terezin guard sentenced to life in prison for killing Jewish inmate | Radio Prague International.

Jezierska, M.E. Some aspects of human physiology and concentration camp realities. Kapera, M., trans. *Medical Review – Auschwitz.* July 6, 2020. Some aspects of human physiology and concentration camp realities | Medical Review Auschwitz.

Story of Hana Greenfield Terezin. Fragments41.vp (bterezin.org.il)

"Anna Lorencova." *Centropa.* https://www.centropa.org/biography/anna-lorencova.

Gilbert, Martin. *The Holocaust: A History of the Jews in Europe During the Second World War.* New York, Henry Holt, 1985.

Bondy, Ruth. *Elder of the Jews Jakob Edelstein of Theresienstadt.* https://www.jstor.org/stable/42941519.

"Bausteine: Ghettos — Vorstufen der Vernichtung." https://www.gedenkstaetten-bw.de/publikationen/ghettos/b08.htm.

"Theresienstadt." *Holocaust Encyclopedia.* Theresienstadt | Holocaust Encyclopedia (ushmm.org).

Czech Hydrometeorological Institute, Branch Hradec Kralove
Provided information on weather for the date Vladimir was born.
www.chmi.cz.

"SS Farm in the Terezin ghetto." Newsletter of the Terezín Memorial
SS farm in the Terezin ghetto | Newsletter (pamatnik-terezin.cz)

"Photos from the town of Terezin today." Pictures of the Hanover
barracks and Jager barracks.
Photos from the town of Terezín today | Folkedrab.dk

"Autumn transports of 1944 from the ghetto to the East reflected in
prisoners' recollections." Newsletter of the Terezin Memorial. (Kitty
may have been one of 32 who escaped transport.)
Autumn transports of 1944 from the ghetto to the East reflected in
prisoners' recollections | Newsletter (pamatnik-terezin.cz)

File:Theresienstadt Ghetto Lagerplan.jpg - Wikimedia Commons
Accessed on July 15, 2023. Theresienstadt Ghetto Lagerplan Circa
1940. Published circa 1940. See page for author. Public domain, via
Wikimedia Commons.